Everlasting Lies

by Barbara Warren

 FriesenPress

Suite 300 - 990 Fort St
Victoria, BC, V8V 3K2
Canada

www.friesenpress.com

Copyright © 2016 by Barbara Warren
First Edition — 2016

Edited by Tanis Nessler

Ornamental henna design by Freepik

All rights reserved. the use of any part of this publication reproduced, transmitted in any form or by any means, electronic, mechanical, photocopying, recording, or otherwise, or stored in a retrieval system, without the prior written consent of the copyright owner, is an infringement of the copyright law.

ISBN
978-1-4602-7768-3 (Hardcover)
978-1-4602-7769-0 (Paperback)
978-1-4602-7770-6 (eBook)

1. FICTION, ROMANCE, ADULT

Distributed to the trade by The Ingram Book Company

Dedication.

Firstly to my life partner, John who always has encouraged me throughout our long life together, to take chances, be what I wanted to be. Because of him I became a teacher, after our children all entered school. He put up with long nights of my studying, performing in University plays, and all the rehearsals and time away from family.

Also for sharing, a life of adventure and travel with me.

Secondly, to my three daughters and their families, for their constant interest in whatever I undertake! I am a very luck dame.

Barbara Warren. January 2016.

Prologue.

"That's the final straw!" Alfie yelled as he walked into his father's office. "I have asked you many times to allow me to learn the business side of running the colliery, but you refuse to give me even a menial office job."

At forty-six, John William Fletcher was part owner of Nonrev Colliery and the father of nine children, including Alfie. He was a slim, mild-mannered man who rarely showed any temper—unlike his third son, who was as tough as a pickaxe and unafraid of his gentle father.

Alfie's face was red with anger and his eyes were on fire as he looked at his father. "I have worked in this mine since I was sixteen, starting at the bottom and slowly working my way up to a hewer. But you won't pay your own son a fair wage!"

John's face was now ashen, but Alfie didn't give his father time to interrupt.

"What the hell do you want from us? You and your big ways and ideas. Yet you are cheap with us, YOUR OWN BOYS. You have me and Abe and Arthur, and soon little John will be old enough to work for you. But you drove Dicky away, expecting us to work longer hours than the other workers for less pay, and now he is working for someone who will pay him what he deserves."

With this John rose, pulled his slim body out of his leather chair, and moved around his desk with fists clenched and raised as if to strike his son.

Although Alfie's slight, short body was trembling, he took a breath and challenged his father. "Pa, if you lay one hand on me, I will leave like Dicky. But unlike him, I will never darken you doorstep again."

John stopped and instead spat in Alfie's face, then slowly turned his back on his son and returned to his desk.

Alfie pulled his blackened kerchief out of his pocket and wiped the spit from his face. Looking at John, he said, "I am leaving this company and will make a life for myself! I want nothing from you, and you shall have nothing from me!" He was sweating with rage. "I disown you as my father." With this the nineteen-year-old stormed out of his father's office and slammed the door, never to be seen again.

Chapter 1

John watched as Alfie charged out of his office. Taking his kerchief, he wiped his mouth. Why had both Alfie and Dicky left his office in anger? Hadn't he done everything possible to provide for his family? He had bought a beautiful home and had fully staffed it, including a governess to educate all his children.

When the boys were old enough, he got them started in the mines—not at eight years old like he'd had to, but after they had reached a standard of education. He blew his nose, deep in thought. Sure, he had them working as hewers, but that was how he had learned mining. If it was good enough for him, surely it was good enough for his sons.

John walked to the window and watched Alfie striding towards the mine house.

Alfie was muttering to himself as he walked away from his father's office, but he couldn't help remembering how close he and his father had once been. One day, when he was about twelve, he and his father had sat in the garden at Crosvu, their beautiful home, as his father told him how he and Alfie's mother had met.

"Alfie, you never know when you will meet yer soul mate! One evening I was walking home after a long day at the mines when I noticed a young woman in front of me. I couldn't take me eyes of the sway of her slim hips. As I drew level with her, I doffed me cap and said, 'Evening, miss.' Alfie, she turned to me, and oh, the blue of her big eyes twinkled as if the sun was shining down upon her, and I was quite smitten with the lass."

"Nice, Pa, but were she smitten with you?"

Everlasting Lies | 1

"Alfie, me lad, I was so polite—introduced me self, told her where I worked, and asked her name. 'Esther,' she said. 'Where d'yer work?' I asked. Now we were walking together, what joy I was feeling. I had never really talked to any young women before, except for my sisters. She was a scullery maid up at Farnley Hall."

Alfie snorted at this memory as he pulled his cap firmly on his head and grabbed the few items he kept in the mine manager's house where he lived with his father and his brother Abe when they were working. He strapped them on his bike and headed home to Crosvu.

As he pedalled, he thought back to the first time his father had the family to see this house, none of them realizing that this was probably the biggest change they would ever have in their young lives.

Pa has done well in the mines, Alfie thought as the wind blew directly into his face while he pushed hard up one of the many hills on the way home. He remembered the benefactor, Howard Allport, a distant relative who had made his father a working partner with profit sharing in the mine, which was extremely lucrative. When Howard had bought the Liversedge mine, he had made his father the under manager.

Alfie got off his bike, sat down on the grass, and took in the view. Remembering their first journey along this road, remembering the night when his father came home, it felt like yesterday.

John had come in one evening, as Esther was busy in the kitchen. As soon they were all sitting at the table eating their meal, John told them that he had to go to Liversedge the next day, inviting them all to go with him so they could see the house they were going to live in.

Alfie remembered that Abe had looked at him, telling him they would no longer be living in a small miner's cottage. "Maybe it will have more than two bedrooms, then all of us might not have to sleep in the same room like now, boys in one bed, girls in another!" Alfie had asked his father about this, and he told them that it was a much bigger miner's home.

So the next morning they put on their Sunday clothes to accompany John to his new job.

They clambered off the train, which was in itself a very exciting trip for the family. Then John loaded them into a pony and trap that was waiting for them at the station. They could all see the mine come into view ahead, but John turned the pony trap away, explaining that he wanted to show them some of the countryside first.

Gently jogging along through the countryside, everyone felt so peaceful, except for Alfie's mother. "What a lovely surprise! A ride in the country! How pretty it is. Listen to all the birds. Eh, look at those big houses—what huge gardens! As they reached the gate for Crosvu, his father turned the horse into the driveway. "Eh, what you doing, Pa?" Esther said.

Alfie, lying on the grass, smiled as he remembered those moments.

"I know the couple who work here, and as the owners are out of town I said I might drop by just to show you all one of the big houses." With that John arrived at the front door. He jumped out of the trap and came around to help his mother down, saying, "Do ye have any idea how much I love ye? Come on, bairns, out you get. Now, I want you to behave."

John turned as the door opened and Alfie saw a short, rotund woman with a broad smile standing in the entry. "Good morning, Master Fletcher and Mistress Fletcher. Oh, and all the little 'uns! Welcome to Crosvu, come in, and make yourselves at home. I am off to the kitchen, Master, I'll make the tea and get the cake ready whilst you take the mistress and children around. Henry be working in the attic, he'll be real happy to meet the mistress." With that she disappeared through a door.

Esther looked at John with a frown. "Strange woman. I thought she was your friend. Why was she calling me—"

"Let me show you around," John interrupted.

Already Alfie and his siblings had taken in the grand staircase, and as John led them into the large reception room, Esther and the children let out a gasp at the beauty of the room with its subtle blues and golds, grand furniture, numerous paintings, attractive rug, and large fireplace.

Esther smiled and said, "A real ladies room, should we be wandering around? Don't touch anything, children. Oh, look, Pa, out this window!" She called the children to come look as well. "Aren't the gardens wonderful? Whoever lives here? Oh, I think we should leave..."

John smiled at his wife and children;

"No, Ma, it is fine, I know the owner well. In fact so do you."

"Naw, I don't know anybody who would own a place like this! How many bedrooms here?"

"Five," John answered simply.

Esther turned back to John. "Five? I certainly don't know anybody who has five bedrooms."

"Aye, you do pet, because it is us."

Esther stopped just as she was peeking into the dining room. "Us?"

John just nodded.

Tears welled up in her eyes as she ran into John's outstretched arms. "Us." She shook her head. "How can that be?"

John gently took her and the children to the settee and they all sat down while he told them the whole story. Then they all wandered, Esther and John arm in arm, around the whole house. They met up with skinny Henry in the attic, where he was fixing and painting the quarters for he and Peggy. They had eventually ended in the kitchen, where Peggy had told them she had lunch laid out for the master and mistress in the dining room but would keep the children in the kitchen with her.

Coming out of his reverie, Alfie stood up and surveyed the land, many thoughts rushing into his mind as he climbed back on his bike and started pedalling homeward. Was he foolish to be running away from this place? Why was he so hot-tempered? It would be hard for him to leave his little sister, Lily.

My sweet little Lily, he thought. *Yes, it will be difficult to leave her. I think she was sent from heaven. I can live without my other brothers and sisters. On second thought, I will miss Abe.*

He remembered that when Abe started working at the mine, he would tell Alfie of the arguments that he had seen between Dicky and Pa. He could hear his voice now.

As much as Alfie was reflecting on his actions, so was his father. John turned from the office window, unsure how long he had been standing there after Alfie had disappeared from sight. He suppressed a sob as he remembered Alfie disowning him as a father and promising never to darken his doorstep again. Did he really mean that? Sure, Dicky had left, but he kept in contact with the family. John sat at his desk, his head in hands, and sobbed as he wondered how he would tell his wife. Alfie had the potential to be a manager—John knew this—but he was lazy physically, and John knew you needed to be strong in both mind and body to earn the respect of the miners. That is why he had made him stay in the mine. He always had his sons' best interests at heart. John wondered if Alfie would really leave. He knew Alfie liked the good things in life; he had the attitude of a well-educated gentleman. At the moment his only experiences had been in the mine...would this be enough to get him the lifestyle he had become accustomed to?

Arriving at Crosvu, Alfie carefully put his bike away for the last time, thinking about where he would go. Interestingly, after Alfie began working at the mine he felt a lot more sympathy for Dicky. He understood why is elder brother had moved to Durham. Alfie had a much shorter temper than most, and having worked for his father, he really had made little advancement. Yes, he was a great hewer as he was small. But he was also well educated and bright and was management material, and his father refused to acknowledge this. *His loss!* thought Alfie.

Alfie stormed in the door, much to the surprise of Lily and her twin brother, John, who were with the governess in the smaller reception room that was used as the schoolroom during the day.

The door slammed and little Lily, who had a soft spot for Alfie, said, "Eee! What's up with you? It's only Wednesday and you boys don't come home until Friday. Are you sick? Hard to tell with your black face and all."

Alfie mumbled something, but Lily only heard the end: "...sick and tired of the way I am treated! Where is Ma?"

Lily smiled at her favourite brother. "She is over at sister Mary's and won't be home until five."

With that Alfie rushed upstairs to the bedroom he shared with Abe when they came home. He tore off his filthy clothes and washed up, muttering, "All I do for everyone here, I am not appreciated. I can do better without this whole family. They won't miss me, and they don't care about Dicky. I told Pa that I disowned him, and I do."

Everlasting Lies | 5

Alfie looked around at the luxury he had become use to but vowed that he would continue along the path he had started on back in his father's office.

Opening a suitcase, he packed what few good clothes he had along with some miner's clothing, a shaving kit, and all his shoes. Then he packed the cash he had saved up. He looked around the room and searched in his brother's drawers, pocketing the cash he found there. He needed more money. Where could he find some in the house? His mother was out, so he went to his parents' bedroom and took some of her jewellery along with a gold pocket watch that belonged to his grandfather Fletcher and some old coins that had been stashed away. He would be able to sell these. In one of the side drawers of his father's dresser, he came across a wallet full of money, which he pocketed as well. He then went into his sisters' room and managed to find some of the money they earned by working in service.

Alfie went back to his room to pick up his suitcase and took a last lingering look at this his family home. As he came out of his door, he came face to face with his mother, who looked at the suitcase with astonishment. "Lily told me you were here, why are you home?"

There was a long silence as Alfie shuffled from one foot to another. He opened his mouth to speak, yet nothing came out.

"Alfie, I asked you a question, and I expect you to be respectful and give me an answer. Right now!"

Alfie couldn't repeat the argument he'd had with his father to his mother. He couldn't tell her how his father had spat in his face or that he had disowned him as a father and would never see him again. He loved his mother and didn't want to make it any worse than his leaving would already be.

"Pa and I had a disagreement," he replied simply, "and I have decided to do like Dicky and look for work elsewhere."

Esther looked horrified. Little did she realize that this, in all probability, would be their last conversation.

"So, I will say bye for now, Ma. I will write when I am settled."

"Where do you think you will be going?" said Esther, looking at her son and following him downstairs.

"Somewhere further south. Like to try something new, don't want to stay here in Yorkshire, time for a change, Ma," the lying Alfie said.

"What did your Pa say?"

"Nowt really. I be nearly twenty, it is time to move on." Alfie was now downstairs, noticing young Lily looking distraught as she eyed his suitcase.

"Now, Lily, no tears, it won't be long before you see me again."

With that Alfie place his suitcase on the floor of the hall and cuddled his twelve-year-old sister, smelling the sweetness of her hair while John looked on at the scene before him.

Alfie stood and gave his mother a quick kiss, picked up his suitcase, and went through the front door and out along the driveway, saying to himself, "You make your bed and you lie in it, only I will have to suffer the consequences.

Chapter 2

Alfie travelled by train to Durham. He was a small man, and many would say not a good-looking one, with unruly ginger-blond hair and puny blue eyes that were piercing and unfriendly. His veined cheeks, caused by the strain of working at the coalface, didn't help his looks. Though for a small man, his hands and arms appeared big and strong.

Alfie was deep in thought as the train moved along the rails with a click-clack. He wondered if his quick temper had made him do the right thing. He inwardly sighed. He was so unlike his father, who was a kind, gentle man, a good provider for his family. Alfie, knowing of his father's poor background with no schooling and the need to start work in the mines at eight, wondered how he ever did learn to read. Because of this ability, his father had become the union head and eventually a partner in ownership.

With a jolt, the train pulled into Durham Station.

Alfie settled in a room just outside the station in a small row house that looked exactly like every other house. His room was tiny, with a single bed, a washstand, a small chest, and a chair. His window looked out onto the railway lines. Finding a place to live was easy as there were plenty of rooms for rent here. But he needed to make plans, find a job, and change his name so he could sever all ties with his family. He really didn't want to have their name anymore. He didn't think they would come looking for him, but he didn't want to chance this. Alfie knew he was a fighter and he didn't care what others thought. As far as he was concerned, life was all about him.

He continued to reflect on his family and was certain there were only three that he would miss: Ma was a good mother and had always tried to help him and definitely put up with his moodiness. Abe was a special brother, very caring towards Alfie ever since he had been born. He was his protector—though Alfie wondered what Abe got out of the relationship! Then there was little Lily, who adored her brother Alfie and loved him unconditionally. He also adored her, and he hoped that one day he would have his own little Lily.

Sitting in the drab room, Alfie felt alone and somewhat afraid, which was something he didn't normally allow himself to feel. He knew he would probably have to work in the mines—after all, what else did he know? He pondered on what he could change his name to. He knew Fletcher was a fairly common name in these parts, and as his father was fairly well known as a part owner of a mine, this too would have to change.

Alfie found a piece of paper and a pencil in his room and wondered where to start. He thought of his father and the story about the naming of Nonrev Mine—what a silly name that was! His father had tried to explain why this name was so important to him. Made no sense to Alfie. Most mines had simple names. Smiling, Alfie wrote the letters N-O-N-R-E-V going down the page, thinking that if he could come up with mines for each letter, maybe it would give him an idea for a surname. *Let's see what I can come up with for N...umm, there is one called Nunnery in Sheffield.* He smiled as he didn't think that would work as a surname. He studied the *O*; there was the massive Oldham Coalfield. Northcroft was another mine. *Wow, I am a brilliant chap! Ravenslodge—wasn't that in Dewsbury? East Ardsley, that was in Barnsley. Last letter, V,* he thought, pacing. He simply couldn't think of a mine beginning with a *V*. He was getting mad. He wasn't used to not getting things right away. *Let me try again backwards.* So on the opposite side of the page, Alfie wrote V-E-R-N-O-N. A smile crossed his face: Vernon. "Vernon," he said aloud, "that will be my new surname."

Now what was he to use as a first name? Alfie Vernon was too common. He wanted his name to be strong, one that suited his personality. Why not use the name of his baby brother, who had died before he was three months old? "Charles Vernon," he said. It had a nice sound. Then he tried "Charles Alfred Vernon," and that was the moment of his

Everlasting Lies | 9

rebirth. He would simply have his parents as John and Esther Vernon and have only one brother, Abraham, and one sister, little Lily. And so it was decided. He now had a perfect family.

Alfie—no, *Charles* brought out the loot he had stolen from his family. He was surprised to find that his father's wallet held 733 pounds, and together with what he had taken from his brothers and sisters, he now had nearly 740 pounds. He was a wealthy young man. The old coins would be worth something, but he needed to find a way to sell these. Then there was the jewellery—many necklaces and a small ring—which he thought would not be worth much but might come in handy in the future. He laughed in the belief that many people did not have his thought process. He felt he had taken what was rightfully his. He felt absolutely no shame.

The next day, Charles travelled to Wingate Grange Colliery in Durham County and applied for a hewer's position. This was a big mine that employed over twelve hundred men and boys in various shifts and was on the edge of the northern coalfield. Charles was a small man, not standing five feet tall, which made him perfect for a hewer as the space they worked in was extremely small. Because of his stature and experience, he was assigned to the Low Main seam at 110 fathoms down. He found lodging at a recommended home close by.

Most of the hewers working in the lower main were older men, and he worked closely with George Bloomfield during the 4:00 a.m. to 10:30 a.m. shift. The Wingate Grange Colliery had not had a serious accident in sixty-six years when Charles started work there in 1905.

Charles soon got the reputation of being a quiet young man who kept to himself. He worked hard, but many saw him as a man with a big ego. He never denied this, and in fact worked at getting this reputation. He didn't enjoy his work or the men and feigned illness often. He became known as a shirker or lay-about, but why shouldn't he be? This was menial work for him as he felt he was a man destined to be great. He was not well like as he talked down to the men and was abrasive and argumentative. He would never answer anyone who called him Charlie, exclaiming, "My name is Charles. Unless you call me by my rightful name, I will not reply!" And he didn't reply until the person talking to him called him Charles!

"Hey, Charles, you sick again yesterday?" George would say.

"What was it this time, Charles?" Another man would call out.

"Ah, Charlie he must have choked on his own spit trying to tell someone to call him Charles."

Much laughter arose from the miners at these times. However, not being liked proved to be an advantage for Charles in October of 1906. Charles was having a more difficult time with his team and had decided to take a few days off. He arrived at the surface the morning before the disaster at the Wingate Grange Colliery, feigning sickness. He was a master at doing this: he had used rouge on his face and body and had arrived at the office breathless, coughing, and sniffing. *I should have been an actor*, he thought. His manager took one look at him and said, "Charles, you should stay home, you are so flushed." He nodded and weakly smiled his thanks, the truth being, he simply didn't feel like working the next few days, and the loss of pay didn't bother him.

The following morning Charles heard the explosion as he lay in his bed. He stared at the ceiling, listening to the hooters and wondering where the disaster actually had taken place in the huge colliery. He would later discover the explosion occurred in the lower main where he should have been working. It killed twenty-six miners, including George, his partner at the coalface.

Charles dared not show his face after not going into work that morning. He knew he was not liked by any of the men, who found him to be grating and quarrelsome. He was nasty to everyone as he felt these men were beneath him. After all, though they didn't know it, he had been brought up in a self-made, wealthy family. As he continued to lay there, he decided he would stay away for several days and would make sure his landlady believed he was unwell. Charles was a great manipulator.

A week later he finally went back to the mine. His team were pretty well all dead, and in his selfishness, he didn't even go to any funerals, continuing to feign sickness. It was no surprise that the workers shunned him and, without exception, would not work with him. It was so uncomfortable that he quit his job and decided to go looking for work elsewhere.

That week he left the boarding house, thinking that maybe this was for the best. If he stayed in one place too long he might be found, and that was not in his plan.

"Sorry, missus, just too hard on me to stay here, all me mates dead, I feel so badly."

His landlady liked him as she found him to be a quiet young man. "Where you going, lad?"

"I think I will try my luck in Wales."

"Well, son, I will miss you, you have been a good lad. If you ever return this way, don't forget to pop in and see me."

Charles was a sorry sight as he left with his small suitcase, his old clothes, and some sandwiches his landlady gave him for his long journey. However, he only travelled a short distance to Newcastle.

Charles quickly found another job in Newcastle under Lyme and lived in a hotel.

After the last mine experience, he decided he needed to work harder at making friends. The men here were younger, and Charles thought if he became more likeable, then maybe he might make some friends, meet girls, and be a little happier. So he began answering to both Charles and Charlie and really tried to fit in.

Charles worked in a team with a young man called Joe Paxton, whom many of the men picked on as he was a little slower than most. The bullying got particularly bad when the men found out Joe got his girl pregnant. They teased him that he wasn't man enough to do that, and they tried to get him to tell how and where he got her pregnant. There was one thing you could say about Joe: he didn't take the bait. Over the course of his first few months in Newcastle, Charles Vernon defended Joe quite often, chastising the men and reminding them that Joe was now married and a father, and Joe began to hang out with Charles.

One evening after their shift, as Charles and Joe walked out of the mine together, Joe said, "Thank you for standing up for me again today, Charlie. Why do you do it? It causes the men to be mean to you."

"It is nothing. I just know how it makes a person feel. Really, it is why I left my last job." What he didn't say was that something about Joe reminded him of Abe.

"Where are you living, Charlie?"

"Still in the hotel until I can find somewhere decent and reasonable to board."

"Me ma has a room to rent as me brother Thomas moved recently to find his own way. I live there with me wife, Ethel. The fellows are right, I had to marry her as we now have a little daughter, Helena. We be saving hard, trying to get rent together so we can move out and be more independent."

"Who else lives there?"

"Well, there be me sister Edina—she helps me ma, she is a pretty little thing—and me two younger sisters, Mary and Margaret. Then there is me baby brother, Robert. Pa also works in the mine. Do you want me to ask me ma how much she wants for the room?"

"Aye, I think I do. It would be nice to be part of a family. Hotel life is pretty dull!"

So in early 1907, Charles Alfred Vernon moved into the Paxton household and soon found himself part of this family and was happy.

Chapter 3

Edina Paxton, John and Ellen Paxton's eldest daughter, was only twelve when Charles moved into the house. She was a slight child, wearing her curly, mousey hair in plaits tied with rag ribbons. She had bold blue eyes and the full lips of a woman. She was small for her age but was strong as she was her mother's helper when she wasn't at school. There was always a lot to do with so many people in the house. The family was now down to nine as Thomas, the eldest, had left, and there were three boarders, including Charles. This meant five men were working in the mines, all on different shifts.

Ellen was always busy and Edina wondered how she accomplished all that she did! She rarely saw her mother sit down, what with the babe and all the filthy mining clothes to wash and all the mouths to feed. Miners coming home at different times and needing to wash meant constant heating of hot water on the stove, which had to be carried to the house all the way from a common pump for water down the street. John had built a lean-to against the outhouse where the miners could wash, but it was very cold, especially in the winter. Then there were the meals needing to be served at all different times of day with the comings and goings of the men.

Edina enjoyed school and really liked walking to school with the boy next door. Billy Charlton and Edina had walked to and from school together since they were little. They still walked together most days, but it wasn't like when they were little and they were always together. Though he was just a year older than her, Billy—or, as he liked to be called now, Bill—had recently shot up in height and was a good head and shoulders taller than Edina. She thought he was good-looking, and she loved looking up to his brown face and brown eyes, so unlike the eyes of her blue-eyed family. When he looked down at her and smiled, his face seemed to light up with joy. Sometimes when Bill smiled at her as he talked about his dreams for the future, her tummy seemed to do a flip-flop. Edina didn't understand what had changed. She never used to blush when he told her that she looked nice—why was that?

One day as they were walking home, Edina was sort of skipping alongside Bill when he said, "I've got some news, Edina."

She stopped skipping and gave him her full attention. "What be that, then?"

"Me pa says I should soon be starting to work!"

"What!" Her eyes went wide with surprise and she stopped dead in her tracks.

He looked down into that sweet face. "Aye, he does, and so at the end of this term, I have to find a job."

"That will be good, won't it?"

"Don't think so, as I said I didn't want to work in the mines like me pa."

"Oh."

"Now me Pa is mad 'cause he thinks I look down on him and all the miners."

"Oh."

"Is that all ye can say?"

"I don't know what to say. Me pa, me brothers, your pa are all miners, this be a mining town. I expect to marry a miner." She giggled.

"Then you won't be marrying me, will you?"

Edina blushed as she got that funny feeling in her tummy again.

"I thought you only saw me as a sister."

"Well, I did, until recently! Anyway, what I want to tell you is that I be moving to my uncle's in Yorkshire because he is a railway man and I am going to try to work on the railways."

Tears appeared in Edina's blue eyes, which surprised Bill. He put his hands on her shoulders. "Don't cry, Edina."

"But I will miss you. It won't be the same, without you."

She watched as his brown face came down closer to hers, his lips puckering. He gently kissed her.

"What you do that for?" Her heart was bumping madly; though she sounded cross, she was amazed at how magical that had felt.

"That was a goodbye kiss, 'cause we wouldn't do that in front of our parents when I do leave, would we? He smiled at her as she shook her head. "It is also a promise that someday I will come back and find you, when we are older, and do it again!" He gave her shoulders a squeeze.

She looked up at him, willing him to do it one more time, but he didn't. "Why older?" she said.

Young Bill grabbed her hand and pulled her behind the hedge. He put his hands on her shoulders, looked deeply into her young blue eyes, and said, "Because I really like you." His arms dropped down her back and he pulled her body until it was touching his. She stood on the tip of her toes. He smiled down at her, bent his face to hers, and as their lips were about to meet, he whispered, "This be a promise that someday when I am a man and you be a women, I will come back and do this again." He kissed her and she kissed him.

As they broke apart, she smiled. "I will look forward to kissing you again, Bill, when you are a man." She was totally weak at the knees.

At the same time that Bill left school and went away, Edina's parents decided it was time for Edina to help out full time at home.

Edina took little notice of Charles; she was far more interested in Joe and how he treated his young wife, Ethel, especially after their baby was born. She couldn't understand why things had changed for them. She used to see them in the garden kissing and fondling each other. Never saw them doing that now. Joe often spent more time with that Charles, just sitting and laughing, ignoring Ethel and little Helena and often speaking roughly to her and demanding that she waited on him. Edina often thought that she wouldn't let any man treat her as badly. She felt Joe had a better relationship with Charles than with his wife and that he acted more brotherly with Charles than with Tom, his real brother.

Charles also came to think of Joe as a brother, and he was sad when, at twenty, Joe moved away with his now-pregnant wife and their daughter to the area called Chester Le Street. Charles definitely missed Joe and often went to his house after their shifts together. It came as no surprise to the family when Joe's son was born and he named the little bairn after his friend, except with a twist: Alfred Charles Paxton.

Young Edina was certainly growing into a beautiful young woman, and by the time she was fourteen and no longer had Bill to tease, she began flirting with Charles Vernon. Her mother turned a blind eye to what she thought were childish advances, plus she trusted this small, wiry man of unknown age; after all, he had been part of the family for quite a while.

Charles liked the attention and encouraged Edina. "Want to go for a stroll with me in the park?"

"I think Ma would kill me!" she said and giggled.

"She don't have to know, does she? Tell you what, tomorrow when I get off shift I will wait for you at the top of the park. That is, if you would like to stroll with me?"

"I'll be there, Charles." Her tummy flip-flopped the way it used to with Bill.

They took to walking and chatting in a park close to the house. Charles was flattered by the attention he was given by Edina. He had never had a girlfriend and smiled at the eagerness of this blossoming young woman. One evening as they walked in the park, Charles took Edina's hand in his, and immediately the fire in his belly was lit.

"So, what is it you want to do, Edina?"

"Leave home!"

"What will you do?"

"Probably go into service in a big house. Ma has given me lots of practice. I want to marry and have children like Ethel and Joe."

"You're a bit young to be talking of such things!" He looked into her deep blue eyes.

"I am old enough. I be fourteen." She parted her lips invitingly. She had watched Ethel do this to Joe, which he seemed to like.

Charles looked at this young virgin, feeling his own arousal. "Edina, you better be off before either your ma or pa find out that you're talking this way to me. They would have my hide and throw me out of the house!"

She laughed as she started to run home. "Then I would be coming with you!"

As he continued to walk, he seemed to have no control over his desires and the thoughts that filled his head. He had never kissed a girl and knew nothing of such things, let alone feelings. But he was so aroused, he was hardly able to walk. He liked how this little girl made him feel.

The next day, when Edina was serving him his meal after his shift, she bent close and gave him a sweet smile. He was about to say something to her when her father, John, arrived at the table, having just come in from cleaning up in the lean-to.

"Hey, Charles," John said in greeting as he sat down. "Joe said to say hello to you and to tell you that little Alfie Charles is missing his godfather! He was on his way home after his shift and said to tell you to try and drop by this evening if you could."

Edina placed her father's meal in front of him and boldly said, "Da, if I get me jobs done and it is okay with Ma and Charles, could I go with him to see me brother Joe and Ethel and the bairns? It is a long way for me to go on me own, but I would be safe with Charles."

"I dunno," answered John. "Perhaps you had better ask Charles if he is planning to go there, and if so, then you have to get Ma's permission."

Edina gave Charles the same inviting look she had given him last night in the park. She purposely ran her tongue over her parted lips as she threw her hips forward and said, "So, Charles, are you going to go and see me brother, then? Can I come with you?"

Trying not to show his eagerness or his accelerated breathing, Charles said, "I guess it depends on yer ma saying okay."

With that Edina went into the kitchen, where she very much became a little girl when asking her mother for permission to accompany Charles to visit her brother. Permission was given.

Chapter 4

After visiting with Joe and Ethel and the children, it was time for Charles and Edina to make their way home. Waving goodbye, they set off down the street.

Once around the corner, Charles reached for Edina's hand and smiled at her when she took his. This young girl immediately aroused him as she chattered about her brother's family.

"But they are so young to be parents," Charles said. "They really don't have much fun."

"Whatchya mean?" Edina challenged. "They are in love, what can be better than that?" She squeezed Charles's hand.

"Go on with you, lass, what do you know about love?"

"I know plenty. I be no kid, I be fifteen in October and a woman." She stopped and smiled at Charles, not letting go of his hand. "I used to listen to Joe and Ethel, long before they had to get married. I used to watch them in the garden. I know plenty, Charles, as you must at your age."

With that she swivelled on her foot, let go of Charles's hand, and walked on. "Anyway, I've already had a boyfriend," she shouted over her shoulder.

Charles rushed to catch up with her as fast as his short legs would take him. "Go on, you never had a boyfriend, your ma wouldn't allow it."

"She didn't know anything about it. He was just a neighbour boy, not a man like you. Ma was out. Bill and me were alone in the house, just larking around, when Bill said, 'Come on, give me a kiss,' and I let him kiss me." Edina smiled as she remembered the spark she felt in the pit of her stomach when Bill kissed her as they walked home from school.

"Did you see him again, did you kiss him again?"

Charles was met with silence.

He took both her hands and made her stop as they were getting very close to home. As she faced him with her face turned up, he got lost in the deep pool of her blue, blue eyes. This young lass stirred his sexual being. He wanted to be her first and she his.

Edina smiled sweetly once again, parting and licking her lips and looking at him hungrily. "Naw, he was just a boy, I was waiting for a man," she teased. With that she put her finger in her open mouth and licked it with her incredibly long pink tongue. Then she kissed her wet finger with a loud noise and touched it to Charles's mouth, just as she has seen Ethel do in the garden.

Charles thought he was about to die with passion for this young girl. Her tinkling laughter wafted on the breeze as she ran down her street to her house. Charles was unable to move, his thoughts racing.

As she reached the door, she turned and called out, "Come on, Charles, you be so slow, you old man. Ma and Pa, I am home! Charles is dragging his feet...Aye, we had a grand time, the little ones are so cute. They asked us again for next week."

With that Charles arrived at the door, and John turned to him and said, "Was it great to see your friend, Charles?"

Charles nodded, saying, "Better be off to bed as I have to get up in the morning for my shift."

Once lying in his bed in the darkness of his room, he relived the walk home with Edina and all that she said and did. He felt his desire grow slowly in the shadows, and with thoughts dancing in his head he relieved himself.

Charles didn't see Edina the next morning as he was on the very early shift. But when he got home, she was in the kitchen with her mother. Ellen looked at Charles and said, "Why, you look beat, lad. Go on and clean up, and by that time John will be ready to eat before his shift today."

John was waiting at the table. No sooner had Charles sat down than John started to chat. Charles thought about how well he had been accepted into this family. They saw him as a person. Mind you, he'd had no reason to show them the angry or moody side of his character because he was never asked to contribute to their family life. Which, of course, had happened all the time in the Fletcher family. Charles hadn't thought of his family since he had left. He wondered if Abe was still working with his father. He could be married by now, a father himself. He wondered how his sweet, adorable Lily was; she and his mother had been the only two women who had ever shown him kindness, it was no wonder he held them dear. Or did he just enjoy being loved by them? He didn't miss them, and it seemed that young virginal Edina loved him now.

"Charles, did you hear anything I said you? You seemed to be dreaming, lad."

Fortunately for Charles, Edina breezed in with their food. As she put the food down in front of the men, she said that she and Ellen were coming in to eat with them.

So all four of them sat down to eat together, which was mighty unusual. Edina was sitting opposite Charles, and every time he looked at her, she seemed to have her mouth open and was licking her lips, her eyes twinkling, so that he couldn't help watching her.

"Wake up, Charles," said Edina. "Me ma is asking you a favour, and you be daydreaming about something."

Now that Charles was paying attention, Ellen continued. "I was wondering, Charles, if you be doing nowt this afternoon if you would go with young Edina and pick up Mary from her grandparents. I really don't like Edina walking through the common on her own. It is so deserted, but you never know if someone be hanging around there."

"I would be happy to accompany and protect both your daughters, Mrs. Paxton."

So after Edina had helped her mother clean up, she and Charles set off to the house of the older Paxtons who lived on the other side of the common. Little was said between Edina and Charles as they set off, but once away from the house, Edina turned to Charles. "Cat got your tongue, Charles?" He shook his head in reply.

As they reached the common with its rolling hills and brilliant green trees of early spring, Edina said, "I love spring—the smells, the sunlight, the warmth of the sun on my back." She rushed over to Charles and grabbed his hand. "We should look out for primroses, Charles, we could pick some for Grannie."

"You drive me crazy, young lady. The way you grab my hand, the way you look at me." He laughed. "You're one big tease."

"So are you, Charles, always evading any questions about your family. We really know nowt about you."

They walked on in silence. Edina knew she had upset Charles as his face was black as thunder, though his sandy hair glinted in the sunshine. Edina appraised this young man; most of the time he was, in her mind, handsome, with his twinkling blue eyes. Though he was a small man, it was perfect for Edina as she wasn't even five feet herself. He had great muscles that made him appear bigger than he was. She needed to get the smile back on his face.

"Do you hear the birds?"

No reply.

"They be singing to you." She smiled her coy smile and watched a glint appear in his eyes. She danced ahead of him, saying, "Bet you can't catch me," and ran along the path.

Charles soon caught her; he may be small in stature, but he was like a little whippet as he ran past her, turned, and stopped suddenly so she ran into him and his waiting arms. Their faces came so close that they could have kissed. Charles felt her hot breath on his face and wanted more than that. Dare he? Should he kiss her now? *No, I want it to be special.*

They moved away from each other, both revelling in the moment they had just experienced as they silently continued walking hand in hand.

They were getting closer to the village. As they came out of the common to the final field, Charles helped Edina over a stile, holding his hand out to steady her. As she climbed the stile and lifted her leg over the top bar, she lifted her skirts so Charles could see most of her leg. His heart beat faster with desire. She stood on the step of the stile straightening her skirts, the sunlight catching her curly hair and her twinkling eyes.

Charles took both her hands to help her take the large step to the ground. She faltered, and he caught her in his arms, her body slowly, so slowly, sliding down his, chest to breast. She stretched her toes to reach the ground, and all he could feel was her taut body pressed to his. Their eyes met as she quickly kissed him on the lips, saying, "Thank you, Charles, for saving me from a fall."

If Edina knew what she had just done, knew the depth of emotions she stirred deep within Charles, she did not show it. She simply turned and said they had better hurry as they needed to pick up Mary and be home before dark.

Charles studied Edina. The moment had been fleeting, but he was now determined that this soon-to-be fifteen-year-old, who said she knew a lot about love, was going to be his first experience.

Several weeks passed with few opportunities for encounters between Edina and Charles while he had been working a different shift, but it wasn't long after his shift changed back that Ellen asked Charles again if he would accompany Edina to go and get her sister from her grandparents. This time they left earlier, which would give them more time alone.

It was a beautiful sunny afternoon, and Charles and Edina easily walked hand in hand, as if it were the most natural thing to be doing. Edina seemed extremely happy walking along, even telling Charles how much she had missed their chats. Chatting wasn't on Charles's mind, but he was careful not to frighten her.

"Why don't we go back in the woods and see if there are any flowers for your grannie?" he suggested.

"That would be right grand, as we have plenty of time."

Edina led, bending down under the branches, her little bum close to Charles's face as he gently put his hands on her hips and followed her.

"Sorry, Charlie, pretty thick in here, it's good we both be short." She giggled. "I hope you don't mind me calling you Charlie."

"You can call me Charlie as I love the way you say it. It makes me feel special."

In the middle of this heavily wooded area, they came across a small opening where they finally could stand upright.

Edina lightheartedly said, "So, Charlie, which way should we go now? I am so turned around."

"I dunno know, why don't we take a little rest here and make a decision?"

"Great idea, I am tired of being bent all over and need to straighten out."

With that Charles removed his coat and laid it on the ground.

"What did you do that for, Charlie?"

Everlasting Lies | 23

Charles smiled. "Just didn't want you to get dirty when you straighten out." He gave her a quick peck on her cheek as he moved to sit down on his jacket.

She smiled. "Well, it ain't a very big coat, hardly big enough for two." With that Charles half lay on his side, patting the open space on the coat.

Edina lifted her skirts and settled close to him. Lying on her back, she thought about how she really wanted Charlie to kiss her; her insides were trembling in anticipation.

Charles looked at her lying stretched out beside him, the sun warming his back.

She smiled, licked her lips, and said, "You want to kiss me, don't you, Charlie? I want you to kiss me, and then I want to kiss you back. I want to feel your lips on mine. I want to know what it feels like to kiss someone who likes you." Edina slowly lay flat on her back. It was an invitation.

Charles looked into her blue eyes as he laid his hand across her very small waist, pulling her gently to face him and pressing his lips on hers.

The fire of the moment exploded as she mumbled, "Oh, Charlie." She moved so she was now lying half on him as she kissed him back gently. He slipped onto his back as she followed his body and held the kiss, groaning with pleasure and parting open her mouth. He responded likewise as she ran her tongue around the inside of his mouth. With one quick roll, he was on top of her, thrusting his tongue into her mouth. She didn't try to stop him.

Suddenly they heard some twigs cracking and they quickly pulled apart, both their faces flushing with the pleasure they had just experienced. Charles quickly jumped up and grabbed Edina's hand, pulling her into a standing position and brushing her skirt flat with familiarity. At that moment a large rabbit hopped out of the brush, causing them both to laugh.

"We better get going, Charlie, me gran will be looking for us. We don't want any suspicion about us coming to get Mary because it sure is to our advantage. If me ma had the slightest idea…"

"Aye, you be right. She would throw me out of the house." He gave her a quick peck on the lips. "That would never do, we have to work out how we can be together more."

As they arrived home with Mary, Ellen had tea ready for them all. No one suspected that Charles even liked Edina.

Several weeks passed with no opportunity for these meetings they both desperately longed for.

Edina worked hard looking after the family beside her mother.

"Ma, why don't you take the little ones to see your ma next week and stay for the day? Just think, Ma, a day away from the drudgery of the house. I could manage here at the house with only Pa and Charlie to look after." Edina gave her mother time to let this thought sink in. She was right; the other two lodgers had gone home to see their families.

"In fact with Pa on the late shift, you both could take the little ones over and Pa could go to work from Gran's place, so there would be only Charlie for me to look after," she said, smiling to herself.

"Aye, that would make a change for us all, but that seems hard on you, Edina, me asking you to look after Charles when he gets off shift."

"No, Ma, it wouldn't be that bad. With only one to look after, even I would have some time to meself."

So it was agreed that next Tuesday the family would go over to Ellen's mother's, and that Edina would stay behind to look after Charles and have tea ready for them when they got home.

Edina was outside hanging the wash when Charles came up behind her. "So, I hear that the family are visiting your gran next week and you are looking after me." He grinned, which made him look even more handsome.

"I got to thinking," said Edina, "that you would all be leaving around the same time—you to work and them to Gran's."

"Uh huh."

"Well, if you got to work and then started to feel sick…"

"What, you are asking me to lie?"

"Uh huh," she said with a smile.

"And for what reason, young lady?"

"Thought it might be nice to spend a day together."

"Meaning what, Edina? Do you want to get to know me better?"

"Aye, I do."

Everlasting Lies | 25

Charles smirked; he knew he had her agreement. "Well, it is a plan, but we must be careful your parents don't suspect anything. You have been pretty bold of late—no more touching me when you think no one is looking, no licking your lips at the table, you know that drives me crazy. You know I want you, don't you?"

"Aye."

After everyone left that Tuesday morning, Edina looked at herself in the mirror while she washed. As she smoothed the cloth over her small breasts, they became quite perky with thoughts of kissing Charles that afternoon, her body wanting more. But more of what?

She had watched Joe and Ethel kissing in the garden and could see Joe's hands groping over Ethel's clothes, trying to find a way in. She had watched in awe as Ethel had lifted her skirt and Joe had fallen to his knees and went under her skirt. Ethel had laughed and bent down as if she were trying to sit or lie down. This caused them to move further back into the bushes, not allowing Edina to see what happened next. Really, this is why she had told Charles she knew lots about love all that time ago to tease him.

She dressed slowly, thinking about how readily Charles had agreed when she suggested that he feign sickness and come to be with her while she was alone in the house.

When Charles walked in the door, black as usual from the coalface, Edina turned and said, "There is hot water waiting for you to clean up in the lean-to."

※

A clean Charles strode into the parlour with his hair slicked down and a wicked grin on his face. He look at Edina and could tell that she had gone to the trouble of looking nice, drinking in her beauty and feeling this great need to be satisfied. He sat on the sofa beside Edina and gave her a gentle kiss. "Why don't we lie down here together?"

Edina set aside the darning she had been mending as she waited and bent down to take off first her shoes, then Charles's. He kissed the top of her head, taunting, "Is there anything else you would like to take off?"

Edina simply smiled at this comment as she crawled into his waiting arms. Charles pulled her close as he lay back, watching as she licked her lips with her gorgeous tongue and then said, "Now, where were we?"

Edina flicked her tongue into his waiting open mouth, igniting the fire smouldering in his loins. As they kissed, he touched her clothed breast and met with no resistance from her. He buried his head in her neck, looking for the buttons that he had taken note of earlier. He undid the top button, exposing more of her white neck. She arched her back upwards towards his moving hands as they slowly undid each button. He expected to see some kind of undergarment, but two small breasts were slowly being exposed, white like snow, with small firm nipples.

He felt Edina's hands on his head as her back arched even more, lifting her breasts within his tongue's reach. "More, Charlie," she quietly moaned. "I want more."

Charles touched the tip of his tongue to the bare white skin on top of her breast.

He came up for air, noticing Edina was breathing very hard. "Oh, Charlie," she said as she slipped to the ground and quickly jumped up, standing in front of him with her blouse open and breasts exposed. She taunted, "You want more, Charlie Vernon?"

"You are beautiful, Edina. Your breasts are perfect and so, so kissable. What pleasure you give me, my sweet child."

"Told you before I am no child, I am a woman. I want what other women have. I want to give myself to you. Will you take me?" With that she walked to her bedroom.

Charles picked up their shoes and followed her up the stairs to her bed.

Chapter 5

Charles felt no remorse for encouraging and taking advantage of Edina. He wondered why he had waited this long to put his fantasies into practice. She had been a very willing participant. His appetite, now awakened, was insatiable, and as Edina wasn't always available to satisfy his growing sexual appetite, he now sought out pleasures from others and was willing to pay for this. In fact he became quiet boastful at work with regard to going to brothels. He may be a small man, but not everywhere.

It was an April morning in 1910 when Edina woke up feeling nauseous and dragged herself out of bed to go and help her mother with breakfast for the family. The little ones were growing up. Mary was twelve, Maggie was ten, Bobby was nine, and baby John was seven. When she walked into the kitchen, Ellen took one look at her and said, "What's the matter with you?"

"I dunno," Edina replied weakly.

"Maybe you have a touch of gripe. You look awful. Away with you girl and back to bed, Mary can help me in the kitchen today."

Edina crawled into her bed and started to heave, yet she wasn't sick.

By noon she was feeling better, so she got up and joined Ellen and Mary, who were working in the kitchen.

Ellen looked up. "Aye, me girl, you look a little better. I have Mary, why don't you take the rest of the day to yourself, you don't often get time off."

"Ah, thanks, Ma, maybe I will take a walk over to see me sister-in-law and her bairns, I haven't seen her in a while." Edina grabbed a shawl and set off to see Ethel. "See you for tea, Ma."

As Edina walked over to Ethel's, she thought of the times she and Charlie had visited there together and how their relationship had begun. Charlie really wanted them to be honest with her parents and to ask permission to start taking her out, but she didn't think her parents would allow it because he was so much older than she was. So they continued to have passionate moments together whenever possible and were getting quite good at sneaking either away or into each other's rooms. Although young Mary had caught Edina coming out of Charles's room one early morning after an illicit night of passion.

Ethel was surprised but delighted to see Edina and happy to hear she had a day off. "How are things with you and Charles?"

"Watchya mean?" Edina snapped.

"Well," Ethel said, "I know that you act together like boyfriend and girlfriend. That is when you are around us. But I think at home you are pretending in front of your parents that there isn't a relationship. Why is that?"

"Can you keep a secret?" Ethel simply nodded. "We are a couple, but I am fearful that Ma and Pa wouldn't approve as he is so much older than me. Charlie wants to ask them if he can take me out, but I won't let him. I watched how upset they got with you and Joe."

"That be different, Edina, I went and got myself pregnant with your brother. Your parents have been kind to us because your brother Joe took responsibility, whilst my parents hardly speak to us as they feel the shame of their daughter acting in such a way before we were married. But I have no regrets."

"Ethel, how did you know that a baby was on the way?"

"You silly girl, if you are doing more than small kissing and talking, if you are allowing him to touch you in places that set you on fire, if you allow his body to somehow enter your body and it becomes very, very pleasurable, that is how you make a baby. I am telling you this, Edina, so that you don't get carried away."

Everlasting Lies | 29

Edina thought of the many times this had already happened with Charles. In fact she could hardly wait for the next time. She did not express this but quietly said, "So, Ethel, how did you know there was a baby on the way?"

"I am not sure I should be telling you all this, and I am only doing it to save you the same heartache that I have had with my parents. Joe and I were madly in love. I wanted his body in mine, and I wanted to be his. We were eighteen, not fifteen, we just chose not to follow the rules of our families. Maybe I should call it lust, because it was. I would take your brother into the corners of your garden and get him to explore me."

Edina lowered her gaze, feeling guilty that she already knew all this.

"But I am not answering your question, Edina. How did I know there was a baby on the way? I was tired, but I was a young girl. I woke up in the morning feeling like I wanted to throw up. My mother had never talked about the bleeding that we experience except to show me what to do when it happened. I didn't know that when it didn't happen it was a sign that a baby was on the way. Let me tell you that I shall talk to my daughter about such things. So that is why I am telling you—so you don't make the same mistake. It is better to be open and tell your parents that you and Charles would like to go out together, and when these urges appear, you need to get married to keep your family together."

After that, they spent a great afternoon talking about other things before Edina made her way home for tea.

Tea was ready and Charles was back from the mine when she arrived home. At the table, Ellen asked Edina if she had enjoyed her day off. "Charles, this morning our Edina was feeling right poorly—in fact she spent the morning in her bed, then she went over to see Ethel for the afternoon."

"Edina, are you okay now?" Charles asked. She nodded without a smile, which he had expected. "Was my friend Joe there?" he continued. She shook her head. Charles raised his eyebrow slightly to her, which made her burst into tears, to the shock of the family.

"Are you all right, dear girl?" John asked.

Edina shook her head. "No, Pa, I just don't feel myself tonight, and maybe I was silly to go over to see Ethel and should have stayed in bed. If it's all right with you and Ma and if Mary is willing to help you clean up, I would like to go to bed now."

"Off you go, and have a good night, my child," Ellen said.

Edina smiled a wee smile and went to her bed as Charles watched her from the corner of his eye.

Charles knew something was wrong and needed to talk to Edina, but there was no way that this family would allow him to visit her in her bedroom. He took this as an opportunity to go to the brothel.

The next morning Edina was still not well and told her mother she would visit Rebecca in the village as she was like a medical person. What Edina really planned to do was talk to Charles as he came off his shift.

⁂

Charles was pleased when he came out and saw Edina standing outside the colliery gate. "You can't get enough of me, right?"

Edina simply smiled as she walked quickly away from the mine towards the common.

"Ah, I am right," he teased. "Are we going to the spot where it all began?"

"Aye, to the stile, where I felt your body against mine for the first time."

That wasn't what Charles expected; he wanted to be in the copse where he could lift Edina's skirt and remove her knickers so that he could enter her once more. The mere thought of an encounter with her sent his body into overdrive.

"We have some talking to do, Charlie. Some plans to make."

These words frightened Charles somewhat. What could be on Edina's mind? Why had she come to the mine to find him? She had never done this before.

When they reached the stile, she immediately climbed to the top and sat down, inviting Charles to join her. As he climbed up, he tried to kiss her breasts. Edina took his hands in hers and said, "You need to hear me out."

Charles's mind raced away with thoughts of rejection, which quickly turned to projection. There were many, many more young women who would accept his advances, and this thought made him feel extremely

Everlasting Lies | 31

wanted by others. And more conquests with different women would be exciting; it would be like living his first experience over and over again. Would his body be able to take all this pleasure? Other breasts to kiss and explore, different sizes, different experiences...he could hardly wait.

"Charlie, are you listening to me? Did you hear what I said?"

Charles simply shook his head as Edina repeated, "I think I am with child."

"I didn't think that was possible at your age," he said loudly and angrily. "Why did you let me have my way with you when you knew this was a possibility?"

"Why did you take the opportunity? It isn't like I forced myself upon you."

"I don't want to be a father."

"I don't want to be a mother."

Charles's face was turning black as thunder. "It is not my fault! It is your fault, "he shouted, leaving his mouth wide open.

Edina took this as an invitation, kissing his open mouth with her tongue flicking. This raised both their bodies to a crest that needed to be satisfied. She jumped down from the stile and ran into the woods, where they would be fully hidden. He was so aroused, he followed Edina into the copse to find her lying on the grassy knoll with sunlight shining on her already-exposed young breasts. She pulled up her dress to reveal that her legs were splayed out to him, she stretched out her arms, leaving herself completely open to him.

"You are so beautiful, you are so inviting, I want you, I need you, I love you," he panted.

He rushed to take off his pants and stood there with his face and chest blackened by coal. Lustily, he easily entered Edina and their mouths locked.

Breathless, he rolled off her, and she sat up, holding her knees with her head buried, and sobbed, "I needed to know that it wouldn't make a difference to you, Charlie, me being with child. What are we going to do?"

Dismayed, Charles looked at this sobbing bundle. So childlike herself, how could she be carrying a baby? In his lust, he learned and experimented on what he thought was still a child, unable herself to have children. As exciting as these encounters were with Edina, it really had been a matter of convenience for him: she had been more than willing, even setting up and planning the day they had spent in her house in each other's arms. They had learned together and it was good, but she was inexperienced. Charles's wanted others, not to be tied down. There were many young women for him to enjoy and learn from, and he loved what he received from the women of the brothels. *I want more than this. What am I going to do?*

Edina sobbed, and he turned to her and draped his arm across her shoulder. "Stop that," he said roughly. "I can't think with you bawling." With that he abruptly stood up and offered her his hand. "You go home. I am going to go for a walk so I can think."

※

Edina took Charles's hand as her heart sank. He wasn't looking at her lovingly, and she knew he wasn't pleased with the thought that she was with child. She knew he wouldn't suggest they go tell her parents they wanted to get married as they had been in love with each other since the moment he'd arrived at the house. She had hoped they would marry and live happily ever after. Instead, once she was on her feet he gave her a peck on the cheek and left.

To Edina, it felt like the weight of the world and she cried anew. Then she straightened herself and turned to walk home. She found a stream and washed her face free from the coal that had been deposited by Charles. With each step she took, she felt the dampness slowly coming down her leg. By the time she got home, she had pulled herself together, put a false smile on her face, and carried in the wildflowers she had picked to give to her mother so she would have an excuse for the walk.

Charles didn't come in for his meal that night, and he didn't eat the breakfast they left for him to have before his early shift. Ellen laughed and said, "Charles didn't come home last night for his meal, and he didn't eat the breakfast I left for him. I think he might have a woman." She picked up the untouched plated and added, "He is a nice enough lad and I have been surprised he hasn't done this sooner. He will be home when he needs clean clothes."

Edina was outside hanging washing on the line when Charles arrived home after his shift. "Where were you last night?" she said.

"I told you, I needed to do some thinking about us."

"But you didn't have to be out all night. Where did you sleep? she challenged.

"Nowt to do with you, Edina. I do as I please," he retorted.

"WHAT?" she shouted. She saw her mother looking out at them and whispered, "I am carrying your child and where you be at night has nothing to do with me?

"How do I know you are with child? How do I know it is my child? You once told me you knew a lot and that you were not a child but a woman, intimating that you had experience. So last night, I went and got me some experience as well. It was far better than I've ever had with you," he said hatefully.

Edina stared at him in disbelief.

"These were women," he continued, "not a mere girl trying to trap me with false accusations. All these women wanted was to give me pleasure. They had no concern for themselves, just to pleasure me. You are so inexperienced, all you do is lay there with your legs apart. These women would—"

"ENOUGH!" said Edina at the top of her voice, sobbing. This was the first time, but not the last, that Edina would experience the ugly side of Charles.

"I don't want to know about other women. I thought what we have is love for each other, learning together. I was not some whore you paid for. Ours was a secret that we kept from my parents," she sobbed.

Edina did not see her mother standing close by, able to hear every word she was saying. She glared at Charles. "We both knew my parents would say I was too young to go out with an older fellow. I didn't plan to have a child now, though I was planning on marrying you because I love you and believed you love me back. I do not tell lies, Charlie Vernon. You are the only man who has touched my body."

Charles turned and almost walked into Ellen. "I am off to meet me woman, Mrs. Paxton. I won't be home tonight," he said with a wink and left as Edina scowled at him.

Ellen looked at her young daughter. "Edina, what makes you think you are with child?"

Edina looked up. "You heard?" she said quietly.

"Yes, I did. Let us go into the parlour to talk."

Once sitting, Ellen continued, "Edina, certain things have to happen to your body before you can bear a child. You have never talked to me about bleeding from your body, has that happened?" Edina nodded. "But you never asked me what to do."

"No, I talked to Ethel as she was living here. She helped me."

"Why?" demanded Ellen.

"I dunno, we had never talked about such things. I have only brothers, I am your first girl, I thought it was me and it was something bad. Babies came after me, but really I was too young to understand."

"So why do you think you are with child?"

"Well, I asked Ethel how she knew she was having a baby. She told me the bleeding stopped. Mine has done the same thing." Edina started to squirm; she knew she would have to admit having been with Charles.

Ellen said, "Edina, that is not the only reason bleeding stops. You could be sick, not getting enough food, and, as we are on this subject you have to have...got very close to a man."

Now Edina watched her mother squirm. "What do you mean by that, Ma?"

There was no reply. "Like kissing, Ma?"

There was silence as Ellen nodded. "Well that was why I was telling Charlie—we have been kissing for a long time now."

"How can that be? You have never been out together."

"Aye, we have, Ma. It started when we used to go over and visit Joe and Ethel. Then you used to send us to pick up Mary. When we walked across the common, sometimes we would stop and rest awhile—that is when we got to know that we wanted more than kissing. We taught each other, Ma, and if you mean that I have to share me privates with Charlie—well, I have."

Everlasting Lies

Ellen looked at her daughter as if she didn't know this child of hers. Then she started to cry. "Oh Edina, you are far too young. Your pa and I will have to talk; you go to your room for now. I am going to go and talk to Charles and make sure he is here to answer to your pa."

Edina did as she was bid, and Mary came out to finish hanging the washing. Ellen went to look for Charles, who was nowhere to be found.

Chapter 6

Charles stormed out of the Paxton home, which reminded him of the day he had left Crosvu. He hated being told what to do. That was exactly what his father had done to him. He understood it happening when he was a child, but as a young man his father had still kept him under control, refusing to allow him to advance. He was very bitter about this.

He had hoped he and Abe would someday run Nonrev. But his father was far too controlling. Charles finally began to realize that this was his personality as well. Wasn't he trying to control Edina? His father was always right, and so was Charles—though Charles was not gentle like his father.

How could he be so hurtful to those who crossed him? He hated Dicky because he was hurtful and didn't care what he did to get his own way. Here he was doing the same to Edina. Why had he been so hurtful to her? He enjoyed her. Why did he go and tell her about his relationships with other women? Not only was he controlling and hurtful, he felt it was his right to be that way.

What was wrong with him? He had told his father it was the final straw because his father wouldn't give him, his son, what he wanted. But he had never asked him why. What if he had a good reason? *But whatever the reason, I would not have accepted it.*

Now he was hurting not only Edina but also the Paxton family, who had become his family. He should be back at the Paxton house to help Edina, but the brothel was going to be his refuge tonight.

Meanwhile back at the Paxton home, the bairns were in bed and Ellen had not seen Edina, having sent her tea up to her room. John was sitting smoking his pipe as Ellen sat down with her darning.

He looked up and said, "Edina still not feeling well?"

"No, Charles and she had a big fight."

"Oh." Silence hung in the air. "Is that why he wasn't at tea either?"

"I dunno, he left immediately. I have never even see them together before, but she told him off good and proper."

"You know, Ellen, we have always found him to be a nice lad, but he's not well liked at the mine. Some say he is lying most of the time, and little is known about him. Like where he came from, where he learned his mining skills; he be good, no doubt about that. Many say he has a mean mouth and is quite the ladies' man, and boastful about it too. But that is miners' talk. What were they arguing about?"

"Well, I only heard a little bit just before he walked off."

John looked at his wife and sucked on his pipe as he waited for her to continue.

"Afterwards, I took our Edina into the parlour. She was just sobbing. I sat her down and asked what was the problem? You are not going to believe what she said."

John knew better than to say a word. Sometimes it took his wife a little bit to get to the point, but he was such a gentle man, so he patiently waited.

"She said," his wife stuttered, her eyes filling with tears, "that she be with child—his child."

There, she had said it aloud.

John's face turned dark as he took his pipe out of his mouth. "She said she was with child? Now, Ellen, she not be old enough, is she?" Ellen nodded. "But I have never seen them together, have you?" She shook her head. "Does she understand what it takes to make a baby?" Again he watched his wife nod. "Did ye tell her?" He knew from her eyes that she hadn't. A little louder, he said, "Who told her, then?"

"Ethel."

"Oh no, she wanted our daughter to get in the family way, just like she did with our Joe!" He shouted, "Well I be da—" He pulled himself up without finishing as he never ever swore in front of his beloved wife; he had far too much respect for her to use such language. Clenching his fists, he said, "What did Edina say about Charles?"

He looked at his wife's tear-stained face as she replied, "She said she loves him."

"Could she be mistaken about a baby?"

"Aye, she could, but maybe it explains why she has been off colour the last few days. She is young, maybe she won't carry the baby. We know things happen, as it has to us."

"Would you say that we would be wise to wait and see if indeed there is a little one on the way? Maybe we should be praying to God that she is not strong enough to carry a baby. Do you think Charles will show his face here tonight?"

"Naw, he knows I heard something, he knows I saw them fighting, I do not think he will show his face here tonight."

Ellen and John talked long into the night.

※

Charles didn't return that night or the next. Edina was shocked that Charles cared so little for her. She prayed that some women would hurt him as much as she was hurting.

Ellen had taken Edina aside, suggesting she wait and see if she were pregnant. "Not every relation with a man results in a baby. Maybe you can go over and stay with me ma for a couple of weeks. Let us wait and see if your suspicions are true."

The next day, Joe and Charles came from the mine together. Walking in the back door, Joe called out, "Ma, ye have tea for me and me bad friend here?"

Ellen rushed into the kitchen to see her eldest son with his arm draped across the shoulders of the wayward Charles Vernon.

"Well, I certainly do for you, Joe. As for you, Charles, just because you ain't been sleeping here, you still owe me the rent. Pay up, collect your stuff, and then you be on yer way."

Charles gawped at his landlady.

Joe went over to his mother and, picking the little woman up, swung her around.

"Joe, you put me down this minute."

He laughed. "Not until you say that we can both have tea with the family."

Poor Ellen wasn't sure how her husband would feel about this, and she wanted no nastiness for the young ones to see. Plus they had decided to be in wait-and-see mode.

"Joe, put me down and let me have my say. Look here: Edina be at me parents'; she isn't here. Pa is at the mines, and I think it would only be fair for him to know beforehand. As for you, Charles, what I heard you say to Edina was mean and ugly, so I need you to pay me, collect your stuff, and go back to whatever women you have found to take you in."

Joe was amazed at the forcefulness of his mother. He chided her, saying, "Charles came to us, we have had him staying at our home. He wants to talk to Edina. How do you know that Edina doesn't want to talk to him?"

"I don't." But my bairn is one upset child. "She needs time to recover from such a horrible experience. Charles—and you too, Joe—need to respect me, her ma. Give me three weeks to prepare your pa to allow this meeting and for Edina to feel better. It will also give you, Charles, time to reflect on your words and actions. That is my final word."

Joe knew his mother meant it. "Charles, go and collect your things, give Ma what you owe her." Joe looked kindly at his mother as Charles left. "How is Edina, Ma?"

"Very upset, and so she should be after what he said to her, and she being so young."

"Ma, we will go back to my place and wait for three weeks. I see no harm in that."

Charles walked back into the kitchen—his face as black as the ace of spades and shaking with anger—and threw the money at Ellen, then walked out of the door without a word.

Joe hugged his mother. "He's just angry, Ma. We will see you in three weeks, let me know if three weeks today don't work for the meeting." He gave her a big kiss.

Ellen watched the two boys walk away until she could no longer see them. She fell into the kitchen chair and lifted the apron to her face, thinking, *Well I bought us three weeks, by then we should know for sure if Edina is pregnant and can make plans for how to handle this situation.* She knew that John had asked around about Charles and that he didn't like what he had heard. Charles had all the qualities that John despised: lying, selfish, lazy, controlling, angry, devious, hateful, mean, and a womanizer. As far as John had heard, this man had no redeeming qualities.

Now she, too, had such a bad feeling about this Charles Vernon.

※

Charles was seething with hatred for Ma Paxton. How dare she speak to him like that? She had no right. *I will pay you back, you hateful woman.* He vowed he would woo their daughter away and make her hate her parents, as he did his. *I will punish you Ma Paxton, you wait and see. You picked the wrong guy to cross.*

Chapter 7

Two weeks later, now into mid-May, Ellen walked over to her mother's to see Edina. When she got to the cottage, she was quite shocked at the sight of her daughter, who was glowing with a pregnancy mask. Though Edina was still small, there was no doubt in Ellen's mind that her daughter was definitely with child. She needed Edina home so she had time to plant the idea that Edina could have the child with the support of her mother and father. Sure, there would be shame attached to this decision, but she and John both felt that this was better than a life of misery with Charles Vernon.

"So, Edina, are you ready to come back home? Your sisters and little Robert really miss you, as Pa and I do. Will you come home?"

Edina looked at her mother's pleading eyes, so full of love. She missed her family. "Aye," she said, "how about I be home for tea tomorrow? I have a question, though—is Charlie going to be there? Or will he be working?"

"No, he's gone pet. He is staying with Joe and Ethel."

Edina smiled. "Ma, I will walk you to the stile, I be needing some fresh air."

When mother and daughter reached the stile, Edina helped her mother over and sat on the top to watch her cross the common. As she was sitting there, she couldn't help remembering the first time she slid down Charlie's body. The memory sent shudders of desire through her body. Why hadn't he come to see her? She was sure her brother Joe would know where she was. She sat there daydreaming, feeling the flutters of life deep within her. She closed her eyes and turned her face to the sun.

Suddenly she heard a voice say, "You look so beautiful sitting there."

She opened her eyes and saw Charlie standing in front of her. She wasn't sure how to react. Should she be mad or happy?

"Pregnancy suits you."

Edina stood on the top step of the stile, towering above Charles. "I have nothing to say to you, Charlie."

"That doesn't really surprise me, but I have something to say to you." He blocked her way, so she just stood there. "You are beautiful and you are mine. You are carrying our child, and I want you so badly." He held out his hand to her to help her off the stoop. "Edina, I want you for my wife."

Edina took his hand and immediately her body felt on fire with desire. She stepped down slowly, looking into Charles's eyes that were indeed burning into her soul. Her feet safely on the ground, he gently pulled her to him and his lips slowly descended onto hers. She didn't resist, but she didn't react either. She did not want to appear eager.

"Don't do that, Charlie."

Her body was screaming for her to open her mouth and let his tongue enter, the promise of more. But she stood there with her arms by her side, and as Charles moved slightly back, she didn't move. He let go of her hand and licked his tongue along her lips, his hand slightly quivering as he gently touched her breast.

Charlie paused. "Edina, my darling, mother of my child, tell me to stop and I will."

She slowly opened her mouth as she tried to get as close to him as possible.

Charles breathlessly said, "Oh, Edina, how I have missed you. I want you to give me a sign that I am forgiven."

Edina opened her eyes, frantically looking for cover so they could make up and make love. "Charlie, let's move over to the hedgerow."

※

Charles took Edina's hand as they walked, his thoughts focused on getting Edina to hate her parents. When they reached the hedgerow, they slipped down into the dip at the roots below eyesight. Realizing the moment of intense ardour had passed, they slipped comfortably into each other's arms. Charles had come to understand through his experimenting with others that it was up to him to rekindle her fires.

"Edina, you are so beautiful and the only girl ever for me. I am so sorry if I hurt you and promise it will never happen again. I want and need you, I want you to have our child."

As he buried his head into her hair, he brushed her hair aside to expose an ear. "I love the smell of your hair and how, when the sun shines on it, I can see blonde lights. Then there is your beautiful ear, so small and perfect." With that he licked the edge of her ear, gently biting the lobe. These were all moves he had learned during his nightly visits to the brothels.

He felt her body arch towards him as he ran his tongue down her long, lean neck to the sounds of, "Oh, Charlie." He showed he had learned his lessons well as his hands moved to the buttons of her blouse, one knee coming over her body to gently rest on her pubic bone. With each button undone, he pressed a little on the bone with his kneecap. First one breast, then the other was exposed.

"I want you to understand what I feel, when I touch you." He showed her how to delicately stroke her own breast. Edina writhed with desire.

Charlie tore off her shirt, and her white skin shone with expectation. She pushed him flat on the ground and lifted her skirts. *Oh yes,* thought Charles, *this is right, keep going Edina, follow your instincts.* This had happened to him many times in the brothels, but he said nothing as he lay there. Every now and again he would put his hands below her small behind and lift her upwards—not only for his pleasure but also because he had been told by the whores that they liked it. It was obvious that Edina enjoyed this too. She undid his shirt to expose his flesh and kissed his nipples.

Edina fumbled with the buttons of his trousers, but Charles had other plans—he wanted to show her what else he had learned from others.

"Edina, I want you to remove your skirt." She did this willingly, and then he pulled her knickers off. She lay flat on her skirt, her breasts and nipples hard as once again he kissed them.

"Charlie, I don't think I can wait another moment, I want you now."

"Wait, my love." He nuzzled and flicked his tongue over her stomach.

"I don't think I can wait, Charlie."

He quickly flipped around and at the same time, like a magician, he removed the rest of his clothes. She cried out with pure pleasure as their bodies contorted and climaxed once again.

They lay naked side by side, smiling at each other. Charles was completely forgiven. He, on the other hand, did not need forgiveness; but he did need revenge, though the Paxtons had welcomed him into their home and had always been kind to him. Revenge would be his when he made Edina hate her parents and family.

After they were dressed, they stood holding each other and Edina asked him what was next. He shared with her his plan.

Chapter 8

Edina moved back to her parent's home and it was now obvious she was pregnant.

"Edina, we are so happy to have you home," Ellen said when just the three of them were alone.

"You are looking right bonnie, lass," John added. "Charles and Joe came over three weeks back and asked for a meeting between us all. Not really sure why they want this meeting, but I want to know if this all right with you?" He looked to Edina for an answer.

"Aye, that is fine,"she said, her thoughts drifting back to her last meeting with Charles.

"Remember, my dear, how badly and cruelly Charles treated you. He is a rough and, at times, cruel person. He walked away after you told him you were pregnant. From what I hear, he likes to go to brothels. He has no shame. We will support you. You are a beautiful lass and someone else will want you for his wife."

John carried on, saying, "A cousin of mine got herself into trouble a number of years ago and her parents sent the boy packing, and now she is in the poor house—unmarried with a seven-year-old son. But you have our full support."

※

Charles and Joe arrived on the appointed day and they were all very civil over tea. The adults, which included Edina, moved to the parlour while the children cleaned up the kitchen.

John started the conversation. "Charles, you took advantage of living here, getting our confidence and then proceeding to seduce our daughter, who was only fifteen."

"How do you know that I was the seducer?"

"Because she was a child and you, a man."

"That might be true, but Edina hungered for attention from me. It was she who arranged for you all to visit Grannie, which was very convenient for her, as she had been telling me often that she was no child but a woman. When it is laid out on a plate for you, a man must and will feed. Indeed, wouldn't you feast? What a banquet your daughter gave me. Giving herself, totally to me and crying out for more. If your wife is anything near like her daughter, you indeed are a very, very lucky man, John."

Edina kept her eyes on the floor. Charles had told the truth about it being her idea, but telling of Edina's sexual desires and the details made her angry. He didn't even consider her feelings.

"We as a family are advising our daughter not to marry you," John spat.

"Why is that?"

"Because you are not the right person for our daughter. We know nothing about you. We know nothing about your family. Lately we have heard many in the mine tell stories of you and your womanizing. In fact my own wife heard you tell Edina that you had the right to the joys of any willing woman." John's voice was rising.

"Pa," said Joe, "I think you are being unfair to Charles. He is here because he loves Edina and wants to do the right thing by her."

"He loves himself," John spat back.

Charles looked at Edina's father, his eye's blazing with hatred. "I really don't care what you have heard at the mine. I would have thought that you of all people would judge me on how I am within your family."

"I am, Charles, I am," the normally mild-mannered John shouted. "You sneaked around and got our daughter pregnant. You didn't have the decency to pick a woman, but a mere child."

"Maybe that is so,—or what you think,—but as I said before, Edina was willing. I never had to force myself on her. I am here to tell you what we have decided."

Everlasting Lies | 47

"Who is the 'we'?" Ellen inquired. "I was talking to Edina about you a few days ago, and she said nothing about ever seeing you or any decisions that you both may have made."

"Be quiet, Ellen," John said quickly, which really shocked Edina, as she had never heard her father speak roughly to her mother.

Charles carried on. "Edina and I are going to get married on the eighteenth of June, which is three weeks away. I am leaving this mine and have already arranged our accommodation and a new job in a mine away from here. We are willing to tell you where we will be living depending on the outcome of this meeting."

"You...you young reprobate," said John. "How dare you speak to me in this manner. Edina, do you see this fellow here? Tell me, what do we know of him? What do you know of him? What do you know of his family? This fellow, who treated you disrespectfully is lewd, from what I hear. Edina, do you want to commit your life to someone with these kinds of behaviours? Do you want to marry this man, who speaks to your pa as he just did? Edina, we told you that we are here for you and your child."

Edina glanced at her brother Joe looking for support, but she saw he had his his head on his hands, as if he wanted no part of this. She looked at Charles, who stared back at her with his beady eyes as if to say, *You had better choose me.* She looked at her mother, who seemed so small as she sat weeping. Edina lowered her gaze; she really was still a child who had never had to make decisions before.

Joe got up, scraping his chair across the floor and shattering the silence. "Come on, Charles, let's be off. Pa, Charles has been staying with us ever since he left here. He leaves next week as he starts his new job at—"

"NO!" Charles shouted. "Don't tell him where I am going, nor where I will be living with my new wife unless he plans on giving his blessing to his daughter, and therefore me. It is now up to Edina to say what she wants."

Edina looked at Charles and gave him a wee smile. "Pa, Ma, I want to have this child with the child's father beside me. So yes, I am going to marry Charlie."

John stood up. "Then, me girl, you make your bed, you lie on it. I will have nowt more to say to you, so you best gather up your belongings and leave now with this scoundrel. I cannot care anymore for you, your life is yours, but without this family."

Ellen fell back in her chair. "No...Noooo, you can't mean that John, she be our first girl."

The children were now peeking around the kitchen door.

Edina stood up and said, "Will you come and help me, Charles? I really don't have much that belongs to me. Joe, can I come home with you?"

Joe nodded as Edina and a smiling Charles left the room, then turned to John. "He's not a bad man, Pa. He has a new job and already has somewhere to live. The wedding is planned as he said. He loves Edina."

John continued to scowl in silence; he could now hear his other three children sobbing quietly.

Edina came in, looking somewhat ridiculous in a heavy winter coat and winter hat that it was certainly too warm out for. She had a small bundle wrapped in one of her shawls and Charles held a bigger bundle.

She looked at Ellen, but not John. "Well, we will be off, then," she said brightly as the little ones ran over to her. "We be married on the morning of the eighteenth at ten o'clock at the Pilgrim Street registry. We both would be happy to see you there and celebrate with us. Now this, Pa and Ma, will be your decision, but I hope you will come."

Edina was very proud of how strong she was being. She kissed Ellen and the little ones, the tears flowing down her face and dropping on their heads. She turned to kiss John, but he purposely turned his back to her.

Edina picked up her bundle, put her arm through Charles's, and they walked out the door together.

As Joe, Charles, and Edina walked down the road, Joe took Edina's bundle and put his arm round her. "Come on, sis, don't take Pa to heart, Ma and I will work on him. Your Charles is a good man, you should see him with my little ones, he loves them. He loves you, Edina, and will stick with you through thick and thin, just like he has me. He be like a brother to me. When the men at the mines get on me, he is always telling them the best sides of me." He bent down and kissed the top of his sister's head. "Just think, by the eighteenth, you'll be Mrs. Charles Alfred Vernon, living in your own house."

Ethel and the children were waiting at the door as they had been watching for them to arrive. Ethel opened her arms to her future sister-in-law, who fell into them, sobbing.

"Right, fellows, it won't be the first time you have done this. I want you to get the bairns ready for bed and get them to sleep. Then, if there is no noise from the bairns after fifteen minutes, you can go down to the corner pub for a drink."

"Right, ma'am," they said in unison.

"Meanwhile," Ethel said, putting on her most posh voice, "we ladies will withdraw to the 'drawing room.'" She turned to Edina. "Which means you and me will sit in the kitchen over a cuppa, and I be hearing the whole bloody lark, firsthand."

With that the men laughed loudly at Ethel and started gathering the children so they could get to the pub.

Chapter 9

On June 18th, 1910, Edina Paxton, twenty-one, and Charles Alfred Vernon, twenty-six, were married at 10:00 a.m. with just brother Joseph and his wife, Ethel, as witnesses. The marriage certificate was full of lies. After all, this was twenty-four-year-old Alfred Fletcher marrying fifteen-year-old Edina Paxton. Unknowingly, Edina was now caught up in the lies.

Charles had provided them with a sparse, simple home in Seaton Burns, and he worked at the mine in Killingsworth. Edina spent many hours sobbing while Charles was at work. She had lived in hope that her parents would come to the registry office. She missed her mother so much; they had always spent time together as she was the first daughter. She also missed her younger brothers and sister. She remembered how angry her mild-mannered father had become; she had no idea how strong he really was. She already regretted her weak decision and vowed never to be that weak again. She was going to teach herself how to be strong because she could see that if she was to have any happiness, it was in her hands.

After they had been married just a month, Charles arrived home from the mines and barely grunted acknowledgment of his new wife. Edina expected more, though she realized they were living much the same as they had always lived since he had been a lodger at her parents' house.

"Charlie, when you come home I would like you to treat me like your wife rather than a servant," she spoke out boldly.

"What are you talking about, lass?"

"Well, I be your wife—"

"You are my bloody servant," Charles interrupted, "and don't you forget it, girl. I expect my meal on the table; I don't expect to lift a finger here to do anything in the house or garden. I go to work, and it is bloody hard work. I put my life on the line every day to give you shelter."

Tears welled up in Edina's eyes.

"Stop your bloody snivelling. What the hell are you crying for? I treat you like a wife in bed, don't I?"

"Aye, you simply take whatever you need, whenever you want to," she spoke up strongly. *Where is the Charlie who used to whisper lovely things to me? Caress my body? Kiss me all over until I was on fire? Where has that man gone?"*

"You're lucky I take any notice of you at all. You're just like a big heifer, it's getting increasingly difficult for me to gain any pleasure from you."

"Why did you marry me, then, Charlie?"

"To pay your bloody miserable parents back for being rude to me. Pay them back, I did. Now, woman, get my meal on the table, and after I have eaten, I will see what else you can do to make me happy. Don't stand there gawping at me, MOVE."

"Get your own meal," Edina said, picking up her shawl in defiance.

"If you leave…" Charles was shaking.

"What? You will take to physically beating me? You do it very, very well with words, I am sure you could do it equally well with your fists."

He lunged for Edina just as Joe and Ethel walked in the back door with their two children. Joe noticed Charles's clenched fists and looked at his darling wife. "Mind if I take Charles to the pub?"

"I think that would be a very wise thing to do right now." Ethel put her arms protectively around Edina.

The men left and Edina sobbed, saying, "I have made a terrible mistake. And as my pa said, you make your bed, you lie on it."

"What's been going on?" asked Ethel kindly.

Edina repeated, almost verbatim, the last fifteen minutes.

"Oh, Ethel, he won't tell me how much he makes at the mines, doesn't give me enough to buy food. Surely, as a wife, I have a right to know this. He is so secretive—besides wages, I know nothing about his family, I don't know where he was born, I am not sure he is telling me his right age. He won't help around here in any way. He attacks me for his own pleasure—it is nothing as beautiful as when we were courting."

They continued to chat until the men returned. In the following weeks, there was little that Joe or Ethel could do to help, and they slowly saw less and less of Edina and Charles.

Edina had made some friends who lived close by, and one of the women was a midwife who would deliver her baby. Her pregnancy was uneventful, and Charles was home the night she went into labour. But she had a lot of trouble getting him to walk the two doors down the street to get the midwife on the cold, snowy October night.

"Charlie, do you expect me to go and get her?" she asked, bewildered by his lack of care and close to tears as she wished she had her mother close by.

With that Charles slammed the door. Edina picked up his slippers and placed them in front of the dying fire. She threw some kindling onto it before carefully placing some small coal in the hope that it would catch and Charles would be pleased that she had done this for him.

Charles came back with the midwife, Isabella Tailford, and her daughter Nora, who was twenty and still single and didn't work except to help her mother deliver babies. Isabella knew a lot about birthing. She had gone through eleven births herself and knew a lot about helping mothers who had a child die as that had happened to her three times.

Isabella looked at Edina. "What are you doing bustling over the fire?"

"Oh, I was making it comfortable for Charlie."

"It is time, lassie, to think about you, not him," she said sharply. She had watched this couple since they had moved in in June and really didn't like this wee man, who insisted on being called Charles by everyone but his wife. Most of the men who lived in the cottages were farmers, but Charles was a coal miner with big ways, strutting around in a suit with an expensive gold watch tucked in his waistcoat. His slicked down his blond hair and ogled the young women when he had a pretty young wife already, who certainly didn't look as old as Nora.

"Come on, Nora, let us go and get Edina comfortable and see what kind of wait we are going to have." They went upstairs to the bedroom, where Edina had a basket ready for the child. This cottage, unlike

Everlasting Lies | 53

Isabella's, was pretty small. But it had a box room, which, in a pinch, could be turned into a small room for a child.

"Okay, Edina, let's get ye undressed and take a look at you."

This was a terrifying thought for Edina as she had never, with the exception of Charlie, shown anyone that part of her body.

"Now, lassie, we all be the same. You not the first for either of us. We need to see how far your pains have taken you, or if are we in for a long wait," Isabella said in a very matter of fact voice. "Nora, get the towels from the dresser to lay under Edina."

A strong pain made Edina grimace, and Isabella instructed her to sit on the towels. "Now, Edina, I want you to spread your legs and then pull your knees up. I need to look at your vagina. Nora, grab the lamp and bring it over here so I can see what I'm looking at."

Edina shuddered with embarrassment.

Isabella looked at Edina. *My girl, you are not twenty-one years old. You're not much older than me child Mary, who is nearly fifteen.* As Isabella moved closer to Edina, she said, "Where is your ma?"

Edina knew this would be coming and Charles had said to make something up.

"She is in Newcastle."

"Why isn't she here?"

"Me poor old nan is lying at death's door and me ma cannot leave her." With that Edina started to tear up.

"Now, now, child, you have me and Nora to look after you. Okay, open your legs, Oh my, Edina you will be a mother very, very soon. I can see the top of the bairn's head! You are a natural, Edina, I have only seen a few grimaces from you and here you are all ready to birth. Any time you feel the urge to push as if you want to go to the bathroom is fine with me. Nora, bring us some hot and cold water, you will soon have a baby to wash."

By the time Norah returned to the bedroom, she could see that her mother was already holding a wee head and shoulders in her hands. "One more push, Edina, and we will know if it is a boy or a girl."

With a little grunt, Edina said, "I am hoping for a girl."

"Aye, and that is what you have."

Edina heard her new daughter wail as she was gently laid on her stomach. "Now, one more push when you feel like it as I need a complete afterbirth."

"What is that, afterbirth?"

Nora smiled at the perfect little girl lying on her mother's stomach and covered her with a towel to keep her warm. "Oh, you really are a city girl," she said with a laugh. "Have you never seen anything born, like a dog or cat, even?" She watched as Edina shook her head. "Well, it be the sack that surrounds them. There is a long cord from the sack that is attached to the mother and the baby, which makes the baby grow." She took Edina's hand. "That is why we all have a belly button."

Edina was tired, but she grunted one more time and the placenta was removed. After mother and daughter had cleaned up the room, Edina heard Isabella saying, "Come on, honey, I need to tidy your hair, ready for the father of this bairn to come in and see the new addition to his family in his wife's arms." As she finished brushing Edina's hair, Isabella again wondered what Edina's story was.

Nora came over with Edina's new daughter and placed the small bundle in her arms. Edina looked down at her daughter and marvelled at how tiny and beautiful she was. Nora ran out of the room and called to Charles, as it was now time for him to come and meet the new family member.

The first rays of sunlight were peeking through the curtains and shining on mother and daughter as Charles walked through the door. Edina's smile was radiant as Charles gingerly walked towards the bed. "Here, Charles, is your daughter, what shall we call her?" Isabella and Norah waited to hear the baby's name; what they didn't know was that Charles and Edina had never discussed this.

Charles looked down at his daughter. "We shall call her Lillian—Lily—after my sister."

Edina gasped. "You have a sister called Lily?"

"I do."

"Why have you never told me?"

Isabella, shaking her head, grabbed her daughter's hand and left the room so the family could continue their conversation.

Everlasting Lies | 55

"I don't want to speak about my family—ever. And, Edina, I don't want you to be asking me questions. This is a closed subject."

"Then we will call her Lillian Mary, after me little sister closest to me. I pray to God that me family will talk to this little one. I don't want her to grow up without the benefits of grandparents, aunts and uncles, and cousins. Children need a strong family. I am tired, Charlie, will you please take Lily and place her in her basket as I really need to sleep."

He took his daughter, saying loudly, "This better not become a habit, Edina. I am not a nurse, nor your servant." He placed Lily in the basket, and then looked back at his child bride and mother. She hadn't heard what he'd said as she was already fast asleep.

※

Life was tough for Edina now as a married woman and as a mother. She had written to her mother to tell her that little Lily had arrived safely but heard nothing back.

Edina had been a mother for just a few weeks when Charles arrived home from his shift while she was bathing their baby. "You playing with that damn child again?"

"If you mean am I bathing *our daughter,* the answer is yes. Because I wanted to be able to give you my attention when it is time to eat. Why don't you go and get cleaned up, and by that time I will have tea on the table," she said, smiling at him, but inside she was wondering why he was rarely kind, polite, or even helpful.

As she had promised, by the time he was ready, so was tea. Charles paid little attention to Lily, demanding to know why she was in Edina's arms. Edina ignored this and managed to serve him some hearty soup along with the bread and fairy cakes she had made.

"Tell me what your sister Lily was like. Do you have other brothers and sisters? Where were you born, Charlie? I really want to know about you and your family."

Charles's face turned purple with rage. "It is nothing to do with you, Edina, why all the questions? My family has nothing to do with you—or even, for that matter, Lily. You are my family now, and you are here to serve me as your master and do whatever I bid you immediately."

Edina, smiling and ready to tease Charles, curtsied. "And, Master, what are you going to bid me do then?" He grabbed her roughly at the neck—he may be small, but he was very strong. "You mocking me, woman?"

Edina was shocked at his roughness. "No, Charlie, I asked a simple question about your family. Then you turned nasty, treating me like a servant rather than your wife. Take your hands off me," she said coldly. Lily lay in her arms, her eyes wide. "Don't you ever touch me again when I am holding our child. You scared her." She laid Lily down for safety reasons.

Charles glared at her. "She was younger and a twin. Nine of us children altogether. I disowned my wealthy family." Then he shouted, "I am your master and you will do my bidding. You have kept to yourself for far too long. Remember, you belong to me, I have my rights." With that he pushed her towards the bedroom.

"No, Charlie, no," she begged as he threw her roughly on the bed, lifting her skirts and forcing himself on her for only his pleasure. As he adjusted himself afterwards, he spat out the words, "I am off now, I'll see you after work tomorrow. With that he marched out of the cottage.

Chapter 10

Edina heard the door slam as Charles left. Slowly, she got off the bed and went to her sweet Lily. She picked her up and buried her head into her, sobbing. When there were no more tears left to cry, she quickly washed her face with a damp rag that was laying beside the crib. "Little Lily, if he comes back, which I doubt, he won't see my tear-stained face."

Then Edina heard her next-door neighbour, Sarah, call out from the direction of the back door, so she and Lily followed her voice to the kitchen. Sarah was kneeling in front of her two-year-old son, John, wiping his nose.

"Just saw Charles leaving looking black as thunder, thought I would come over and check on you. Andrew and I often hear him shouting at either you or Lily." When Edina didn't answer, Sarah looked up at her friend and noticed her red eyes. "Oh, luv, what's the matter?"

Edina burst into tears. Sarah promptly put her arms around Edina and Lily.

"Now, Edina let me put the kettle on for a cuppa. We will make ourselves comfy and I will see if I can bring a smile back to your face." Lily squealed with delight at Sarah's closeness.

Tea was made and the two children were placed on the floor. Little John was fascinated with baby Lily, and she with him.

"So now, tell me what is bothering you, Edina. You shouldn't be unhappy, and if you are, you shouldn't bottle it inside of you."

This unleashed the stories from Edina, the main ones being that she knew nothing about Charles's family and that she hadn't seen her family for nearly a year. Even though she had written to them and told them about Lily without Charles knowing, they had never acknowledged her letter.

Sarah, though she was unaware of this fact, was eighteen years older than her friend. She was wise and said, "Edina, you need to go and see them, and it's not that far away. You need to show your mother her grandchild. You cannot live like this—wanting to make amends and not doing anything."

"Aye, it is easy to say, but I have no money to go and see them. Even if I did, Charles would be extremely angry at me if he knew."

With a glint in her eye, Sarah said, "Then let's tell him you want to come with me to visit my parents. Do you think he would give you some money for the fare under those circumstances?"

"I really dunno, Sarah. He is very tight with his money, and secretive. I don't know how much he even makes at the mine."

"You're his wife, Edina."

"Aye, but he treats me like a servant. I do as I am told. I look after all his needs at his bidding."

"Edina," said Sarah, "that isn't how marriage should be. How did you get into this situation?"

With tears in her eyes, Edina looked at Lily on the floor with John and then at her friend and simply said, "Passion."

The two friends talked most of the evening, the children falling asleep on the floor together. They decided that they would plan their journey for the following week, which would give Edina enough time to ask Charles.

However, Edina had other plans that she thought might work better. The next week she was extra nice to Charles, and as she hung up his clothes, she searched for money in his pockets. Little by little, even stealing from him at night, she gathered enough money to go see her parents.

The day before the planned trip, she asked Charles if she and Lily could go see Sarah's mother the next day. She told him Sarah had offered to pay for her as she wanted the company. Charles granted permission.

The two young mums set off early on that sunny morning to catch the train. Though it was already hot, they had quite a bit of walking ahead of them, so Edina brought a shawl so she could swaddle and tie her infant to her body.

As they travelled, Edina told Sarah all about her family and spoke with joy.

As they closed in on Chester Le Street, where Ellen and John had moved to be closer to Joe and his family, Edina began to get nervous. "My pa should be at the mines," she rambled. "I always loved it around here as it is close to the River Ware, do you know my family has lived here for centuries? So I've been told. Chester Le Street is used by many of the coalmines as the coal is transported on barges on the river. Then there is the beautiful Lumley Castle..." Edina was having a great time telling Sarah all that she knew.

As she got closer to her parents' house, which she had never been in, she looked in panic at Sarah, who smiled at her friend. "Don't worry, Edina, the worst is that she will shut the door in your face."

With that Edina marched up to the door and knocked. The door opened, and very quickly Edina said, as strongly as she could despite her knocking knees, "Ma, it is me with my friend Sarah, and I have brought your granddaughter Lily to meet you."

Ellen opened the door, her eyes shining with the tears. "Come in, oh come in, Edina, my child, and let me see the bonnie wee lass. Sarah, welcome to my home, I am so glad you came with Edina."

Ellen took Lily from Edina, promptly putting the child comfortably on her hip, and they all followed her into the kitchen, where she grabbed the kettle to make tea.

Edina went to her mother, smiling. "Here, let me make the tea whilst you talk to Lily, Sarah, and her little Johnny."

"Hinny, being a mother suits you. I sure have missed seeing you, dear. Is Charles fine? How is his new job? I guess not so new now." Ma laughed at her own silliness. Your brother Robert is having some trouble at school, bright lad. But he and his dad are always arguing. I hate that. So much so that Robert is living with Pa's sister, Rachel Glaspher. She lives at 18 Lambert Street, Stockton, on Tees Durham. Now, I am sure he would love to see you and Lily."

Edina smiled, but she was shocked to hear her pa had had words with Robert.

Time together passed quickly and easily.

"Ma, do you think that Pa would mind if I tried to make a visit when he is home? Mind you, I will have to save for a while for the train fare, but I would like to see you all. Meanwhile, if you wanted to, you could come for a visit to me."

"I think your pa would be ready to see you again, child, and I know your two sisters would love to see you and Lily. I certainly could come and see you, and meanwhile we can write."

Besides really wanting to establish contact again with her family, Edina had another reason for coming—one she hadn't even told Sarah. "Ma, that would be wonderful. Before I leave I want to tell you one more thing—Lily will have a little brother or sister soon."

There, she has said it aloud for the first time.

"How wonderful! I am happy for you. Thank you, dear child, for having the courage to come and make things better between us. I heard news from time to time from Joe but was really worried about how Charles would react."

"I think, Ma, it would be best if we kept it the way it is now. Charles carries grudges for a long while."

Ellen took her newly found granddaughter in her arms. "What a bonnie wee girl you are, Lily. Nan's little darling. Now, you look after your Ma until I see you both again."

She handed the precious bundle back to Edina. Mother and daughter hugged and cried.

"Nice to meet you, Sarah. Thanks for coming with Edina. Friends are so important."

As the women and children left, Edina turned many times to get one more look at her mother.

When the house was no longer in sight, Sarah turned to Edina. "Well, your ma was plenty happy to see you. What a wonderful lady, and it was great learning about all your family. Wow, and that is great news, when is the baby due?"

"November. Sorry I hadn't told you before, it just seemed Ma was so pleased to see us and I wanted her to be the first to know."

"What you mean, Edina: *first to know*? You haven't told Charles yet? Why?"

"I haven't because I think he will be unhappy with the news. But I will. Or maybe I will wait until he notices..."

Chapter 11

By July of 1914, living in the small cottage in Seaton Burton was very busy for young Edina with her two active children; Lily was just over four years old and John was soon to be two. Their young neighbours, Andrew and Sarah Patton, also had two children. Sarah and Edina had become very close and Andrew and Charles got along well.

One afternoon as the four children played outside together, the women chatted as they watched over them and the men relaxed inside.

"Charlie is still so upset with me, Sarah, now that Ma and Pa are back in my life."

"Good job they are—at least your ma helps you with the children."

"Aye, that be true. Charlie takes little notice of them and definitely would never put them to bed or play with them."

"Andy and I have noticed that he acts like you are his servant. We often hear him shouting at you. I don't know why you put up with it."

"You know very well, Sarah, that he is not an easy man. He is never wrong and loves to argue—and if not winning, simply puts you down. But as women, what choice do we have?"

"Um, dunno, but I am not sure I could do it."

Meanwhile, Charles and Andrew discussed the situation of conflict in Europe over a smoke and beer.

"You know, Charles, I read that the heir to the Austro-Hungarian throne and his wife were assassinated when driving through the streets of Sarajevo in Bosnia. Our press is reacting with fear over European peace. When I read that, I turned to Sarah and said that this is not a good situation."

Charles sighed. "I would never allow Edina to have an opinion. I don't know, Andrew, with all the doom and gloom in the papers, it sure doesn't look good." He dragged on his pipe. "I can see why Britain is siding against Germany. I mean, we have never been very fond of the Krauts, have we?"

"I couldn't agree more, Charles, but we should be okay. Though chances are we will be at war, we are fathers and have responsibilities."

"You reckon that will make a difference? We be young," said Charles, puffing out his chest.

"Aye, but I don't want to be leaving Sarah and the bairns."

"Your wants aren't going to be a consideration." Charles took a swig of his beer. "Russia and Germany are each looking for dominance in Central Europe. This country won't allow Krauts to take that. Mark my words, war over there would affect our food supplies. In fact if war be declared officially, I would join up, Andrew. I am not enjoying being a father, the children take Edina's focus off me, and she wouldn't notice if I left."

"You be a selfish bugger, you would miss the joys of your pretty young Edina," Andrew said with a wink.

"Nah, a man in uniform can get plenty."

"Even a short little bugger like you? After all, your not be as tall my wife." Andrew got up, laughing. "You must have been the runt of the litter. Your sisters, if you have any, would all be taller than you. Nah—your ma and pa took one look at you and said 'No more.'"

"Laugh as much as ye like, but women fall over with joy after an encounter with me." Charles picked up a rock to throw at Andrew.

"You are a little liar." Andrew dodged behind the hedge separating their cottages.

⁂

Charles had obviously been watching the papers because on the first of August, the navy was mobilized and the army was on war footing. On August 4, Great Britain declared a state of war on Germany.

Charles came home from the mines towards the end of August. Lily sat beside him while he had his tea as Edina was getting young John ready for bed. As Lily jabbered away, Charles nodded every now and again, not listening at all. *What a bloody life this is,* he was thinking, *tied down with children and a wife who does her best to refuse me whenever I make advances.* He was aware he was never really very nice to her, belittling her whenever possible and making fun of her in front of her girlfriends. She just wasn't his equal, intellectually. Anyway, if the truth was known, she was just twenty and he was already thirty.

Edina came into the kitchen. "Lily, it's time to get ready for bed. Say goodnight to Pa and give him a kiss."

Charles felt his daughter's kiss on his cheek and then watched Edina carry her to bed.

When Edina came back in, she said, "Well, that's them down. I see you didn't bother to clean the things from the table."

"I am not doing women's work." He settled into his chair with his pipe and the paper.

"Well, I will go and wash up the tea things and then wash your miner's clothes. Is there anything you need, Charlie?"

He gave her a look. "Yes, you."

He was a frustrated man; he needed to be the centre of attention. It had been a long time since Edina had looked at him in adoration.

Eventually Edina came and sat down beside the fire after finishing in the kitchen.

"How was your day, Charlie?"

"Bloody hard work," he retorted.

"Charlie, you know I don't like you using language like that."

"I be damned if I will have you telling me how I should talk. It is bloody hard work on the face, and you are lucky that I work hard and support you and the children."

"I am, Charlie," she said, getting up as she watched his face turn red yet again.

"Where the bloody hell are you going?" Charles said. "You just sat down."

You don't treat me right, thought Edina, *you verbally abuse me, you take no notice of your children, and I am better off in the solitude of my kitchen.* Instead, she said, "Why do you ask? Do you have something to tell me about your day? I know you work hard in the mine, and I don't

Everlasting Lies | 65

want to make you angry. There is always work for me to do in the kitchen, just thought I would leave you so you can read your paper."

"Come back here and sit down."

The unkind way Charles said this sent a shudder through Edina. The thought that he was going to want to make love to her again made her tremble. The last time he was so rough and forceful, he had hurt her and there was no joy for her. His lovemaking had become directive, making her do things she didn't want to do.

"I want to tell you something." He waited until she sat down before he continued. "I have decided to enlist. Tomorrow after work I am going to Newcastle to see if I can join the Northumberland Fusiliers. It will give us a steady income. If I join the reserve corps, it will be unlikely I will be sent overseas. If I wait and I get called up, I will be put in the Army, then for sure I will be sent abroad. There will be no discussion on this as I don't want to be killed. This is what's best for me, I am protecting my own interests."

Charles waited for some kind of outburst from his young wife.

Nothing.

"Well, you have nothing to say?"

She shook her head. Still nothing.

"Why the bloody hell not?"

"You already told me there was to be no discussion as this is what's best for you."

"I'll be going into work early so I can leave early. Make sure my suit is ready."

Edina turned, saying, "I am off to bed now, our mornings are early enough."

When Charles finished work the next day, he got cleaned up and caught the bus into Newcastle. With the state of war declared and Lord Kitchener's new form or short service introduced, there was a long lineup of fellows all ready to volunteer. In theory, these early volunteers could choose the regiment they joined. Charles wondered if they were all volunteering for the reserve.

After a two-hour wait, he sat down for his interview.

"Well, Charlie, where are you looking to enlist, then?"

"Thought about being in the reserve. Please, my name is Charles."

"Why the reserve, *Charles*?"

"I got to thinking that this way I would get some good training, and therefore be more useful," Charles replied, feeling quite smug with his answer.

"Well, here is the form, I will leave you to fill it in whilst I interview someone else. I will be back with you shortly so I can go over what you have written."

Charles filled out the form. His only true statement was the date: Monday December 14, 1914.

When he turned in his form, he was given number 34233, told to put his affairs in order, and to report to East Boldon on Monday January 4, 1915, at 10:00 a.m. for six weeks of training.

When Charles walked into the cottage all dressed in his suit, Edina looked at him in surprise.

"I didn't think you meant what you said last night."

"You are a stupid woman."

"Charlie, don't be so hurtful. How did you get on?"

"Nothing to do with you, my dear woman. What I do, where I decided to go, has absolutely nothing to do with you." He was now shouting at her angrily.

"It does, if I have your meal ready and you don't turn up, it has everything to do with me."

"Don't you raise your voice at me, I am your master."

"Charlie, let me tell you that you not very good one."

The back door opened and Sarah called out, "Yoo-hoo! Edina, you there? Well, God bless my soul, look at you, Charles…in a suit. Where you been? To see the Queen?" Sarah started to laugh.

"As a matter of fact, I have just joined the reserve."

"You what, Charlie?" said Edina.

"Watch my bloody lips, Edina. I. Just. Joined. The. Reserve. Army. I report to East Boldon on January the fourth for six weeks of training."

"Hey, hey, Charles, there is no need to talk to Edina like that, I was the one who asked you."

Well, you want to know, Sarah, I "don't like you barging into my house and interfering with the way I talk to my lazy wife."

Both women looked at Charles as he pulled himself to his full height.

"As there is no tea waiting for me and it is unlikely you will have any time for me, I am off to find me a woman, a real woman—that is unless you, Sarah"—he smirked at her—"are willing to fulfill my desires? Don't wait up, Edina, I won't be needing you. In fact don't expect me home until after my shift tomorrow. Whoever I find, I shall spend the whole night with her."

"You are a dirty bugger." Sarah couldn't help saying this to Charles.

He turned, grabbed her by the shoulders, and kissed her hard as he fondled her breasts. "Ah, you sure you wouldn't like to fulfill my desires? I would like that, and you, for once, would experience a real man making love to you. Edina, look how she cannot resist me, there is no fighting from her." Charlie's mouth once more covered Sarah's.

Sarah, now recovered from the shock of Charles's attack, shoved him away with all her might and spat in his face.

With that Charles walked out the door, laughing. "I will see you, sweet tasty Sarah, you will be begging me to make love to you soon." He turned and blew her a kiss. "Next time when you are on your own, I will have my way with you, you will be begging for more. Maybe we could make Edina watch. Or better yet, Andrew could have her."

"Oh, Edina, I am so sorry, I could hear him shouting and thought it better if I came over. Now I have made it worse. However do you put up with him?"

Edina was crying. "Thank you, my dear friend, I am happy you came over. He is such an unreasonable man at times. I am sorry he treated you the way he did."

"He is disgusting, Edina. Did he mean it about finding another woman?"

Edina just nodded.

Chapter 12

Christmas came and went quietly in the Vernon household as Charles flatly refused to spend time with any of Edina's family, and so they were alone with their two children. Though Edina was very unhappy about this, she knew that once her husband went in the Army, she would see a lot more of her parents and the rest of her family.

The morning of January 4 came and Charles had to be off pretty early. He kissed the tops of the children's heads and gave Edina a peck on her cheek. She gave him a sweet smile and told him to stay safe. Holding John in her arms, she gaily smiled as he left.

Edina knew that her life would be more peaceful now. Her children were far less demanding than her husband, who she had found to be very selfish and needy over the last four years. He was unkind to her, often making fun of her speech and lack of education. He argued every little point with her, and if she tried to defend herself in any way, he began the name calling and swearing. Edina became more and more quiet around him. She was happy he was leaving. Not only would her life be more peaceful but now she would also be in control of running her house rather than always having to beg for money. She would not have to watch Charles turn his back as he got out his wallet so she could not see how much was still left after he gave her a pittance for the needs of the family. Now the Army would be giving her a daily reserve pay for her to feed and care for the children, herself, and the home.

She would also be able to help Isabella with her midwifery; one of Isabella's youngest daughters was able to look after Lily and John whenever Edina was needed as a midwife. Charles had always scoffed at the idea that Edina had any brains to do this.

Everlasting Lies | 69

Edina also had major plans to start growing more of their food. Charles was always against this idea as he felt it might involve him; though he worked hard at the face of the mine, he was a lazy man and expected to be waited on. Edina wondered how he would survive the Army.

Meanwhile Charles arrived at Bolton and went to the registrar's office, where he received his uniform, had his head shaved, was inoculated, and then was shown to his tent and allowed to rest. Charles looked around and nodded his head. *This is all right,* he thought.

The next six months were spent marching, learning gun control, and saluting. His fellow soldiers soon named him D.W., which, he eventually realized, stood for dogging work, or they referred to him as the runt; although he was amazingly small, he had a tendency to walk about like someone important.

Charles sometimes wondered if he might meet up with his older brothers Dicky or Abe. He did miss Abe; not only was he his brother, but he had always been kind and helpful to Charles. Yes, indeed, he would like to see Abe again.

Most of the men, when they were able to get into town on a few hours' pass, wanted some good food, but Charles and a young fellow, Sid, were always looking for the joys of female company—another kind of feeding frenzy.

One evening in town, they met up with a young women called Maggie, who simply said, "Are you soldiers looking for a good time?"

They both nodded.

She smiled. "You want a threesome?"

Sid and Charles looked at each other and then back at this young women. Sid said, "What do you mean?"

"Silly boys, I mean I will take you both to the heavens at the same time." They looked at her in astonishment. Now, young Sid had never been to a prostitute before, so he was looking at Maggie and was already excited. Maggie looked at Sid and said; "I can see you like the idea." She looked over at Charles. "What about you?"

"I don't know, I kind of like the idea of having you all to myself. I like the satisfaction it brings me when I have all of a woman."

"I tell you what, if I don't please you both, then it's free."

Sid nodded, saying, "What have we got to lose?"

※

"Wow," said Sid as they left Maggie, "what an experience that was. There were times when I didn't know whose hands were on me."

"It was okay."

"What you mean? It was bloody fantastic, Charles."

"No, Sid, it is better alone."

"How so?"

"Well, you get all the attention. I have been with about thirty women, not counting my wife."

"Thirty?"

"Aye, and everyone taught me to be a better lover."

"Does your wife say that?"

"Aye, I have told her that I sometimes go to prostitutes. She gets hurt by this, but I want to hurt her so that she performs to keep me. I want her to know that I can get any woman, so she better keep me happy by pleasing and pleasuring me. Of course, she has no idea how many prostitutes I have visited or how many other women I have had, but I learn from these women and take these ideas home with me and get Edina to do the same things. That's a benefit for her. I can tell you sometimes she becomes crazy with desire after a little suggestion here and there—this way we both get benefits from my research."

Sid rolled his eyes.

"I have rights as a husband, and if hurting her keeps her in line, that's to my advantage."

"Why isn't she enough for you?"

"Can you ever have enough?"

"I dunno."

"Well, for me I would enjoy having sex once or twice a night. In fact us talking like this makes me very ready for more. I tell you what, let's make a wager. I bet I can get any woman from the next pub we come across to kiss me and leave with me."

"You're on. How much? And it has to be completed in fifteen minutes."

"Five shillings says that the woman will leave the pub with me within fifteen minutes."

The Black Bull came into sight. As they walked in, Charles said, "Watch a master."

He swaggered up to the bar next to a young brunette and her girlfriend. "Hi, lassies, can we buy you a drink? What are your names?"

"Lovely. Ta, mine is Ann and this is Liz."

"We are Charles and Sid. Sid here is just an ordinary bloke, but me, I love experiencing new and different things." The barman set down four drinks in front of them. "Now, which of you ladies likes to have fun?"

"That would be me, Charles," said Liz.

Charles moved over to Liz as Sid looked at his watch.

"Then, let us have a toast, Liz." He encouraged her to link arms while they toasted each other. Charles forced his way between her legs as she sat on a stool, placing one hand on her upper thigh. "To an evening of pleasure." He squeezed her thigh, allowing his little finger to move upwards with a stroke. She moved closer to him, her eyes shining as she gently moved her hips up and down.

"I certainly will drink to pleasures of the night." Laying a hand on Charles's face, she let her little finger touch his lips as he swallowed.

He panted, whispering, "Liz, you are very desirable," and he moved as close as was possible. "You look like you have perfect breasts that need to be kissed, and your thighs are telling me that you can hardly wait for excitement. I may look small in stature, but I am told that I am hugely manly. Would you like to play explorer with me?"

Liz quickly poured her drink down her gullet. "Oh yes, indeed, I would love to explore and be explored. Shall we leave now?" She slid from the bar stool, maintaining contact with Charles's body.

Charles winked at Sid. "We are off, Sid, see you back at the barracks." Liz was now kissing Charles as they walked out of the bar.

※

Charles managed to get home on an illegal overnight pass in mid-April. He was able to catch a bus, and because he was in uniform, he got a free ride. Edina did not know he was coming home. He had not written at all since he had left, and she did not know where to write.

Charles really wasn't sure how to approach his own house after being away so long. After all, when he left for training, it was almost as if Edina was glad he was leaving. As he walked up to the front door, the memory of the first time they made love, back when Edina had managed to get her parents to leave her in the house on her own, came back to him. He remembered how passionate she was. He decided to knock on the front door; this way, he would be able to see her reaction.

Rat-a-tat-tat went the doorknocker. He stood on the stoop with his cap in hand and his blue eyes shining. The lights were on in the living room, and he could smell the smoke of the coal fire. He heard someone walking towards the door and watched the handle turn as Edina called out to ask who it was. He said nothing, and the door opened a crack and Edina peered out into the darkness. When she saw Charles, she flung the door wide and put her arms around his neck. She smiled and then kissed him lustily. "Oh, Charles, what a surprise! I have dreamt about you coming home. I was real worried as I hadn't heard from you, but you are here." She pulled him into the coziness of the living room.

Edina took his cap and greatcoat. "Sit down. How long are you home for? Do you want some tea? Oh, how I have missed you. The children are growing so fast." She stood in front of him, the firelight catching the tears in her eyes.

Charles looked up at his young wife. She was indeed beautiful. "I have an overnight pass and have to be back tomorrow. I want you, Edina, as I have missed you as well." He pulled her towards him and she did not resist as she slowly sank to the floor in front of the fire.

"Come lie here in the warm, Charles. Bring down some cushions for us." She licked her lips, which set him on fire. He crawled beside her and gently laid his hand on her breast, then kissed her softly, brushing his hand through her hair and murmuring to her about how much he had missed her.

Edina ran her hand over his coarse serge pants, feeling for the buttons and saying, "Your clothing is rough, let me remove it for you." He lay still, letting her do what she wanted. Her small hands struggled with the

Everlasting Lies | 73

buttons of his trousers, but once she had them undone she pulled the pants aside, exposing his underwear and the largeness of his member underneath them. "Lift up your buttocks, Charlie," she ordered. She pulled his trousers to his knees, then lifted her skirts and straddled him, moving to get comfortable she reached down to his feet and unlaced each boot, and as she moved back and forth, he felt every movement of her body. Once the boots were unlaced, she gently rolled to the floor and removed the offensive boots, then pulled his trousers off and looked adoringly at him. She slowly, so slowly, moved back up his body.

※

All the while, Edina thought about how she needed Charles to make love to her. She had missed her monthly time and was convinced she was pregnant.

As she continued to undress Charles slowly, she thought back to the chance encounter she'd had with the boy who had lived next door when she and her parents lived in the Joyce Buildings. She was back to see her parents when she bumped into Bill Charlton, who had also visited his parents while he was home on leave. He decided to visit the Paxton's as well, as he had been wondering about Edina. How lucky that she was visiting them the day he dropped by. He offered to help her get her children home as Lily was going on five and John was a tiger at three. Plus, she had an armful of goodies that her mother had made. Edina willingly took the offer; after all, Bill was a handsome young fellow and just a year older than she. She was really missing male company and had not had a word from Charlie.

Once she and Bill were back at her cottage, she gaily said, "Bill, do you have time for tea?"

"I would love that, Edina. How can I help?" This astounded Edina as in all her married life, Charles had never offered to help.

"How good are you in the kitchen?"

"I can do whatever you ask me."

"Well, if you make our tea, I will get the children ready for bed. Then maybe after I have put them to bed, we can catch up on old times and I can find out if you ever did get to work for the railway. Do you remember telling me you were moving to your uncle's? That is, if you have time to stay?

"I don't have to be back until six tomorrow night. Tell me what you want for tea and I will get busy in the kitchen."

Edina showed Bill where things were and got the children ready for bed very quickly before tidying herself up. By the time she and the children went back to the kitchen, Bill not only had the tea ready but he also had a cozy fire going in the fireplace. The four had tea together, and it was obvious that both her children liked Bill, who actually talked to them and picked them up and made them laugh. Edina smiled. Her home sounded like a happy place.

After tea, she bustled around cleaning up while Bill played with the children. When she had finished washing up, she watched him with the children and laughed. "Okay, you little demons," she said, "it is time for bed."

Out came the cries from the children. "No! We want to play with Uncle Bill."

"I tell you what, little ones," said Bill, "if you go off to bed now, I promise I will come back and see you both before I leave tomorrow. Is that a deal?"

The children were now screaming and jumping.

Edina smiled at Bill before turning to the children. "Off you go...go peepee and I will come and tuck you in."

"Edina, I am just going to pop out to the off-licence and pick up some beer for us," said Bill. "Do you like wine?"

"I don't know, I have never had any. I'll get the children settled, just walk back in, Bill."

The fire blazed and Edina sat knitting as Bill let himself in the back door.

"Hey, luv, where are your glasses?

"I will come and help you," she gaily called back.

"No, don't get up, I will bring it in to you. Do you happen to have a tray?" he called.

Everlasting Lies | 75

"Yes, there be one beside the cooker." She got up and dragged her only side table into the centre of the room so he had somewhere to put the tray.

In he walked, looking handsome in just his khaki shirt and serge pants, holding aloft a tray topped with wine glasses, cheese and crackers, and a posy of anemones. As he placed the tray down, Edina said, "Ah, what pretty flowers! Where did you get them from? I have never been given flowers before. Where ever did you find the cheese and crackers?"

Laughing, Bill replied, "It's amazing what people will do for us soldiers. Anyways, hang about, I couldn't get everything on the tray." With that he went back into the kitchen, came back with a bottle of wine and a bowl of grapes, and then he poured the wine and sat in Charles's chair.

They caught up with their lives, she telling him about Charles, he telling her about joining up. She asked him about girlfriends and he said he had none in his life, especially now as he knew he was soon going over the pond. He laughingly told her how, as a teenage boy, he'd had a crush on her. Bill queried why she sat on the settee while Charles had his chair much closer to the fire.

She tried to explain that Charles liked the best seat in the house.

"Up you get, Edina," Bill demanded.

By the time he had finished, Bill had moved Charles's chair, placed the settee so that Edina and the children could sit and get the most benefit from the fire, and put the table within easy reach. "Now, isn't that better, Edina? Come sit and be nice and cozy by the fire. And now we can sit together."

"You better not be getting too comfortable. You should soon be on your way back to your ma's as you promised you would come back and see the children tomorrow."

"Ma's not expecting me. In fact I was wondering if you would mind if I kipped here on your sofa for the night. Or would that cause you some problems?"

Edina laughed. "No, it doesn't cause me any problems."

Charles lay on the floor, looking up at Edina. "You certainly seem hungry, Edina."

Edina was glad she had been able to fool Charles into believing that it had been a long time since she had made love. With the number of love bites she noticed on his body, she was sure it wasn't the same for him. As she settled on him, she said, "Charlie, though I am ready to explode, I want to remember this moment—gently, gently."

It was enjoyable as she was directing the movements to Charlie, but she was in control of her mind and could think only of the time with gentle Bill, as she knew she was his first. She lay beside Charles, dreaming of Bill—kind, gentle Bill—the man she knew was the father of her next child. She would be able to get away with this as long as Charles wasn't around for the birth. She remembered making love to Bill, who had declared his love for her and promised to write. Even though she thought he would already be in France, he would never know he had fathered a child.

✧

Charles was back at the barracks with the soldiers he had been training with when they were told to pack up their gear as they were going to be stationed in Sunderland, which was closer to the coast. This meant that they would be marching in full gear as if they were in combat; there would be no leave before this departure.

The march from East Boldon to Sunderland was very interesting. Men carrying the regiment colours marched from the barracks through Boldon, followed by men who marched four abreast, the shortest soldiers in front, many of whom looked like underage boys. This was where Charles, a mere five feet one and a half inches, marched—he liked to say the best led the pack—each group behind him increasing in height. The men marched with full battle kits and helmets slung behind, all of them wearing their great coats and carrying their guns. They took each step in unison, a single sound rising to the heavens as if to say *We will win, we will win*, the sound echoing in the streets as people rushed out of their houses to cheer these brave men on.

Once out of town the march continued, but the soldiers now marched two by two so traffic could pass them. They sang songs to keep the rhythm and to help take the soldiers' minds off the distance they had to travel. Songs such as "Pack Up Your Troubles" and "It's a Long Way to Tipperary" floated across the countryside.

They marched to Sunderland's square, where the men would be organized and sent either to their quarters or to the tent area.

Charles was not liked by the men of the Northumberland Fusiliers and was unhappy, so he asked for and was granted a transfer. He joined the Newcastle-on-Tyne 184th Machine Gun Corps on June 28, 1915. He was given a month's leave as he was a reservist, and he was told to put all of his affairs in order as it would be likely that, as a member of the regular army, he would eventually be going abroad. He was to report for service on July 26, 1915.

Chapter 13

Charles wrote to Edina to tell her that he was changing regiments and that, because of this, he would have some time away from the army and should arrive home on June 28, although he didn't know for how long.

This was Edina's first ever letter from Charles since he had left.

Dear Charlie,

I was surprised to get a letter from you as it has been so long and I had no idea where to write.

The children are excited that their daddy is coming home.

You managed to leave a gift with us when you were last home…I am with child once again and the baby is due in December.

Things here have been tough with little money, so the children and I set to and made us a garden. The tough digging work was done by one of the lads from the cottages, as I couldn't do it all. Believe it or not, we are growing runner beans, peas, potatoes, carrots, beets, parsnips, a few cabbages, and brussel sprouts. The farmer down the lane gave me some tomato plants, which I planted, I set lettuce and radishes. We will have vegetables and salad all summer.

The farmer is going to help me make a root cellar in the garden, so we should have vegetables most of the winter, which will save us money.

I hope that we will see you soon.

Your wife, Edina, and Lily and John.

When Edina told her mother and father that Charles had made her pregnant the one night he was on leave, they shook their head in disbelief. Then she told them that he was moving to the regular army and should be home around the end of June. Her father told her he would come over in the autumn to help her gather and store the vegetables.

When Charles arrived home, he could see Edina and the children working away in the garden. As he came through the gate, the children came running. "Daddy! Ma, Daddy's home," cried Lily, with little John following closely behind her.

"What's all this, then?" said Charles, totally ignoring his children.

Edina looked up from her planting. "It is a garden, Charlie, I told you about it in my letter—to help get us through the winter. It be some work, but it will be worth it."

Charles looked fiercely at Edina. "Well, don't you be expecting me to give you a hand because I won't."

"No, the young lad and the farmer have promised to help."

"What do they get in return?"

Edina was well aware what Charles was intimating.

"Anything they want, though the farmer's not my type. The young lad of sixteen has quite the body and likes to hang out with me and the children." Edina smiled inwardly, ready to play Charles's game.

"Why you doing this? You are pregnant, and how the hell did you get pregnant again?"

"Well, that is a funny question coming from you, Charlie. You seemed to be a very willing participant in the making of this child." Tears welled up in her eyes.

"Well, you caught me off my guard."

"'You mean I caught you with your pants down. Really, Charlie, you better not come near me if you don't want the consequences."

"Why can't you be like the whores and do something to protect yourself?" With that Charles marched into the house.

Edina turned back to her garden, fell to her knees, and sobbed, wondering how long this man was going to be home. Lily came over and hugged her mother.

Charles stayed for nearly a month—a month of hell for Edina. She managed to keep him at bay, repeating that her condition was his fault. When he could not get his way with her, he would shout, raising his hands as if strike her.

"You are denying me my rights, you witch. Get these brats over to your mother's. If you don't do this, I will have to visit the whorehouse."

The threats, shouts, and name-calling left her emotionally damaged, but she said nothing.

"I am leaving for a few days. You are driving me into the arms of those who will satisfy my needs," he would say, slamming the door as he left and cursing so loud that the whole street would hear. She would be relieved when this happened because he would be gone for two to three days at a time.

Eventually Charles left to begin his new career, which was in the coastal defenses with the MGC on the east coast. Charles told Edina there was a feeling that the Jerrys would attack the coast and try to interrupt the mines. As he left, Edina was cool, as were the children.

The very next day, young Bill Charlton came knocking on the cottage door.

"Hello, Edina," he smiled warmly. "What a lovely garden you have. You must have worked very hard to get that all planted. What a bonnie lass you are, in fact a picture of health. Are you going to leave me on the stoop, or are you going to invite me in?"

Edina looked at his smiling face and moved back so he could step in.

"Uncle Bill!" cried the children. "Are you staying?"

"Only if your ma says I can." Bill winked at Edina.

"Can he, Ma? Pleeease, can he?"

"Now, now children, Uncle Bill won't want to sleep on the settee. He is far too big to be comfortable."

Lily looked at her mother with imploring eyes. "He could have our bed and we could sleep with you, Ma. That would work, wouldn't it, Uncle Bill? You would have your own room then."

"Aye, I would, and that would be mighty kind of you, especially as this is my last leave before going to France. I have five days off, and spending it here with you youngsters would mean a lot to me. But it is up to your ma to say yes."

With that three pairs of eyes turned to look at Edina.

"How can I refuse with an offer like that from my children? Bill, I can't tell you how much we all would like to spend this time with you."

"Good," he said.

"So, Lily and John, if your ma says it is okay, let's move you over to her room and make a space for me."

Edina laughed. "Off you three go. Lily and John, make sure you keep my room tidy. I will see what we can have for tea." *What a different feel in this house with Bill here rather than Charlie,* she thought. *I can't remember one time the children laughed when Charlie was around.*

After the children were in bed, Edina came downstairs to the living room to find it changed back to a cozy configuration, with wine already poured.

Edina started the conversation. "When do you leave for France?"

"Not really sure, pet. Either July or August. There's a lot of movement of divisions into brigades, and we have been told that this is probably our last leave before setting off. I just had to come and see you and the children again. Spending my last five days here with you would be perfect as long as it won't cause problems."

"Well, Charles was just home on leave as he has changed into the MGC as home defense. He said he didn't think he would get back again until later this year."

Bill, taking Edina's hand, said, "You know I love you and your children, don't you? But times are so uncertain right now. If I come back from this war, you will be the first to see me. Then we can make plans."

"Aye, I know that, and I love you, Billy. Let us make the most of these five days and pretend like we are family."

"Isn't it a bit dangerous? What will your neighbours think?"

"It is all right, the children already told them all about you, their fun Uncle Bill. I told them you are my brother, and as long as you introduce yourself as Bill Paxton when you meet them, there shouldn't be any trouble."

"Good enough," Bill said, placing his arm around Edina and pulling her close. He tipped her head back as he placed his mouth to hers, pushing her backwards and running his hand lightly over her breasts.

Bill, Edina, and her children spent five glorious days together, going for picnics, walking in the countryside, and playing games together. Then there were the evenings together. It was so different from when Charles had been home for a month. He had hardly spoken to the children and had snapped at Edina whenever she spoke.

On their last evening together, Bill and Edina sat drinking tea after the children had once more gone to bed in Edina's room.

"Bill, these last few days have been the happiest in my life. I should have listened to my parents, who tried to persuade me that Charlie was not a nice man and not to marry him. I truly regret that I did marry him. He does not make me or the children happy."

"Shhh, Edina, you know I love you and the children. Who knows how long this war will go on? Already it is closing on a year. The losses of men are unbelievable. I am just so happy that we have had the chance to have such a wonderful time together and to really get to know each other." He winked and smiled at her.

"Yes, we certainly have done that. But I need to tell you something." Edina paused, but Bill waited and didn't interrupt her as Charles would have done. "I will always have a piece of you with me…I want to tell you, Bill, that I am pregnant and it has to be your child."

Bill's eyes grew large and sparkled as he looked at Edina and gently touched her stomach. "Our child is within you? Oh, Edina, I am ecstatic. But what will Charles do?"

"Well, that is the hard part to tell, but I allowed him to have relations once when he was home. I already knew I was pregnant and I didn't expect to see you again. So I made sure that he could think it was his. With a bit of luck and his total disinterest in our children, he will be too stupid to work it out, and I will tell him that the child is early. I have no feelings for him, Bill. The whole time he was home, he flaunted going to the whorehouse, thinking he was making me jealous. I was relieved that he wouldn't try to touch me." The tears were rolling down her cheeks as Bill gently took her in his arms.

"What wonderful news, Edina, to be blessed with our own child. If it is a girl, I want you to call her Edna—I love that name as it sounds like yours—if that is okay with you?" he said, kissing her.

"If it is a boy, it will be named William after you."

"Come, Edina, let us off to bed and enjoy our last night together for who knows how long. I want to show you how much I love you so these few days will last until the next time we can get together."

The next morning, Bill packed to leave and helped Lily and John move back into their bedroom. There was much giggling going on with the children.

Then came the time for Bill to leave. Picking up the kids one at a time, he gave them each a big kiss and then gave them a second kiss to give to their ma. He smiled at Edina with the remembrance that he had already given her a way to keep in touch with him. "You will write, won't you?" he said. "I will write to you whenever I can, Edina."

She couldn't answer. She picked up little John for security and then managed to say, "Let's all blow Uncle Bill kisses to send him on his way." But young Lily was sobbing into her mother's apron and John was sobbing into her neck.

Bill turned at the gate, "See you on my next leave."

Chapter 14

William G. Charlton left England for France in August of 1915. He was part of the British Expeditionary Force in one of the six divisions, which was part of the "big push." They were joining France and Belgium, as they seemed to be losing the battle against Germany.

In November, Edina had a second daughter, whom she duly called Edna.

Charles A. Vernon was now with the MGC, which was based on the coast in Tyneside to protect England against attack from the sea. Tyneside and Wearside were of strategic importance as the coal exporting ports were located along this coast. Anti-invasion obstacles were set up to prevent this area being used as a landing site.

Charles's shifts were spent most often in pillboxes or bunkers, which were erected on the edges of built-up areas or on scrubland. They came in all shapes and sizes and afforded protection for soldiers with slits for them to use either rifles or machine guns. These were placed not only along the coast but also at riverside. Charles was attached to Frenchman's Point and later to the Sunderland Wave Basin. Prior to his deployment to France, he went to the barracks and trained at the Whitburn Rifle ranges.

November 30, 1915

Charlie,

I am writing though I never had a reply to my last letter after you had been home and had wondered, very rudely, how I had got pregnant, knowing full well that your expectations of me are constant and often.

I am very disappointed with your lack of interest in your children and, for that matter, your caring for me. It really doesn't take long to put pen to paper. To say that I am upset is stating the facts mildly. However, I know full well that rather than come home to a pregnant wife that you have probably spent your leaves at the brothels.

Because I am far kinder than you, I am telling you that you have a second daughter, born earlier than expected. This was a very difficult birth with pain that was almost unbearable—probably from all the stress you cause me. I named her Edna.

Edina

It was very difficult for Charles's commanding officers to grant him a leave for several reasons. Mostly, it was because he often feigned some kind of illness and was getting the reputation as a malingerer. He'd had several short-term leaves because of illness, which he had never spent at home with Edina but instead always went off somewhere else with other companions. Another reason was that no one knew that his wife was pregnant, so when he out of the blue asked for a leave, he was denied and told he couldn't possibly have a leave until after Christmas. So he sat down and wrote to Edina.

Edina,

I received your letter with the news of our daughter's arrival and how strong the pain was during this delivery.

I didn't appreciate the tone of your letter.

I applied for leave only to be told that it would have to wait until after Christmas as there is a very strong chance that our MGC is going to be sent overseas in 1916.

Yours, Charles

Edina, of course, had also written to tell Bill the news of his first child.

My darling, beautiful Edina,

I am so happy that we have been blessed with a child—"a love child"—and that you followed my wishes and called her Edna.

I dream often of our first time together, the gentle fondling, your patient teaching of how to play with you, and how you made me feel. I recall watching you that night when you started to remove your clothes, encouraging me to do the same and you helping me. I so well remember my first glimpse of your small but perfect white breasts and how your nipples stood out, inviting me to taste them, nibble them. This was my very first experience of taking someone with my body. My heart will surely burst as I think of how much I want you now.

What a wondrous joy I am feeling. I only regret that I can tell no one, that I may not share this with my family at home. I long to tell everyone that I am a father of, I am sure, an exquisite daughter.

I hope by the time you get this you have both recovered from the drama that a birth must cause.

My sweetheart, do take care of yourself and all of the children. Give a special kiss to Lily and a hug to John from Uncle Bill, and to Edna, whisper in her ear that her daddy loves her.

I long, Edina, to nuzzle your ears, and to again kiss your lips—all of them. I want to make you a part of me once again. I long for that day; hopefully this dreadful war ends and that day will be soon.

Yours as long as you will have me, Bill

※

Charles became worried when he did not hear back from Edina as he really had expected to. She probably was busy, his mates would say to him with a smirk. Most of them believed he was making up the story. *Mind you,* he thought, *she probably is busy.*

Christmas came and went, and he still heard nothing from her. However, he didn't write again—after all, it was her turn. He requested leave again and this time a day pass was granted.

Charles walked in the back door unannounced, startling John, who was in the scullery with his mother. John screamed, waking baby Edna, who started to cry. Edina said to John, "It is your pa. Go on, give him a hug. Sorry, Charlie, we weren't expecting you." She bent down to pick up Edna from the laundry basket she had been sleeping in.

"Well, I wasn't expecting this mayhem in my own home."

Edina decided it was best not to react to his anger. She walked across to him, pecking him on the cheek. "Here is your daughter Edna." She held out the baby to him.

"Why did you call her Edna?" he said, glancing at the baby.

"I thought it would please you, as it is what my parents really wanted me named." John was now clinging to his mother's skirts, and she ruffled his hair affectionately. "How long are you home for?"

"I have to be back by midnight. I had to beg to get them to give me a leave. They wouldn't believe me when I told them you'd had a child."

Edina wondered why anyone would have trouble believing such a thing, but she dared not ask him about it.

"I should get a longer leave if we are to go overseas. I am hoping that this damn war will be over before we are sent, I don't want to be fighting in the trenches. How come you didn't reply to my letter?"

Edina looked at him in astonishment. "To be perfectly honest, Charlie, that is only the second letter I have had from you. All my friends' husbands seem to have more leaves than you do, so I have wondered why you haven't come home more often. I am really busy with three children, and most nights I have been too exhausted to write. If you were worried, why didn't you write again?"

"Who do you think you are talking to? How dare you question if I am coming home or not." Charles had raised his voice at Edina, and young John started to scream. "Make that snivelling child stop screaming. Have you no discipline with the children? What kind of mother are you? Where is Lily, get her to take care of him."

Edina placed the baby, who was once again fast asleep, back in the laundry basket, and then picked up John, who immediately stopped screaming. "Charlie, John rarely cries, he is a peaceful child. He just isn't used to someone shouting at his mother. Lily is now at school and will be home for a bite to eat before she has to go back for the afternoon. Now, John, why don't you go and find your top and show your pa how you can make it spin, and I will put something together for us all to eat when Lily gets home."

John peered at his father and shook his head violently.

Charles scowled at this domestic scene. "I don't want the snivelling child. I want you to make me a cup of tea, I want you to be a wife to me, I don't want to eat with three children. I am the master and should come first."

"I will make you tea, Charlie. As for the rest, our children are here and their needs are first and foremost in my mind. Lily will be happy to see you when she gets home."

"Well, that isn't going to happen. I am warning you that when I get my leave before going overseas you had better make some arrangements for the children. Send them over to your mother's. I will expect you to be at my beck and call, I will expect you to be a wife to me, to look after my needs day and night, night and day, do you hear? Stop that child's screaming. I can't stand it here. It wasn't worth my effort to come home to this. I wanted comfort, and I wanted love. How can that happen, will it happen today? Edina, I am asking you for my rights today as your husband, will you accommodate me?"

Edina looked at this man—her husband—and wondered what she had ever seen in him. He was being so cruel and unkind. She hated being shouted at, she hated being belittled, so with her eyes full of tears, she said, "Charlie, all I can offer right now is family time—you being a pa to the children, us all laughing and playing together as a family, Right now it is not about you and I and our needs. John will settle down when you stop shouting and badgering me. We can be a family together, I can keep Lily home this afternoon so we can all be together. Let me make you tea. Take off your coat and come in, sit down, I will light the fire in the parlour—"

Everlasting Lies | 89

"You daft woman, I want and need feminine company. If I can't get that here, then I be off to find it for myself."

Charles expected her to beg him to stay. She didn't. He stuffed his beret back on his head, turned, and walked out the back door, slamming it loudly.

"Good riddance," said Edina as she buried her head into her sobbing son.

Chapter 15

There was lots of talk about being sent to France but still no official word. Charles was on duty the night the zeppelin flew over Sunderland, dropping twenty-one bombs and causing severe damage to shops and houses.

The soldiers were mobilized just after the bombing, which was just before midnight on April 1, 1916. "How come our boys didn't manage to shoot the buggers down?" said one of the boys in the tent as they fumbled to get dressed in the dark—they dared not turn on any lights as that would make them a target. "Because they were fooling around," said another soldier with a laugh. They could all hear the *thump, thump* of the soldiers gathering in the square.

Every group of soldiers was assigned an area and given a first aid bag. They were told where central command was and to work in a pair of their choosing. Charles didn't have a buddy, so he ended up with Greg, another young soldier who wasn't liked. Then the sixteen men from their tent set off in formation for the area where it was thought the bombs had been dropped.

It was chaos: Houses and shops were on fire, people wandered around in a daze, and children screamed for lost family. Those not hurt were sitting with those that were, waiting for someone—anyone—to help them.

Bob, who was in charge of their group, barked out some orders, then looked at the two misfits together and said, "All right, you two, I know how you are both not sociable people, so I am going to give you the tough job of moving the dead over here. When you pick them up, see if someone around them knows who they are. By the time you get back with your first body, I should have some sheets for you to cover them with.

"If you come across someone who needs medical attention, call out 'Medic' and stay with them until you are relieved, then continue your search for bodies. If you hear someone shout 'CG here,' that is a call for you as someone has found a body for you to collect.

"Got the instructions, everybody? With the exception of CG, everyone is a medic. Okay, fellows, remember: we are a team, we are sleeping buddies, and we care about each other, right? Let's get out there and help these poor buggers."

Although it was not a pleasant job they had been assigned, Charles and Greg worked well together. Neither of them was ready for what they saw and had to do.

As they were working, Greg said to Charles, "Why here, Charlie?"

"My name is *Charles*. They are after the docks, and then the blast furnaces northwest of town, in all probability. Remember, they attacked Tyneside last year and, I don't know, maybe the winds made the Huns attack here. Here—pick up your end, lad, and we will take this body to the central place."

"Okay, Charles. What is this, number ten?"

"About that, I reckon. But there are a lot of people injured. I hate seeing kids hurt. I heard someone talking about the railway station being hit as well."

After a night's sleep, all the men gathered. First, Bob congratulated the members of his tent, who now seemed much closer after going through the disaster together and coming through. Then he informed them that twenty-two people had been killed, twenty-five had been seriously injured, and more than one hundred had been slightly injured. A tram had experienced a direct hit, and the conductress had been injured and an inspector had been killed. Soldiers were still needed to help clear the rubble, but when they were finished, they would be given a short leave before moving south for some more intensive training in the trenches. Then they would be leaving for France for an unspecified term. He told them that when they went on leave they should make sure that they had all their affairs in place for their families.

Edina,

I have just come through dealing with the bombing in Sunderland with my mates. If I had my choice, this is as close as I would be to the war.

We have just been told that we are all being given a leave before going for more training in the south somewhere, then leaving for France for an unspecified time. We were told to put all affairs in order, which I did when I first joined up. Pretty simple, really, as we own nothing.

The last time I was home wasn't the best of times for me. Three children in the house means you have little time for looking after my needs. So I need to know if you will make some arrangement to have the children looked after?

Let me know one way or another.

Charles

Edina read this letter and then sat down and wrote back immediately.

Dear Charles,

I received your letter this morning. I had no idea that you were involved in that bombing. In fact I know very little of your life in the army as you rarely write. You wrote about your mates, but you never said their names, and this is the first time I have heard you have friends.

I am very grateful for my neighbours as it is a rum way to live without a man to look after us and him to do the things that I am unable to do. Isabella's poor husband, old Ralph, watches over not only his own family but also both Sarah's and mine as we have no menfolk to look after us. Both his sons, Thomas and Joseph, have joined up, and Thomas is already in France.

We all would love to have you home so we could be a family for a few days, I think Lily would like to take you to school to show off her soldier pa. I know that is not your plans and that you too are craving attention, but I cannot send our children away because they have a need to see their pa.

I am hoping you understand that this war affects us all. And you having to go to France, which probably means you will be in the trenches, is a scary thought for me. The uncertainty of our lives is so hard to live with, and I would welcome time as a family as this hasn't happened since Edna was born.

But I know that you will do what is right for you. I would like it if you would tell me what your decision is as I would like to prepare our children if you are coming home and will plan to make some memories together.

I remain your obedient wife, Edina.

Edina read through her letter to Charles, which she had now decided to call him as *Charlie* no longer felt right, and sighed.

Charles, upon receiving this letter, turned red with anger. *How dare she refuse me? I don't want to be surrounded by snivelling children.* He did not write back—no need to prepare his children because he was intent upon spending whatever free time he had off base in the company of those who would be prepared to please him.

Within the week, Edina received another letter, but this time it was from Bill. As she opened the letter, a ten-shilling note fluttered to the ground.

Edina, the girl I dream about whenever I have the chance to sleep,

I am thinking of you reading this letter in the parlour, sitting in our favourite place together, which holds so many wonderful moments for us—in fact the place where our little daughter was conceived.

How are the children? Is Lily enjoying school? Will John be going to school soon? Can you get these two to draw something for Uncle Bill? I can tuck it into my helmet and always have part of you close to me. Edna—how big is she now, does she sit up, crawl? I have no idea what happens to a child in their first year. I wish I could see you all.

If I was a cussing man, I would be cussing often at the futility of the war we find ourselves in. When I get a chance in my little bugwarm, I think of the Jerrys sitting in the trenches on the other side—they are men just like us who are in this situation not of their own choosing but because of their government. They are fathers, sons, and lovers just as we are.

Edina, it is funny—we even get to know each other's names and play tricks on each other. The other afternoon, one of my pals put his battle bowler on top of his gun and held it up so it was just showing above the trench, and then he moved it as if he was walking. Now, before he did this, there were bets on how long it would be before one of the Jerrys shot at it. The closest bet to that time won the money. Up it goes as someone starts the stopwatch, and ping the bullets come flying.

Guess what? I won the other day—made myself ten shillings. Immediately after this, one of the Huns called out, "Hey, Tommy! How much was the bet? Will you buy some plonk with it and share it with us over here?" Edina, there was much laughter from all the trenches—theirs and ours. So this is why there is ten shillings here for you all. I hope it helps a little.

I tell you these stories so that you understand that if we have to shoot to kill we do, but there are the moments when we all know that this wretched war is not of the people's making. We are the enforcers, but maybe not the believers.

Well, my love, dare I ask if you have seen Charles lately? If I survive this war, I intend to make you my own. But at the same time, I know that you must not give Charles any cause to doubt your love for him.

Don't forget the pictures for me. I promise they won't get shot.

Love, sweetheart, to you and the children. Till we meet again, Bill

When Edina read this letter she cried and laughed and wondered again why she hadn't looked at Bill more closely when he was living right next door to her.

Everlasting Lies

Chapter 16

At the end of August 1916, Charles received notification that the MGC was being sent to Lyndhurst in the New Forest before embarking for France.

Charles, of course, had not used his leave days to go back to Edina as he had been so angry that her letter implied she only wanted him home if he was prepared to be a father. He was now regretting that decision as he did not know when he would see her or his children again.

He and Greg were sitting in the canteen after returning from leave.

"Well, Charles, did you go home?"

"No, life is so busy back home."

"Oh…I am feeling pretty scared about going to the battlefields," said Greg.

"Aye, and so we should be scared. We all remember what happened to the 'Immortal 7th Division' in the battlefields of Ypres. Of the fifteen thousand soldiers who arrived, only about twenty-four hundred were still alive within a month of going into action. I am no bloody hero, this godforsaken war terrifies me."

"Charles, did you read the news coming out France of the bloody battles in Somme? The opening battle on July first was reported as the bloodiest battle so far. Fifty-seven thousand were injured and over nineteen thousand were killed. I'm bloody scared."

September 18, 1916

Edina,

I believe I owe you an apology for not coming to see you before we leave for France. I realize I was being selfish when I took my leave and went elsewhere.

I guess I am a selfish bugger, which my family always used to tell me. The fact is I didn't even write to tell you that I wasn't coming and just left you without knowing what was happening.

By the time you get this letter, I will be on my way to France and the trenches. Only God knows what my fate will be there. From all accounts, it won't be pretty.

I may not write often as I am not sure when or if I will have time. But I implore you to write to me and tell me about our children and how you are coping.

I am sorry if I have hurt you. You are a good lass and deserve better than the likes of me. I always carry in my mind the beautiful courtship we had.

Charles.

On September 19, 1916, Charles boarded the HMS Cardiganshire for the short crossing to France. The voyage was not an easy one for the troops as conditions were extremely crowded, with many men from other regiments stuck with them in a hold and everyone holding absolutely everything they owned. Charles reflected that, because of how he had joined up, he had been able to delay his leaving for France. The thought of an attack by a U-boat and death in the cold Atlantic made this journey for Charles much more difficult. The voyage over the Atlantic gave him time to reflect on his life, which made him very glad that he written to Edina.

It was so congested as they docked in La Havre that it was difficult to unload the soldiers. Charles did as little as possible, though he took the time to look at the French people who were watching the British soldiers with great interest.

"Gawd, mate, look at the beautiful mademoiselles."

"They aren't going to be looking at little runts like you, Charles."

"Look at the legs on that one, I do believe they go all the way up to her arse."

"Okay, soldiers, fall into line and move along," someone screamed. "We are not here to ogle the ladies."

Eventually ready, they marched through the streets with many French people waving and calling out to the men. The town was large and had very wide streets.

"Christ, look at that woman over there."

Someone shouted, "Eyes right!"

They marched, eyes right, as a woman waved, bent forward, and lifted her skirts. Many of the men gave wolf whistles. "Cor blimey, I would like a piece of that."

They marched for hours; even the songs didn't seem to help. Finally, they marched into a large field, where there were some stables and huts that had obviously been used recently. Judging by the items scattered all around, the occupants had left in a hurry. After a meal, they were told to rest. "What you mean, *rest*?" someone called out.

"That's what I mean, soldier—we will be moving out shortly to take advantage of the cover of darkness."

"Charles," said Greg, "let's sit back to back. At least we will have some support."

Around midnight, the men who had fallen asleep were awoken and everybody got ready to march again. There were grumblings amongst the men.

"We have to march again?" said one fellow.

"I have had no sleep since leaving Southampton," complained another.

"No worries, men, in about half an hour we will be at a goods station," said a sergeant. "There will be a train waiting. Okay, left...right...left."

There was no platform when they reached the train, so the men had to scramble onto the train as best they could. Once aboard, there was a roll call to make sure everyone was present. With that done, the train slowly moved off. Nobody knew where.

"Look, Charles!" Greg could finally see some pretty countryside, with no signs of a war going on. Passing an orchard, he said, "Look at them apples. I'd buy some if someone would go pick them."

As the train wasn't moving fast, it wasn't very long before some of the young soldiers jumped off the train, picked some apples, and then ran like the breeze to catch up with their buddies. Once back on the train, they offered to sell the apples to their mates.

But the carefree spirit soon dissipated. As darkness descended, the men were still shut up and extremely weary.

The train came to a halt and the sleepy men peered out, only to be greeted by wind and rain. The sky was continually lit up by flashes from guns, and they could hear the guns' constant *boom, boom, boom*.

Charles quaked in his boots and turn to Greg beside him. "Bloody hell, this is worse than I expected."

The soldiers were commanded to get off the train and start unloading and packing again to be ready for another march. There was a lot of shouting going on and someone called out loudly, "Where is Vernon? Where is that short little bugger?"

Someone shouted back, "You mean Shorty? Why, what do you expect? Vernon is a master at dodging the columns every opportunity he gets. He has cold feet."

After three hours, the soldiers were ready to move off to the unknown. *Thump, thump* went the men's boots as they marched for about an hour before coming into a field that was to be their camp area. As dawn rose, it found these men hard at work putting up their tents, setting the mess tents up with the equipment for cooking, and building the latrines. Once finished, all of the soldiers fell into their beds for a well-earned sleep. They were in Pernes, a small village in the Somme district. This is where they would stay before moving to the front.

※

After four days and nights, the gunners and signalers gathered before dawn to move out for the front line. A voice came through the darkness. "Well, this is what we trained for, right fellows?"

After they had been marching for a while, the ambient light in the sky began to reveal the scarring of the land around them, shell holes everywhere. The road was so thick with mud it was barely passable.

"What a disaster this landscape is," someone said, lighting up a fag.

"Jesus, I need a parachute to get through here," said another as he dragged on his fag.

"Come on, fellows, the Jerrys will see you coming."

"It's still as black as the ace of spades out here, don't be daft."

"He's right, bloody daft is that man."

"Aye, I might be, but you should be standing beside me."

"Why, you silly arse?"

"Look at you stupid, naïve blokes. You look like a bloody red line weaving about in the darkness as you all puff on your fags. You're going to have to learn the hard way, I guess."

Suddenly, there was a huge yellow flash and a high-velocity shell crashed on the roadway close by with an ear-splitting explosion. All the soldiers scattered.

"Put on your bloody tin hats, you silly buggers," someone shouted. "Get in the ditches, lay low, protect yourselves." They all put on their tin hats and dove for cover somewhere—anywhere.

The flashes were blinding and the sound was deafening as the shells continued to rain on the men as they wallowed in mud. Then the shells stopped.

Charles was up to his thighs in mud whereas everyone else was only up to their knees, and he couldn't get out. A couple of the taller guys passed him and said, "Take our hands, you little squirt, and we will set you on your feet." But this wasn't as easy as they thought as the mud clung and seemed to be sucking Charles down. As they struggled to release him, they could hear screams from those who were wounded, the pitiful cries of grown men.

As Charles and the others tried to find their battalion, they realized they still were not at their destination: "The Line." This was just a taste of the hell to come. It seemed impossible to believe that out of this chaos order could be retained.

A week later, the soldiers who had not been severely wounded or killed were in the trenches. As much as these soldiers had been trained in the trenches, this was real and felt very different. The men all seemed to realize that something big was about to happen.

Every morning in the trenches around 5:30 a.m., though still dark and fairly quiet except for the occasional burst of shells from the machine guns, some Kraut would call out, "Hey, Tommy, you still there?"

Someone would answer, "Sure thing, Squarehead, just waiting for you to show yourself and we will blow your head off."

Then silence until the senior officer on duty at the time arrived and roused all the gunmen on duty; all guns, large and small, were involved. Every man knew his post and waited for the signal: the officer would call out, "One...two...three...four...five...six," and at exactly 5:45 a.m. he would command fire. All the gunners would let the shells rip as fast as they could for the next fifteen minutes. At precisely 6:00 a.m. they would stop. This happened along about fifteen miles of trenches in this area. When they stopped, the Jerrys would retaliate; however, this really kept the Germans in a state of hesitancy because they thought something was afoot. But what? They looked for soldiers coming over the top, but nothing happened. Yet.

There had been small attacks on the twelfth and fifteenth of September, keeping the Germans on edge, never knowing what the English and French armies were planning. The English knew the big push was close.

There were times when the men just sat around chatting and, of course, smoking....

"You know, I got around to thinking: here we are in a place we have never been to, and all we think about is blowing the head off some Jerry, and he's sitting over there thinking the same bloody thing."

"Yep, the worst of it is, he is just like us, with a wife and kids at home that he loves."

"Or not."

"We are at war because we have been told we are at war, but what for?"

"Peace."

"At what bloody cost? We have been at war for over two years now."

Everlasting Lies | 101

"We know we have lost a lot of men already and a lot of women have had badly injured men returned to them."

"I bet they have lost a lot too."

"Bloody well hope so or we aren't doing our job."

"God help the Squareheads when we get told to go over the top. After all, it's them or us."

"What about the carnage they have done to the villages around here? These people didn't ask to have their homes destroyed by invaders, we are their protectors."

"That's why we have to push the buggers back into their own country and fight there—damage their homes, their people."

"Ah, come on, let's change the topic. Anyone for char? Then let's talk about the fairer sex." This soldier was pelted with stones.

It started to rain as the soldiers continued to wait for orders. But obviously tonight was not the night as gunfire was served. The lucky men who were no longer on duty were able to crawl into their fleabag in a bug warmer to stay dry, hoping that sleep would come quickly and that it would last longer than a couple of hours.

At 5:30 a.m., the fifteen-minute volley began.

"Jesus Christ," said Charles." I can't imagine what that is all about, a bloody waste of ammunition if you ask me."

"Get real, Vernon, no one is about to ask you anything." This comment was accompanied with laughter.

"Did you get out of the wrong side of the bed, Vernon?"

Life is hard, Charles thought. *Umm maybe it is my fault. I did have a soft life, and because of my angry, rough ways and the fact that I like to be in control and be right, I left my family. I wonder if they ever think of me? Why should they? I never think of them!*

"No, I had a great sleep in my bug warmer and my flea bag. How was your sleep standing up?" Charles would retorted.

"Ah, great, I spent me night keeping you safe."

Charles continued with his thoughts. *I feel not liked or respected here as well. I am even awful to my wife and three children, hardly knowing them.*

Charles decided it was time for him to take a walk to the biffy. He needed a stretch and chose to go to the furthest one.

"Where you off to, short arse?"

"Thought I would take a long walk in the country."

As Charles started off down the line, he could hear laughter behind him rather than the usual insults.

As Charles was returning, the Jerrys suddenly started throwing hand grenades and shooting from their trenches. The soldiers, hoping that it was just a few moments to stop the boredom, hunkered down, and Charles took shelter with another platoon.

"So, mate, where are you from?"

"Northumberland."

"Well, you be a short little bugger."

"Hey, I had a brother like that—short he may have been, but he had grandiose ideas."

"Surely he wasn't this short? You're tall."

"I can't see the little bugger. Anyways, I am not from Northumberland."

"Well, that means nowt these days," someone shouted.

"I am from Yorkshire, it means a lot. Hang about, I'm coming to look at this runt."

"Why?"

"Well, maybe it's me long-lost brother, who ran away."

Charles's eye were wide. *That voice.* But before he could move, a soldier came over on his hands and knees and said, "Alfie? Alfie, is it really you?"

Charles turned and looked into the eyes of his favourite brother. They grabbed each other as Abe said, "Hey, this is my long-lost brother I haven't seen for—" And with that he and Charles broke down and cried as they clasped each other.

Abe's mates suggested that the two go hunker down in the closest bug warmer and catch up with each other.

"Don't you brothers worry, we will cover for you."

Charles, being so small, settled right at the back of the bug warmer. Abe was taller and had more weight on him than Charles and had to settle near the entrance. Abe looked at Alfie and asked, "Why did you leave?"

Everlasting Lies | 103

Charles shook his head. "Don't know, really. Guess Pa never trusted us boys to do more than menial work. I told him what I thought, we disagreed, and I lost my temper."

"Huh, you were always doing that. Especially when you didn't get your own way. Pa was mighty upset in his quiet way."

"What you mean, Abe?"

"Oh, he blamed himself for not recognizing that you and Dicky were management people."

Charles sighed and shook his head.

"Well, you knew Mary was married—her Flo is now fifteen and the twins, Doris and Ethel, are thirteen. Young John died when he was three, but young Joseph is seven and a handful. Will is a baker and seems to be doing great. They're living in Burton on Trent, Staffordshire."

"How are Ma and Pa?"

"Ah, well, you disappearing like you did was really hard on Ma, but she is well considering she is in her early fifties. Pa, he is such a gentle man. When the war be over, Alfie, you should visit them, they are living in Sacriston County Durham."

"No, I have made a life for myself. I don't need them and they wouldn't appreciate me. What about you, Abe?"

"I married Dora and we have two sons—Harry, fourteen, and Norm, twelve," he said with a smile.

"They're different names, Abe."

"Yes"—he proudly showed his brother a photo of the family—"they are her family names. What about you, Alfie, you married?"

Charles nodded.

Abe shook his head. "Well, do you have children?"

"Aye." Charles smiled at Abe's enthusiasm. "Three. Lily is nearly six, John will be five next year, and Edna is the baby."

"I not be surprised at the name Lily, she was always your favourite. Why was that?"

At that moment a hand grenade landed in the trench. Abe fell on top of Charles. Charles heard the firing of machine guns and a soldier shouting "Take that, you bastards" from the trenches alongside screaming and sobbing from all the injured. It was mayhem.

Charles pushed Abe off him. "Hey, Abe, you all right?... ABE?" Charles struggled to his feet and looked down at his brother. All he could see was bone, blood, and flesh. Abe's back had been blown open as his body filled the entrance, affording Charles protection from the explosion.

"Medic! Help!" he screamed.

Somehow, Charles managed to get closer to Abe's face and put his hand close to his mouth. He felt nothing. He screamed, "Man down! Medic! We need a medic over here now!"

"Abe...Abe, speak to me...It's Alfie...It's me, your brother."

A medic appeared in the entrance. He tried to peer in over Abe's body. "You all right in the back there?

Slowly, Charles pulled himself together. "I'm all right, how is my brother?"

"He looks like a goner to me. There is nothing left of his back, blown right open—the poor sod wouldn't want to live. We are going to try to pull him out of the way and get you out."

Charles was sobbing as the medics dragged Abe by the legs.

"Come on, don't lollygag, soldier. We need to get you out before the firing starts again. No use sobbing back there. This is an order. You are putting us at risk. CRAWL. OUT. OF. THERE. NOW.

Nothing.

By the time Abe's dead body had been removed, Charles had passed out in the fetal position. So he, too, had to be dragged from the trenches.

Chapter 17

Charles lay in a hospital, often screaming out at night as he relived his brother's last moments—their last moments. Most had no idea what Charles's problem was, and some doctors believed Charles was playing sick; but trauma was difficult to treat.

In the bed beside Charles lay a young fellow named Bert. The nineteen-year-old signal officer was telling Charles how tanks were now involved in the war.

"Charles, these monsters look like they might topple on their noses."

"Noses? You are delusional."

"No, Charles, listen up. That was my impression of the tank. But at the back, at its tail, there were two little wheels, which kept it level. These monsters have two sets of continuous tracks and huge bulges on each side, Charles. Inside the bulge is a machine gun on swivels. Beside the gun, there is, like, a tractor seat where a man can sit."

"Gore on with you, you're making up this tale, Bert."

"Na, I'm not. Anyways, we had twenty-five of these monsters waddling towards the Jerrys. It was a right laugh, Charles. The Jerrys kept popping up and down like little rabbits in a hole, obviously not knowing what to do as these monsters beared down on them with machine guns blasting."

The two soldiers started to laugh. "What did the Jerrys do, Bert?"

"Got up and run, what would you have done? But the tanks just shot them down as they fled and kept going—dead or wounded were squished into the ground."

"Oh my God."

"These trenches had been held so long by the Jerrys," Bert went on.

"So how did you get hurt?"

"Well, we were running over to the Jerrys' trenches, heads down and ready to claim them—claim our victory—but, Charles, these bloody monsters leave a huge footprint, and in this mud the tracks are sometimes deeper than they look, so I broke me leg."

Before any more conversation could happen, Dr. Lowe came in. "We are going to let you go this afternoon, Charles. Your brigade is in camp, so you will have a few days to get stronger with them before you all return to the front, which is now further into enemy territory, and all hewers like you are going to be needed. Best of luck to you, Charles."

※

Charles was back in the trenches with his regiment—trenches that, until recently, had been occupied by the Germans. There were many underground tunnels that were of no use as they led back to trenches behind the line of German control. The objective was to build tunnels towards the new line in the trenches that the German's had established. They would dig under the new lines so that explosives could be detonated and blow the Germans into kingdom come.

Charles was with a group of four men who had all been miners. Once the initial tunnel had been charted to a lower chamber, it was up to the hewers to get into these tunnels, which were so tiny that even they, small as they were, needed to lie down as they worked in order to move the tunnel forward, inch by inch. Even they struggled with the demon claustrophobia and the musty air and darkness.

The day of the accident, the tunnel was some fifteen feet long under no man's land and was progressing slowly. Charles was lying at the face when he heard something and stopped digging.

"Quiet...shhh, everyone."

The team lay quietly in the darkness, listening to the muffled sound of other pickaxes hard at work. *The Germans*, they mouthed.

Hardly daring to breath, they decided to move back, but that was easier said than done as there was a whole pile of dirt blocking their exit.

"Jesus Christ," whispered George. "The bloody dirt hasn't been cleared away yet."

Charles squiggled closer, saying, "Shhh...can we push it back quietly with our hands?" Working together, they began clearing the exit.

"Gore on, Charles, see if ye can get through." As Charles pushed with his toes, his little chest acting like a scraper, he thought, *It is no wonder they call us sewer rats or moles, that is what I bloody well feel like.* With an extreme effort, he got through and got to his feet, walking doubled over in the small space, his mates following close behind him. As they neared the trenches, lamps lit the way and they were able to walk upright.

Once they had made it to the trenches, their CO questioned them.

"How close were they? Which direction were they coming from? Do you think they will find our tunnel? How long is our tunnel? If we blow it up, can we cause damage? Deaths? Do you think we can still use this tunnel? Is it better protection for us to blow this tunnel up? How much dynamite should we use?"

Not once did the CO ask if his idea posed a risk to the men who would eventually lay the lines for the explosion.

He commanded Charles and the rest of his team to go back and bore some chambers towards the oncoming tunnel, and then pack these chambers with explosives.

Someone whispered, "We don't have enough explosives for the holes we bored."

"Maybe we could put fewer in each hole."

"Don't be daft, man, then we will have a half-arsed job. No, someone has got to go back and get more explosives."

"Whatchya mean, *someone*?"

"Well, it would be daft if we all go back."

"Let's send Charles, he be the smallest."

"Bloody hell, why should I go whilst the rest of you have a nap?" Charles whispered fiercely.

"Hands up. All those who think Charles should go."

※

Once more Charles awoke in a hospital bed, an angel looking down on him. He was screaming, "Where are me mates? George, Robbie…" Then sleep took a hold of him again and the pain no longer existed.

A nurse looked down at Charles and whispered, "You be the lucky one, Charles—the only one in the tunnel to survive the explosion. You be the lucky one."

Charles moaned and groaned as he was forced to relive the nightmare explosion again and again as he slept....

He was crawling and crawling and just starting to stand up when the explosion hit the tunnel, which was caused when the Germans blew up their tunnel, which of course detonated the explosives they had just laid in their tunnel's chambers.

This explosion threw Charles to the ground and completely knocked the wind out of him, but he was a miner and knew instinctually to, no matter what, get up and flee...run... run... r...u...n. He could hear the explosion was chasing him. It was as if he were trying to get away from a mad bull. *Crash!* He was on the ground again, with dirt and timber falling around him. He was swimming, pushing the waves of fear away, trying to stay on top of the dirt and water that were now in the tunnel and throwing his body this way and that. He felt hands on his shoulders pulling him...*Don't pull*, he wanted to scream....

Indeed, Charles was alive, and the British now occupied the positions that the Germans had held in the summer. As the weather closed in, the Allies had taken an area of around 120 square miles. Though thousands had been killed, Charles was alive.

Charles lay in his hospital bed, slowly recovering from the emotional turmoil that he had been through since arriving in France, knowing that he did not want to go back into the trenches.

Every time a doctor came to examine Charles, Charles would play the idiot.

"What is your number?"

"Don't know."

"State your name."

"Alfie."

"What regiment are you in?"

"Trenches and tunnels."

"Soldier, are you married?"

"Nope."

Everlasting Lies

With that the doctor would walk away and write his report.

In the next bed to him was one of his mates from his regiment. "What you playing at, Charles?"

"I want to be sent home," Charles said simply.

However, this ruse did not work and Charles was returned to the trenches for a second time. But he was taken off tunnelling duty for the time being.

The soldiers spent a lot of time just hanging around in the trenches, both sides bored and cold.

A German soldier shouted across to them, "You guys got anything to smoke?"

"Cheeky bugger," Charles said, as a chorus of his fellow soldiers called out, "Sure."

"Will ye gimme the makings?" came the retort.

"Only if you come and get them."

With that a young blond German fellow stuck his head and shoulders above the trench and put his hands on the top of the trench...

"Blimey, he is coming over!"

The young German with a month-old beard ran crouched across the flat land that separated the trenches. Lying flat, he peered into the British trench. In perfect English, he said, "Where's the cigars?"

"Bloody hell, you sure got some nerve, you damn Jerry," a British soldier said with a laugh. "Here, take these damn French cigars off my hands."

The German took them and said, "Then, Tommy, I had better say *merci*." With that he stooped low and ran back to his trench. Charles and his mates laughed at the antics of the young blond-bearded man, now safely in his trench.

It wasn't long before this same young man called across and said, "This cigar is great."

At this a number of the British soldiers playfully threw rocks towards the German trench.

"Hey, you Tommie's, you seem like a decent group of fellows. I am going to bring you a present."

"Yeah, gore on," up went the cry from the British.

"Will you shoot me if I come over again?" He didn't wait for a reply. Once more, he catapulted out of the trench, this time carrying what looked like a bottle of plonk. It was French Champagne. "Here, Tommy... enjoy." He ran back with both sides cheering and laughing.

Much later that afternoon, the Germans shouted across to let them know that this young soldier had been killed because he kept sticking his head up during what the soldiers called business hours.

Charles said to his mates, "We need to remember the good nature of this young German, we need to make something to remember him by. He gave us a laugh, which don't happen often these days."

So down the line straw, string, and toilet paper were collected, and the soldiers set to and fashioned a wreath from the straw, with toilet paper flowers attached. During the night, they placed the wreath a few feet from the British trench facing the German's trench. They had written the words *Rest in Peace and Thanks for the Good Memories.*

At daylight, the Germans saw the wreath and started to clap. In unison, fine, rich male voices sang "Deutschlandlied" for their fallen comrade, who had given such entertainment to the enemy. Once finished, it was time for the British to clap and cheer for their enemies.

Several soldiers came to Charles, saying, "That was a great idea, mate."

The soldiers would hear snippets of news from other soldiers who had received newspapers in their care packages. There seemed to be trouble in parliament. Men who were in the trenches up to their knees in slimy mud with little cover from the rain, sleet, and winds couldn't be bothered to worry about this. The weather had become bone-chilling, and they had not been issued better clothing to ward of the cold. The food was god awful and was rarely served warm. The men were a sorry sight.

Charles was constantly coughing and groaning. Then he started to have stabbing pains in his chest that spread through his shoulders. If he happened to sneeze, he would scream in pain, and his breathing was getting shallower every day. It wasn't long before he was carried out on a stretcher back to the hospital, where he was diagnosed with pleurisy. It was believed this was caused when he was crushed in the tunnel during his last accident. The medics surgically removed the fluid buildup in his chest.

During this stay in hospital, Charles decided that it was time to write to his wife and tell her what his life was like now.

※

When Edina read Charles's letter, she burst into tears, startling Sarah, who walked through the back door at that moment.

Sarah noticed the letter in Edina's hand and rushed to her friend. "Edina, luv, what is it?"

"I just had a letter from Charles."

"Surely that is a good thing, Edina, you have been complaining that he has had no contact with you."

"True, but the letter is all about him, he didn't even ask anything about us—how we are doing, how the children are…nothing. Does he even care about us?"

"He wrote, didn't he?"

"Yes, but only to complain and to tell me that he has received orders but doesn't know where to. He didn't say anything about missing each other. Asked nothing about his offspring."

"Wait a minute, Edina, do you ever write to him? Do you ever enquire about him? You can't lay all the blame at his door. Unless he has done something to kill your feelings for him? That, I don't know. I will agree that from what I have seen he has shown little affection for you, but you have three children. What happened?"

Edina turned to her friend. "I was very young when we met. I was his first experience, and he mine…But he would think nothing of taunting me with the prostitutes that he would go to. He wouldn't come home if he was angry over something, and he would tell me he was going to find others and then leave. I know nothing about this man. I have never met any of his family, nor will he talk about them—tells me I shouldn't poke around in his business. When he is here, I feel that I am a convenience for him and that there is no love, just his satisfaction."

Sarah said simply, "Are you going to reply?"

Chapter 18

January, 1917

Charles,

Thank you for your letter. I was very happy to receive this.

The children are growing. Lily is at the local church school and doing very well. She is now 7, which I find hard to believe, and loves reading and drawing. She is becoming a great little knitter and loves to help me around the house. John will go to school whenever I can get him in. It is a safe place for the children to be. He will be 5 in February and is the image of you. I think he could be a bit of a problem as he is very active and could do with a man in the house. Edna is certainly developing a personality. She is a determined child and is already walking.

The children have loved helping me in the garden during the growing season, which helps us keep our food bills down and gives us lots of fresh food. I am now keeping a few laying hens and often have extra eggs and produce to sell.

This awful war that keeps families like us apart. When will it end?

I guess when you can you will let me know where you are.

I hope you have returned to full health.

Your wife, Edina

When Edina wrote this, she couldn't help but think of the lack of letters from her own husband and the mountain of letters from Bill

Charlton and how they expressed his fondness for them, always enquiring how she was doing and even writing notes to the children.

Bill and Charles were both in France. Charles as a gunner and Bill with the Tank Corp. Edina knew so much more about Bill's life in the Tank Corp as he was proud of their first efforts in these tanks. He had told her many tales of his adventures, but he omitted the dangers. She dragged out some of his letters and began reading.

Edina, darling,

> *You can't imagine how lucky I am as I get to decide to work with either a male or a female—that is a tank, of course. Our Mark 1 tanks are male, and they carry two Hotchkiss 6-pound guns and 4 machine guns, whereas the perky little female has 5 machine guns. Yes, I am sticking with the female tank. There was something strange about seeing the male tank with its long muzzle of the Hotchkiss gun stuck in the mud as they were going down the muddy banks. No, my love, I will stick with the female that I love and intimately know.*

This brought a smile to her face.

She picked up another letter, and the tone of this one was different.

Darling Edina,

How are you all?

> *I had the strangest encounter the other day and it impossible to give you place details.*

> *We were back from the line on leave. These days, there can be all kinds in the camp at the same time—by that I mean different regiments, different jobs. It is a few days of respite from the heavy work at the line.*

> *Anyways, there were some soldiers picking on one soldier, pushing and shoving him around, calling him a liar. In fact it was getting very nasty. So my mate and me went over to settle things down—God only knows there is enough fighting without it happening between us. We*

got the rowdies to leave. The soldier who was being berated sat there with his head down on his arms.

Me mate rolled his eyes and told me to deal with him and went off to get himself a drink.

So I sat and waited at the table, saying nothing. Finally the soldier lifted his head, looked me in the eye, and asked me if the buggers had gone. I just nodded. He sat up and stared at me. He asked me my name. When I told him he nodded cordially. He told me he was a gunner and asked what I was, and I told him. He commented that we really had nothing in common unless I was a miner. That wasn't even a fit for me, being in the railways.

He asked why I helped him. I tried to explain and eventually I asked his name. Will you guess who it is? Right, your husband, Charles Vernon.

So I asked Charles why they were fighting with him. Apparently Charles wanted to go to town and that was not allowed. Eventually he got up to leave, telling me that I seemed like a nice enough bloke and asking me my name. Then he thanked me and said, "I shall remember this, Bill Charlton."

But Bill didn't tell Edina all of their conversation.
"So, Charles, are you married?"
"Never married. However, right now I want a woman—actually, it is so acute that I *need* a woman. Do you ever get like that, Bill?"
"Like what?"
"Like you need a woman?"
"Naw, I have a beautiful young lady back home."
"That's right—back home—not here and now. Come with me and I will find you a nice mademoiselle."
"No thanks, my girl is amazing."
"How so? I need to find me an amazing woman."
"My girl is the sweetest, kindest girl."
"That's okay, but can she perform?"
"Oh yes, when I get home she takes the time to strip me, caress me, allows me to do the same to her. She makes me want to scream out with

passion. She has a bully of a husband, who really rapes her for his own pleasure. But with me, because I love her, it is gentle and amazing. We have a love child together."

"You make her sound very special."

"She is, Charles, too bad her husband doesn't appreciate her. His loss, my gain."

"I would like a woman like that."

"Would that be enough, Charles?"

Charles shook his head. "Does the husband know she is unfaithful?"

"Well, he is unfaithful, does it really matter?"

"Why don't you come with me tonight and we can finish this discussion."

"No thanks, Charles, you go have yourself a good time."

When Edina read Bill's letter, her stomach flopped. She hoped that nothing had been said to show that Bill had knowledge of Charles. How strange that they would meet. She picked up another letter.

Dearest Edina,

How are you and the children making out? It must be so difficult for you to have the whole responsibility of your family. Sure, it is no fun for soldiers over here, but we only have one to look after. So I want to thank you from the bottom of my heart for all you do for our daughter. I love hearing stories of her development. Don't get me wrong, I love the stories of Lily and John and what they are doing too. They both seem such a help to you.

When this damn war is over, and if I am lucky enough to survive completely, I would be happy to somehow make you my wife. By "survive completely," I mean having all my limbs, all my faculties, and—most of all—my manhood. I would not in any way want to be a burden to you. I can hardly believe that we have been fighting for more than two years. Whenever will it end?

With tears in her eyes, Edina closed this letter and thought, What does the future hold for me?

Chapter 19

Because of the sheer number of dead and wounded, things changed really quickly as different battalions were combined. All Charles knew was that he was well enough to travel and that they were going to be sailing on the HS Sicilia.

The Sicilia was a hospital ship, though it would, on this journey, act as a troop ship as well. To start, Charles was to be travelling in the hospital part to be sure that he recovered completely from his pleurisy, though he would be one of the "walking sick." One of his battalion soldiers would pack everything for Charles, and they would bring his kit bag to him once on board.

Charles had never been on a ship travelling for days and so had no expectations. Though of course there was great deal of discussion about what dangers could be encountered because of submarines, aircraft bombings, and mines in the area.

The soldiers got on the HS Sicilia at Cherbourg and started their journey staying pretty close to the coastline.

In the hospital area, Charles was the closest he had been to women for quite a number of months. He enjoyed the smell of a woman, enjoyed her gentle hands tending to his incision, which had become infected out in the field hospital. He oozed charm from every pore, and he was careful not to appear to be getting better, otherwise he would no longer have this contact.

Charles was drawn in particular to a nurse from Australia called Alice. Not only was she young she was also pretty and had a body that seemed to Charles to be crying out for attention.

On the third day at sea, Charles's body reacted to Alice's gentle washing of his wound before she put on a fresh dressing. He lay there wishing that she would allow her hands to roam all over his body. "So, Alice, tell me why you became a nurse and chose to be involved with this damn war and travel these dangerous seas when you could have stayed safely in Australia."

"Just a sense of adventure, and to do my bit for the war. My parents are from England, and both my brothers enlisted in the Australian Army. My parents brought me up to be independent and strong, to make my own decisions. I was already a nurse, so it became my way to help the war effort."

"So, you don't have a young man in your life, then?"

"No, most of the young men came this way to help in the war effort. I was too focused on becoming a nurse. What about you? Girl? Wife?"

"Not me." With that Alice patted Charles. "Up you get, soldier. Dressing done for today. You need to get outside, do some deck walking, and build up your strength because in a couple of days, we have to do some vaccinations and inoculations for typhoid. You can come back here tonight to sleep, but my guess is that this will be your last night here.

"Will you be on duty tonight?"

"Yes, little rest for us nurses."

Charles picked up his pass, went up on deck, and started walking. It was chilly in the wind, but he felt good to actually be out of the ward. Leaning over the side of the ship, he watched the rhythm of the waves as they washed against the side of the ship and thought about how long it had been since he had been with a woman. He thought of Alice; she was a pretty young thing, and she had implied that she had never had a boyfriend. This excited Charles as he contemplated teaching her and taking her for himself. He wondered how he could make this happen.

He met up with some of his buddies from the trenches, who were surprised to see him up and about. As Charles was talking to one of the soldiers, he noticed the young man didn't look very well. His face looked quite pink, and he seemed to be sweating. "You all right, mate?"

"Nope, I feel kind of dizzy and really, really hot," the kid answered.

Right at that moment, Charles spotted one of the medics he knew. "Hey, medic! Come and take a look at this soldier, he is such a pink colour."

The medic took one look at the young man, gave a slight gasp, and said, "I want you both to come with me."

"Me as well! Look here, I just got let out of that hospital hole, why do I have to come back down there with him? I don't even know him."

"It looks to me as if he might have measles. If that's the case, you'll have to go into quarantine—it's the only chance we have of stopping an epidemic. Highly contagious and an enormous danger to the army in these crowded conditions." They walked towards the hospital hole. "Measles in adult life is usually a severe condition."

With that Charles was isolated in a large room with some other men as the young man was taken to see one of the doctors. The room was hot and smelly simply due to its depth in the ship.

The door opened and a doctor came in, saying, "Sorry, guys, you all have been exposed to measles. Have any of you had measles as a child?"

Charles and two others raised their hands. "Well, you will all be staying together, but you three will probably be out of here in a week if at that time you are still well. You others will need to be here for two weeks before we can be sure you are okay. By the time we land, all of you in this room should be okay as our journey will take roughly just a little under a month."

With that some of the soldiers started to shout, "Where the hell are we going?"

"I think the captain will be announcing that to everyone on board this evening," the doctor said before he turned and left.

At 1800 hours, the ships speakers started to crackle. Everyone—staff, soldiers, doctors, and nurses—stopped in the middle of what they were doing, turned to look at the speakers, and waited.

A disembodied voice boomed out, "I have a message from Major-General Stanley Maude to tell you all that we are travelling to Basra. MG Maude has been told to hold the existing line. However, he sees an opportunity for advancement. He eagerly awaits your arrival. So with the help of every one of you, we will do our best to capture Baghdad.

The men already here have had success, according to MG Maude, as they seized Khadairi Bend in December and at that time managed to establish their trenches a mere four hundred yards from the enemy's front line.

So, gentlemen, MG Maude wants you to take this time to strengthen your minds and bodies. Stay well, and we will see you all in a few short weeks."

That was the end of the message.

The men looked anxiously at each other. "I thought France was bloody awful."

"Aye," says another, "bloody cold and muddy."

"Now we are going to the other extreme—a hell hole," someone else shouted.

"God, we are shut up in this room in quarantine," said Charles. Silence fell on the men as they now remembered why they were here.

The speakers crackled again. "Ladies and gentlemen, this is the captain of the H. S. Sicilia. Doctor Williams has just reported to me that we seem to be in the midst of an outbreak of measles. He has had thirty-five cases today. If you are feeling unwell, report immediately to a medic. In these crowded conditions we are travelling in, this disease can spread quickly. Do not put off coming to a medic as the risk of death to young adults is much higher than for children."

Outside in the ward, Nurse Sally turned to Alice and said, "Looks like we are in for a long journey, dear friend."

Alice smiled. "We better start fumigating with sulphur to try to keep the air quality as high as possible."

When a few days later the first two young men died of measles, it seemed horribly sudden. An announcement was made over the speakers once again. The captain said that as the risk of spreading measles was too high, they did not want the men to gather; instead, the sea burial would be broadcasted over the speakers.

Arriving at Basra, the soldiers, many of whom had either been ill or in quarantine, disembarked. They were weak and yet were faced with a forty-mile trek to Qurna, where the two rivers, Tigris and Euphrates, meet before flowing into the Persian Gulf. With no roads, all transportation was done on the rivers.

The goal was Baghdad, some 570 miles upstream.

Charles's regiment was amalgamated with an Indian company. These East Indian soldiers were the few who were allowed to fight in France alongside the British. It was an interesting combination for the military, to have their brown brothers fighting whites. The Indian Army preferred men from Nepal or Punjab as these men appeared more "manly." Being under General Maude, everyone communicated in English. The British were in a camp to recover from the journey, which was a relief to most who had travelled on the HS Sicilia.

Once settled in camp, Charles caused a lot of problems. During a conference of doctors, they discussed him.

"I am not sure what to do with this soldier."

"Well, judging by his records, he seems to be a shirker."

"True, but what about the nightmares? My God, this man has had some pretty rough traumas in the trenches."

"The screaming. The aggressiveness. I agree, I don't think he is faking his illness. We can't leave him in the tent with the other soldiers, it is not fair to them."

"Perhaps we should transfer him to Deolali?"

The consensus of the doctors was that he should be transferred to Deolali in India., which was a transit camp for British troops who had gone "doolally." Deolali was set in the hills, a hundred miles or so from Bombay. It was an awful place, and it was thought that those who feigned illness would get better quickly just to get out of this place.

Chapter 20

The hospital at Deolali had an Australian matron, Alma Louise Bennett. Most of the nurses were Australian rather than British because they could stand the heat. There were enough beds for three thousand soldiers but only a very small staff of around seventy-four, and only fifteen nurses came from the Indian Nursing Service.

"Gertrude, I don't know how we are going to cope with most of our nursing staff sent elsewhere."

"I agree, Alma. Maybe we will have to turn to more locals to help us."

"Great idea—not everything has to be done by a nurse. What is happening in the wards where the outbreak of small pox has occurred?"

"Well, all nurses have had their vaccinations, which is a blessing. We are trying to assess who has and who hasn't had vaccinations. Alma, there is some talk of nurses and soldiers becoming intimate. Do we need to do anything with these rumours?"

"We have enough problems without dealing with rumours. It is not difficult for me to imagine the distress that charges of behaving in a sexually promiscuous manner would have on our unmarried women if we start to act on these accusations."

"I agree. Quite honestly, there is little time off to engage in such shenanigans."

"Though, I do perceive a problem with orderlies—because we don't speak the language and really know nothing about their culture, we have to sign or show them what we want them to do. I worry if this is right? We are in a very male-orientated world here. I would hate to offend."

So this is where the doctors had decided to send Charles as soon as there were others assigned to Deolali and transportation could be arranged.

Charles arrived at Deolali on May 9, 1917. He was immediately put into solitary confinement, where he could not disturb others and where it was believed that not being in a ward would help to settle patients like him. In addition to the isolation, he was subjected to a restricted diet and drugs that could cause a coma, convulsions, and hypnosis. This was not what Charles had expected. However, in his mind, anything was better than fighting.

After a month, Charles was placed in a ward that was run by Australian and Canadian nurses.

"Charles, this will be your bed in ward 11."

"Thank you, Nurse Margaret." Charles looked down at a skinny cot with a very thin mattress covered by flimsy sheets, a light blanket, and a pillow. Over the bed, a tied mosquito net hung.

"There are twenty-four beds in here and, like you, all these soldiers have recently left isolation."

Charles nodded as she left. He placed what little he owned under the bed and looked at the man beside him. "Hello, where are you from?"

"London."

"I am from Northumberland."

"I be a Geordie," someone called out.

Charles smiled. "So, fellows, can we go outside?"

"No, not till we are assigned a companion."

"What do you mean?"

"Well, it's like this, fellow," said someone down the ward. "You have to appear cured. Meaning no dreaming, screaming, or losing your temper. The shrink comes to evaluate you every couple of days. Two weeks of good evaluation and they give you a companion and you get to go sightseeing."

Another soldier piped up, "I hear tell that there are some pretty good sights." He collapsed into laughter. "I am not talking about trees and buildings, but a bit more about the birds and bees."

"Gor on with you, how do you know?"

"'Cause I managed to get out once."

"And?" said Charles.

"Got this amazing young woman, who was very satisfying. But I wanted to go out more—like every day. Lost my cool and got put back into solitude and treatment again. Won't happen this time."

"I reckon he is kidding," Charles said.

During the week, Charles noticed the nurses were wonderful, but he was fascinated with the Indian women who did the cleaning. They were slender, strikingly beautiful, and dressed in wonderful saris, which were colourful and sometimes quite transparent. His dreams changed from those of terror to ones of lust. With these thoughts, he made quick gains and was soon allowed to move around the compound and eventually out onto the streets with a companion.

Charles was assigned a companion named Esha to show him around. Esha was at least six inches taller than he was, and when he looked up at her, he immediately wanted her. The first morning she arrived to take him out, she was dressed in a white sari trimmed with blue. The thin silk material was wrapped tightly around her slim body, showing off her dark yet luminous skin. The sari top was simple: one layer of material thrown loosely across her shoulder and pulled over her shining black hair. The top draped over her perfectly formed breasts and displayed her large dark brown nipples through the white silk. He gasped aloud at this vision of beauty, his eyes resting on those nipples with sweet thoughts of taking one large nipple in his lips and using his flicking tongue to make it even larger, if that was possible.

The doctor looked at this little runt of a soldier and said to Esha, "I want you to take him for a rickshaw ride around the city. Show him the sites, give him a meal, and have him back here by three. If he becomes angry or rude, then you are to bring him back immediately, you understand?" The woman simply nodded.

Once outside, Charles immediately felt his spirits lift. He helped Esha into a rickshaw and climbed in next to this beauty, feeling the heat of her body against his. In the hospital, there had been talk among the soldiers that having sex with an Indian woman was an amazing experience—not at all like having sex in England and much better than any brothel.

As the rickshaw driver pedalled Esha and Charles around Deolali, Charles said, "So, Esha, are you married?"

"No, I live with my family."

"Close?"

"Just outside of Deolali."

"How old are you?"

"I am thirteen."

"You are working?"

"I help my parents as there are ten children in my family."

Charles said, "Esha, what is your job exactly?"

Esha turned her lithe body towards him and fixed her large brown eyes on his small blue ones. "My employment is to make sick soldiers recover from whatever ails them."

"So what does that mean? What training did the hospital give you?"

Esha asked the rickshaw driver to stop at the small park they were passing. "Charles, let us get out and walk for a while to build up your strength." She hopped quickly down and came round to Charles. "Here, take my hand, let me help you."

Charles didn't need to be asked twice; he was longing to touch her. He took her brown long-fingered hand and once again was amazed by her height, her gracefulness, and her beauty. He slipped to the ground and smelled the scent of a woman rather than a girl. They both turned as the rickshaw quickly left.

Still holding his hand, Esha drew Charles towards a lake in the park and said, "I will try to answer your questions as we walk. As I said, my goal is to help you to recover. That is what I am employed to do. Women really don't need to be trained to make men happy. I have watched my mother all day, every day, at home. My father works as little as possible, my mother works very, very hard. We daughters are taught to do everything for our brothers, who are also lazy. We watch our mother make my father happy whenever he demands her to. Our teaching is done through watching. We women have very good instincts." With that she moved in front of him and walked toward the lake, and he was mesmerized by the rhythmic swaying of her hips.

Everlasting Lies

"Look, there is a small island in the lake, let us wade out and see what is there."

"But I will wreck my uniform," he said stupidly, regretting it the moment he said it.

"So strip down to your underwear, and I will bundle your clothes up and carry it on my head. Come on, it will be good for you." With that she dashed into the water, her white sari becoming more transparent and clinging to her beautiful legs as she stood thigh deep.

Charles quickly undid his belt, removed his shirt, and dropped his pants, folding them carefully into a small bundle. He added his socks and shoes and enclosed all this within his shirt and passed this to Esha. She placed these on her head and simply said, "Come on in and join me, Charles."

As he reached her, she brushed her lips across his.

"I liked that, will there be more?"

They reached the island but it was slippery, so she took his hand and pulled him up. The pulling made her fall, which caused him to slip on the mud as well. As they were falling, she had the presence of mind to quickly throw the bundle towards the dry grass so his clothes would not get damaged. Charles landed somewhat on top of her.

"You are beautiful." He then kissed her.

"You are very large for someone so short." She moved her lower lip back and forth, knowing full well she was giving him a throbbing kiss, one that should stimulate his desire.

Quickly, Esha got up and ran into the water. Charles sat up to watch her. She started to remove the sari from her head, slowly unravelling the yards of material and exposing her beautiful naked body.

"You had better come in and wash the mud off your underwear, then we will find a sunny spot to dry in."

This beautiful thirteen-year-old sashayed past him. He ran quickly into the water.

"Over here! It is a perfect drying spot."

What a vision of loveliness greeted him. Esha's sari was hanging around some trees, making a circle. She sat in the middle of the circle wearing his army shirt. She could see that he was fatigued and patted a place beside her.

"In this country, sex is public. We are taught Kama Sutra and watch and learn from others. We women want the pleasure, and when someone is sick like you, we will take the place of the man and work hard for us both to have enjoyment." With that she gently rubbed her hand over his lingam as she removed his underwear, watching the erection form.

"Umm, she said, "though I know you are fatigued, I see you are interested. Do you want me to continue?

Charles nodded.

As Esha stood up, she purposely stepped over him, making sure that he had every opportunity to see her.

"You are beautiful, Esha."

In all the brothels Charles had visited, never had he experienced anything as good as this. He was totally exhausted; Esha curled around him while he napped.

As Esha returned Charles to the hospital and a waiting nurse, she said, "I hope today has helped you to feel better."

"It has, will you get to take me out again?"

"I don't know if it will be me or some other worker."

"Nurse, can I request to have Esha take me on my next outing?"

"I doubt it, Charles, we have so many young girls working for us, and I understand from the soldiers that they are all wonderful at their job. Anyways, it is better not to get reliant on any one person, don't you think? This way you are not setting yourself up for a disappointment."

"Then how long is it before I get taken out again, Nurse?"

"Depends, Charles—if you do not regress and if the doctor deems it necessary, you could go again very soon."

"What makes it necessary?"

But the nurse had already left, so Esha answered. "I can tell you, Charles, that you will be taken out fairly quickly if you do not fall back into your old ways. I hope today was fun for you." She smiled and left.

Everlasting Lies

Chapter 21

Charles had many outings for his recovery over the next eight days. He met Manjula, who took him to the Pandavleni Caves.

"Charles, these caves date back to ancient times, do you notice that they look yellow in colour?"

"I do. They match the colour of your sari."

"Right, the Buddhist monks who lived here wore yellow robes."

Charles thought this was probably one of the most interesting places he had been taken to. He looked back on this as a golden experience.

The more he saw of Deolali, the more he was shocked by the filth in the streets. There was manure from the sacred cow everywhere, barely-clothed children were dirty, and grimy people sorted through the many mucky piles of rubbish, trying to eke out a living. And the evocative smells left behind by the camels and elephants wandering the streets only served as a reminder of what he'd thought when he'd first arrived.

But with his different companions showing him the sights—Manjula, Inda, Reshima, Kanti, and once more with Esha, oh, the pleasure he'd felt.

※

The day before Charles was about to be returned to his regiment, he went to see a nurse.

"Nurse, I was wondering if you could give me something for this rash."

"Where is it, Charles?"

"On my feet, buttocks, and now on my hands. I think it's some kind of heat rash."

"Does it itch?"

"No."

The nurse took his temperature.

"Any other symptoms, Charles?"

"A sore throat, and I feel headachy," he replied.

"I will get the doctor to look at you."

The doctor soon diagnosed syphilis, which was not a surprise. Having this much sex and experimenting with different women was the cause of Charles's syphilis. He was returned to a hospital, where his case became very severe. After three weeks in hospital in Deolali, he started to show signs of recovery. It was now July, and he had not written to Edina since the beginning of the year.

July, 1917

Dear Edina,

Life has been very difficult for me and I have been unable to write.

I was still in hospital when I was aboard the ship. Aboard we had an outbreak of measles on the ship so we travelled in quarantine. All of the troops were extremely weak when we arrived.

I was transported to Deolali as I'd had a nervous breakdown. Things were not pretty, but my times in the trenches and then the accident in the tunnel and losing all my friends was too much for me to cope with, and the quarantine on board gave me too much time to remember.

I was doing quite well until three weeks ago—I wasn't having nightmares anymore and had begun dreaming that maybe they would send me back to England and to you. I was being allowed out of the camp accompanied by a local Indian, and we would go for walks and eventually was taken to the Indians' home to meet the family. They taught me their ways of doing things, so very different from our ways. In fact I was a willing learner and this whole experience was most enjoyable. I think we all had a good time together.

Charles re-read this part, and the memories of the women made his body react to past pleasures. But he read it carefully to be sure that there was nothing that would make Edina the slightest bit suspicious before he continued writing.

> Oh, Edina, how I long to see you again so we can continue with our lives rather than living as part of this war. But let me continue with my health issues.
>
> Then I suddenly became desperately ill again, this time with dysentery, and I really have not been well or conscious of what has been going on around me for the last three weeks.

Charles really didn't want to tell Edina that he had syphilis and thought dysentery sounded better.

> My battalion has been amalgamated into an Indian company. I have been told that I am to be sent to the hospital where they are as soon as I am seen fit to travel. Obviously, I am expected to continue my career here.
>
> Charles.

※

Edina received the letter in late August of 1917. She was sorry that her husband had been so sick and noticed he seemed to know little about the war other than in his little world. She wondered if he knew or cared that the Americans were now involved, that there were Americans now in Britain, and that their forces had arrived in France at the end of June. There was much talk in her village that maybe there would soon be an end to this awful war.

She sighed as she continued to gather beans and peas from her garden. Charles had not asked one question, not one. He showed no interest in his children. What kind of man was he going to be when he came back?

Sarah poked her head over the fence. "Just made a cuppa, Edina, come sit awhile. Bring Edna with you and she can watch the antics of our children."

Edina scooped up a giggling Edna, saying, "This is such a happy child."

"What is new with you, Edina?"

"I finally had another letter from Charles. He is in India."

"India! What's he doing, running away from the war?" Sarah grinned at her friend. "Andrew used to say to me that Charles would wiggle his way out of the war." The ladies giggled. "Now, did he ask anything about you or the bairns?"

Edina shook her head. "So how is Andrew doing?" She was thinking about the fact that Andrew was forty-one now and what a tough life that would be for him.

"He seems to be recovering, though according to his letters it appears he has lost sight in one eye. But he is cheerful enough and wrote a funny letter to the kids saying that they will always have to be on his right side so he can see them because if they are on the left, he won't know what they are doing. Methinks he is setting them up for some kind of disaster. You know what a ham he is."

"I do that. Is he out of rehab yet? What will he do? Surely they won't send him back in the trenches?"

"Gawd no, he probably would shoot his own side." The children stopped to watch their mothers laughing. "No, seriously," said Sarah, trying to pull herself together, "they are talking about putting him in the cookhouse. Imagine—he is left-handed and has lost sight in his left eye." With that the ladies screamed with laughter, each adding on to the story.

After they had pulled themselves together, Sarah said, "Let us get back to Charles. So why India?"

"Well, he left France on a hospital ship that was going to somewhere and he said the ship had problems with measles and they travelled in quarantine. They all arrived in poor shape, and though he didn't actually say this, we all know that when soldiers are killed there are a lot of amalgamations, and I would guess they were amalgamated into a British India unit."

"Ah," said Sarah, "I remember reading that The British Indian Army is part of the Siege of Kut, so that makes sense. But how did he get to India?"

"Apparently he had a nervous breakdown and was taken there. He pretty well has been recovering ever since. He sure has been in hospital a lot."

"When will this war be over, Edina? It has been going on for over three years now. When will get our men back?"

"That's if you want them back."

Shocked, Sarah looked at Edina. "What are you saying?"

"Well, I manage pretty well on my own, don't I? Charles has no interest in the children—or me, for that matter. Do I care if he comes home? I could get a job tomorrow they need women workers. I reckon I could learn to drive. I could work on the land. Women are pushing for our rights, we will be able to rent and own property and, I hope, soon some will be able to vote. I don't want any more children, so I don't need Charles. I was young when we met, it was lust, not love for either of us. My parents warned me that Charles had a bad reputation. I was too young—I lied about my age on my wedding certificate. There, I finally said it to someone."

Sarah just stared at Edina as the silence spread between them. Edina waited and waited....

"Oh, Edina, you have managed to always hide all this."

Edina shook her head. "Not much love between us. Charles is in love with Charles. Charles—even before we were married—went to brothels and boasted about it. How do I know this illness, he wrote me about wasn't caused by having sexual contact with other women? Probably was. Do I want him to bring diseases home to me? The last time we had sexual relations was not pleasurable to me, it was all about his pleasure. In fact he physically hurt me."

Long silences. Smiles from Edina.

"It's all right, Sarah, I have had a long time to adjust to this. I just don't know what will happen next. I pray that I am strong enough.

With that Sarah gave Edina a much-needed hug. They called the children over and Sarah said, "So, little ones, shall we all have tea together? Both of us mummies will see what we can bring to the table, and then how about a game of cards all together? There was much excitement from the children and grateful glances from Edina to her friend Sarah.

Chapter 22

"Edina! Edina, look! Come here and look at this morning's paper," Sarah shouted as she rushed into her friend's home. She held a paper in her hand. "Listen up, Edina," she said as she read, "Lloyd George appeared on the steps of 10 Downing Street, smiling at the crowd that had gathered. 'I am glad to tell you that the war will be over at eleven o'clock today, November 11, 1918.' He waved his hand and disappeared."

"He disappeared? That is all he said?"

"Wait a bit...ah," continued Sarah, "he spoke again. 'You are well entitled to rejoice. The people of this country and our allies, the people of the dominions and of India, have won a great victory for humanity. The sons and daughters of the people have done it. They have won this hour of gladness and the whole country has done its duty. It has achieved a triumphant victory that the world has never seen before. Let us thank God.' Well, nice words, I guess."

Edina laughed at her friend.

Sarah sighed. "Rejoice. But what about all those people, who lost family members during this awful war, how will they cope? How many have been killed or injured in the last four years? I would think some men would have psychological problems."

"Not only men," claimed Edina. "What about women? Look at those who went to work filling the jobs men left. You think these won't be given back to the men? Think of it, Sarah, women are even employed in government jobs. Look, we have women as bus and tram conductors now. Many of us have worked on the land, you and I included. Look at all the women in the munitions industry and even other industries. Many women do heavy work like unloading coal—even building ships. Sarah, it was a matter of survival, we needed paying jobs. What about all the nurses? They went and looked after the soldiers in the most awful of conditions. We women are capable."

"Edina, I am going to get you a soap box."

With that both ladies laughed.

"Mark my words, Sarah. There are many more changes to come."

"Like what?"

"Look at the last election."

Silence from Sarah. Edina sighed. "Remember when I came back from my tea room meeting at the Fenwick Café? You know, when I got to meet Dr. Ethel Bentham with Lisbeth Simms?"

Sarah nodded, inwardly smiling at her friend's passion.

"In 1917, the laws caused problems."

"No, I don't remember, what do you mean, Edina?"

"The problem was that, according to the law, only men who had been resident in the country for the twelve months prior to the election were entitled to vote."

Edina looked expectantly at Sarah.

"Oh, and this made the soldiers who had been serving overseas just like us women—unable to vote. Fortunately, some of the arguments put forth by suffragette Millicent Fawcett led to a minority of women getting the vote. Though I didn't, because I am not thirty, the vote for women *is* coming—I just feel it in my bones—and we will all have it soon. We will be emancipated."

Sarah shook her head and smiled at her friend, whose eyes were shining brightly.

Lately Edina had been very active in women's rights and the women's vote, and she was fortunate that Sarah would watch her children when she was at meetings. The country was being taken by storm by strong women looking for the vote; they wanted an equal partnership with men.

"Thanks for the education, I'll put the soap box away now." Sarah left, laughing.

Edina was particularly interested in divorce rights for women. As it was, there were very few divorces because only men could divorce their wives. She pondered this. Marriage was considered to be the very basis of society, something to be held together no matter what. The only ground for divorce was a woman's adultery. Because she'd had relations with Bill, Charles had legal grounds to divorce her and prevent her from ever seeing her children again. She could get a separation as long as she could prove cruelty or habitual drunkenness.

Now the war was over, what would she be faced with?

✦

A few days later, she heard from both Charles and Bill.

September 1918

Edina,

Well, I did recover from my depression and rejoined my regiment but have been several times back in hospital.

I have had several bouts of dysentery and had problems with adhesions and adult colic. I have spent at least two months, on and off, in hospital.

Now that it looks like the war may end, I thought I should inform you I still have a commitment to the end of 1919. As far as I know, I will be spending the rest of the time in India.

Just wanted to tell you that you shouldn't expect me home anytime soon unless I get a medical discharge.

I have to tell you that I love India. It is a very different life here. Much easier than coming back to work in the mines—not sure my body could take it.

Charles

November, 1918

My dearest Edina,

The war is over and, my darling, we are both alive. I am sure there was a celebration in the village. But for us still here at the front, there was none. Many of us didn't really believe it.

At 11 a.m., we laid our arms down and there was this silence. The quietness was unnerving.

After these long months of strain, always thinking of the enemy, all I could think about was coming home to you. Though, sweetheart, I have to tell you I soon fell into an exhausted sleep, as did many others.

The big question is, Now what? You know I love you and all the children and really want to make you my wife. Will this ever be possible? Will we have to run away all together?

I know already that I will be back working with the railways, which was my job before this dreadful war. I would be able to ask for a transfer. We could live anywhere.

Can't wait to hold you in my arms again and have hugs from all the children.

Lovingly, Bill

What decisions would she have to make now?

November 14, 1918

Darling Bill,

It is wonderful to hear from you and I am wondering when you might be home.

I had a letter from Charles, and unbeknown to me, he signed on till the end of 1919.

He tells me he is pretty sure that he will be in India for the rest of the time and that he likes it there, though he mentioned a medical discharge and in the same breath said he could not go back to the mines. As I have been telling you in other letters, I have become very active in women's rights, and especially divorce. But at the moment there is no way a woman can get a divorce, only a husband can divorce his wife.

So I think I shall write to Charles and request that he divorces me. Which, my darling, would then free me to marry you.

Charles will never make me happy as he does not want to be a family man. My parents pleaded with me not to marry him and, honestly, I think he did marry me to spite them.

No matter what happens, if you want us all, I am willing to follow you wherever you work, but I understand that with Charles still around this could become very distasteful for us all.

Waiting to hear your latest news.

Very lovingly, Edina

Edina folded the letter and put it thoughtfully into an envelope, addressed it, and turned to write a letter to Charles.

November 14, 1918

Charles,

Thank you for your latest letter. I had no idea you signed on till the end of 1919. Why did you not tell me before? I know you wouldn't have thought to discuss this, or think about how I feel about this.

Other lasses are expecting their husbands' home very soon to become a family with their children once again.

You might wonder why I haven't written sooner, especially as you seem to continue with ill health. But I have been doing a lot of soul-searching. I find myself worried about how life will be when you return. You seem to have no love or interest in our children—you never ask how they are, what they are doing, nothing, Charles. Do you even remember their names and how old they are? Lily is 8, John is 7, and sweet Edna is 3. They take a lot of time and energy but are wonderful children.

So, Charles, this is a plea from me to you. Will you please divorce me and set me free? I know it is not possible for me to divorce you, though I have plenty of reasons to divorce you for your infidelity during our marriage. I am sure I could find proof. Even now I suspect you are not faithful to me. But this isn't the reason I want a divorce. I do not want our children to see you angry with me, nor do I want them to grow up knowing that their father frequents brothels.

I am begging you to give me a divorce. You can reverse the tables on me and ruin my reputation I really don't care.

I know it is possible to start this process even whilst you are still in the forces. When you come home, you will be a free man. You can start life over again with someone who is willing to shower you with attention, think about it like that.

Edina

She put this letter in an envelope, called to little Edna, and said, "Let's walk to school to pick up Lily and John."

Edna, a little ball of a child, ran squealing and laughing to her mummy as she said, "Come on, Mummy."

Edina couldn't help but think Edna was a delightful child.

Walking back from school, Edina bumped into Sarah. "What made you come out on such a grey November afternoon?"

"Oh, I had letters to post to both Charles and Bill."

"I haven't heard you mention a letter from Charles, any idea when he is coming home?"

As the children ran ahead and played tag, with smiling Edna saying "Wait me, wait me. I it," Edina told Sarah the story.

Sarah shook her head in disbelief. But she stopped dead when Edina told her she had asked Charles to divorce her.

"You did what, Edina? How will you survive without a man at your side and three children?"

"Oh, Sarah, you are so old fashioned. Just like I have been doing during this war. I will get myself a job. I will be happy. The thought of Charles coming home terrifies me. What if he be cruel to the little ones? In fact maybe I will see if I can get myself a housekeeping job as a live-in. I really need to move if he won't give me a divorce. I need to protect us all."

"I think, Edina, all this women's rights stuff has gone to your head."

"It may have, but I want my children to have a happy life."

As they reached their homes, Sarah turned to Edina and gave her hug. "You be one special lady."

"Don't know about being a lady." Edina laughed as thoughts of Bill flew into her head. "Come on, you little rascals, we have jobs to do. John, go get stuff from the shed, your job is to get the parlour fire going. Come on, young ladies, let us see what we can find for tea."

Edina waved to her good friend as she closed the door.

Chapter 23

Christmas came and went with Edina and the children spending it at the Paxtons'. New Year was spent at home with Sarah and her children. Though officially the war was over, there had been no change in the lives of these ladies.

On the eighth of January, Edina had a letter from Bill.

January 6th, 1919

Darling,

Just a quick note to tell you I should be back in England by the 10th of January. Not sure how many days it takes before I am released. When I know more, you will be the first to hear. I suspect I will be in Ripon. As soon I am released, I will be on my way to you.

All my love. Bill

Edina started to cry. She picked up Edna, as the other two were at school, threw a warm shawl over them both, and rushed over to Sarah's.

Pushing open the back door, she called, "Sarah, it's me and Edna."

"Edina, is there anything wrong?"

"No, no, I came to share that Bill will be back in England in a few days."

"How wonderful, that your brother will be home so soon," Sarah said as she went to put the kettle on. "I see that little missy is sleepy. Do you want to lay her down on the children's bed? Then we can chat over tea."

By the time Edina had Edna settled, tea was ready and was served with digestive biscuits. The two friends sat at the kitchen table because it was nice and cozy by its small fire.

"Ah, your ma and pa will be thrilled to have their son home. How long is it since any of you have seem him?"

"Back in 1915." With that Edina burst into tears.

"My oh my, this is good news, Edina."

"Oh, Sarah, I need someone who I can be honest with, someone who will just listen, someone who is my best friend."

"Go on, Edina."

What was Sarah committing to? Already tears were pricking her eyes.

Edina confessed that Bill was not her brother but her lover and the father of Edna, then she went on to explain how she had tricked Charles into believing Edna was his.

Sarah was frowning as she tried to follow the story.

After a moment of stunned silence, Sarah said, "Why did Charles think Edna was his?"

"Well, when he came home unexpectedly, I already knew I was pregnant, so I literally pushed myself on him. I was shameless. Charles went off angry.

"What about Bill?"

"He didn't know, but when he came and spent his last week before going overseas with us, I told him I was pregnant with his child. He was very happy. Charles isn't that bright. He believes Edna is his." Edina sighed and looked at her friend.

"I just told you that Charles doesn't come home until perhaps the end of the year. Remember I wrote Charles before Christmas and asked him for a divorce."

" Have you heard anything?"

"No," said Edina, shaking her head. "I'll be lucky if I hear back in a couple of months."

"What you going to do, Edina?"

Edina shook her head. "I love Bill, he loves all my children, and they love him. I have no love for Charles—he is cruel and selfish. I have been thinking for a long time, Sarah, about nothing else. What will I do? Well, if Bill asks me, I will run away with him. I would follow him anywhere. He is a kind and gentle soul."

Sarah gasped. But as a friend, she did not pass any judgment.

"Am I terrible to want happiness, not just for me but also for my children?"

Sarah didn't know what to say, and Edina took her silence as judgment.

Fortunately for both women, Edna woke up and gaily called out in her little singsong voice, "Ma? Ma, where are you? I am here, where are you?"

Both women laughed and this broke the tension. Edina quickly picked up Edna and wrapped her shawl around them both, then smiled at Sarah. "Thanks for the cuppa and bickky, and especially for listening to me. I just needed to say what I was thinking out loud, and you got lucky, Sarah." Edina giggled. "I picked you."

※

A few days later, the children had just come in from school when there was a loud knock at the front door.

"EEE!" said little John. "Who could that be? Nana wouldn't be knocking at the door, she'd walk in the back door, right Ma?"

"There is only one way to find out, John, and that is to open the door." Edina strode to the door and opened it a crack. The wind came swirling in and brought in big flakes of snow. It was almost dark, but she could see a tall figure standing in the snow with his back to her. The snow deadened all sound. John was clutching and peeking from behind his mother's skirts as she enquired, "Do you need help?"

The man brushed the snow off his great big overcoat as he turned around very slowly and moved towards the light coming through the doorway. "Thought I would drop by and surprise you."

Edina heard that beautiful, deep, melodious voice, and her heart skipped a beat.

John ran head down towards the man, screaming, "Uncle Bill, Uncle Bill, you're home." As John barrelled into his body, Bill picked him up as if he were a feather.

"Come in why don't you, Bill? Come in, oh, come in out of the cold."

John was now perched high on Bill's shoulders, shouting, "Lily! Lily, Uncle Bill is here, back from the war, standing right here."

There was a girlish scream and thunderous racket as both girls came running. Lily flew into Bill's arms. "Oh, Uncle Bill!" she said and started to cry."

Edina watched with tears streaming down her face as Edna puffed her way into the room to see what all the excitement was about. To find a man in their house that was a very rare occurrence—she stopped dead and fell down on her bottom, much to the laughter of the four watching. She smiled a great big smile and pointed her fat finger straight at Bill. "Who's dat?"

Lily said, "That's your Uncle Bill, get up and say hello."

The little barrel called Edna pushed herself back up to her feet and waddled towards Bill, who was now crouched down. Without a care, she planted a great big kiss on his cheek.

Bill gently picked her up and said, "My, Edna, you are growing into quite a little roly-poly." With that he buried his head in the child's shoulder, thinking, *Hello, my little daughter, you are one cute little girl,* as he put out his arm and gathered Edina to his side.

There was much laughter in Edina Vernon's home that night. Unfortunately, they learned Bill only had a 24-hour pass. He told the children that he had managed to hitch a ride part of the way, then travelled on the train, taking him a little over three hours, so he would have to leave pretty early tomorrow if he was not to be late getting back to Yorkshire. But he announced that he would be finished and home by the twentieth of January.

Once the children were in bed, he and Edina sat side by side in the parlour.

"It is so good to feel you close to me again, Edina."

"Mm-hmm," Edina agreed. "It was so good to see the children's reaction to you coming through the door."

"It was that—and our little dumpling of a daughter seemed happy too."

"She is such a happy child, she makes us all laugh." Edina snuggled closer.

"You realize, I have to leave pretty soon after breakfast tomorrow, pet. I came to see you so we could get some plans into place. I can have a job on the railway, and this could come with housing if I want, so we really do need to talk."

Edina looked at Bill, thinking there were many things she would rather do than talk.

Bill smiled at her, saying, "I can tell what you are thinking, but we have the rest of our lives and so little time now to make these plans. My employers have told me that I shall be working at Bridge Street Station. They have property on Bridge Street and offered me a three-bedroom home in terrace housing. I want to know if you and the children will move in with me?"

Edina wasn't at all surprised by this request, knowing full well they both wanted this. "Bill, how do I explain this to the children? They think you are my brother. I want to be able to sleep with you, I want us to be seen as husband and wife, I want you to be recognized as the children's father. I have written and asked Charles for a divorce."

"You have?"

"Yes, I told him that he can divorce me and lay all the blame on me—I don't care, I want to be with you."

"Does he know about me, then?"

"No, of course he doesn't, so me moving in with you would be perfect. If he hasn't already divorced me by the time he comes home, he will want to divorce me then, right?" Edina smiled lovingly at Bill.

"What will we tell the children? Why, suddenly, is your brother sharing your bed?"

"I don't know, we will just have to answer the questions when they come. Don't you think that would be best?"

Bill smiled at Edina. "Darling, you are so practical, and willing. So I take it that you will start packing and laying the plans to move into the terrace as soon as I know the date?"

She nodded.

"So, sweet one, is it time for us to turn in? Or do you want me to add more wood to the fire?" he said with a twinkle in his eye.

Gently kissing him on his cheek and taking his hand, Edina said, "I think it is bedtime." Bill stood up, gently lifted Edina into his arms, and walked to the bedroom.

Chapter 24

Bill went back that Sunday morning. By Tuesday, Edina had a letter from him stating he would be demobbed on the tenth of January and would be home some time that day. He was able to start work on the fifteenth. He also said he had a three-bedroom terrace house on Bridge Street, which was about a ten-minute walk from the cottage Edina was living in now. He wanted to know how soon they could be ready to move.

The next few weeks were a flurry of activity; the children would not have to change schools for the time being. They were told that they were going to live with Uncle Bill as their ma was going to be his housekeeper. The children were happy to be moving to Uncle Bill's bigger house. They didn't find it strange that Edina and Bill shared a room.

Life was idyllic until the day that Edina received a letter from Charles in mid-February.

January 15, 1919

Edina,

What the hell are you talking about, a divorce? Who ever heard of such a thing?

I don't have to have an interest in the children. You are right; my interest is in you, just you.

I will never set you free. NEVER.

Just because I have enjoyed the company of other women—and certainly continue to do so with the beautiful women of India—these whores are not someone I want to marry. You are my wife. This gives me respectability. You are mine and I will not give you up to anyone else. Remember your parents' words: You make your bed, you lie on it.

So, Edina, you are stuck with me, as I am with you, but I have the advantage of being a man and it being acceptable to have affairs.

I will never, ever, give you a divorce, and nothing you do will ever make me.

Charles

Edina wondered, *whatever is going to happen?*

Once the children were in bed and she and Bill were sitting in the parlour, she passed Bill the letter. When he was finished reading, he folded the letter and handed it back to her.

"Oh, my love. I am sorry there are such men in this world. But we won't rush into any plans, we will think about this and make our plans not as a reaction, but sanely. I have a good job, one where I can apply for a transfer. We have no idea when he is coming home, but we know he signed on until the end of the year and, darling, it is only February—you don't have to write back to him for a long time, as there really is nothing to say at this point. Though when you next write, I think you should start having letters sent care of the post office, and you need to start getting his allowance sent to the PO as well, that way he can't trace where you are living. This will really put him off balance."

Bill was now rambling and Edina started to giggle. "Did you say that we wouldn't rush? And what was that word, *sanely?*"

They started to laugh and just hugged each other. They were both so happy.

Life was good. Edina and family would often go to Newcastle to see her parents and her siblings. They could now travel on the train for free as Bill worked for the railway.

One weekend Edina and her children were getting ready to go for a visit when young Lily said, "Ma, why doesn't Uncle Bill ever come with us and visit his ma and pa?"

Everlasting Lies

Innocent words from a nine-year-old, but words that pierced Edina's heart, which actually stopped beating for a few seconds.

"Why won't you let me talk about Uncle Bill in front of them?"

Edina had worried when this situation would arise and always prayed that she would be able to come up with answers. But this was a bigger mountain than she was prepared to climb.

"Um, sweet Lily, those are all mighty big questions. Can we perhaps try to chat about this after a visit to your grandparents as they will be expecting us?"

"Okay, Ma, but don't think I will forget."

"I know you won't, and we will talk when we get home, is that okay?"

There was a nod of Lily's head.

With that the little family made their way to Bridge Street Station.

John took his grandchildren to the ice cream store, allowing mother and daughter to spend some time alone.

Ellen made tea for her daughter and herself. Edina looked at her and said, "I am glad Pa is taking the kids, Ma, because I desperately need to talk to you and seek your advice."

Ellen raised her eyebrows.

"Not really sure where to begin, Ma, and we don't have a lot of time."

Edina tried to fill in her mother as much as possible—from her first encounter with Bill, to the difference between Bill and Charles before they both went off to war, and on and on to the present day. Edina told Ellen that she had asked Charles to release her and recounted his mean, gruff refusal. Then to today's question from Lily. Ellen and Edina spoke softly to each other; there were no reprimands, just two women talking about a problem. A plan was discussed.

John entered with three squealing, giggling children. Edina quickly said, "Come on, you three, we better be off home, we don't want to be missing the train. Give your grandparents a big hug and kisses."

As the little family set off, Ellen said, "Next time you come, bring Bill with yer."

Edina waved and smiled as she watched her pa look at her ma and mouth, *Bill?*

※

Once everyone had had their tea, Edina turned to Bill and said, "Would you mind getting John and Edna ready for bed? Lily and I have some talking to do."

Lily gave her mother a great big smile, which Bill noticed. "Sure, I can do that."

Edina looked at Lily and said, "Let us go and get cozy around the fire."

"Oh, Ma, you remembered your promise."

"Promises are really important to keep. But I want you to tell me something first, if that is okay?"

Lily nodded, smiling at her ma.

"Lily, what do you remember about your pa?"

"My pa? Not Grandpa?"

"Aye, that is what I mean, Lily."

Lily frowned as if she were trying to conjure up something. "Not really much, I suppose. It has been a long time since we saw him, hasn't it, Ma?"

Ma nodded. "Yes, you were at school—just around five or six."

Silence.

"I remember him shouting at you, cussing. I know he didn't like me, or little Johnny. We seemed to be in his way, Ma. He made you sad. I know we never talk about him, why is that, Ma?"

Edina hugged her daughter closer, and they both stared into the fire.

"I want you to know that your pa loved me very much in the beginning. But, sweet Lily, he isn't cut out to be a father. He wants me to himself. If that doesn't happen he takes to cussing. Yes, indeed, he made me very sad. Because of all that you said, Lily, and the fact that Pa isn't going to be home until December, maybe. Also, he has shown little care or love to us for a number of years. I have decided that no matter what happens, we will not be living with your pa anymore."

This statement was greeted by Lily staring at her mother with her blue, blue eyes. Somehow she knew that there was more to come.

"But you asked about Uncle Bill and why he doesn't come and visit Grandma and Grandpa with us, right?" Lily nodded. "I was wondering why you asked that?"

Everlasting Lies | 149

Lily looked at her ma and squirmed in her seat, but Edina continued to wait.

"I guess it is because...because he does everything else with us."

She looked at Edina, who continued to say nothing but appeared to be waiting.

"I really like him, Ma, he treats me like he is my pa and I know he isn't. But I don't know my own pa, I hardly remember him. I like Uncle Bill, John does as well, but he is your brother, so he should go and see his ma and pa, and then they never ask after him."

Edina nodded. "You're right, pet, they don't because they aren't his ma and pa." She paused to allow Lily to think about this." You know you call Sarah your aunty but my ma and pa are not her ma and pa, right?"

Lily said, "No, she is your friend, right? Is Bill your friend, then?"

"Yes, he is a long-time friend. In fact, Lily, he and I went to school together. He does know my ma and pa because we used to live next door to each other when we were kids."

"Really?" Lily said, smiling at her mother. "Were you my age?" Edina nodded. "Was he a good little boy, or did he pull your hair like the boys at school?"

Bill was standing at the door, having put John and Edna to bed. Edina shook her head at him and he left as silently as he had arrived.

"Yes, he did. Do boys still do that to the girls?"

Lily nodded. "I think they do this because they like you. Does Uncle Bill like you?"

"He does, and he loves all of you."

Lily pondered all that she had heard and said, "Does he love you?"

Bill was still listening at the door unseen by Lily. He looked at Edina, asking if he could come in and be part of this conversation, and she nodded.

"Young lady, did I hear you ask your ma if I love her?" Lily, smiling at Bill, nodded.

"Well, not only do I love your ma but I also love all you children. So, missy, what do you say about that?"

"So the next time we go to Grandpa and Grandma Paxton's, will you come with us?"

Bill quickly looked at Edina, who was nodding. "That I will," he answered with a grin.

Lily got up and said, "Think I will go and get ready for bed. If that is all right, Ma?"

Edina, smiling, nodded.

"That went easier than I expected, Bill. "

"I heard that. However, what are your ma and pa going to do when I come to their place? I promised Lily, as you heard."

Edina then set to and told him what had happened in the afternoon when she had time alone with her mother.

"I bet my pa got an earful tonight," Edina said with a smile.

"So they know about me, then. Or perhaps I should ask, sweetheart, what do they know about us?"

"Pretty well everything...Um, they don't know that Edna is yours. But they know I have asked Charles for a divorce, which makes Ma very happy."

Chapter 25

The summer months passed, with no more questions from Lily and no more letters from Charles, but plans were made. The children went back to the same school for the time being.

Bill put in for a transfer. Edina wrote to Charles in early August.

Charles,

I thought it was time I sat down and wrote to you.

As you probably know, the army is now paying me my allowance to a post office because we no longer live at the cottages. I do miss Sarah, but after your last letter I had to make some decisions.

I am unsure when you will return to England, or what you plan to do when you are demobbed. But from your last letter it was obvious that I would be the last to know. I have never been privy to your decisions.

My decision is to disappear. Once you are out of the army I understand there will be no support for me, but I have my own plans to support the children and myself.

I would ask that you do not bother my parents as they know nothing of my plans. They are aging and they don't need to be worried.

I know disappearing is possible as I know nothing about your life before we met, so obviously you managed to do this.

I wish you well.

Edina.

Edina knew full well that it would probably be at least a month before Charles received her letter and, if he even bothered to write back, she might not hear until close to Christmas.

※

Meanwhile, Charles had had many bouts of illness during his year in India. This often left him wondering why he had ever joined the army. He had suffered early in the year with syphilis, but he had continued contact with Indian women. This disease and bouts of malaria eventually led to myalgia, which made him suffer from a lot of muscle pain. He was hospitalized many times in Mhow.

Considering that Charles was only in his thirties, he was in pretty poor shape. But he was grateful for the care given to him by the army. Though he had thought many times of deserting during his career, he knew that with his ill health he was better off in the army.

At the end of September, the army loaned him to the Barrackpore Coal Company to complete his service. The Army's commitment to the Empire after the war ended was to help companies to get back to full power. This was a perfect place for Charles; he had become very comfortable in India with its culture of white supremacy, which fit his personality perfectly. He was put into a supervisory position and now lived in the lap of luxury. Though he was still paid by the British Army, he certainly had a taste of the good life.

Charles appreciated that the custom in India was that men were dominant and always right and that women did the hard work. So women from lower castes also worked in the mines. These women were seen as illiterate and pliable, which, to many of the white men involved, was a benefit.

Charles had been surprised that he did not hear back from his wife after the last letter. So when he received the letter from her in September, he couldn't believe what he read and was furious as he wrote back.

October 1919

Edina, how dare you write a letter such as this to me?

*I can assure you that—no matter what—**I will find you. You are my wife and I have no reason to divorce you.***

So you have left the cottage, really? You must be still close by as you are having the cheques sent to a post office in Newcastle. See, that wasn't too hard for me to find out, now was it?

As long as you need money I will be able to track you down—even if it means sleeping on the doorstep of the post office.

I need you to know that I am passionately in love with this country, India, and am planning on looking for a job here and bringing you and the children to live here. I will make sure that their schooling or a governess will be included. We will live in a house that is provided and will have servants. My dear, you will become a lady. You will have a better life and definitely more time for me.

At the moment I am on loan from the Army and running a mine for Barrackpore. They seem like a good company and there will be some great managerial positions for next year, which they have asked me to apply for. I already have and am waiting for the interview.

We will be able to start our lives afresh in a new country. The children will be well educated—perhaps in boarding school so you can donate all your time to me.

I recognize that I have not been a perfect husband, but we will have a new start when I come to get you and bring you back to India.

So, Edina, I am begging you to let me know where you are as I don't want our new life to start out on a nasty note. But it will if I have to come and find you. No matter what has happened in the past to either of us, that is in the past and I want us to look forward to a bright future here in India.

But I also want you to know I will find you. And no matter what circumstances I find you in, my dear, you are my wife and you will return to India with our children and me.

Your husband, Charles

Charles sat back and read the letter and was quite pleased with his letter-writing abilities. It was to the point and demanding, but he felt kind. He knew his wife was a sexy young thing, which was why he'd had his way with her when she was so young. She still was in the prime of her life as she was only twenty-six now. He allowed his thoughts to roam to Edina's body; this was quite an arousal for him.

Maybe in the last four years she'd had encounters with others as well. He really wouldn't be able to act shocked if this was so; after all, he had lost count of how many women he'd had relations with. Especially since he had come to India.

This country was so different: it was teeming with people and with many different cultures, religions, languages, and attitudes. There were so many rules within the caste system; frequently, they were identified with distinctive marks or garb, and they were usually forbidden to marry, or even to associate with, persons of different caste.

Untouchables were generally forbidden to come into contact—even indirectly—with members of other groups and were, accordingly, forbidden to enter many temples or public buildings, to draw water from the public wells, or even to allow their shadows to fall on any person of a different group. They were also subject to other restrictions, all designed to avoid a personal pollution that could be removed only through religious rituals. However, Charles worried about none of this. But he did have to be aware of the different situations if he was to be a manager.

There were so many religious groups: Hindus, Muslims, Christians, Sikhs, Jains, and many pagan animists. Their beliefs reflected amazing social behaviours, from bestial activities to self-sacrifice. Charles had often watched anal intercourse between men during the war, he had seen a man in India have sex with his dog, and he had heard tales of shepherds who had sex with their goats. Interesting, Charles thought, but not for him.

Charles had watched Sati self-sacrifice rituals, which, though banned, still happened. A widow would throw herself onto her husband's pyre and be burnt to death.

Charles was standing at his office window when a young woman caught his eye. He called out, "What is your name, woman?"

"Vallabha."

"You finish at three?"

She nodded.

"Immediately from work, come to my office. I need to talk to you about your work."

※

There was at tap at his door, then the woman covered in coal dust walked in.

"Use my shower in the back before we talk."

Vallabha came back out in a wet sari.

"Come over here and sit on me."

These women wanted their jobs, and this man was white, so they would readily walk over and sit on Charles's lap, unbuttoning his shirt, bending forward, and mouthing his nipples—as Vallabha was doing now.

"More, I am in your hands."

She pulled Charles to a standing position, unbuttoned his trousers, and removed them, then she gently pushed him back into his chair so he could watch as she slowly removed her clothing to expose the full glory of her body.

"Am I pleasing you?"

Again she sat on him with her back sliding against his chest, his hands groping for her breasts as he ran his tongue on her damp back. Charles, who gasped for air, moaning, "What is your name?"

"Vallabha is my name," she whispered as her arm folded back to caress his head.

"Ah, Vallabha, move faster, sweet girl."

With that they both exploded. She took his hand and guided him to caress her breast. She sighed. "So, Master, is my job secure?"

"Vallabha, only if you can get me totally aroused again."

"Then, Master, may I take you to the floor to sit with me there?"

Charles moved very willing to the floor.

"Master, as I wrap my legs around you."

"This is amazing."

"Prepare yourself, Master, as I lift your leg."

"I can't wait—ahhhh."

"Now, Master, you have the control of our copulation. Move just like this. Slowly, slowly," she purred.

Charles gasped. "Vallabha, I'm moving you out of the mine and onto my staff to an easier job in the office. This way you can visit me often."

Charles really liked working for the Barrackpore Coal Company. The manager was too old and his son, who was to take over, needed help. Old Partha Kumar liked Charles and recognized that he knew a lot about mining, and his son, Sugata, respected Charles. They had welcomed Charles into their family, which was quite unusual as the British were typically despised.

At a family gathering in November, Charles was surprised to see Vallabha there. Partha introduced them, saying, "Charles, this is my sister Aaina's youngest child, Vallabha. She is one of my favourite nieces, is she not beautiful?"

Charles smilingly agreed.

Vallabha introduced him to her mother, who was a widow. Sugata joined in the conversation, telling Charles that his aunt Aaina had been his children's ayah and suggesting that if Charles was to return to India to work permanently and had young children, Aunt Aaina would be perfect for him. Charles, smiling at Sugata, said, "I would need to have a job to come to."

"I know," said Sugata. "My father and I have talked at great length about this, and we should all meet tomorrow so we can present you with a proposal we have in mind."

Charles stared at Sugata. "Really?"

"Really, Charles, let the three of us talk in father's office at ten on Monday morning. But enjoy this night with my family." With that Sugata wrapped his arm around his aunt and they went to go find Partha.

Charles was left with Vallabha.

"I live quite close by with my mother, would you like to see where we live?"

"Will anybody be there?" Charles asked as his breathing quickened.

"No, my mother will be busy here with the family. I can show you our place, and then we can come back and tell them we went for a walk around Partha's property."

Charles immediately was excited about the prospect of going with Vallabha, and he prayed that she felt the same way he did.

She did.

Chapter 26

Monday, December 1, at 10:00 a.m., Charles arrived at Partha's office, where Sugata was also waiting.

"Sit down, Charles," Partha began. "We are very happy with the work you are doing with us, and we are very aware that you are on loan to us from the British Army. It is obvious to us that you are very knowledgeable and want to keep you. We are willing to offer you a mine manager's position, which would include a fully staffed manager's house, with a cook, servants, and gardeners. We would also include food and education for your children in the best schools possible. We would employ an ayah, if you would need one, and pay you a good salary."

Charles looked at the two men as they carried on. "We would require that you sign a five-year contract that would be renewable yearly after that by either you or us. We will pay you a salary of one rupee a day for the first five years, and we will then negotiate each year thereafter."

This was far better than Charles could earn back in England, and he would have five years guaranteed. He was very excited when he heard that he would manage the Raniganj Mine in Bengal.

Back in his office, he sent for Vallabha. He was delighted when she appeared and eagerly told her his news; she smiled but seemed distracted.

"What is it, Vallabha?"

Big tears welled up in her eyes. "You will be moving away from here. I will no longer be working for you. You will bring your wife and family and I will be cast aside."

"No, no, I already have a plan, if you are willing? That is why I asked you to come to the office. Like I said the other day, I want to train you to work in the office for me. We have to start immediately so that I can tell

Partha. When I finally sign the contract later this month, I want to take you to the new mine with me. I certainly do not want to cast you aside. True, I will be bringing my wife and family back to live with me. But this way there will be no suspicion as you will be already set up to work with me. I certainly feel I cannot live without the deep pleasure you give me. Will this be agreeable to you?"

"I would love that, but what about my mother?"

"I will ask Partha if she can be part of my household staff. He already said he would provide an ayah. That way you will be able to continue to live together."

Vallabha looked at Charles. "You seem, Master, to have thought of everything. When do I start?"

"Right now."

"Now? I am dirty from the mines."

"True," Charles said. "You must go and have a shower, and then I will get you to work in the office, where they will train you in all the business matters—that is, after we have done some training together." Charles laughed. "I am wondering how you are going to train me now. Don't be long as my need is very great after living with the exciting memory of the visit to your home on Saturday."

Vallabha returned, her sari around her waist. Charles was sitting at his desk, and the blinds were drawn. "Stand up, Master." She removed his pants, and just then there was a knock at the door. He stood there looking like a business man from the waist up, yet like a lover from the waist down.

Quickly, he said, "Hide under the desk." As he sat down on his chair, he called out, "Just a minute," and began struggling to put his pants back on.

"No, Master, just sit in the chair. No one will be any the wiser, I will be very quiet."

Charles was sitting behind his desk as he called out, "Enter."

His foreman hurried in, saying, "Master, there is a problem with some men outside."

Charles heard nothing the man said as he was very aware of Vallabha under his desk was now licking his feet and running her long tongue up the inside of first one leg, then the other.

"Could you repeat that?" Charles tried to concentrate on what was being said and even picked up a pen to make notes. But now Vallabha's hands were moving slowly. The ecstasy must have registered on his face as he began to sweat. "Aah, ah!"

"Sir, are you all right?"

"No, no, I...am a little overcome with heat right now. Would you mind if we continued this conversation later this afternoon?"

The foreman got up and walked to the door, turned and said, "Is there anything I can do for you, or anything you need?"

"No nothing, I think once I am able to lie down for a while this will pass." Vallabha started to giggle quietly. The door closed.

※

Edina was at the post office picking up her mail and there, laying on the top of the pile, was Charles's letter. She caught the bus back to her home with Bill. As she sat on the bus, she relived the previous night.

Bill and she had the children settled and were sitting side by side, having a nice cup of tea by the fire while Bill read the newspaper and she knitted. *Click, clack* went her needles as Bill put his paper down with a laugh.

"Whatever are you knitting so industrially, my love? Something for one of the children for Christmas?"

"It is for one of the children, but not for Christmas," she had replied with a smile.

"Ah! John's birthday is coming up after Christmas, are you knitting him a cricket sweater?"

She had laughed. "Why do you think that, darling?"

"Because it is white, I can only think, knowing how scruffy John is, that it has to be for cricket."

Edina laughed as she turned to Bill and lightly kissed him on his nose, which sent shivers through his body.

Everlasting Lies | 161

"Put the knitting down, Edina, and give your lover your full attention." Bill smiled.

"Willingly," she laughed as she snuggled into his arms. "In fact I wanted to have a chat with you."

"About what?" Bill teased. "You need more money to prepare for Christmas?"

Smiling, she shook her head. "You are such a good provider and a very good pa to the children. You give me plenty, and I have easily managed on what you give me."

"Edina, you are an amazing woman, the love of my life. You know that, don't you?" He kissed the top of her head. "I was wondering if it is time to go to bed?" he said with twinkling eyes.

She giggled. "That is just what I want to talk about..."

Bill rolled his eyes. "We have to discuss if we are going to bed?"

"No—wondering."

"What? My pa said women always talk in circles. Aye, that's what you are doing now. I have no idea what you are wondering about."

She sighed. "I was wondering how you would feel if we were to have another baby of our own? That is, we could try. Would it make you unhappy if I was to get pregnant again with your child?"

"Unhappy? No, I would be a very happy man if you were to get pregnant.

Edina had sat quietly, smiling in the warmth of his arms. "I was at Doc's the other day. He told me that I am with child and the baby is due in May."

Tears had welled up in Bill's eyes as he had said, "That is the most wonderful news I have heard since the last time you told me. This time I will be with you, knowing that this child is ours. Oh my love, I couldn't be happier. Now I know who you are knitting for!"

Edina looked up and out of the bus window and saw that she was nearly to her bus stop.

Once home, she took out Charles's letter and read it aloud.

"Edina, how dare you write a letter such as this to me? I can assure you that—no matter what—*I will find you. You are my wife and I have no reason to divorce you...*"

Oh, this isn't a good start.

"I need you to know that I am passionately in love with this country, India…"

Oh no. She skipped ahead, thinking, *I am not going to that godforsaken country.*

"We will be able to start our lives afresh in a new country. The children will be well educated—perhaps in boarding school so you can donate all your time to me."

Thinking about himself again, she thought.

"I recognize that I have not been a perfect husband…"

Well, finally something we can agree on.

"No matter what has happened in the past to either of us, that is in the past…"

Oh my, when he gets back to England, the past will be very much the present. What will he say when he finds me big with child. Surely he will agree to a divorce then?

She started to cry softly as she read, "But I also want you to know, I will find you. And no matter what circumstances I find you in, my dear, you are my wife and you will return to India with me and our children."

Charles has made up his mind—he will get what he wants. She shuddered at the thought.

⁂

Later that night after the children were in bed, Edina turned to Bill and said, "I had a letter from Charles today and I think you should read it."

Bill took the letter and read it slowly, every now and again glancing at Edina. He noticed that her eyes shone in the firelight with her tears that were ready to fall.

"Oh, my dear, there is no need to worry. Once he finds you with child, he will be willing to let you go."

"Bill, you don't know him." She shook her head and the tears rolled down her face. "He will still expect me to leave with him, knowing how much this would hurt both of us, which would give him pleasure. He has such a mean streak."

"I won't let that happen," he said, trying to comfort Edina, though he wasn't feeling very confident.

She sat there shaking her head. "I know him, he will threaten to take the children from me, and I couldn't bear that. Bill, what can we do?"

"Nothing right now, sweetheart, we will have to wait and see what happens."

Chapter 27

Charles was enjoying his time in India. He loved coming home from work and being served a nice cold beer as he sat on the wide veranda that surrounded his house and kept it cool. He wouldn't be able to do this in "jolly old." The average temperature here, even in December, was around twenty-seven degrees Celsius.

Charles was deep in thought as he watched the birds that visited the gardens. Golden orioles and the funny hoopoes—striped in orange, black, and white with crests on their heads that looked like fans–all flashed high in the treetops. He loved watching the green parakeets, which made quite the racket when masses of them came to roost in the woods behind this particular property. There were also mynah birds and bee-eaters, and he loved the weavers that made long, stringy nests.

There was quite an expat community and plenty of life at the club, especially as young women, laughingly called fishing fleet girls, were now coming to India from Britain to look for husbands. Charles sniggered to himself. *Silly men, why bother with these cold women who know nothing about lovemaking?* All the Indian women he had encountered were definitely not cold. They had watched and learned from their parents and were eager to try these moves to perfect them. Vallabha was a master at innovative moves.

However, Charles knew British men needed wives for respectability. He wondered how Edina would fit in. After all, most of the fishing fleet girls and the women who were already here were from the upper class. However, he knew it would be good for his children in India as they would receive a much better education in the wealthy church schools here.

Charles was now back in the office after celebrating Christmas and the arrival of 1920, and he was wondering when he would be returning to England when there was a knock at his door.

"Come."

"Sir, the owners wish to meet with you on Tuesday, January 6, at ten o'clock." The young man then handed Charles a letter.

"Thank you." He opened the letter as the messenger left.

Good morning, Charles,

At the meeting we wish to discuss the details of your contract. If there is anything special you want in the contract, now is the time for all negotiations to be settled as this contract will be binding for five years.

We will visit the mine and your new home for you and your family together.

Sugata

Charles called Vallabha into his office, telling her to bring her notebook. He was sitting at his desk when she walked in. He requested her formally to sit down. Vallabha's eyes opened wide as this was not his usual greeting.

"Don't look so worried, Vallabha. I want you to take notes and make sure that I ask for everything."

"I think, Master, that I need to tell you something that might be important to your requests."

"You haven't changed your mind about moving with me, have you?"

"No, Master, I have not. I have already discussed it with my mother and she is happy to come and work for you in whatever capacity. But I need to give you the opportunity to change your mind, Master."

She quickly carried on before he could interrupt. "I need to tell you, Master, that I am with child, your child. I don't want to embarrass you, so you might not want us to come now."

"Vallabha, how could this happen, I thought you took care of such things?"

"The first time, Master, I was not expecting a relationship with you. I think it must have been then. This could be quite a complication with your wife and family coming."

"Why would Edina suspect anything? Anyway, when is the baby due?"

"I believe it will be a June child, Master. Of course I would want my mother to bring up this child, but now she will be working for you."

"Ah, that is good, Vallabha, the child will be born after I return and I can pretend that at this time I know nothing of this blessed event. I will just change your mother's duties after this child of ours is born. I can see no reason my wife would have any suspicions."

"Oh, dear Master, that is wonderful."

"Now let's get down to work and put my side of the contract together. I would like my eldest daughter, Lillian, to go to the Loreto Convent in Darjeeling as a resident. I would like my son, John, to go to St Joseph's, also as a resident." Charles paused. "I will need a governess for my daughter Edna for a few years before we will be prepared to send her, as well, to the Loreto Convent when she is seven. Because my daughter Edna will be with us, I request that Vallabha and her mother, Aaina, come with us to Bengal. Vallabha will work in the office as I have been training her to do this. Aaina will be my daughter's ayah." He paused again. "I would like a membership in the British Empire Club. I would like transportation and a driver provided with the house. You have already offered me a mine manager's house, including staff for both house and garden.

"Now, Vallabha, you see that your mother will be able to look after our child along with my child and no one will be any the wiser."

⁂

This contract was signed and arrangements were made to visit the mine and the house with Sugata. They travelled there on Wednesday, January 7, and planned to stay for a week.

Sugata and Charles boarded the Coalfield train in Howrah.

"This station looks fairly new, Sugata,"

"It was built in 1905 and has fifteen platforms. You and your family will take this train all the way to Raniganj. Look down—that is the Hooghly River. We used to bring all the coal down the river until trains took over. In fact Barrackpore Mine is close to the river.

Travelling throughout the countryside, Charles admired the lush green trees that went all the way to the horizon. Sometimes they travelled close to the roads and saw hundreds of people walking, riding in rickshaws, or pedalling on bikes. They stopped at Durgapur Station, and it seemed to Charles that these stations were huge and very, very crowded.

"Sugata, as we were travelling towards this station I saw what appeared to be a number of small demonstrations—mainly men and boys who seemed to be chanting what sounded like *Gandhi*."

"Yes, Charles, it is Gandhi—Mahatma Gandhi. I think in the next few years we are going to hear a lot about this man. He is trying to start a non-cooperation movement to abolish the use of British goods. Gandhi has always been a political man. He was around during the Boer War. He wants independence. He doesn't like taxes."

"Well, he has my vote," Charles said and laughed.

The train struggled to get going. Charles got up and grabbed the leather strap to lower the window. He poked his head out and could see many Indians hanging onto the side of the train. The women jammed on the platform of the small station were all wearing bright, beautiful saris, and Charles could not help thinking of the joy each one of them could give him. The train was belching black smoke into the air as it worked to gather speed. He shut the window and sat back down.

As he looked out the window beyond the tracks, he saw a large stupa, a place of worship, alongside totally unkempt buildings and signs that were so dirty you could barely read them, though many were in English. The streets were filled with people, many of them two to a bike, pedalling past dogs and cows so skinny their rib cages showed and children with no clothes on. Squalor everywhere.

The train chugged its way into Raniganj Station through papers floating everywhere along the railway lines. Lots of people were milling around this very dark and dirty station. It was chaos outside: street sellers were selling fresh vegetables and prepared food for those going on the train. Big pots of boiling oil bubbled for rolls of dough to be fried. The scent of all the spices was overwhelming. Bikes, rickshaws, and men pushing carts were everywhere, everyone crowding around them. There was no order to the chaos, but Sugata quickly found someone to help them with their bags and confidently moved towards a horse-drawn carriage.

Once they had settled in the carriage, it immediately took a small side street. "We are going towards the mine. We will be staying in a house much similar to what you will be provided with."

On the way they stopped at the club to which membership would be provided. "Charles, this hall is where members hold dances, eat, and have a drink in the bar. There are meeting rooms for different clubs and organizations, such as a Masonic Lodge and recreational and sports clubs for cricket, polo, badminton, archery, and croquet. Will be great for your family. You will have membership here and at the sister club in the hills around Darjeeling. We intend to enroll the older children in schools in Darjeeling and your family could live up there in a somewhat cooler climate in the hot and rainy season. This is all part of your contract."

They drove to a bungalow surrounded by a shaded, vine-covered veranda. Charles smiled to himself when he saw the name as they drove through the gates: Ivy Lodge.

Staff came out to greet Sugata, who quickly introduced Charles as the mine's new manager, and then their bags were whisked away. "Charles, meet me back on the veranda in an hour for a pre-meal drink."

Charles was shown to his room, where his bags had magically been unpacked and clean clothes awaited him on the bed. His room was furnished much as his house had been when he was a child, though it was much, much darker as the windows were small and the veranda kept out a lot of light. But the room was amazingly cool and welcoming after more than five hours on the train and an hour in the pony and trap. He unfolded the dhoti laying on the bed. It was a rectangular piece of unstitched cloth, about five yards long. He wrapped the white cotton about his waist and legs, then knotted it at the waist and went out to the veranda.

Sugata, who was also wearing the traditional dhoti, smiled at Charles as he sat down. "You look very comfortable in your dhoti, and I can tell that this is something you wear regularly, not something to please me."

"True, for some reason I have found it very easy to embrace the culture of India. It is almost like a homecoming. Quite honestly, I love the dhoti as you do not need to wear undergarments, which makes me feel very free. I love the thinness of the fabric, and I know women like that too! But I like to wear a long white cotton shirt with it, otherwise in the rain it could become very revealing!"

They smiled knowingly and drank their beers in comfort in the cool of the veranda as they discussed their plans for the week.

※

When Charles and Sugata returned to the Barrackpore office on the sixteenth of January, there was a letter waiting for Charles demanding that he report back to the Army on the seventeenth in full uniform as they were to begin their journey back to England on the eighteenth.

Charles looked at Sugata." Well, they didn't give me much notice, did they?"

"Do they say when you expect to be home? Do you have any idea how long it will be before you will be able to return to us?"

"From what I read there is a process once I get back to England. I will write my wife informing her of our return to India. So it will be a matter of getting ready and arranging our crossing and then a train journey to Calcutta. I will let you know as soon as I have details. In my mind I plan to be back by May."

"That is great, Charles. Once we know your dates I will arrange for you to stay in Calcutta in one of the mine homes, perhaps for a week or two, before you and your family do the journey that we have just completed. Your contract will begin the moment we see you here in Calcutta. We will do all the arranging of your travel once you arrive in Calcutta. You will then be a company man with all the benefits we discussed at our meeting. We will have sent Vallabha and her mother ahead, and they will be waiting for your return in Raniganj."

Chapter 28

Edina's hands were shakings as she read the letter.

Darling Edina,

I am writing this on the way home and will mail it as soon as my feet hit British soil.

I am coming home. That is right, home to you. We have lots of planning to do. Our journey to India will be long and, I am sure, arduous, with lots of culture shock for you and the children. But our lives will be so much better.

Before I left I visited the house we will be living in. It is big, with five bedrooms for us and has a staff of five who live on the grounds and will be at your disposal night and day. There is a nanny, a cook, and several servants and gardeners. We have membership to the British Empire Club, and the children are enrolled in school—that is, all except Edna, who will have a governess to start with, and the governess will live off-site.

We also have at our disposal a summer home in Darjeeling, just in case you find it too hot in Raniganj and would like to stay closer to where Lily and John will be going to school.

Now, I know that at the moment you have not told me where you are living. But why don't you make this easy and tell me where you are? This, dear, is a fresh new start, and it would be far easier if it started without any difficulties rather than on bad circumstances. Because you know I will get my way.

When I arrive I will be at Ripon and have requested that the pay they owe me be placed at the same PO where your allowance is being sent. You could leave me your address, which would be the right thing to do as we move toward rebuilding our marriage.

I shall look forward, my dear, to once again becoming your lover and taking you to new heights of ecstasy. Oh how I have dreamed of our first tentative encounters. Both of us will have the joy of relearning. Yes, it has been many years since I have enjoyed the sweetness of your juices, and I am aroused simply thinking of your slim and delightful body.

I am begging you, Edina, to make this easy for us both—it is in your hands rather than mine. Speaking of your hands, I can hardly wait until I can feel your hands on me.

I am and will remain your husband,

Charles

Edina knew every word he said about getting his way was true. What would he do to Bill? She would put nothing past him. Should she share this letter with Bill?

The children were involved with both men—what would the three of them say about Bill?

She was pregnant and due in May. She decided to go and talk to her mother the next day and say nothing to Bill. Her mother knew she was pregnant and was horrified.

Edina left Edna with a friend and arrived at her mother's very early the next morning. She walked in the back door, calling out to her mother.

"What you doing here so early?"

"Oh, Ma, I just needed someone to talk to."

"You sound troubled, child," said Edina's sixty-two-year-old mother.

Edina smiled. It had been a long time since this twenty-six-year-old had been called child.

"Well, I had a letter from Charles yesterday He is now home in England. He will be coming to Ripon and will be demobbed from there. He could make a lot of trouble."

"Do you have the letter with you?"

"Aye, I do"

"Will you read it to me?"

Edina had forgotten that her mother had difficulty reading. So she didn't have to share everything. Ellen was scurrying around the kitchen, making tea. "I will, Ma, when you are sitting down."

Ellen brought over the tea, sat down across from Edina, and waited expectantly.

"Before I read his letter to you, I have something else to tell you."

"About your pregnancy?"

"No, I am fine, everything is quite normal."

"Except the parentage," Ellen said quickly.

"That is the point, Ma. You see, Edna has the same parentage." Edina sipped her tea as she watched her mother process what she had said.

"Edina, you telling me that Edna is Bill's child?" She stared at her daughter. Edina nodded her head in agreement, tears welling up in her eyes. "How can that be? Why does Charles think she is his? How could it be Bill's?"

"Oh, Ma, Charles is the wrong man for me. I suspected that I was pregnant with Bill's child, so I tricked Charles into making love to me when he was home on leave. He thought Edna was early, so it all worked. I wasn't intending to tell Bill, but I did when he came to be with me before he went overseas. Charles hardly ever wrote, and Bill was always writing. He wrote love letters, always asked about the children, and he came home to me. I now live with him and am pregnant with his child again. I know I must be a big disappointment to you, but Bill is a great father to all the children. I wrote and asked Charles for a divorce and received a very threatening letter. Now this letter."

Edina wiped her eyes and read the letter to Ellen.

"He wants you to live in India? Who has ever heard of such a thing? The children would get to go to private schools? Sounds like he has a good job. Sounds like he wants a fresh start with you."

"True, Ma, but did you hear the threat?"

"What threat?"

"He said, 'Because you know I will get my way.' That is a threat, Ma."

Everlasting Lies | 173

"But he is begging you, Edina. He wants you to start over."

"But, Ma, he doesn't know I am pregnant."

"But he doesn't want to divorce you, Edina, so maybe he will forgive you. You said he used to go to brothels—well, you forgave him, right?"

"What you say is true, Ma. But I worry what he might do to Bill."

"Well, if you leave Bill and move in with us, I can get your father to say you have been living here with us. Then Charles wouldn't know anything about Bill."

"How did I get pregnant?"

"Um, you went out one night with a bunch of girlfriends...and...and... some guy raped you. Yes, that is it, you got raped."

"What if Charles wants to talk to these girls?"

"You only knew one of them—surely you get a friend to help you with this?"

"What about Lily, John, and Edna? They are bound to talk about Bill," Edina said, quite surprised at her mother's ability to make up such a story.

"That is a problem, isn't it? Why do the children think you are all living with Bill now?"

"Because I work for him."

Ma looked at Edina. "Edina, you don't want Bill to get hurt, right? The children think you are there as his housekeeper, right? Do they see you sleeping together? Has anyone asked why they call him uncle?"

Edina sighed. "You are right, Ma, I don't want Bill hurt, he is such a gentle man and has been so good to us all. I truly want to marry Bill, but Charles is so spiteful, he would do and say anything to be sure it didn't happen. Yes, the children know I look after Bill and cook, clean, and wash for him. Lily knows the truth about Bill, but John and Edna think he is my brother. That is why he starting coming here with us to visit you."

"There you go, Edina, you just have to get Bill to agree to our plan."

"But, Ma, I really don't want to go with Charles. I don't love him. I love Bill. I want my children to be brought up by him, I don't want them to grow up in India."

"Then, Edina, I have given you my story, which I think you came here for. You will have to talk to Bill and make a decision. You believe Charles won't divorce you, and you know how violent he can be. It is your decision to make, but it is one that will have to be made quickly, my girl, you are running out of time to make this work."

"Oh, Ma, you have been helpful—and with such grace, not judging—you have no idea how lucky I feel to have you and Pa as my parents. But I had better be on my way. I will let you know what we decide." Edina stood up to leave. "Would it work if you kept the children this weekend? I could bring them over after school on Friday? This way I could work this problem out with Bill without the children there. If we decide to go with your plan, I can bring all our stuff back with me on Sunday so we can live with you—I would tell the children that Bill no longer needs me to look after him. Would that work for you, Ma?"

Ma simply gave her daughter a big hug. "Take the weekend, and hopefully you will both see my plan is the best."

Chapter 29

When Bill arrived home that Friday evening, Edina told him that she had taken the children over to her parents.

Bill followed Edina into the kitchen and said, "Are we going over to pick them up tomorrow? It's my weekend off."

"No," Edina said and smiled. "I thought it was time for you and I to have a weekend alone together."

Bill grinned. "That sounds nice. I see you have a nice fire going."

"Copper too. I thought you might be chilled to the bone and would appreciate a bath. I'll run your bath for you." She started to hook up the lid. "Your pajamas are warming by the fire." Bill rushed over to give his short lady a hand to hook the bath. He leaned his body into her back, and she giggled. "You're going to make me fall in."

"That really is the idea."

"You don't want this pregnant lady sharing your bath."

"Oh yes, I do, my dear." He gently turned her around to face him.

She bent to turn the water off. "We won't need so much water, then."

Smiling, Bill turned the lights out so the kitchen was bathed in the warm glow of the firelight. He gently began to undress her, an amazing look of adoration on his face as he tipped her face and kissed her lips tenderly. Edina was immediately aroused.

"I love you, Bill."

He moved back and began to take his clothes off, and as his gaze washed over her protuberance of a stomach showing the love child yet to be born, Edina felt no doubt that he loved and wanted her.

Bill stepped into the bathtub and gave her his hand to hold as she stepped into the tub. She settled herself between his legs, feeling him on her back as he kissed the top of her head and then nibbled her ear. She settled comfortably into him as his large hands explored her body, slowly soaping her breasts, her legs, and between her legs. "You are such an amazing lover, Bill." She slowly turned to face him on her knees as she washed his body, the water splashing up the sides of the bath as he moved with her touch. She bent to kiss his body as he tried to direct her face to where he wanted to feel her lips.

"Oh, Bill, let us get out and go and dry in front of the fire, I have towels over there that we can lay on."

They stood up in the bathtub, and Bill moved his hands over Edina's body to get the excess water off her. She followed his lead. He got out of the bath and gently picked her up, carrying her across the kitchen floor to where the towels were already laid out. He went down on one knee and gently laid her on the floor. Arranging a pillow for her head, he placed a leg on either side of her body and ground his bottom into her. She squealed with delight. "I think it would be better if we changed places."

"Show me." He lay on his back as she moved to his side to kiss him, flicking her tongue into his mouth as he groaned.

They lay wrapped in each other's arms in front of the fire.

The next morning Edina woke up to the smell of breakfast cooking. By the time she arrived downstairs, breakfast was laid out in front of a blazing fire. She looked out the window and saw snow was gently dancing its way to the ground.

"What a winter wonderland it looks out there."

Bill smiled. "Yes, I thought breakfast in front of the fireplace was—or perhaps I should say *might be*—as nice as last night round the fireplace."

"You must have got up early."

"I did, because I thought you must have something on your mind as the children are not here. So, I thought a good breakfast might be helpful."

"You are very observant. Let's eat this wonderful breakfast you have made and wallow in this moment." Edina kissed him.

After they had cleaned up, Bill said, "So, pet, what's on your mind?"

Edina handed him Charles's letter. "You said that we wouldn't rush, that we would make our plans sanely. The time has come."

Everlasting Lies | 177

She waited while he read the letter.

"Well, pet, he obviously has fond memories of you."

"Bill, he has fond memories of many women. He will have himself a woman now. I am sure of that. I would become the older woman. I love you, Bill, our life is peaceful and full of each other. Not only do you love me but you also love my children and our child." She paused. "I don't want to live in India, in that godforsaken, dirty country."

"Sweetheart, you are not an older woman."

"Bill, I am being serious. You have read his letter—he has a mean streak, he has a horrible mouth, and what if he were to take it out on the children? Or worse yet, the baby that is not born yet? He is so determined—as he says, he will get his way. I am frightened."

"Edina, have you talked to anyone else?"

"Me ma."

"Was she helpful?"

"Well, she suggested a plan of action. But I asked her to take the children so we could talk and make decisions without interruption."

"Tell you what, let us both take some time and write down some of what we are thinking, and then we can share this with each other and make some plans. But I do want to hear what your ma thought as well."

They kissed gently, and then Edina found paper and pen while Bill stoked the fire.

"We both have to be honest, and nonjudgmental, of any idea put forward. Agreed?"

Edina nodded.

EDINA'S LIST

Charles will do anything to get his own way.

He will try to ruin both Bill and me through lies.

He could kill if made mad enough. He might harm the children.

I am pregnant—this has to be taken into consideration.

I love Bill and want him to be involved with the children.

The children love Bill.

If I left Bill, how would I explain this to the children? Perhaps I could say I lost my job.

I don't want to live in India.

Charles has made sure the children will get a good education, probably better than Bill and I could do here.

I worry about why I wasn't enough for Charles and worry this might happen between Bill and I.

I worry I will be lonely.

I have often felt abused by Charles but have never felt this with Bill.

Ma's idea has merit as no one but me will be blamed.

BILL'S LIST

I am prepared to do whatever Edina thinks is right.

Edina is my soulmate.

I don't know Charles except for that brief meeting in the war, but he seems like a mean man.

I would like to see my children growing up. If Edina decides to go back to Charles, for whatever the reason is, will I still be able to see my children?

Could I get a transfer to India? Would Edina want this?

Will Edina let me set up a bank account for my two children?

How will Edina explain why the children call me Uncle?

They exchanged lists. No comments were made.
"So, what did your ma think we should do?"
Edina carefully told Bill what Ellen had said, prefacing it with how many times Ellen said that Charles would not give Edina a divorce.
"You know, Bill, that I want to spend the rest of my life with you, don't you?"

"I don't want you or the children to get physically hurt, that is a major concern of mine. Do you think he would believe the rape story?"

"I don't know the answer to that, but I am sure he will hold this story against me and will badger me, saying I must have asked for it or wanted it. But I can handle that because I shall ask him why he would go to brothels."

"Looking at our lists, it appears that we both want to be together."

Edina nodded. "Yes. Yes, I want to be with you."

"So, darling, what do you think of my idea of getting a transfer to India? How do you think the children would react to seeing me there? Do you think it would make Charles suspicious?"

"Too many questions, Bill, let's look at each one. Could you get a transfer to where we are? That would be the first question to answer. I think the children would react with pleasure, but I think you should follow quite a bit after us so as not to cause any suspicion—with the children, more than with Charles. I think if I turn up to Ma's this weekend saying you had to let me go and I am very upset, the children would believe me. This part of the story would be strongly in their minds for when Charles comes back into their lives. Oh, my darling, it could work."

They both fell silent, deep in thought Edina asked. "But how are we going to be able to see each other once you are in India?"

Bill picked up Charles's letter and re-read it. "Oh my, he has set it up for us—listen: 'We also have at our disposal a summer home in Darjeeling, just in case you find it too hot in Raniganj and would like to stay closer to where Lily and John will be going to school.' How perfect would that be? You can take Edna and the new baby there, saying you prefer the cooler climate. It is perfect. I will ask for a posting to Darjeeling Station."

"Oh, my darling," said Edina, "this might work—that is, as long as he hasn't killed me for being pregnant! My guess is that he will be in Ripon. If we are to make this work, I must move back into Ma and Pa's house this weekend and write a letter immediately so that it gets to him in Ripon."

"True, you had better write it now so we can catch the afternoon post. As long as you promise to spend this last night together and go to your parents tomorrow."

"That would be my choice, my darling Bill. I am not sure I am able to live without you."

"Get writing, you silly, so we can have a fun time together."

Dear Charles,

I received your letter .

It is true that I haven't told you where I am living, though I am willing to. But I consider that it would be better if you and I met first, without any interference from anyone else, including our children. We need to sort things out, just us, before major decisions are made. I hope you agree.

So continue to write to the PO, and as I have no idea how hard it would be for you to get leave, I will expect you to name a date, time, and place for us to meet. Ripon is quite a way from Newcastle and perhaps I should come to you. I could catch a train and get someone to look after the children.

I have to tell you that you certainly have been diligent in finding us accommodation, schooling, and things to do in India. But, honestly, I am not sure I want to move to India. I hope you can find this understandable. I am presuming a better salary there than you can get here.

Family is important to me and I am not sure how I will manage without their support. But these are all the things that we need to discuss when we meet.

Charles, I don't want you to think that I am going to just jump into bed with you, we need to re-establish our relationship, <u>slowly.</u> I will expect that you will respect this. If you can't, then don't get in touch with me.

Life has changed a lot for both of us. There is much to talk about.

Edina

She handed the letter to Bill, who approved, and the rest of the day was theirs to enjoy, as it would probably be their last meeting for months.

Chapter 30

Edina caught the train midmorning on Sunday after packing all her stuff up, ready for her father to come over and get. She took just enough clothing for her and her children to get by for a few days. She still had a key to Bill's house and knew when he would be working, and they had decided together that it would be easier if she did not see him again and just dropped the key through the letter box after she had collected her things.

Edina no sooner got off the train than she started to cry. This really wasn't what she wanted; she wanted to spend the rest of her life with the man she loved, the man who made her happy. She trudged down the street under the weight of the bags and saw her children playing hopscotch, which they had drawn in the snow that had fallen the previous night.

Lily looked up and saw Edina. "Ma!" she screamed as she turned to her siblings. "Look, it's Ma!" She started running. John wasn't far behind her, and then Edna, who wasn't five yet, waddled behind them. "Ma, why are you crying? Why do you have all those bags with you?" Lily reached to take a bag from her mother, ordering, "John, take that biggest bag from Ma." Edna came barrelling like a snowball into her mother's knees, then promptly fell over. Lily sighed as she picked Edna up. "Here, Ma, John and I can carry the other bag between us, you bring Edna. Whatever is wrong, Ma?"

"Let us get into the house, I am right cold. When we are all sitting down round the cozy fire, I will tell you all what the problem is."

Ellen had been watching from the window and called to John to stoke the fire, saying, "Looks like our home is going to be full tonight. Now remember, John, be surprised and ask her no difficult questions. Let Edina lead us where ever she wants."

The two eldest children breathlessly came in the door with the three bags. Lily said, "Grannie, where shall we put these bags?"

"Why don't you take them to the room you three were sleeping in," Ellen said, looking at her daughter. "Whatever is the matter, Edina?"

The two eldest must have thrown the bags into the room as they were already back in the kitchen, staring at their mother.

Ellen was fussing over her daughter as little Edna waddled over to John with one boot on and holding the one she had managed to pull off. She smiled at him, totally unaware of the drama unfolding around her, as she said, "Help, Grappa" and climbed up onto his lap.

He quickly pulled off the boot, saying, "Hey, little John, come and take this and be a good man and stack all the boots away for us." Edna was now standing on John's lap, squeezing his face and planting a big kiss on his cheek. "Thanks," he said.

Ellen said, "Come, Edina, sit here by the fire and tell us whatever is the matter?"

Edina sat down as young John pushed another chair towards the fire for his grandmother, who promptly sat down and pulled young John to her lap. Lily went and stood by her mother.

"I no longer have a job with Uncle Bill." She burst into tears.

John and Lily looked at Edina as if she were lying. Lily's eyes sparkled with tears. "He loves us all, Ma, he likes having us around, he always says so. So why would he suddenly not want you to work for him?"

"There are several reasons, little ones. He knows your own pa is on his way home, finally. So he knew I would have to leave and we would all become a family again with Pa. He wanted us to be ready for when Pa comes home. Then he told me yesterday that he had found someone else to work for him, starting on Monday, and as you children were already gone that I might as well leave on Sunday morning so the other woman could move in Sunday night."

"He didn't say goodbye to us," John said and sobbed.

"No, he didn't. But it was bad enough he and I saying goodbye. Of course he has enjoyed us looking after him, but as soon as he knew your pa was coming home, he wanted to make it easy for me to leave. He went looking for someone else so he could set us free. He is a very kind man."

"Aye, he is that," said John. "There not be many like him."

Ellen turned to her daughter. "So now what happens?"

"Well, Charles told me in a letter he has a job to go to in India."

"India?" Ellen exploded.

"Apparently so, Ma." Tears once again welled up in her eyes as she thought about leaving. "He is taking us all to India. He has a good job, with a house and servants. He has arranged schools for John and Lily already."

"Good heavens." Ellen now started to sniffle. "I won't get to see you all. Does he say for how long? Does he say when?"

"I dunno, Ma, that will have to wait until I see him. But until that time, can we all stay with you, Ma and Pa?"

Little Edna tugged on John's shirt. "Can we, can we, Grappa, can we? Can we?"

Lily looked at Edina and said, "Ma, can we go back to the cottages and make our home there? Maybe when Pa sees our cozy home, he won't want to go to India, he will want to stay here."

"No, pet, I think it will be best if we wait until Pa gets in touch with us before we do anything."

"What about school, Ma, it is too far for us to go where we were."

"That won't be a problem," Ellen said. "You can go to the school here."

Now it was Lily's turn to cry. "But...but I didn't say goodbye to my friends, Ma."

"I know that be true, Lily, but once we have brought our stuff away from Uncle Bill's, I will take you back to school to say goodbye to your friends."

Both little John and Edna were fast asleep now. Ellen and John decided to lay them on their beds. Lily quickly helped to make it easier for them.

When Ellen came back down, she said, "Lily is such a caring child. I am going to make us some tea."

"Ma, listen quickly," Edina whispered. "I have also got to mention the baby in front of Lily—ask me if there is any other reason Bill decided to let me go."

With that Lily skipped into the kitchen. "Let me help you, Grannie." She set to and pulled a small table closer to the fire.

John walked in. "They're all settled down. Sure is snowing out there, I'll throw a little more coal on the fire. Well, I think you, Edina and Lily, can share a room, and the other two can have the smaller room. Do you have much to bring over?"

"Quite a bit Pa, I have bits and pieces of furniture."

"No matter, we will make it work, that's what families are for—you remember that, young Lily."

"Edina, so this all happened because you told Bill that Charles was on his way home?"

"Well, not really, Ma, I said there were several reasons." Ellen shot John a look, mouthing, *Act surprised.*

"Because I also told him I was expecting a baby, so he knew I would be giving up working before that happened."

"You're having another baby, Edina?" Ellen said.

"Gor on, you can't be," said Pa, thinking, *Why is this happening now? Why are we talking about this now? What is Lily going to think?*

Lily looked at Edina. "A baby! Another baby! Oh, how exciting, Ma."

"Ah, Edina, that explains why this has happened so quickly, Bill dismissing you. Lily, that Mr. Charlton must really care for you all to let yer Ma leave so quickly."

Edina thought that this had all gone well. *Now Lily knows, and she has no idea how babies are made and so accepts there is a little on the way.*

✻

A few days later, Edina was walking to the post office to see if there was any mail as she happily thought about the fact that everyone had settled very quickly. The older children were back at school, her parents had accepted the situation and welcomed them into their home, and Lily had spread the word to her brother about the new baby.

She asked for her mail and was given a letter. She knew it was from Charles.

She sat down in a big chair in the corner of the post office and opened the letter.

Everlasting Lies | 185

Edina,

We arrived in Ripon on February 6th and I wanted to find out roughly what was going to happen. I agree about meeting alone first.

I am due a 24-hour leave starting at 8 a.m. on Friday, February 20. I am not sure you can deny me my rights, but knowing your feelings on us being together overnight, I could meet you in York. If you left Newcastle by train and I left Ripon by bus, these journeys would take about the same time. I was thinking we could meet in York Station. I have never been, so let us say I will meet you at the gate of platform one. Shall we say around 10:30 a.m.?

Please drop me a line to say you agree to this. Perhaps by then I will know more about when I actually get released.

I am truly looking forward to seeing you and telling you all the plans that I have for us in India.

Your husband, Charles

Edina sat staring at the letter, wondering how this meeting would go. *If I am truthful, I really want nothing to do with this man. I really should start thinking of the story I will tell him. How does one get raped? Sounded good when Ma said it, but now that I shall soon have to tell the story, not sure this would be right.*

⁂

Charles sat on the bus to York and wondered how this meeting was going to go; after all, for the last number of years he had given his wife no thought and had enjoyed the flesh of many women. Would she suspect this? Would she suspect that he was about to become a father again very soon? How would this situation work out in India? He mused about keeping two women happy and smiled to himself.

Edina was walking along the platform towards gate one when she saw a very short man in soldier's uniform that she thought must be Charles; he appeared much, much shorter than she remembered him. She pulled her coat tighter around her body. Though far along in her pregnancy, she was small and it wasn't obvious.

As Edina walked towards Charles, he turned and looked at her, five years older and the mother of his three children, and noticed she looked tired. "Edina, over here, my dear." He felt nothing for this woman, she didn't even appeal to him.

They met and she put out her hand to shake his. "Charles, it has been a long time, how are you?"

Charles grabbed her arm and started to steer her. "I looked as I got off the bus and there is a café across from a park close by. Shall we go there?"

"That would be nice, Charles, to get away from the smoke of the trains. You are looking well, so how are you feeling? You have been through so much in the last few years."

"I am really feeling well, partly because my life for the last few months has not been that of a soldier. I have enjoyed managing a mine in India."

They reached the café and found a table just for two, which meant that no one else could join them if the café got busy. The table was close to the window overlooking the park. "This looks perfect for us to get reacquainted, don't you think, Edina?" She simply smiled. "Let me take your coat, I will just go and hang these up."

Edina watched him go over to the coat stand as she slowly peeled off her gloves, leaving her hat on her head. He sat down and she smiled and said, "I guess we have both changed a little in the past few years."

They ordered tea and biscuits. After the waitress left, Charles reached across the table and took her hands in his. "So, Edina, how have you and the children been? What about your parents, how have they faired during this awful war? Unfortunately, you may have noticed that I am not much of a writer."

The waitress returned with their order, and they both sipped at their teas. Edina looked up into Charles's blue, blue eyes that were staring at her. "You are right, Charles, I spent a lot of time hating you for not writing, not asking about the children, and seemingly not caring about us."

Charles took her hand again yet said nothing, just waited expectantly.

"Lily and John know I was coming to see you today. They know you are still in the Army and that at the moment it is impossible for you to come and see them. They are both like school and are doing well. Edna has no concept of you. Times were very difficult for me, partly because I felt you didn't care as you didn't write. Life was difficult and very lonely. I was very, very sad when other fellows came home and you couldn't or didn't—I felt abandoned. I found myself a job as a housekeeper where I could have the children live with me. This gave us some extra money and me some extra time, which allowed me to become involved with women's rights and to meet other women in the same situation as myself. It was a very lonely life, Charles. Ma and Pa have been a great support to me. But what about you, Charles?"

Charles talked for the next half hour. He talked about France and his life in the trenches, and then he talked at length about his terrible journey to Mesopotamia and his time in India. Edina tried to show interest by asking questions, but he dismissed her questions as stupid.

"Let me tell you about India. The people are so amazing—they may be poor, but they are beautiful. It has an amazing past, many different cultures, and a caste system, and women are there to look after and please the men—some women encourage their husbands to have more than one wife."

"You sound like you approve of this. Can a woman have more than one husband?"

"That would be silly, women are here for men's pleasure. When a woman is full of child, she loses interest in pleasing her husband. Men need to feel wanted and be loved at all times."

"Women don't have the same feelings?"

"In India women know their place, and that is to pleasure their husband, and it is not uncommon for a man to have more than one woman in his bed. Women have learned how to satisfy all in such a bed." He looked hard at Edina for a reaction, thinking, *you are going to have to get used to sharing me sexually.*

"Anyway, let me explain our life in India. I will be managing a coalmine, and you will live in a beautiful house with servants, including a nanny for Edna. Lily and John will attend boarding schools in Darjeeling, where we have a summer home, and you may find, in the heat of summer,

Darjeeling maybe a better place for you to live." Vallabha popped into his mind, images of her body interrupting his thoughts.

"Why would our family all want to live separately, we have already done this for five years? Or is that what you want?"

Charles decided not to answer and looked out the window. "It is not very nice out there, is it? But I will do what you want—we could brave the weather and take a walk in the park, or we could have a bite to eat here in the hope it clears up and walk afterwards."

"Let us eat early and walk afterwards." They ordered their meal and sat in silence.

"You said you worked as a housekeeper for a family, are you still doing this?" She simply shook her head. "Why not?"

The waitress placed their steak and kidney puddings in front of each of them along with another cup of tea. Edina picked up her knife and fork and said easily, "They let me go a few weeks back, umm, for several reasons, really. Well, I had your letter saying you were coming home, and I knew that I didn't want to go to India. You had refused me a divorce and told me that no matter where I hid you would find us. So I was about to make the move to hide from you. My employer had been good to me, but I didn't want to give them any trouble. I didn't want you coming and finding me there and making a scene. I really had no reason to leave except to hide, so I told them I was pregnant."

Charles burst out laughing. "Wow, funny they would believe *that*."

"Why?"

"Well, my dear girl, think about it. It is not like you are some kind of prize—look at you. Used goods you are, and not beautiful either. You have three children, who on earth would be attracted to you—dumpy, short, and a little fat." He started to laugh loudly. "Who on earth would ever want you?"

"Apparently you do, as you won't divorce me." Angrily, she stood. "I am going to the ladies, and then I am leaving and catching the train back."

Charles waited until she came back, watching her as she came towards him. As he held out her coat for her, he wondered about her being a little fat. "Edina, I am sorry. Let us take a stroll in the park, it is sunny now and we can finish talking and making plans."

Everlasting Lies

She nodded.

"I have to tell you that you be a feisty woman, and creative too. What a great story you told them, you being pregnant with no husband. They believed you, I take it?"

"They had no reason not to believe me."

"Well, my dear, let us make plans for our return to India, I have a job to get back to."

"So you are fine that I am pregnant?"

He stopped and went white.

Edina kept walking.

He rushed up to her, grabbed her, and turned her to face him. Her shoulders were downcast as he said, "Are you telling me the truth? Are you pregnant?" She nodded as he shook her violently and spat in her face. "You are no better than a whore."

"I am no whore. You wondered how I got pregnant with Lily and said if I had been a whore, I would have known what to do about such things. So they know a lot more about this than I do. This, like Lily, is a love child. I am asking you again for a divorce."

"NEVER! You and your bastard child are coming to India, even if I have to drag you there by your hair. If you don't agree to coming with me, I shall find you and I shall abduct my children and take them with me, leaving you here with your bastard child. You have no choice, Edina, but to come, and I will do my best to try to accept this unwanted child. Or you will lose all your children. You may have been a bit of crumpet for some shite, he may have enjoyed your minge, but I am sure he only shagged you once—after that encounter, he would have preferred to wank as you—"

"Enough! You and your filthy mouth, your filthy mind, and your disgusting soldier talk. I am catching the next train."

"Edina, Edina, I am sorry, I am being unreasonable. I can't bear the thought of anyone else having you, touching you. Will you please come to India with me? Will you allow me to make amends to you and our children and give you a better life in every way? I promise to be kinder and nicer. I love you and will love this expected child. Please forgive my outburst. What do you say?"

"Why is this so important to you? I know you are capable of doing all the things you threaten. I love my children and could not survive for a moment without them, but I never want to hear you speak to me as you just did. Yes, I got lonely, just as apparently you always have. I will not deny that I did enjoy someone else who treated me kindly. We have a great deal to sort out and come to terms with. I will come to India with you as I feel I have no choice. But you also have no choice but to change if we are to have a chance at a life together. You must show me you can be kind not just to me but to the children as well. Otherwise you will find that I am not afraid to leave and show you up as the man with no feelings."

"Are you threatening me?"

"Yes, because now I know I am desirable to others, and I enjoy male company—that is kind. So even in India I am sure I could disappear and find someone willing to take care of me. Yes, it is a threat because I am willing to put the past behind me—mine and yours. I am ready to try to make us into a family.

There was a pause, so she went on. "Yes, in your words I can be a great piece of crumpet, if that means having sex—seems to me we are made from the same cloth. I am telling you I will not put up with your filthy mouth ever again. Those are the terms for me coming to India."

Charles looked at Edina and smiled. "Terms accepted." He sealed the contract with a kiss to her hand.

Chapter 31

Travelling back on the train, Edina thought about how she had stood up to Charles and his filthy mouth. She'd known she would have to be very strong so he understood that she, too, was strong and had expectations.

When she got home that evening, the children were already asleep. Ellen had food ready for her and made her eat.

"So, lass, how did the meeting go?"

"Well, it was quite a shock when I met him. He has aged." Edina recounted their meeting in detail. "When I called him on the filthy language, he realized I meant what I said."

"I am surprised you agreed to go."

"I don't want anyone to get hurt—you and Pa, Bill, my children—it all rests with me."

꧁꧂

A few days later, Edina met up with Bill on his day off. He wasn't surprised at her decision because it really had been their plan; he was looking for details so he could apply for a transfer to India. He was very worried for Edina and the children's welfare. There was no telling what a man like Charles would do.

"Bill, I have to get home to the children. I will write as much as possible once in India. Whenever I have details, I will send them to you. I will let you know when our child is born."

"Remember, Edina, if you get there and know that you need to come home, I will pay for your return. Or, if I am already on my way to India, I will be your knight and whisk you and the children away and we will all go into hiding."

It wasn't long before she had a letter from Charles saying that he would be demobbed on the twentieth of March but needed to stay close to Ripon as he had applied for a disability pension. Also, he needed time to arrange their trip overseas. All this was fine with Edina as she did not want to live with him any sooner than she had to. He asked to come and see the children.

A meeting was arranged, and Charles hitchhiked his way to Newcastle. Edina had decided it would be best to meet him in a park in the city. She didn't want her children to see the rather frosty relationship between their father and grandparents.

"Now, children, when you meet your Pa, you must be very polite. I know you remember little about him, but he is your pa and he laid his life on the line for all of us. He is a war veteran."

Arriving at the park, Edina and the children walked towards Charles, and when Lily spotted her father, she ran to him. "Pa! Oh, Pa, is it really you?" Lily put her arms around her father, but he made no movement to embrace her. "How are you, Pa?" Nothing, just nothing, came from him to her.

Edina walked up to him, her heart breaking for her daughter, who had now run behind her mother.

Edina kissed him on the cheek and then said to her son, "John, shake hands with your pa." John did as he was bid but said nothing.

Little Edna cowered behind her mother. "Don't…like him…Ma. He made Lily cry. Bad man, don't like him," she said, shaking her little head.

Charles took them all to a café, telling them that they were going to this country, India, that was part of the British Empire and how lucky they were. He had arranged their travel to London on April 30, where they would board the P&O called ss Mantua on May 1 and sail to India. He watched their faces, but the children just sat silently.

❧

On April 30, 1920, Edina, Charles, and their three children stood on the Newcastle Station Platform. Their luggage already on the train, they were saying goodbye to Ma and Pa Paxton, the children giving their final hugs to their grandparents.

"All aboard!" the porter called.

"Charles, would you please take the children on the train and get them settled whilst I say my goodbyes to my parents?" Charles, for once, did as he was asked.

Edina turned to her mother and father and took them each by the hand. "Stay well and look after each other, I will write often. I have no idea when or if we will return. Know I love you and am very grateful for all of your help and also sorry for all the unnecessary worry I have caused you. I will write when the baby is born."

With that she threw herself at John, tears streaming down both their faces. "My child, are you doing the right thing?"

Edina kissed him and shrugged.

Ellen hugged her and said, "Come home if he is not good to you. Somehow, we will find the money to help you." She kissed her daughter. "Come on, my luv, on the train or your children will be anxious." Both women sobbed.

Edina, in her pregnant state, was ungainly climbing the train steps. She moved to her children. Charles had put her and the three children in four seats together facing each other. He sat across the aisle in another set of four seats with a women sitting by the window and facing the engine.

When Edina sat down, little Edna immediately climbed on her mother's lap, saying, "Don't cry, Mama. 'Member, we are going on a a'venture." She waved to her grandparents, who were standing outside the window.

The whistle blew, and the train jogged to a start, rolling along the platform. John had his arm around Ellen, and it seemed to Edina that he was holding her up. Edna climbed off her ma's lap and settled into her seat. Edina rested her head on the window as the train slowly moved along the platform. The three children had no awareness that it would be many years before they returned.

Edina reached into her pocket for a handkerchief to blow her nose, but she kept her head resting against the window as she gazed towards the end of the platform. She could see a lone figure of a man. She held her breath. Was it? It couldn't be, surely? But it was Bill Charlton, standing at the very end of the platform, waving his large handkerchief high in the air. Her darling Bill was there to see her off, the father of her child within, the love of her life, a man gentle, polite, and caring, who made her feel important all the time—unlike Charles, who at every turn made her feel and look stupid. She raised her hand in acknowledgement.

"Who you waving to, Ma?" little John asked.

"Nobody in particular, couple of people standing right at the last of the platform," she lied. "I guess I was pretending they were there for me." She smiled at her son.

She was feeling most uncomfortable. Charles had insisted that she bind herself tightly so no one would suspect she was close to having a baby, as women in their final months were not allowed to travel. He had lied about her due date. She looked at him and said, "Would you mind changing seats with me as I am so tired and would like to sleep?"

His face was as black as thunder as they switched positions. "I am not prepared to look after the children. That is your responsibility. But if you must, I will give you an hour," he snarled.

She immediately settled down and closed her eyes. Breathing deeply, she pretended to sleep so she could take the hour he said he would give her, but Edna started shouting, "Don't touch me, mean man, I want Lily." She left Charles's side and sat on Lily's lap and glared at the man she was told to call Pa. Charles called across to Edina, "Come and take care of your brood."

The lady across from Edina gave her a sympathetic smile. Edina struggled to her feet and changed places with Charles.

Once away from the children, Charles beamed at the lady and tried to engage her in conversation. She scowled at him and said, "Young man, it would be far better if you took at least one child off your wife's hands and entertained him on this journey. Maybe you could play cards with your son rather than disturbing me."

Charles glared at the women and totally ignored her.

It wasn't long before Edina told John to go and sit with Charles as she wanted to put Edna to sleep. John was almost as sulky as his father at being told what to do.

After the long train journey, they boarded the ship, which would set sail early in the morning, with a porter's help with their many trunks.

Everlasting Lies

Edina had no idea what she was going to, so she packed every perceivable item she thought she might need. There were two wardrobe trunks as she had decided on one for the children and one for her and Charles. These would always be accessible no matter where they stayed, and it would save her a lot of unpacking and packing. There were drawers on one side and a place to hang clothes on the other, and there was a place for shoes. Once packed, these were extremely heavy. Then she had packed metal trunks as well with bedding, kitchen wear, and dishes. All these and the many suitcases were handled as baggage, and once on board, they would not see them until their arrival. Everyone carried their own small suitcase with what they considered personal items, such as books, games, and special toys.

They had a pretty small cabin on D deck, far forward in the boat, with two bunk beds, numbers 351 to 354.

"Now, you two girls can share a lower berth, and John, you will be on the top berth."

"Edina, I will take the other bottom berth," said Charles.

"Charlie, I really am unable to climb to the upper berth in my condition. If you are on the bottom berth, I will be expecting you to look after the children."

"Edina, you are to refrain from calling me Charlie. My name is *Charles*, and that is all I will answer to." He glared at Edina as he moved to the upper berth.

Their cabin contained a small chest with a mirror and two small chairs. There were two fans hanging from the ceiling, and Edina, who was suffering with heat, wondered how helpful these would be. She was pleased that their cabin was close to the bathrooms. Charles was going to have to get used to looking after John.

※

"Hey, Ma, come and look at the lifeboats," called John, who thought it was exciting to explore the boat.

Lily said, "I hope we don't have to get in them, ever."

"Me too," Edna said and nodded wisely, hanging onto her mother's hand. John giggled at his little sister.

It was fun for the children to be outside on the promenade deck and to meet other people who were already on board. They were in wonder when they saw deck tennis.

They were about to go downstairs when a crew member came up to them. "Ma'am, make sure you get the children on the tours we have of the kitchens during our time on board. You know we do all our own baking, I think the children would enjoy it. The times will be posted on the notice boards."

"Thank you, young man, I think it is something I would enjoy too."

The family walked past the saloon smoking room on B deck and saw Charles sitting in there in a leathered upholstered chair. To Edina, he seemed to be trying to look important. There also was a music room and a tiny nonsmoking saloon, but it did have tables and chairs and a piano, with beautiful carpeting on the floor, which gave the whole area a homey feel. The children were fascinated with the curtains that adorned each porthole.

"Ma," John said, "will they close these at night? Who do they think will be peeking in?"

This brought laughter from his older sister. After seeing their cabin, Edina suspected they would be spending a lot of time here.

"Quick, Ma, look." John was peering over the gallery and looking down on the dining room. "Now look up, Ma." There was a beautiful glass dome. The ship had skylights that brought filtered daylight into various interior spaces.

Downstairs was the second-class dining room on C deck with long, banquet-style tables that could hold fourteen people. They would later find out that the circular chairs were bolted to the deck through their cast iron base and had revolving seats to allow them to take their seat. This dining room was right at the front of the boat and Edina hoped it wouldn't feel rough. The first-class dining room was at the back of the boat on the same deck but had twice as many tables.

Edna seemed quiet overcome and tired, so Edina said to the children, "Let us go and find Pa in the smoking room."

Charles was in deep conversation with another man when they arrived. Edina told John to go and stand beside Pa and not to speak until he was spoken to. "When you get a chance, ask Pa if he can spare a minute to come and talk to me. We will wait in the music room for him."

John dutifully did as he was bid, but Charles paid no attention to him. Finally, one of the other men looked at him and said, "Well, young fellow, is there something we can do for you?"

"Yes, I wondered if I could talk to my pa."

"Who would that be, child?"

John looked at his pa, so Charles had to admit to being the father.

"Well, you have a very nice, polite boy here."

John smiled at the man as Charles gruffly said, "What you want with me, John?"

"Ma asked if she could see you for a minute."

Charles got up and excused himself. When he had found Edina, he said, "Don't you ever send your son over to interrupt me like that again."

"Ma, I didn't interrupt. I waited until I was spoken to—not by Pa, but another man."

"Amounts to the same thing, John."

John cast his eyes down.

"Well, it was me who wanted you, Charles, John was helping me," Edina said defensively. "I need to put Edna down for a nap, and I am not feeling that great, so I wanted you to entertain Lily and John so I can have a rest as well."

"I will do nothing of the kind." He spat the words out.

The two elder children watched in horror at the rudeness to their ma. Edna snuggled closer to her ma, whispering, "I don't like him."

Lily looked at Charles and said, "It is okay, Ma, John and me can play a game on his bunk whilst you and Edna rest."

"Good," said Charles. "Remember this, you may never expect me to help you with the children, that is totally your job. I don't give a brass monkey what you want. You must remember, in my eyes you are no better than a servant, my servant. You are here to look after me, to look after all my needs and to service my desires. I will always come before the children."

Lily looked at Edna. "Edna," she said, "take John's hand and see if you can take us all back to our cabin. There's a good girl. I will give Ma a hand as she is looking awfully tired and upset." With that she glared at Charles. "We have managed for a long time without you, Pa. We are capable of looking after each other." Lily immediately placed her arm around Edina and followed Edna, who was chatting to John as he led the way. Edina, tired as she was, allowed herself to be led by her children.

Edina thought it was wonderful how Lily had put her own father in his place.

Chapter 32

As the family got up and dressed, they noticed they could not feel the boat moving.

At breakfast, they were told the ship had been delayed but should be leaving around 10:00 a.m.

"Wow, that's good," young John said. "I really wanted to see us leave port. Do you think there will be people on the dock waving us goodbye on our adventure, Pa?" This was greeted by stony silence. "Ma, can we all go up and watch as we leave? Maybe Lily and I can go and grab some chairs so if you are not feeling well, you and Pa can sit and watch us?"

Edina smiled at her excited son. "That sounds a grand idea. Edna and I will go down and get our jackets, and then we will join you wherever you have found a place. Will you be joining us, Charles?"

"Maybe, and maybe not."

A few minutes later, Edina was climbing the stairs with Edna helping by carrying the jackets. "Which way, Edna, do you think John and Lily went?"

"Dis way, Ma, they want to see the dock."

Edina marvelled at her little daughter for remembering that detail. As she walked, she really felt a sense of sadness, knowing she had left her family, her lover, and her native land. With Charles not wanting to be part of the family, she felt lonely, forlorn, and unhappy. He really didn't want the family, and she saw them all in a pitiful state. Why hadn't she been stronger? Big tears welled up in her eyes as she held back the sob in her throat.

"Hey, Ma, over here, I have deck chairs." John had found two wooden deck chairs that were bolted to the deck. "We can share these."

Lily looked at her Ma. "He be excited, Ma," she said, rushing to help Edina. As they were settling themselves, a sailor came over.

"Why, Ma'am, what nicely behaved children you have. Can I bring you some blankets to make the chairs more comfortable?"

"That would be nice."

The sailor quickly came back with blankets and a tray of tea and biscuits. "Now, Ma'am, can I take your son for a little tour and show him what we have to do to cast off?"

Before Ma could answer, Lily said, "Can I come too?"

"I can't see why not if you are interested and as long as your ma says it is okay."

With gleaming eyes, the two children looked at their mother, who gave her consent.

There seemed to be a lot of activity after the children returned from their tour. Charles, too, arrived on the deck as he also wanted to observe the departure. Slowly, with a lot of cranking, the ss Mantua moved away from the dock. Those on board took their last look at their homeland, many waving their hankies above their heads at those standing on the dock and many crying, not knowing what the future held for them. As the body of the ship moved away from the land, some passengers began to sing.

By the end of the song, many were crying and most husbands were comforting their wives, but this was not true of Charles. He simply lit up a cigarette and looked at Edina, who had her arms wrapped tightly around his children.

"Join us, Pa," John called, and Charles deliberately turned his back on the family. "Ma, doesn't Pa like us?' John asked.

Edina was at a loss for words.

※

Life on board ship was very different from what Edina had imagined. She hadn't expected she would constantly be hurrying along the corridors in her dressing gown every time one of the children needed to go to the water closet. Bath time was a chore as they had to go to bath cubicles where an Indian bath attendant filled a tub with hot seawater. They had to use a special soap because of the salt water, and once soaped, Edina had to rinse with fresh water get all the salt off. By the time she helped her three children, she often had no energy left to do this for herself. She was saddened that Charles never once offered to take John with him.

On entering the notorious Bay of Biscay, Edina felt some anxiousness. She had earlier been talking to some of the sailors, and they had painted a bleak picture of this part of the journey. But she said nothing to either Charles or the children.

It wasn't long before she could see the waves growing larger and hear the winds getting stronger. Then the ss Mantua was pitching and rolling as the waves tossed her around like a matchstick. Little Edna's eyes were wide with fear.

The sea grew so large and menacing that everyone was ordered to stay off the deck. Edina and the children lay in their cabin listening to the boat hit what seemed like the bottom of the ocean, all of the while fearing for their lives. It wasn't long before they all became nauseated and paralyzed. Seasickness became a horror.

"Ma, where is Pa?" John said in a weak voice.

"I have no idea, John."

"He should be here with us so we wouldn't be worried about him."

Once out of the Bay and rounding the bottom of Portugal, life seemed better. The children enjoyed the decks and sunshine as they played quoits and shuffleboard and skipped constantly around the boat. Often the crew set up games for the passengers, and the children enjoyed not only playing but also watching adults play like children. The egg and spoon race was their favourite. It seemed that many adults enjoyed the potato sack race. This all helped to pass the time away.

Sometimes they would get to watch the antics of adults going to the fancy dress dance. John particularly liked the men who dressed up in so-called kilts, made from bath towels and with sponges and shaving brushes hanging like a sporran.

"Pa, I would like to see you dressed up like the Scotsmen," John said with a twinkle in his eye.

"You will be waiting a long time, lad."

Edina was amazed that her son never gave up trying to include Charles in the family, and eventually it seemed to be working.

Edina was beginning to feel the heaviness of her pregnancy, but she was still binding herself tightly so she would not show. "You are going to be one squished baby."

"Are you talking to the new baby, Ma?" said Lily.

Edina smiled at her eldest.

"Tomorrow we are due to land at Gibraltar. Our sailor friend told us the passengers would be allowed off the boat."

The children looked at their father with the question in their eyes.

"Yes, we will get off for a short while," Charles said, "but there will be no spending of money."

John looked at Lily. "It will just be nice to see trees and houses again."

Edina smiled and nodded. She had been reading some of the information posted by their ship and could hardly wait to do this herself, so she set about to tell the children what she knew.

"Do you know that many different people from many countries have lived on the Rock of Gibraltar? This has been happening since medieval times. We think we are clever, but our ancestors travelled far and wide. Even before my ma and pa were born, ships were stopping here from England. Which means that when we are walking, we should see both Protestant and Catholic churches and also mosques brought by the Arabs—even Jewish synagogues are there. Now, I really think it's great that obviously there is respect for other faiths and beliefs. Remember that, children, as we are going to live in a country that also practises religions different from ours. Remember, we must be always respectful."

Charles looked at Edina, astonished.

"You could also, depending on what we do, see your first apes."

Young John jumped up and looked at Edina. "You're kidding me, Ma...right?"

"No, I am not, John. I am telling you that you should be careful—from what I have read and what one woman who has been here before was telling me, you better not have any food in your pockets because they will come over and steal it. These monkeys aren't shy. You ask anyone to tell you stories about the monkeys—ask your sailor friend, he will

Everlasting Lies | 203

tell you. There is a legend about the monkeys that says as long as there are monkeys on the rock, it will remain British territory. That's enough information, we will explore when we get there."

"Ma, can we go for a walk about?"

"Of course you can, as long as you take your little sister."

The three children went off hand in hand, and Edina smiled as she said to Charles, "Bet they have gone looking for their sailor friend."

Charles looked at his wife, this stranger who was carrying someone else's baby, who really was beautiful when she smiled. "You have done a great job raising our children. They are polite, respectful, and well behaved."

"Thank you, Charles, for saying that. We really should have some fun tomorrow. Both Lily and John are always interested in their surroundings, and walking costs nothing."

By the time they got up the next morning, the boat was already docking. The children and their parents hurriedly ate their breakfast, Charles urging them to eat lots.

Once off the dock and walking, it was just like any English city. There were lots of tall, narrow houses just like they had in Newcastle, and the paved streets were really clean. However, the children soon noticed that the people were not speaking English. Many men doffed their hats to Charles and Edina, saying, "Buenos dias, señor, señora."

John quickly said, "Bet that means 'Good morning, Mr. and Mrs.,' but what language are they speaking?"

Charles answered. "That is Spanish, and you are correct in your assumption, John."

The children looked at Charles with utter bewilderment as it was the very first time that he had entered into a conversation with his children.

"Wow, Pa, you are really clever," Lily said.

The noisy streets were full of bikes and horse-drawn wagons and carriages, most carrying fresh vegetables. Then they saw a donkey pulling a large music box. A man was winding the box and, to the delight of the children, it began to play Spanish music.

"Me like that Ma," said little Edna, clapping her hands.

Charles bent down to his little girl and whispered to her. She looked at him wide-eyed and nodded. He picked her up so she could see the workings of the music box. As he put her down, she said, "Thanks, Pa, dat was nice."

Edina smiled. The charms of her children were bringing Charles closer.

While they were walking, they found the Alameda Gardens, which were within the city. The children enjoyed the freedom of running around among cannons and fountains. But most of all, they were intrigued by seeing flowers that were new to them. Bougainvillea and hibiscus of all colours, beautiful white lilies, ginger blossoms, and candytuft flowers that seemed to grow right out of rocks.

The children lay on the grass as quiet as mice, watching birds in the bushes and trees and whispering to each other. One of the groundkeepers came along and sat with the children. Edina and Charles were sitting on a bench watching them when Charles got up and joined them, saying, "Edina, you stay here to rest, you look a little tired, my dear."

"Thank you, I will, if you don't mind."

"I certainly don't mind, my dear." He strode to join the gardener, who was telling the children that the Rock was a very important place for migratory birds and who then took the time to explain what this meant.

In a whisper, the gardener said, "Where are you looking? Tell me what you see."

John was quick to reply. "On that branch of that big tree, there is the strangest bird I have ever seen. He is bright yellow with black stripes on his back, and he looks like a redskin Indian because of the feathers on his head. I expect him to dance and whoop." John giggled.

"Good description. He is a hoopoe, and the redskin feathers are called an erectile crest. This bird is native to Gibraltar. Good spotting."

"I see one too," said Lily. "He looks like a bandit—see, he has a black mask over his eyes, but he is pretty. Look, his back sort of looks like a mixture of orange and red and he has a beak like a parrot, doesn't he?"

"Another great description, you children are observant. That is the red-backed shrike, also a native of here. Do you notice his head is a little grey? Shrikes are not always a nice bird. Sometimes they eat smaller birds or frogs and will impale the corpses on thorns or barbed wire, so this practice has given them the nickname of 'butcher bird.' You can see these birds in parts of England."

Little Edna, not to be outdone, said, "Cuckoo, cuckoo."

"I hear him too, little girl. Well, I had better be off. Are you off the ship that came in today?"

"Yes," they all replied.

"You are a couple of days late, so we were all happy to see you arrive today."

Charles said, "I think the storm in the Bay of Biscay delayed us, it was a big storm. Thank you so much for spending time with the children."

They walked back to Edina, and Charles said, "How about if I leave Edna with you, dear, and we'll go and see if we can find something to eat and drink. We can have a picnic in the gardens as the children seem to be having such a good time."

Edina was shocked by this statement but smiled and said, "That would be lovely."

After lunch the children spent a long time at the edge of ponds observing turtles and huge goldfish. They loved all the waterfalls that meandered slowly over the rocks, making music for their ears.

When they left the gardens, Charles made sure they went through the old gates located in the fortifications of the Charles V wall. "This first gate was built in 1552," he told the children. "That was 368 years ago."

Edina smiled because that was hard for even her to imagine, but the children looked at Charles in wonderment.

"The second one was built in 1883, which," he pointed out, "was built about the time your Ma would have been about as old as Lily."

All this, though interesting, was nowhere as fascinating to the children as the gardens.

"Let's away back to the ss Mantua, we will all be ready for a meal tonight, right?" The children all nodded as Charles started to lead the way.

John ran up to Charles and shyly put his hand into his father's, saying, "That was a grand day, Pa. Really fun. I am glad you are home."

Charles looked down, astounded at his son. Then he looked across at Edina, who was trying to carry a very tired Edna. Walking back to his wife, he peered at Edna, who, for the first time, gave him a smile. "My little hinny, would you like to ride on your pa's shoulders? I can see my wee girl is tired. Would you like to do that?"

Edna looked at Charles and nodded, and he lifted the four-year-old up onto his shoulders, holding tightly to her hands. She promptly laid her head on her father's, and within two or three steps was fast asleep.

So the little family marched back to their ship, which was ready to sail away through the numerous boats and smaller sailing ships heading for Algiers.

Chapter 33

Algiers had been a very quick stop to let a few passengers off at their destination and to pick up some fresh food. Though most food would be acquired at the next port of call.

The Vernon family was excited about going to Marseilles. They were going to be there for some time as fresh food needed to be procured, coal needed to be loaded, and the passengers who had chosen to travel overland rather than face the perils of Bay of Biscay needed to be picked up. All passengers were required to leave the ship as the time-consuming task of loading the coal got underway.

The family descended the gangway, young John leading the way. "Before we leave, Pa, can we watch the loading of the coal for a while?"

They already knew that all portholes and doors were sealed against the coal dust.

Charles managed to find something for Edina to sit on, and they watched the porters—mostly men of colour and naked except for loincloths—as they loaded the coal.

"Look at that, Pa, there is no space between them when they are walking up the gangplanks."

"Those baskets filled with coal on their heads look mighty heavy," Lily said, "I am surprised their necks can take that load."

"True, Lily, but see how they bend over? Their backs are also taking the weight," Charles pointed out.

Little Edna wandered over to Charles and pulled on his trousers, "Day singing songs…right?"

"Look, everyone," John said, "it looks like a big black caterpillar as you watch the running legs and black bodies going up the gangplanks."

"Come on," Charles said. "Let's take the tram to the Notre-Dame de la Garde, which is a Catholic basilica built on the highest natural point, just on the south side of the Old Port. The tram will take us to the funicular."

"What is a *fun...funic*...whatever you said, Pa?"

They got on the tram, and Edina smiled as the children listened to their pa not only as he tried to explain what a funicular is but also as he talked about the sights they were passing. He really was well educated and seemed to be enjoying the children.

The children couldn't believe their eyes when they saw the funicular after they got off the tram.

"Pa, Pa, we really going on that?" said John, rushing over to his father.

"Is it safe?" asked Lily.

"Well, it was built in 1892 and hasn't had an accident yet, and it is a long walk up the hill."

"I bet more people go to church now," John said.

Charles smiled at Edina. "Honestly, I am not sure how his mind works."

The funicular had two floors, and they found themselves on the upper floor. Each floor had a guide to point out places and to explain how the funicular worked. John managed to squeeze close to the guide as he explained that the two cabins circulated on parallel cogged tracks, and each cabin had a twelve-cubic-metre tank of water that was part of the hydraulic balance that caused the movement of the cabins. He went on to explain that the two cabins were linked with a cable, and as the water from the ascending cabin emptied, this caused the other cabin to lower. John quickly put up his hand.

"Well, young sir, do you have a question?"

"Yes, I don't understand because once we are at the top, we have no water, in the tank, right?"

"Quite correct, young sir."

"So now the cabin at the bottom has all the water, it is impossible for this cabin to make the other cabin move because water doesn't run uphill. So how do the next people get up here and we get down?"

"We don't." There was laughter from the crowd. "After all, young fellow, you need to get off."

John looked expectantly at the guide and politely waited.

"When you get off and we reload passengers, the water from the cabin below has the water from her tank pumped back up the hill and placed in our tank. As long as I have set the brakes, we won't move. Young fellow, for us to climb from the bottom to the top in this here cabin takes roughly two minutes, but it takes about ten minutes to pump and fill the tank back up here. What's your name, young fellow?"

"John Vernon, sir."

"Well, young John Vernon, where you be travelling to?"

"India, sir, we are moving to India."

"Young John, it has been my pleasure to have aboard such a polite and bright young man, who asks great questions."

John smiled and doffed his cap to the porter.

"Aye, John, you asked some good questions. Can you explain it to me now so I can understand?" Lily said.

Lily and John walked ahead on the footpaths that lead to the basilica, deep in conversation. Charles said, "Those two do you proud, Edina, they get on so well."

"You seem to be enjoying them."

"I am."

When they got to the church, they found out it was built in 1864. There were many mosaics, which really seemed to fascinate Lily. The nave was very beautiful. It had three cupolas covered with identical mosaic tiles making up fields of flowers and lots of doves. The first cupola was made of white flowers, the second had blue flowers, and the third had red flowers. Lily spent time showing little Edna, who promptly lay down to look, which made the whole family laugh as they stood in a circle protecting her and asking what she saw.

"I see all the flowers—like the red best. Um, I see an ark...look, there is a rainbow, lots of birds..."

"Edna, get up now, please, and let's go outside and look at the view." Edna got up, but because she was a little tubby, it was difficult and she had to do it in a not very lady-like way.

Though interesting, the basilica certainly didn't hold the children's attention like the gardens had at their last stop, so they decided to walk down and wander past the shops. Charles noticed Edina was looking very tired so suggested they stop to have an ice cream. "Why don't you sit here with Ma, Edna, and I will take Lily and John for a wander. Then we will come back to you and we will catch the tram to the boat.

"Thank you, dear," said Edina, "I am feeling very weary. I may go inside as it is sunny here."

Charles opened his wallet and gave her some money. "Buy drinks for you and Edna, and I will do the same for us before we come back. Do you need me to take Edna as well, darling? You look so tired."

"I need Edna to look after me, right young daughter?"

Edna gave Edina a big kiss.

After a busy day, everyone was glad to get back on the ship.

✥

By the time they docked in Port Said, Edina wasn't feeling well and had taken to her bed. An ayah took care of Edna while Lily and John went to the library to do a puzzle. Charles came in to see his wife.

"Charles, I cannot keep binding myself anymore. Besides the heat, it is causing both the baby and myself stress."

"I don't understand."

"Well, if I am honest, I think I am very close to delivering this baby."

"You can't, I signed a paper saying you were no further along than five months."

"I will tell them I lied to you. There is no way, if this baby decides it wants to come, that we can stop it. I understand this very difficult for you. I am extremely sorry for this whole situation because you seem to be really enjoying the children and I think that John is very excited to have you in his life."

"Yes, he and I seem to be getting along well. I worry we have such a long journey ahead of us, and a baby will make it even more difficult for us all."

"You don't think I haven't been worrying about this? But to be honest, I would rather have the baby aboard this ship than on a train. Do you think you are capable of delivering a child on a train? At least here, there are doctors and nurses to take care of the baby and me. I am sorry to have let you down so."

Everlasting Lies

"You know, Edina, that I have been no angel either."

"True, I know that. I pretty well knew every time you were going to a brothel. But I also knew that you would not set me free. So here we are on our way to India, with me carrying a bastard child. Facing a train journey right across India with four children. The point is, if we women make a mistake, we carry the burden. I have no idea if you have other children because on you, it doesn't show."

Edina's words stung Charles's conscience. He was about to have his first child with his Indian lover. How did he feel about Edina? Would he be willing to give up Vallabha, an amazing, sensuous woman who was carrying his child? Edina and he had kissed only once since his return—almost as a seal on a contract. He'd had no relations with her as she was pregnant and had not allowed him in her bed. He shook his head. This was hardly true as they had been travelling since being back together with all the children. He was making excuses. Would he feel different about Edina if she allowed him to have relations with her? Could he enjoy their bodily contact? This was definitely an unknown. How would she react if she knew he was about to become a father? Should he tell her? Or should he wait until they had copulated to see how this affected his feelings? Could he handle two women? With all the sexual fantasies going on in his head, he felt he should bide his time and see what happened after this bastard child was born.

Edina watched Charles. It seemed to her as if he were weighing up a dilemma, one he didn't disclose.

"Well, my dear, I will leave you in peace. Would you like me to arrange for food to be delivered to you? Then you can stay here unbound and maybe this feeling will pass.

"That would be good, but what about the children?"

"Have no fear, their pa is here."

"Will this journey never end?"

"It will when we get to Bombay."

The children return in time to hear the end of the conversation.

"Pa, I thought that was the beginning of the train journey," John said innocently.

Charles smiled at his son. "I think your ma wants some encouragement, not to hear what more lies ahead. Be off with you. Take your sisters for a walk along the deck, and if you see your sailor friend, tell him that your ma would love a cooling lemonade."

"Righty-ho, Pa." John saluted. "Come on, sisters, we have a mission to complete."

"You are looking very white, Edina, and you feel very hot."

"Well, I am having labour pains and this worries me."

"Why, you have done this three times before—given birth, that is. So you have a baby on the ship, I don't think they will make us get off. Is that what you are worrying about?"

"No, I think I worry more about having the baby after we get off."

"Then relax. Let's get you moving more, and maybe the little blighter will come soon."

"Can I ask you a question?" He nodded. "How do you feel about this baby?"

"You mean because it's not mine?"

"Mm-hmm."

"I don't know, really, I try not to think about it. Maybe I could ask you something. How would you feel if you knew I had other children?"

"That is different."

"How so, Edina?"

"Well, as you put it, I wouldn't have to look at the little blighter every day, I wouldn't have to bring the child up. So it is very different. I am asking you to support this child, hopefully learn to love this child as if it was yours. Yet every day there will be a reminder of my unfaithfulness."

"I see your point. But what would your reaction be if I did have a child that you saw every day and that I asked you to share yourself with?"

"Have you got such a child?"

"No." After all, such child was yet to be born.

"I suppose, Charles, that this would depend as to how much you loved and were committed to me and the family, and how much I loved and was committed to you. However, I do feel that if you continued to have relations with the birth mother—or me with the father—that would be the end of any trust, would you agree?"

There was no answer from Charles.

"I do know this," Edina said. "We have this opportunity to start over, and for this to work we both have to be willing to do this and to be faithful to each other. This trip has been a great opportunity for the children to get to know you, and yes, to love you as their father, which I see developing strongly. I am willing to make this commitment to you. Are you willing to as well?"

Charles looked at his still-young wife, still very much in her prime. How could he know what the real Edina looked like when, ever since they had re connected, she had been pregnant? Looks, he guessed, were really important to him—when a beautiful woman made love with him, it was very good for his ego, being a small man in stature.

"Edina, I am willing to try."

"So no more brothels? Prostitutes? Affairs of any kind?"

Charles nodded.

"I can make this commitment to you easily, Charles, as I have known only one other than you. All the years you were in the Army, I was faithful to you." A little lie, but good for her cause. "I will forget all your digressions as long as there are no more. From this day forward, our slates are clean."

"Before this happens, I have to make a confession to you."

Edina's heart dropped.

"I didn't lie when I said I didn't have a child…yet. I have had relations with a young Indian woman, who is with child—the child to be born around June. So, Edina, it is like we are both pregnant."

"Will you be seeing this woman when we get back?"

"Yes, she works for the same mine company, and her mother is a member of the staff at the house we live in."

"Will you be supporting this child?"

"She is unmarried, I think I owe her that, don't you?"

At that moment the sailor arrived. "Your beautiful children, who, if I might be permitted to say, are so well behaved, asked me to bring you lemonade."

"Thank you so much," Edina said, and the sailor left. "Yes, I think you do need to support the child. Are you giving support at the birth?"

"I don't think so, Edina, her mother will give her that—after all, that's women's work."

"What about afterwards?"

"Well, as it happens, I would suspect that my child and your child will be looked after by her mother. She will be the ayah to both. Will that be all right with you?"

"I can handle that, Charles, but I cannot and will not share you with this woman. Will you be able to control yourself if you are working together? If you have the slightest relationship with her, we are done. Forever. It would give me the right to do the same—by that, I mean to have sexual relations with other willing and desirable men, of which I am sure there are many. I would like us to have a legal agreement on this. That if either stray from this marriage in the future, a divorce must be given."

Charles looked at Edina, wondering how she got so strong and demanding. He thought of the beautiful Vallabha, of all the amazing sexual encounters they'd had in the past and how he was craving more of these in the future.

"I will agree to this after, and only after, we are back sexually together. How do we know if we are still compatible? Just maybe we are not."

"I understand this concern as I feel the same way about you. But as my pregnancy and our present sleeping arrangements prevent this from happening right now, can we both agree that until such time as this is a possibility, neither of us will stray?"

Charles's heart sank; he would have liked one more time with Vallabha. "Agreed." He bent down to kiss his wife, and she reached for him. As their lips met, she gently probed his mouth with her tongue, slowly moving it in and out of his receptive mouth, then thrusting it in deeper and with a promise.

When they broke apart, Charles looked at Edina and said, "I can hardly wait, my love."

Chapter 34

"Hey, Pa, look how many ships are around," John said. He, Lily, and Edna were with Charles as Edina rested in the cabin.

"Look, children, we are passing a great big statue. Any of you know who this is?" They all shook their heads. "Well, here is an easier question. Do you know what it is made of?"

"Gold," Lily said.

"No, bronze. It is a statue of Ferdinand de Lesseps, who was a French diplomat and developer of this canal. See, his right hand is welcoming us to the canal, and in his left, he holds a map of the canal. It was erected just over twenty years ago."

"So it's not very old, is it Pa? But why was the canal built?"

"Before the canal, ships from Europe had to go around Africa to reach Asia. Now they sail through the canal and save many days of sailing."

"So, Pa, if this wasn't here, we would be going around Africa?"

"Right, Lily. There is quite the story about the opening. On the official day of opening, the French yacht L'Aigle was to be the official first to go through. But in the darkness of the night before, Captain Nares managed—without lights and through the mass of waiting ships—to navigate the HMS Newport until it was in front of the French."

"Whoa." John laughed. "That must have caused a lot of trouble, didn't it, Pa?"

"Well, of course. The French always want to be ahead of us Brits. I understand that Captain Nares received a reprimand—but also an unofficial thanks—from the Admiralty."

Lily and John found this to be funny, so Edna joined in the merriment.

"Nares was a smart man. If he had told any official what he was planning, they would have stopped him. Sometimes it is better to ask forgiveness than to ask permission."

Their sailor friend brought around drinks. "I couldn't help overhearing your story to the children, sir. Did you know that the first P&O liner through was—no, not this one, but the ss Delta. Children, we travel in convoy as we pass through the area. On a typical day there are two convoys travelling south and only one north. Just the canal will take us around sixteen hours. Then we will be in the Red Sea."

By the evening of May 16, Edina knew she was in labour and asked Charles to get the doctor to see her.

"Mrs. Vernon, we are going to have to move you to the hospital. Do you think you can walk there or do you want to go by stretcher?"

"No, I shall walk. But I would like to have a few words with my husband first."

"Of course. I'll be waiting just outside."

"Charles, I would like you to be at my side as they take me to the ship's hospital, and I want to talk to the children before we go."

"I will go and find the children."

"And..."

"And of course I will walk you to the ship's hospital."

"Will you be all right with the children?"

"I am their pa, aren't I?"

How the war had knocked off his rough edges. He was so respectful to all he spoke to. Could they re-establish their marriage? It was the first time she had even considered this a possibility.

"Ma, you wanted to see us?" Lily said.

Edna was now scrambling up next to her ma.

Edina looks at Lily "Indeed I do. It is time Lily." Turning to John and Edna "You know that for some time I have been unwell. John and Lily, it is something we have been through together before. I am about to have another baby."

"A baby? Another baby! You're going to have a baby while we are on board the ship?" John exclaimed.

"Where da baby?" Edna said, touching her ma's face.

Everlasting Lies | 217

"Baby is in my tummy. Come here, the three of you. I want you to put your hands on my belly. Can you feel the bumps of the baby? You might feel it move. Pa is going to take me up to the ship's hospital and the doctor is going to help get the baby out."

"I feel it!" Edna squealed.

Lily and John looked at each other with wide eyes as they felt the child within.

Charles said, "May I join this baby-feeling part?"

"Over here, Pa, I have a great spot. It feels like the baby is kicking right at my hand."

Charles knelt down, laid his hand next to his son's, and smiled at his wife. "I wasn't around before, but I am this time."

"Now, children, I need you to be good for Pa."

All three nodded, then John said, "Ma, I want you to make sure this baby is a boy."

"Sorry, John, I cannot make that promise."

Charles jumped up. "Did you feel the baby move?" he said to his children. They all nodded again. "I think it is time I took Ma to the hospital. I want you to stay here and get cleaned up as it will soon be time for us to go and eat. Can you do that?"

"Love you, Ma." The children all hugged and kissed Edina.

"Well, Mrs. Vernon, can I escort you to the hospital?"

"Mr. Charles Alfred Vernon, I would be very happy if you would take me there." Edina stood up and Charles gave her a gentle, loving kiss.

John turned to Lily. "Did you know Ma was having another baby?"

"Yes, Ma had told me," Lily said with importance.

"Won't this make our train journey more difficult?"

"I would think so, for all of us."

"I bet it is a boy, I hope it is a boy."

✻

At the ship's hospital, the doctor greeted both Charles and Edina. "Not much you can do, Mr. Vernon, if we need you we will come and find you. I know you already have three children, so once you have them settled in the cabin, come back and see how your wife is doing. Do you need any help with the children?"

"No, I think we will be fine. I will see you later, dear."

The doctor examined Edina and told her he didn't think the child would be born until the next day but her husband could come see her again that night. She lay comfortably in bed and thought about Charles. He had become so much gentler and he showed interest in the children, which was so amazing. He had told her about the woman who is expecting his child. He seemed to want their marriage to work. He didn't go into a physical or verbal rage when Edina gave him her boundaries. Maybe... She fell fast asleep midthought.

Charles popped by around 11:00 p.m., but she was sleeping. The nurses said they would not wake him for the birth unless something was going wrong.

Edina woke up around 6:00 a.m. in a lot of pain. The nurse came to her and said, "You had a very restful sleep. Maybe walking together will help you. Up we get, on your feet now. How many pregnancies have you had?"

"This is my fourth."

"No miscarriages, stillbirths?"

"No."

"Lucky woman."

"Ah! That was a big contraction..."

"Your waters haven't broken yet. How on earth did you manage to get on board this close to your birth? P&O line is very particular about pregnancy."

"I was unsure of my birth date."

"This is yet another postwar baby. Mind you, with the number of men killed during the war, we need lots of babies."

"True. I hope they are right—that this was the war to end all wars."

They walked and walked, and talked and talked. Around 7:30 a.m., Edina's water began to dribble.

"So what is your guess, a boy or a girl?"

"My son wants a boy as he already has two sisters."

Everlasting Lies | 219

"I expect Mr. Vernon would like another son to carry his name forward."

Edina gasped. She had not thought of this.

"Was that a contraction?"

"No, I am just getting weary."

"Let me take you back to bed, then."

Edina lay in bed with her thoughts. *If it is a boy, it will get Charles's name, but it is not his. If it is a girl, she just borrows his name. If it is a boy, I am sure Bill would want his son to have his name.*

The more she pondered the problem, the more she hoped she was carrying a girl and that Charles's lover was as well. That way his rightful son, John, was his only heir.

※

"Come, Edina, push. Two more pushes is all it should take, then you will be cleaned up and ready for a well-deserved lunch."

"Lunch would be great."

"It's a girl," the doctor said, laying the baby on Edina's stomach for a few minutes before she was cleaned and swaddled and handed back to Edina.

Tears welled in her eyes as she looked at this daughter, Bill's second child, and thought about how he would have no idea of this for some time.

"Let us get you cleaned up and looking pretty, and then we will call the happy father in.

Charles arrived to see his wife sitting up in bed holding a wee bundle.

"My, Edina, you actually look much better than you have the last week. You're a bonnie lass. So let's look at the new daughter in the family."

Edina loosened the bundle, and there snuggled was the small, dark-haired child.

"Would you like to hold her, Charles? You have missed many births."

He came over and sat on the edge of the bed. "I don't know, Edina. Did I ever hold any of the other children?" He looked down into the baby bundle and moved his finger down until it lightly touched her face. He smiled, putting his army around Edina's shoulder.

"No, you didn't, Charles, so you can hold her and pretend she is the others as I am very doubtful that there will be any more."

"You are still young, darling." He stood up with the child in his arms. "This is not so hard. What are you going to call her, Edina?"

"Perhaps we could both name her."

'No, I think this is up to you."

"Well, I was thinking I would like to name her after my ma's mother, Elenor Watchman, and then we could also name her Mantua, after this ship...she could go by this name as I think we have enough names beginning with E. Do you like that?"

"I do, though I think Mantua is a big name...maybe we can shorten it to Manty?" The baby stirred in his arms.

"Perfect."

"Here, take Manty back. I am going to get the children so they can see their new sister, and then, my dear, you can have some rest."

Within five minutes, Charles was back with the three children. The girls immediately rushed to their mother. Lily automatically helped Edna onto the bed, and Edna, wide-eyed, crawled towards Edina.

"Is that the baby? Can I touch her?"

"Better than that, Edna, you can sit beside me and hold her."

Edna crawled into the crook of Edina's arm and held the baby in her arms.

"Cootchie-cootchie-coo." Everybody laughed. "No, don't laugh at me, Lily used to say that to me." Lily kissed the top of Edna's head. "You want to hold baby, Lily?"

"When you have had enough."

"I finished."

Lily, like an expert, took the baby. "She is very little, Ma, what are we calling her, then?"

" Elenor Mantua."

"After this ship," John said.

"Absolutely." Charles was grinning. "Your Ma and I decided we would call her Manty, for short."

"Oh." John looked horrified. "I can hear it now. Batty Manty, Catty Manty, Fatty Manty..."

Lily laughed at her brother. "Here, you can hold Fancy Manty."

"All right, Manty, back to Ma as they both need to rest. Off you go, it is time to eat anyway."

The children kissed Edina and the baby, and Charles did likewise. "Rest well whilst you can, Edina. We will be back later to see you, but I will check with the hospital staff first. Thank you for making me hold Manty, I still feel manly with Manty. Good thing John didn't hear that."

He kissed Edina gently on the forehead. Her eyes were already closed.

"Thank you, Charles...."

Chapter 35

On May 20, just after leaving Aden, Elenor Mantua Vernon was christened in the first-class saloon, using the ship's bell as a font.

As the made their way toward the saloon, Charles supported Edina, who was holding three-day-old Manty,, and John walked between Lily and Edna.

"Now, remember that we are speaking on behalf of Manty," said Lily. "As we have no other family or friends on board, we three are godparents."

"Lucky for us she's a girl," John said.

"Why dat?"

"Every child to be baptized has to have three godparents." John stated importantly. "At least two must be girls like the baby—see, that's you two."

"You no girl."

"Right, Edna, but one has to be a boy—that's me."

By now the family had arrived at the bell font, where the ship's chaplain waited.

He bent and whispered to the three children, and they nodded. He whispered more, and only Lily and John nodded.

A chair had been brought for Edina, as she was still weak from the birth.

"Dearly beloved, forasmuch as all men are conceived and born in sin, and that our Saviour Christ saith, none can enter into the kingdom of God, except he be regenerate and born anew of water and of the Holy Ghost." The chaplain held his hands high.

Edna's eyes grew larger.

"Beloved, ye hear in this Gospel the words of our Saviour Christ, that he commanded the children to be brought unto him."

The wise chaplain gave cards to the children, even Edna, with the written part they would have to say. He also gave some to Edina and Charles, whispering, "I would like you to say the answers with your children." The parents nodded and smiled at their children.

"I demand therefore, dost thou, in the name of this Child, renounce the devil and all his works, the vain pomp and glory of the world, with all covetous desires of the same, and the carnal desires of the flesh, so that thou wilt not follow nor be led by them?"

The family replied together, "I renounce them all."

"Wilt thou be baptized in this faith?"

"That is my desire."

"Wilt thou then obediently keep God's holy will and commandments, and walk in the same all the days of thy life?"

Lily quickly whispered the answer to Edna, and her voice could be heard above them all as they said, "I will."

This brought a smile to the faces of the first-class passengers who were in attendance.

Lily took Manty from her mother and over to the chaplain. She looked back and held her hands out to John and Edna, who took them as they watched what the chaplain did next.

Taking Manty into his hands, he looked at the three children and said, "Name this Child."

Lily squeezed their hands, and in one voice, they said, "Elenor Mantua."

The chaplain couldn't help but smile at the three as he held Manty over the bell font and dipped her head into the water, saying, "Eleanor Mantua, I baptize thee in the Name of the Father, and of the Son, and of the Holy Ghost. Amen.

After the prayers he finished by saying, "That as he died and rose again for us, so should we, who are baptized, die from sin and rise again unto righteousness, continually mortifying all our evil and corrupt affections, and daily proceeding in all virtue and godliness of living."

The passengers clapped, and then the first-class passengers presented Edna and Charles with a silver bowl, which was engraved with the child's names and the latitude, 19-40 N, and longitude, 39-10 E, of her birth. This would forever be a keepsake.

After the celebration Edina and Manty returned to the hospital area so that Edina could be well rested for their arrival in India two days later.

Charles realized that Edina was going to need a few more days to rest before getting on a train. The temperatures in May would be oppressive, and they would be doing a train journey at the worst time as the weather moved into the rainy season. It was going to be hard on all the family. So most unlike Charles, he decided they would spend a week in a hotel in Bombay to give Edina time to get her strength back and for them to all acclimatize.

"Captain," he said, "I was wondering if it was possible for me to get off the boat early? I have decided that, with my wife in her delicate state, it would be best to spend a week in Bombay before embarking on the train for Calcutta."

"Which hotel were you thinking of staying at, Mr. Vernon?"

"I thought perhaps we could get a suite at the Byculla Hotel."

"Good choice, Mr. Vernon, let me tell you what I can do. When you wake up tomorrow morning we will already be docked. As soon as we are docked, I will send one of the sailors out to alert the Byculla Hotel of your impending arrival."

"That would be excellent, sir. A weight off my mind indeed."

"Also, Mr. Vernon, if you would like to make the decision to stay on the ship until the last, then I can again have one of the sailors assist you with your luggage to the hotel, which could be to your benefit as the sailor could tell the Byculla Hotel that your arrival will be late afternoon when he books your room."

"That would be splendid, Captain, and I am indeed indebted to you for all your help."

"Think nothing of it, Mr. Vernon. You have a lovely, polite family, which I have heard of often through the staff. I know the staff will be pleased to help you and your family. Whilst you are waiting we will still feed you and your family."

Charles went to tell Edina, who was sitting up in the hospital area trying to answer all her children's questions. He told them all of his conversation with the captain.

Edina looked very relieved as she said, "That makes me happy as I am so tired and was wondering how I would cope with the next few days. It is very thoughtful of you, Charles. So what are our plans now?"

"Well, instead of leaving by train immediately, we will not leave until next Friday. I think we should try then to do the journey as quickly as possible. I had planned that we would stop half way, but with little Manty this seems a waste of time and energy for you. The sooner we get to Calcutta, the better. It is going to very hot, humid, and difficult as you have never experienced this kind of heat.

"As luck would have it, on deck the other evening, I met a man from first class who was at Manty's christening. After talking for a while, he told me about the Calcutta train. We will have a large and spacious suite with a private bathroom, and where our meals can be served to us."

"Wow, it sounds first class, Pa."

"It is, John."

What Charles didn't tell the family was that this first-class passenger worked for the railway and had arranged this as a gift for the family.

Edina and the girls started laughing at John and Charles. Edina, cradling another man's child in her arms, was quite shocked at Charles and his consideration for her and Manty. She was also impressed by his flair with the children and the relationship he had cultivated with them during the past three weeks.

"Pa is funny."

"Yes, he is, sweetie."

Edna hopped down, causing Manty to stir, and went over to hug Charles's legs. He bent down and picked her up. "What was that for, young lady?"

"'Cause I love you."

"Well, well, that is the best news I have heard in a long time."

"Come on, youngsters, time to leave Ma and Manty for a well-earned rest. Darling, we will drop in before the children go to bed for the last time on the ship. Rest well."

There was a chorus of goodbyes from the children as they all left.

Edina snuggled down and Manty latched on to the breast presented. There was a sigh of contentment from them both.

Chapter 36

"Mr. Vernon, good morning, sir. The captain sent me to tell you that the hotel is all arranged and that we will come and get you and your family after all the other passengers have left. If you would go to the purser's office and identify all your luggage, we will get this all loaded and ready to take to the hotel later this afternoon."

"Thank you, that is most kind of you."

"Also, sir, I have a letter here from one of the first-class passengers. He said you would know all about this. He was sorry not to see you this morning, but he and his wife left early as he had a train to catch to Delhi."

Charles took the letter, tucked it safely into his jacket, and said to the children, "Let's go to the purser's office and see to the luggage, and then we will go and see Ma."

*

The nurse came in just as Edina finished feeding Manty. "Let me take the baby for you and Nurse Roberts will get her ready to leave the boat and then put her down for a nap. Now, Mama, let's get you ready for your new life in India."

"What are your plans?" asked Edina. "Sounds like you have some."

"We do, with your permission. This is the first baby any of us have had since working for the P&O Line, so we want to give you a gift. We have the hairdresser at our disposal to do your hair. Mr. Vernon kindly brought your suitcase last night, so I took the liberty of making sure all your clothing was clean and pressed."

Edina's eyes glistened with tears. "Sounds like I am in good hands, and why should I spoil a well-made plan?"

Edina was bathed and dressed in her undergarments, which miraculously fit again. The hairdresser appeared. Walking around Edina with her hand on her chin, she said, "Um...hmm. My dear, when was the last time you went to the hairdresser?"

"I have never been."

"Just as I thought. Do you know much about India? Like how dreadfully hot it is going to be?"

Edina shook her head after each question.

"Well, you might have four children, but you are a young woman. I want to know if you are willing to let me bring you into this new era, the postwar years. Are you ready to embrace the new styles? In fact I want to know if you will let me have my way with you?"

There were giggles from the staff standing around watching.

How could Edina refuse? She simply nodded.

With the staff clapping, the hairdresser went over to them and whispered her plans.

Edina's long, slightly reddish hair hung half way down her back as the hairdresser began. *Snip,snip,snip* went the scissors to the *oohs* and *ahs* of those standing watching or passing by.

"Are you going to leave me any hair?"

"Do you know how hot it is out there? You are going to be glad all these tresses have gone. People are going to look at you with four children and say, 'There goes a woman not hampered by the past.' Edina, if I may call you that, you will look beautiful and modern."

"But will I be able to look after this myself?"

"Don't worry, it will be easy, I will show you how."

When her hair was finished, others came in with clothes for Edina to wear.

Edina looked at the grey skirt they brought to her. It looked familiar but different. "Is this my skirt?"

"Yes, ma'am, it is, but we took the liberty of shortening all you're clothing so you would look thoroughly modern with your new hairstyle."

"Really? How wonderful! I had wanted to do that, but I was so busy getting ready for leaving. Oh, what a treat." She slipped into the skirt, which now fell a little above mid-calf.

Everlasting Lies | 229

"As you are short yourself, this new length makes you seem taller."

"It feels so comfortable, and it seems I still have a figure."

Edina slipped on a white blouse that was now embroidered with red silken thread. The thread matched her lips, which had been painted a brilliant red.

"Close your eyes, Mrs. Vernon, let me lead you to the mirror. When I tell you, you can look at the new you."

Edina stood in front of the mirror, her eyes tightly shut, and giggled as the ladies fussed over her.

"You may look now, Edina."

Slowly, Edina opened her eyes and saw a slim, modern women staring back at her with this amazing reddish bobbed hair, which made her look girlish, and bright red lips, which were a strong contrast to her blue eyes.

"Oh, I love it. How can I ever thank you?"

A young girl of about sixteen came forward. "I made this for you from one of the hats you had in your trunk." It was now a cloche hat, the latest style. "See the green ribbon on the cloche? Well, what I have done is designed it so you can change the colour. See, I have this red one that matches the red on your blouse." Her deft hands quickly popped the snaps, removing the green ribbon and replacing it with the red.

"How very clever."

"Madam, would you sit on the chair, please?" The young girl then proceeded to put on the close-fitting cloche, which went on easily over Edina's newly cropped hair. She pulled it well over Edina's eyes so no forehead showed. "Now, madam, I would like you to walk and show everybody."

Because the hat was so far over Edina's eyes, she had to lift her head to see, which immediately made her look and feel taller. Everyone clapped.

Edina, smiling, turned to the hairdresser. "But what have we done to my beautiful hair?"

"Very easy to fix, Edina. Go to the mirror. Now take off the cloche hat and shake your head hard. Great. Take your fingers and fluff your hair. Excellent, now rub your palms together hard, and with your hand smooth your hair into the basic bob."

"That was easy. How can I thank you all for your thoughtfulness and the good care I had here with my new baby?"

"Well, we had told your family that you would meet them for lunch, which will be served to you in the library. We would love to look after little Manty until you are finished."

Edina walked out, looking and feeling beautiful. Reaching the library, she walked towards her family. Charles looked up and held back a gasp. He stood and went to greet his young wife and presented his arm to her, which she took with a smile. He put his hand on hers, and said, "My dear, you look amazing. You are so beautiful, young, and fresh. My heart is beating widely with desire for you. If I had a chance, I would take you somewhere and rekindle our passion for each other."

"I would really like that, Charles. It would be so nice to have dinner alone without the children. It would be wonderful to talk and catch up our lives with each other. But we are still unable to do all that our hearts desire as Manty is but six days old."

The three children looked at their parents as they approached the table.

"Ma, you look so different, you look skinny, you look beautiful, doesn't she, Pa?"

"She certainly does."

"Your hair is so short, Ma."

"No, no, son, if you make a comment like that, you must add something like 'And I really like it.'"

"Your hair is really short, Ma, and I liked it better when it was long—that was my ma."

"That is not nice, John," said Lily. "What if Ma turned to you and said 'I liked you better when you were a baby'?"

"All right, you two."

Charles pulled out Edina's chair for her. She sat down, thinking that Charles had never ever done this before.

"Your mother has had a very trying journey, but she is showing you she is ready to embrace this new life, in a new country, away from all she knows. I am so proud to call your ma my wife and I think she looks ravishing, and I am the only one who has a say in this matter."

Everlasting Lies | 231

Little Edna said, "Pa, I don't think Ma looks like a radish, she looks really pretty."

Ma kissed the top of Edna's head. "Thank you, sweetheart. Let us all join hands together and give thanks for our safe journey to Bombay."

At 3:30 p.m. the Vernon family were all standing ready to make the trip to the Bycullah Hotel.

Charles was in his best suit, and Edina was now wearing her cloche hat and holding baby Manty.

"Ma, you look like royalty in your posh new hat."

"Very pretty, Ma."

"Most fetching and enticing. I love you, my dear."

"I like it, Ma." John had decided it was worth the effort after his last attempt.

They all said their goodbyes to the captain and the hospital staff, and their favourite sailor was coming to make sure all their luggage had been loaded on a bullock cart.

Halfway down the gangplank, Edna began to scream. "Me no like it!"

Charles bent and picked her up.

"Look at all the people, Lily," John said, grabbing for her hand. "Whatever happens, Lily, don't let go of me."

"Oh, John, why did Pa bring us here?"

"What are the ladies wearing, Lily?"

"Look over there, John. There is an almost-naked man with no legs on the ground. Oh, I am scared."

"Who do those cows belong to? Lily, I am afraid, they all look so different, why do so many men have their heads bandaged?"

"I don't know." She shook her tight blonde curls with blue ribbons. She had taken her hat off as she was so hot.

"Lily, put that hat back on at once or you will get sunstroke." Ma was behind, carrying Manty. She too was having the same feelings and questions as her children. She looked at the women in bright, colourful saris with children strapped to their bodies and the almost-naked men. The smell was overwhelming; it smelt like a farmyard.

"Pa, I want Ma." Edna was sobbing. "Me frightened."

Charles paused as the sailor had told him to wait at the end of the gangplank. Edna took her father's face in her chubby hands, and with her big blue eyes she stared into his. "Let's go back on ship."

John and Lily, still holding hands, were now beside Charles.

"Why is it so hot, Pa?" John started to sob, sweat running in rivulets down his face. He buried his face into Lily's shoulder, who was doing her best not to cry as well.

"Why have we stopped here, Pa?"

"The sailor has gone to get us our carriage."

Edina and Lily said together, "Carriage?"

"Charles, why aren't we going by taxi? I see cars and buses. A carriage, you mean like with a horse?"

"Well, because all our luggage is on a cart with a bullock, which is slow moving. We need to travel together and that wouldn't work with a car."

Lily was now holding onto Edina's skirt, with John hanging tightly to her hand, as a Hindu man with a stick eyed the family and held out a withered arm and a gnarled hand, begging and touching Edina's skirt.

"Memsahib, Memsahib," he said.

Edina looked at this old man; it wasn't fear she felt, but pity. But with three children all hanging on to her, she said, "Charles, please do something."

"Chale jao."

"What did you say to him, Pa?"

"I told him to go away, John."

"I didn't understand what you said."

"Well, I was speaking Hindi."

"Sir, the carriage awaits, as does the bullock cart with the luggage. Really, sir, I believe there should be someone up with the driver to make sure he follows, as I really should be in the back for protection of your luggage. Do you think young John would come with me? He could sit with the driver and I would be right there? Then you could go with the ladies."

"I so doubt it, but we could ask him. Let's get to that carriage and that cart so he can see his options."

Everlasting Lies | 233

"My, sir, you are an impressive father to think like that."

Charles tried to talk to the family once they arrived dockside at the wagon and carriage.

"So it is like this—Ma has to travel in the carriage with Manty and Edna. What you need to know is the wagon will follow the carriage so we will always be in sight of each other. Now, we need one person to go on the wagon with the sailor, who will sit with the luggage, and that one will sit beside the driver."

Everyone turned to look at the driver, all dressed in white with a white turban, which was a contrast to his chocolate skin.

Lily looked at Charles. "Does he speak English?"

Charles looked at the sailor. "Yes, he does, and he was born here in Bombay so he knows a lot."

"Well, I am prepared to go on the wagon, and the rest can go with Ma. But I wanted to give you older two the opportunity." Charles watched John slink closer to his mother, trying to pull Lily with him. "Because if I am in the carriage, I can answer some of the questions you might have. Any takers for the wagon?"

John already had the door of the carriage open for his mother and would not make eye contact with his father.

"I would like to do it, Pa, would it be a problem as I am girl?"

"I don't know, Lily, let us ask the driver and let him decide if he can take you or needs to take me."

"Would it be all right if I came with you so my Pa could answer questions that the rest of the family have? That is, as long as you will answer my questions?"

The driver gave Lily a toothless grin. "As long as your pa is comfortable having you travel with me, I would be happy to have you up here with me, little miss."

"So can I, Pa?"

Charles spoke to the driver in Hindi, then turned to his daughter. "Let me help you up beside Kautik."

The sailor climbed in the back of the wagon and Charles helped Lily up beside Kautik. He gave her a gentle hug and kiss. "I am very proud of you, Lily."

Kautik looked at Lily and shook her by the hand, got her comfortable, and handed her a bright yellow umbrella. "You need to use this, missy, against the sun."

Lily took the small umbrella, opened it, and carefully held it over her to create shade. "Kautik, my name is Miss Lily, and thank you for agreeing to let me come with you. Do you know I have never ridden in a wagon, let alone with a bullock pulling it?"

Kautik just smiled.

"Charles, is she safe going in the wagon?"

"Just as safe as we are."

For Lily, this would turn into a ride of a lifetime. The bullock and wagon pulled ahead of the carriage. Little Edna smiled and waved.

"Kautik, this is very bumpy."

"Yes, Miss Lily, as we are on cobblestones, but once out of the docks the roads will be better."

"It is very noisy here."

"Busy place, Miss Lily. We have ships that bring people to visit or come to live and work in our fine country, and we have ships bringing and taking good to and from other places in the world. Look around, Miss Lily, at all the workers carrying items and the selling and buying that goes on in the docks. This all makes noise. See all those bales over there? That is cotton going to Europe."

"Lots of weird smells."

"Well, Miss Lily, we just went by spices that are being sold—just look over there, they are selling spices for abroad."

"Oh, Kautik, look at all the bright colours...different yellows to oranges and then reds, don't they look pretty? What ever are they?"

"Saffron, different degrees of hot for the curry powders from yellow to red, chilies, cloves, ginger, cumin, paprika, coriander. All used for cooking. I understand that your pa works in Calcutta, —your cook in your home will use many of these spices and she will be able to tell you lots more."

"Oh, how exciting. Kautik, do I smell tea?"

"Miss Lily, I am sure you will be going to Darjeeling, which is a big tea-growing place."

"Why are you so sure I will be visiting Dare..."

"Darjeeling. Because that is where many white people live during the heat of the summer. It will be quite close to you."

"Have you been?"

"No, Miss Lily, I have never been out of Bombay."

"Where do you live, Kautik?"

"I live in chawls."

"I have never heard that word before."

The sailor was sitting close enough to hear the conversation.

"I don't know what you would call them. But lots of people are crowded together. Mainly poor workers—it is overcrowded and unsanitary."

"Sounds a bit like British slums."

"Well, that is where I live, but it is better than the really poor who have to sleep on the streets."

"What do you mean, 'on the streets?'"

"Miss Lily, you see the man on a bike over there?"

"You mean the Indian man who is taking the well-dressed white man sitting in the back under cover?"

"Yes, Miss Lily, you are very observant. Anyway that is called a rickshaw, it is like a taxi for one. It is unlikely that man has a home and he will have to sleep on the street tonight with his only possession next to him. In fact he may sleep in his rickshaw as that way no one can steal it."

"So he has no family?"

"Unlikely."

"That is a dreadful state of affairs."

Kautik just smiled at his passenger.

"Kautik, I love the way the ladies are dressed, what are their dresses called?"

"Saris."

"They are beautiful. Oh, look at the clock tower over there, what is that place? Look at the carvings. I could almost believe that I am in England."

"Miss Lily, that is called Crawford Market, completed around 1869—older than your pa. You should get him to take you there. There are some wonderful paintings of Indians in the fields. See over there, Miss Lily? That is your hotel, Bycullah Hotel."

"Golly, that looks very grand to me, are you sure we are staying there, Kautik?"

"That is what I was told, Miss Lily. Now, young lady, you enjoy your time here in India. Will you be going to school?"

"I am sure I will, Kautik, but I don't know anything yet. But I expect to be in school by September. I like school."

"You asked some very good questions, Miss Lily."

By this time they had drawn up outside of the hotel and footmen came running to remove the trunks and suitcases from the wagon. Kautik jumped down and ran to Miss Lily's side as she was closing the beautiful umbrella. He reached up to help her, and she took his hand as he lifted her down: a picture of East meeting West. She hung onto his hand and dragged him over to the carriage.

"Let me present my pa and ma, Mr. and Mrs. Vernon. My ma is holding the newest member of our family, Manty, then this is my brother, John, and little sister, Edna. Family, this is my new friend, Kautik, who has taught me so many things."

Kautik bowed to the family, saying, "I have to leave now, Miss Lily, the footmen don't like me here really. Stay safe on the rest of your journey. Welcome to India."

Lily rushed over to Kautik, her finger encouraging him to come close and bend down to her as if she wanted to whisper something; instead, she planted a big kiss on Kautik's cheek. "Thank you, Kautik, for allowing me to travel with you. I hope that one day soon something special happens to you and you get to move away from the slums."

Kautik smiled and shook Miss Lily by the hand. The sailor paid him on the behalf of Mr. Vernon and Kautik rapidly left. Lily stood watching him leave as the rest of the family moved into the hotel. The sailor also paid the carriage driver. He then escorted Lily into the hotel. "Lily, you are a very special girl, never ever lose the kindness that you have in your heart."

Everlasting Lies

Charles came over to the sailor to reimburse him for what he had spent and to pay him and give him his fare back to the ship. They shook hands, and the sailor left to go back to the ss Mantua.

Lily moved over to the family. Edina was looking at all the luggage and deciding what needed to come with them to the bedroom and what could be stored. John and Edna were sitting in a great big chair, John looking decidedly uncomfortable holding a squirming baby. Lily picked up Manty and watched her mother. She thought Edina looked elegant in her shorter grey skirt, pretty blouse, and cloche hat.

Lily looked at John, still sitting where he had been placed to look after his sisters. "Well, John, let our new life begin."

John glared at his sister.

Chapter 37

Manty woke early the next morning. Charles quickly picked her up and handed her to Edina, who started to feed her daughter so all was peaceful once again.

Charles settled back in bed. "So we seem to have survived our first night sleeping together," he whispered.

"Indeed."

"I thought you looked really beautiful yesterday in your shorter skirt, pretty blouse, and fetching hat. Hard to believe you gave birth only a week ago, you are looking very desirable."

"Thank you for arranging this beautiful room for us all. It should work well for us over the next couple of days, with the two single beds for the children and chairs for you and I to sit in—cozy and adequate for us all. The hotel even put a supply of games in this room for the children."

"Yes, I agree, but I want you to rest as much as possible. I will take the children out, preferably early as it is cooler then, to do some exploring. I suggest that after lunch we all have a siesta as it is so hot."

"I had no idea it would be this hot. Unfortunately much of what I have brought will be too warm. Once we are settled in our own place, I will set to and make clothes for the girls."

"You have just given me an idea. When we are out and about this morning, we will go and look at cotton. Do you have any idea as to how much material you would need? It would give us something to do, and I think the girls would be excited to pick material. If you tell us what colours you would prefer, we could buy material for you."

"Great idea."

"We will go right after breakfast, can you get the amounts for us by then?"

Edina nodded.

Edna stirred, her head popped up, and then she waddled over, looking like an unmade bed. Charles pulled Edna into bed with them. It wasn't long before all six were in the same bed.

※

Lunch was soon to be served, so Edina was down at the main entrance sitting with Manty cradled in her arms. The family arrived back, and over lunch Edina heard of their travels to the market to look at material. John pouted as he had little to say.

"So where is the material you bought?"

Edna shook her head and spread out her hands. "Don't know, all got none."

"We don't have any," Lily corrected.

"Why don't you have any material?"

"Lady got it." Edna smiled.

"The lady has it," Lily corrected.

"What lady, girls?"

"The lady at the material shop said she had sewers and could make three dresses for me, three for Edna, and three for you, Ma. And she would also make you cloche hats to match."

"But we leave early on Friday."

John decided he had better get into this conversation. "The lady is going to deliver them at five o'clock."

"John, you made a mistake, that is nine dresses and three hats in a few hours."

"That's what she said, Ma. Right, Pa?"

"Yes, it is, son. In fact, Edina, if you don't like any of the dresses made, we will not have to pay for them. There are many women working at sewing, and they are used to women arriving here in Bombay with unsuitable clothing for the tropics."

"Golly, I can hardly wait to see what material you picked."

"Pa picked out your material, Ma."

"Even more interesting." Edina laughed. "What about you two boys?"

"I had churidars, which are trousers that are loose around the hips and thighs but gathered tightly around the ankles, made for John and myself. She will also make John a sherwani, which is a long coat that falls just below the knees. It is traditionally formal, but she wanted John to feel special.

"Are you feeling like leaving the hotel with us all and having our dinner out with the children all dressed up? Not that it is cold, but it certainly is cooler then."

"I think that would be a fitting end to today. If it is too far to walk, maybe we could take a couple of rickshaws."

"What a great idea, but I also want to make another suggestion. I made enquiries at the hotel, and we can get an ayah to look after and feed the children. As long as you feed Manty before we leave, we could have a dinner in the hotel tomorrow night, just the two of us. If they need you for Manty, you would be close by. It would give me great pleasure to take you out, and perhaps we can close the gap of years that we have lost."

"Indeed, I would be very delighted to do this. There is so much I want to ask you.

"All right, everyone. Listen carefully, ladies and gentleman." John started to giggle at his pa.

We will have a siesta this afternoon. After we have delivery of our clothing, "I want you ladies to pick out your very favourite dress that was made today. John and I will dress up in traditional Indian garb. I have found a very traditional Indian restaurant, and we will have the adventure of eating there tonight, travelling by rickshaw. How does that sound?"

"Wonderful, Pa."

※

The family arrived at the restaurant, excited to experience traditional food and entertainment.

Some of the food was very strange to the family. Charles was in his element. "This is biryani with mutton."

"Why is it so yellow, Pa?"

"Spices—mostly saffron, and the meat will have been marinated in the same spices. Hot spices make you sweat, which in turn helps to keep you cool. This dish here is chole bhature, these are curried chickpeas, and the bread is called chapati. Those roundish things are pani puri, filled with potato and onion. Look at the tandoori chicken."

"You mean that red stuff is chicken?"

"Marinated for hours and hours in a mixture of yogurt and spices and baked in a clay pot. Ah, and bhindi masala fry...okra, tomatoes, and onions in spices. And for dessert, gulab jamun is dried milk made into balls and boiled in sugar syrup. Now, everybody, I want you to try a little of everything because this is the type of food the house staff will cook for us."

When they were finished eating, Lily said, "Actually, Pa, I really liked it all."

Little Edna's face was quite red as she said, "Bit hot, Pa."

"Well, when we are living in the house, we can ask the cook not to make it as hot for you, little one."

Once the food was cleared away, the dancing began. Lily and John made Charles sit beside them. Six young maidens made their way onto the floor in the middle of the tables, and each one posed.

"Look, Pa, they have trousers like yours. They are all in orange and yellow," said Lily.

"Like oranges and lemons." John giggled.

"But look at their gorgeous crowns, all golden, Pa, and no one is in the same position. Look, some are standing and some are crouched, but no two are the same, Pa."

"The basic square stance is known as Chauka or Chouka and symbolizes Lord Jagannath. See the Pakhawaj drums? The different sizes make different sounds. Then there are the bamboo flutes, do you see them? If you look closely, you will see some of the girls have metal cymbals on their fingers. And the big instrument is a sitar. Sit back and watch how the girls will move their feet to the drumming by stamping."

At the end of the dance the Vernon family clapped wildly.

After the amazing meal and entertainment, they decided to squeeze into one rickshaw; it might be a little squishy, but it was worth it to be together.

"All right, Ma, let me get John settled on my lap and we will take Manty, otherwise you soon won't be able to straighten your arm."

"Wonderful, Charles, that way I will be able to cuddle my other two girls."

Lily sat between her parents with Edina's arm wrapped around her, and Edna snuggled on Edina's lap and promptly fell asleep as soon as they started moving.

"Golly, he is very strong to be able to make this rickshaw move with the six of us," Lily whispered.

"I could do that." John smiled sleepily.

"You couldn't even reach the pedals, brother dear."

But John wasn't awake to hear.

"Why are all those people lying on the pavement?"

"Ma, that's because they are homeless. They can't even live in the chawls. So every night you will find many people sleeping in the streets," Lily announced as Charles smiled.

"How do you know that, Lily? What are chawls?"

"Kautik told me, he lives in a chawl, which sounds like a tenement in a slum. Most rickshaw drivers are homeless," she whispered.

"There are hundreds sleeping on the street. Look—men, women, and children. Will it be like that in Calcutta?"

Charles nodded. "This is a country filled with haves and have nots. You are all in for an education of a different sort."

Chapter 38

The Vernons watched as they chugged out of Lahore Station on Friday morning. They'd had a wonderful rest in the hotel and had learned to be a family again.

"This is amazing," said Edina. "I can't believe we are on a train. With a living room and a place for the children to play and the fact that we can have our breakfast served here with the children is all very special."

"Pa, have you seen the bathroom? There's a bathtub in there," Lily said.

"Pa, I will get a bed all to myself. The girls will have to share a single bed and they will bring in a basket for Manty to sleep in. You and Ma have a room all to yourself."

"Well, John," said Edina, "I am not sure you will always have a bed to yourself. My plan is that you will change beds so everyone has a chance to sleep on their own."

"But, Ma, that ain't fair, I am the boy."

"*Isn't* fair! My lad, what makes you think you are so special? One more word from you and there will be no sleeping alone for you, just the girls."

Lily smirked. Charles kept out of the situation. John stared at his mother but knew better than to argue with her because she would keep her word.

There was a knock at the door and an Indian man dressed in very traditional garb and a turban with a very large jewel pinned to it brought in tea, biscuits, and juice for them.

"Ma, we have finished, can we three go to our bedroom and sit on the bed by the window and watch?"

"Of course you can, but don't wake Manty as she is in the basket in our bedroom. Charles, this is wonderful, how on earth did you manage to get this for us? It is like living like the rich people."

"You are worth it. I managed to save quite a bit in the Army and used it for this. Wait until we have our first meal—I used to hear stories about the great food on these trains when I was working." Inwardly Charles was smirking to himself for not revealing how these living quarters became theirs.

"What is it like if you can't afford this?"

"Well, like a regular train you just have places to sit. Or you can have a carriage that can be turned into four bunk beds, but they are very narrow."

"We had so many wonderful times in Bombay, but we never got that dinner alone as promised."

"It was so fun. The children seemed to really enjoy the boat trip and their first Indian city and loved learning and experiencing anything. This train journey will be long—that is the reason for the comfort. Maybe we can have that meal alone together on here. Let me see if I can find someone to look after the children so we can do that. Would that be good for you?"

"That would be special. This train seems to be moving slowly, why is that?"

"It is a mail train. Though passengers do not get off except in Jalgaon, Jabalpur, Kenduijhar, and of course Calcutta, there are many pick-up and drop-off sites, so the train is not a fast train. But with our accommodation I thought it would be a great way to see some of India."

"I am looking forward to the journey, it is giving me time to rest after the birth of Manty. Looking outside I could almost believe I was in the English countryside if it didn't look so burnt up. Then I see cows and bullocks pulling carts and I know we are somewhere very different."

There was a knock on the door. "Memsahib, may I clear your tea?"

"Certainly."

"Lunch will be served in half an hour, how many at your table?"

"There will be five of us—two adults and three children, but I will need space to be able to but my baby in a basket on the floor."

Everlasting Lies | 245

"Memsahib, I will get a table for six ready for you and will make sure the extra chair can accommodate a baby in a basket."

"That would be very kind."

Half an hour later the family followed the Indian, who was carrying Manty in the basket, along the narrow corridor to the dining room.

There were tables for four on one side and tables for two on the other, each by a window, with a large gangway between for serving. But sticking out halfway down was a table for six; the table for two had been pulled across, so the waiters now had a curve in their long run.

"Now, Lily, you sit by the window and I will put Manty in her basket between us."

"I want to sit opposite my wife, where would you like to sit, Edna?"

"Next to you, Pa." She giggled.

"Great, then, John, you go next to the window opposite Lily."

As they were getting settled, their special Indian man said to Edna, "I brought a cushion for you, may I lift you up on it and push your chair in, miss?"

Edna nodded and said, "What's your name?"

"Aadi." He smiled.

"Thank you, Aadi."

John whispered, "This is very posh, Ma, look at these chairs, what's the green stuff?" He was stroking the back of the chair.

"Green velvet, and the yellow curtains on the windows look like silk."

"Ma, what do we do with the white towels on our plates?" Lily asked.

"Those are called serviettes," said Charles, "and as Edna here next to me is small, I shall tuck hers in the top of her dress, like this. Then if she accidentally drops anything, it will fall on the serviette. Now, Edna, please stop squirming."

"You're tickling me, Pa."

"Sorry, Edna. So you can do the same, children, but Ma and I will simply put them on our laps to catch any spills."

"Aren't the plates pretty, Ma? Look, the knife and fork look like they were made from gold."

Water was served in cut glass wine tumblers. Everything was first class.

Walking back towards their carriage after their lunch, John said, "Pa, you know so much about the food of India."

"Ah, Memsahib, did you enjoy your meal? I have left some games in your carriage for the children."

"Thank you, Aadi."

"Let's see what Aadi left," Lily said, skipping into their quarters.

"What's this? A large piece of brown paper with six circles each side and a bunch of stones. What do we do with these?"

"Memsahib, I thought the children would need some instruction, that is, if I may?"

"Of course, Aadi, please do. I have to go and nurse Manty."

"You go, my dear, I shall learn the game with the children."

Aadi sat easily on the floor with John beside him. "Ah, I see I have a partner with Master John. Perhaps the rest of you could sit on the other side. You, sir, have two helpers. Firstly, we split the stones into white and dark. I met someone on the train from Africa and he showed me this game that the children in Africa play. It is called Mankala and is one of the world's oldest games. How many stones do we have of each, white and dark?"

"We have twenty-four white, do you have the same number of dark?" John nodded.

"So now I want you to put four into each of the circles sitting in front of you. Littlest missy, take one of your stones and put it in one of your hands behind your back. If John picks the hand with the stone, we start. If not, you start."

"Aadi, we get to start." John smiled.

"All right, this is a chase game, the first to capture twenty of the others' stones is the winner. So, John, pick up any four stones and drop one in each circle. If one of our stones goes into one of their circles and it contains their stone, we capture them."

John picked four stones in the middle, dropping a stone into positions four, five, and six, and then he dropped the last stone into position with one of Lily's team, capturing four of their stones. John smiled.

"Is it our turn now? So I can start from anywhere on my side? I must go counterclockwise right, Aadi?" Lily went to her far right and dropped her stone onto one, two, three, and four. "So that is four in number one, four in number two, zero in number three, and five in number four equals thirteen."

John gasped. "So if I move this stone that has already won four to the next circle, that will give me eight." Lily quickly moved her four stones away from John, who could do the same.

"Out of danger but no gains."

"I like this game. I will move my number six, which will give me ten more…ahead of you now."

After a long while of chase, Lily then took five more of John's stones. "Tie game, brother. Eighteen to eighteen."

They decided to call it a tie.

Charles looked at Aadi and said; "I think this will keep then amused for a while."

"We should soon be at Jalgaon. If you look out the windows you can see mango groves and banana plantations. It will be a very short stop there. We will then make our way overnight to Jabalpur. We have a major stop there as this is an important junction for the railways. If you would like, I can arrange some things for you to do."

"That would be wonderful."

"Sir, would you and Memsahib like to dine alone tonight? My mother works on here as an ayah, and she would be happy to be with the children, to feed them here, and she is good with babies."

※

Charles escorted his wife to the dining room at 8:00 p.m., when the dining car was reserved for adults only.

"This is a little different from the café in York."

"You look beautiful tonight. I love your new haircut."

"Would you like a cocktail or wine, memsahib

"I would enjoy some wine. Which do you prefer, Charles?"

"Red."

"Then red it is. I often pinch myself to see if this is all true and not some dream."

"I am so delighted you agreed to come."

"Well, you didn't leave me much choice, but I want you to know I am happy with my decision. You have changed. You seem more content, softer."

"When we first got married, it was tough times in the mines, there was lots of war talk, and I felt your parents didn't approve of me—I was all right as a boarder in their house, but not to marry their daughter."

"I was young, we were having to lie, and I was only fifteen when we married—just a mere five years older than Lily is now."

"That doesn't bear thinking about."

"What? Us getting married?"

"No, what you said about Lily. I never regretted marrying you, Edina."

"Can we be honest with each other? We need —or perhaps *I* need— to get the nagging questions I have out in the open so we can start fresh. I am here and I find myself glad that I came, but there are so many questions I want to ask, and I am sure you have some too. This would be a perfect time and place to do this, my love."

"Yes, I have questions too."

"I always thought I had satisfied you before we were married, then after marriage and with me being pregnant, things changed, and I didn't understand why."

"I became addicted to sex and then to sexual encounters. After you got pregnant and had Lily, I didn't think you were as interested. I guess I am trying to say I was no longer the centre of your attention, I was jealous. The boys in the mines talked about brothels, and I felt I had missed out. I used you as an excuse to go to the brothels, telling myself you were withholding sex from me. I had an insatiable need for sexual pleasure."

"That hurt me a lot. Do you still go to brothels?"

"Haven't had to in India. The women want to have relationships with white men. For favours given, they receive some kind of support. Their menfolk take any other money they earn."

"What about now? With me being pregnant and now just giving birth—this may sound strange, but how are you coping?"

"Things have changed, I think, Edina. I no longer go looking for sex, but if sex is offered to me I seem incapable of saying no. No matter who offers it to me. I am being brutally honest with you. Did you only ever have the one affair?"

"Yes."

"That's all you have to say?"

"Yes, but I will try to answer questions if you ask them."

"How did you meet him?"

"I knew him from before, we went to school together."

"Did it happen right away?"

"Pretty well, we were both terrible lonely."

"Did the children know?"

"They saw him, but only as a friend."

"Did they like him?"

"Yes, just as they like you—anyone who takes notice of them, plays with them, they like. Tell me about the schools for the children."

"Lily will go to Loreto Convent, will be a resident. John will go to St Joseph, close by, and he too will be a resident. There will be a house in Darjeeling that you will be able to use when it gets unbearably hot at the mines. I will spend my summer holidays there as well."

"Will you mind me living there? Or will this give you an opportunity to be with your mistress, the one who is having your child? If I find out you are having any relationship with another women, any woman, I want you to understand that it gives me the right to do the same thing. Our marriage would be for my convenience, and until such time that I wanted a divorce, you would support us all. You are bound to give me a divorce if requested. We would both turn a blind eye to the other's relationship. I want this agreement as a legal document."

"When did you become so knowledgeable about contracts?"

Edina laughed. "I volunteered for the suffragette movement. You agree on this point? Before you answer, I want you to know I see a changed man right now and I am willing to make a complete commitment to you to become your wife, companion, and lover. Are you willing to do the same?"

"Yes, I am, as long as our agreement also gives me the same rights—if you stray from our marriage I am no longer legally bound to support you and I will have the right for my children to remain with me. Agreed?"

"Absolutely. Can we seal this agreement with a kiss until we can get the legal document written?"

"Willingly, darling." He got up and kissed his wife. He looked at the waiter. "Please bring us some food and some more wine. Now, Edina, let us talk about our future together."

Chapter 39

In the morning, Aadi served breakfast in their carriage as they were already in the train station. The children ate at a small table and Charles and Edina ate at a separate table in big winged chairs.

"Sir, I have arranged the tour for you," said Aadi. "You will travel by car from here to Bandhavgarh National Park and you will get to see the Madan Mahal Fort. You will arrive back here around five as the train leaves at six. My mother will accompany you beside the driver as she will be at your disposal, Memsahib, to look after your baby so you can also enjoy the sites with your family. Unfortunately, I could not find a wet nurse for you to leave the baby here. I have already packed a picnic for you to take with you."

"Okay, children, eat your breakfast and then get ready. Make sure you girls have a sun hat for going out," said Edina.

"What is a wet nurse?" Lily asked.

"Well, it is the services of a woman who has had a baby herself but breastfeeds another woman's baby."

"Why would she do that, Ma?"

"Not that long ago in Britain it was practised. Mothers' milk is more nutritious, so babies with mothers who had died would have also died before the advent of baby formula, which was around after we were born. So those who had babies would feed others to save orphaned babies' lives."

"But that is taking away food from the mother's own child."

"Not so, Lily. With more demand for milk, most times the mother produces more."

"I think it is…is…is nasty, not right. Surely you wouldn't allow that for Manty?"

"Well, dear child, if I was unable to feed her—let us say I became ill—somehow I doubt we would find formula for her here. Then I would far rather that another woman who was capable of feeding Manty to do so than have her die of hunger. What say you, Lily?"

Tears were in Lily's blue eyes. "I suppose, Ma, that I wouldn't want our Manty to die."

Ma got up and hugged her daughter.

"Well, everybody, let's get ready for our adventure in Jabalpur," Charles said briskly.

Aadi's mother grabbed little Edna's hand as Aadi led the group along the platform to a waiting car.

"Oh, Pa, look," John said. "It is a Crosely car, isn't it beautiful? Aadi, we going in this car?"

He nodded.

"Crickey, look at the crank handle and big lights. Who is going to sit where?"

"Well, it sounds like you would really like to be in the front," said Charles, "which means you would have to share a seat with Aadi's mother."

"Oh, I could do that, would you all fit in the back seat?"

"I think so. Lily can sit between Ma and I, Ma will have Manty, and I will have Edna. Think we should put up the hood, though, to keep the sun off us."

"Oh, Pa, this is very exciting, look at the racing green seats."

"John, you organize everyone into the car, but do it politely. I shall talk to Aadi to find out what he has planned for us."

"Pa, did you see how thin the tires are? This is a Crosely 25/30. Here, Edna, sit on me whilst Pa gets settled. I love the colour green and now with the white hood up it will reflect the sun. Edna, now you sit on Pa's lap."

Edna started chattering excitedly.

"John, if these women in the back keep chattering, you and I are changing, son."

The driver started to pull away.

"Charles," Edina said, "I feel like royalty, do you think I should wave as we move off?"

Everyone laughed.

The chauffeur went around the station and out onto the road and then said, " We will not be going through the city as I need to get out of town to get to our first place, which is a park—Bandhavgarh. I think you will enjoy this place, it is really a game preserve."

"What kind of game?"

"Deer, maybe" John said.

"Sorry, young man, we may see spotted deer, but that wasn't what I was thinking."

Edna smiled. "I know, I know—monkeys."

"We should see the red-faced monkey and langur monkeys."

"Mongoose?"

"Yes, indeed, we should see them. We should also see nilgai—it is like a large antelope—as is the chausingha. Then there is the chinkara, which is a gazelle, and we could see gaur, which is a bison."

There was silence in the car. "Could we see cats?"

"Yes, yes, we should, we have jungle cats. There are leopards but they are difficult to see. But we should see tigers."

"Tigers?" The two older children said together. Edna shrunk and cuddled against Charles.

"I hope so. And we have arranged for an elephant trek for you all. You will be with a guide who is a naturalist."

"We are going to ride an elephant?"

"Very soon, missy."

※

"Pa, look at the elephants over there, they look enormous."

"Memsahib, you will leave the baby with me, it will be far too uncomfortable for the baby," the ayah said.

The family got out of the car and introduced to the mahout and his elephant, Abu, who was a huge male elephant.

"Abu and I have been together since he was born to my father's elephant. My father was also a mahout. I used to walk everywhere with him as he followed his mother. I knew that I would be his mahout. Elephants and their trainers sometimes learn together. Abu is my friend and he will easily carry all of you."

"He is so big. How do you get on him?"

"I will show you later, but right now I want you to come and meet Abu." The small skinny young man took Lily's hand and led her to the elephant. "Put out your hand."

"Look at that, Pa, the elephant is touching Lily's hand with the tip of his trunk," John whispered.

"Stroke his trunk gently and see what he does."

"Oh. Oh, he is making a noise like he is purring."

"Great, he likes you."

With this the elephant began to touch Lily's face and feel her hair.

"Oh, Abu, you tickle." Lily rested her face on his trunk. "Can my sister Edna come over here with me?"

"Yes. Edna, will you walk to me first so I can introduce you?"

Without any hesitation, Edna walked to the mahout.

"May I pick you up, Edna, as you are so small? I want Abu to see you, will you sit on my shoulders?"

"Abu, this is my little friend Edna. Reach out and touch the top of his trunk and rub it like Lily did."

"Oh, Abu, you have such long eye lashes." Edna kissed the elephant's trunk. "Look, Ma, Abu is shaking right on top of his head."

The mahout moved in very close. "Edna, touch his ears."

"Oh, they are very, very big." Her little hand reached for the ear. "It is soft and a little hairy."

The elephant lifted his trunk and touched Edna's face. "He is nibbling my ear." She giggled.

The mahout moved back a little and the elephant reached out to touch Edna's legs.

"Yes, yes, we both like you, Abu." Lily put her arms up to Edna, who sort of fell from the mahout's neck. The weight of Edna unbalanced Lily, but Abu quickly moved close and used his trunk to sort of guide Edna into Lily's arms.

"My, he really likes you girls."

"Can I come and meet Abu?"

"Of course, young man, but I wondered if you would like to sit on him?"

"Sit on him?"

"Let me show you." With this the mahout spoke to Abu in his native language and the elephant lay almost completely down, lifting his leg and making a giant step. The mahout stepped on this leg and dragged himself to the top, sitting very close to the top of the head. The elephant stood up.

The mahout told the elephant to lie down again, and John said, "So you want me to step up on his leg?"

"Yes."

"That is a long way up, I don't think I can do that."

The mahout spoke to Abu and the elephant moved his trunk to make another step. "Boy, just step on his trunk."

"Really, is it strong enough?"

"Step on it and reach for my hand."

As John did this, the elephant lifted him. "I've got your hand," said the mahout. And there was John sitting in front of the mahout, much to the laughter of his family.

"We will meet you at the mounting area, where we will put a cradle on for you to sit in."

"Wow, it is really fun up here. How do you steer the elephant?"

"Look, with my feet behind his ears. Sometimes with the stick, this one here."

"Why does the stick have a hook on it?"

"Well, I never have to use it now, but the hook helped to train Abu when he was young. Just like children, elephants must do as we request, otherwise it could be dangerous." They plodded along, both man and boy swaying to the rhythm of the elephant's walking.

Arriving at the mounting place, the cradle was waiting to be put onto the elephant, which was done very quickly. John scrambled back to the cradle as the rest of the family mounted the stairs to the platform.

"Come on and sit by me, Ma. That's right, you sit and put your legs under the bar, see there is a ledge for your feet. Maybe we should have Edna between us, Ma?"

"Good idea, John."

A small Indian child brought extra cushions for Edna to sit on. "Look, Ma, I am as tall as John now."

"Now, sir, I want you to sit with your back between your two children and facing away from them. We are trying to keep the cradle balanced. So, missy, you sit down with your back to your ma. We are going to slip something like a back of a chair between you all so it makes the ride a little more comfortable. Then we will attach the canopy to give you some shade."

They swayed their way through the forest.

"Lily, do you see that bird? Isn't it a roller?"

"You are right," said their driver, "it is an Indian roller—a little different from the European roller. We have many species of birds in this park."

Abu the elephant continued wandering along the path, every now and again breaking off a branch with his trunk so it would not hit his passengers.

They passed a water hole, where they saw a pair of sarus cranes and also a deer-like animal in the water.

"What...is...that?"

"Oh, that is a sambar." Abu stopped so they could watch it feeding.

The area was alive with bird sounds.

"Look, monkeys in the trees. They have red faces."

"Edna, look—some have babies hanging on."

"Oh, look over there, a spotted deer," Lily said, pointing.

"And another. There are lots more just on the edge of the brush."

"What is that in the tree? See, just above the water, see it on the big branch, Pa? Look."

"Good eyes, young sir, that is a fish owl. See how his wings look spotted? Look back behind the fish owl. Can you see the black-faced monkeys? They are called langur monkeys. Notice they are whitish in colour and very different from the red-faced monkeys."

With this the mahout urged Abu to walk on. Whispering, he said, "There—in the long grass."

They all looked and saw a tiger looking straight at them.

"Look at him, he looks like he is wearing a mask." The tiger was flicking his ears and looking straight at them. Turning his head, he yawned.

"Oh dear, I feel like Red Riding Hood because I want to say, 'My, what big teeth you have," Lily said. There were stifled giggles as the tiger strode across the path to the other side and melted back into the bushes. Then they heard the tiger roar.

"Look at the big footprints in the sand," Charles said.

Suddenly there was lots of screeching and chatter as the red-faced monkeys started flying and jumping from treetop to treetop.

"Look at them go."

"Everyone, I want you to look down at the ground...do you see the footprint?" the driver said.

"Whatever it is, it almost looks human."

"It is the footprint of a sloth bear. We would be very lucky to see one as they are rare."

Travelling on, there suddenly was a raucous squealing as at least ten wild boars popped out and ran down the track with their tails held high.

"What noisy animals, they look so funny, especially when they are running."

Whoosh...whoosh, a peacock with open feathers was dancing towards a peahen. The peahen did not seem impressed but the children certainly were. "What a pretty blue-green colour his feathers are."

"We have seen so many animals this morning."

"We saw lots of birds," John exclaimed.

"I saw butterflies, lots of them." Lily smiled.

"But that tiger we saw—"

With that another tiger walked across the track. "I didn't realize their tummies are so white. How exciting this is," Edina said.

Suddenly they were back at the mounting area. The ayah was sitting under a big umbrella with baby Manty in her arms.

Under the shade of a tree, a picnic had been set up for the family.

Once back in the car, it was a quick drive to the fort, where Edina gave Manty, who was fast asleep, to the ayah. The group walked to the Balancing Rock, where they had quite a panoramic view of Jabalpur, and then walked again from the fort through the lookouts along the ramparts. This was nowhere as interesting to the Vernon group as their morning trip, but they knew they needed to return to the train.

Back in the comfort of the train suite, they welcomed the drinks brought in by Aadi as they were all hot and tired. "So was it a good day?"

They told him it was wonderful and all the children told him their favourite part. "Sounds like a great time," he said with a smile. "In fifteen minutes we will be pulling out of Jabalpur, and tomorrow afternoon you will be in Calcutta."

⁂

Edina gazed out the window at the sunrise as she fed Manty. Looking down at her contented baby, she said, "Not really sure what your life is to be like here, little one. Sometimes methinks it is very similar to home with green fields and wheat growing. Then we pass through a small village with dirty mud huts and thatched roofs, like now—children squatting in a circle, all intent on their morning bowel movement. Meanwhile women are filling large jars with water and carrying them on their heads, skinny dogs following them. Then there are the oxen pulling carts, even camels can be seen doing this."

Manty snuffled in reply as she latched onto the second breast presented to her. "You have been so good since the day you were born. Later today we will be in Calcutta, but I have no idea how long it will be before we get to our own home in..."

"Raniganj," Charles said. "I am the mine manager at the Raniganj Coal Mine, and I promise to get us on the train to there as soon as I can, even if it means I have to come back here to Calcutta for meetings. You need to feel settled in our new home with our children and new baby. Our little one is only twelve days old and you have travelled amazingly well and without complaint. It is the least I can do for you now."

They smiled at each other.

Everlasting Lies | 259

Chapter 40

On arrival in Calcutta on the afternoon of May 29, 1920, the family stored most of their luggage at the station, ready for when they caught the train to Raniganj, their future home. There was a car waiting to take them to a hotel close to the main office of the coal mine.

Calcutta was a huge city, and the barbers in the street fascinated the children. "Look over there, John, three barbers in a row." Three men stood at the closest point to the road with their clients sitting on low stools.

"Fancy having a shave on the street. I find that very strange, would you do that, Pa?"

Charles shook his head. "But I might allow them to cut my hair."

"Really, Pa?"

Again he shook his head, smiling.

"Pa, what are those bottles the men are sucking on?"

"Ah, that is a hookah. As simply as I can put it, it is a water pipe. Smoke is passed through the body and bubbles through the water, and this smoke is cooler, which is thought to be safer. Don't ask me as I don't know."

"Ouch, ouch that would hurt, wouldn't it?" Edna said, looking at a man lying on a bed of nails.

Everyone laughed as they nodded.

When they arrived at the hotel, Sugata Kumar was waiting for them.

"My dear Charles, how are you? Tired of travelling, no doubt."

"However did you know we would arrive today?"

"Charles, you will learn soon enough that India has a great bush telegraph system. Now, let me meet your family. I understand your wife had a baby on board the ship," he said with a mischievous grin.

Charles was aghast. "Mr. Kumar, let me present my wife, Edina, and our newest child, Manty."

"Very pleased to meet you, Edina, please call me Sugata. A very interesting name for your baby, please explain."

"Please to meet you, Sugata. We came over on the ss Mantua, of which I am sure you were aware, so as our baby was born whilst we were on the Red Sea, we named her Elenor Mantua after my mother and the ship. It was Charles's idea to call her Manty."

"Delightful story, Edina, and considering Manty isn't even two weeks old till tomorrow, you both are looking fantastic. I can tell you are the kind of women India needs. You look amazing."

He gave her a perceptive look, which Charles noticed, and Edina shuddered.

"What are the names of your young children, Charles?"

"We have Lily, our eldest, John, our only boy, and little Edna."

"Delightful. Well, I am aware you must be somewhat fatigued of travel. So tonight we have put you into a three-bedroom suite. Your meals will be served in the room, and anything you need our coal company will look after. Tomorrow morning you will catch the train to your new home. Your staff will be waiting for you to help you settle. Aaina, your ayah, has been there for some time preparing the nursery.

"Your other staff—Gopan and Chinpan, both males, and two other women, Belli and Suma—are full time. They are there for your every need and want—in fact whatever you yearn for. Charles, your office worker, Vallabha, is very close to producing a child. Edina, she is the daughter of Aaina and lives in a small hut on the grounds, so I would like you to think about that. Vallabha could continue her work within the company office if you would allow her mother, Aaina, to also be ayah to her own grandchild and bring the two babies up together. No, I don't need an immediate answer, you need to talk this over with Charles as Vallabha is unmarried."

"How ever will I remember all these strange names?" Edina said.

"I will give Charles a list later. If it is all right with you and Charles, I would like to meet with him for a little while this evening—business stuff, this way you can leave in the morning and start your life here in India."

Charles and Edina nodded.

"I do have a question, Sugata."

"How can I help you, dear lady?" He gave her a lecherous look.

"I would like to write to my parents. How do I go about sending the letter? Also, can you give me our new address so they can write back?"

"I will get you supplies, and when you leave, give it to the front desk and I will have made all the arrangements."

⁂

Charles was at his meeting, and each child was sleeping in their own bed for the first time in weeks. Edina decided that she would write to Bill and place his letter in with her parents' so they could mail it to him in England.

May 31, 1920

My Darling Bill,

We have just arrived in Calcutta.

We have another daughter, she is beautiful with blue eyes and almost two weeks old. She is called Elenor, after my mother, and Mantua, which is the name of the ship she was born on as we travelled the Red Sea. She is a very contented baby and has already spent her whole life travelling.

The other three travelled very well and took in all the sights we went to see—there has never been one cross word between the children. They love their new sister and call her Manty.

Charles has been very good with us all and it will be interesting to see how he will be once we settle into a routine. We will be moving into our home tomorrow.

How is your transfer coming?

I suppose my biggest news to tell you is that Charles has a mistress here, who is expecting his child. She is an Indian and works for him. The baby is due shortly. Charles and I have been able to discuss this. Today I met the man that Charles is to work for, Sugata Kumar, who I think knows about Charles's mistress...and now knows about me. He very quickly put it together. Somehow he scares me—he looked at me as if I was available, I think because of his knowledge that Charles and I have not been committed to each other.

Charles and I have agreed to get a legal document put together. I am going to send you what we talked about and wonder if you could come up with a document I could present to him.

What I want is an agreement that states that if, from this day forward, either of us strays from our marriage, it gives the right for the other partner to do the same. Ours would then be a marriage of convenience.

However, if circumstances were that both did not want to divorce, each would turn a blind eye to the relationships outside of the marriage.

If I ask for a divorce because of Charles's misconduct, he must comply and allow the divorce and pay me support for the children and myself.

If Charles asks for a divorce because of my misconduct, he is not required to give support and would have the right to his children.

However, after watching the meeting between Charles and his boss, who knows about Charles's mistress, I feel sure that Charles will falter with her. Meanwhile I have no desire except for you, and I don't know the date of your arrival. My guess is, once I can get this signed it will be to my benefit as I can be waiting for you. I hope it will be soon.

I think, my darling, that it would be better to give any letters for me to my parents and they can send them to me.

I know it will be quite a time before I hear from you. I love you, I love your daughters, and I can't wait to share my life with you.

Lovingly and longingly, Edina

Edina wrote to her family, talking about the new baby and all their adventures, and asked them to forward the letter to Bill.

With this she retired to bed, wondering what the next day had in store for her.

※

By the evening of the next day, they were all standing on the porch of Rose Lodge. The staff—Gopan, Chinpan, Belli, Suma, and Aaina—were waiting to greet the family.

Aaina rushed up to Edina. "Memsahib, let me take the baby to her nursery, this way you can organize the staff and the luggage. Why don't I take all the children and show them their rooms so when the staff bring their luggage, they can start unpacking.

"Thank you, Aaina, that would be most helpful."

"Charles," said Sugata, "it sounds like we men can go to the back veranda and enjoy a refreshing drink until my staff has our meal ready over at Ivy Lodge next door. This will free your staff to get you all settled. Edina, please join us once you have the staff organized. Just sit and relax and rest, and let them do the work for you."

"Now come, Charles, we have many things to talk about."

Edina stood looking at her surroundings and thought how grand it was. She had noticed how isolated it was as they drove to the walled garden and came through the large, imposing gate. "Who looks after the gardens here?"

"We all help, Memsahib," Chinpan said, "though Gopan and I do the labouring. We have a vegetable garden as well."

"From what little I saw, the gardens looked very well kept, Chinpan. I used to grow a lot of my own vegetables in a very small garden in England."

Gopan and Chinpan gathered the children's suitcases and took them to the rooms where they would be unpacked. Belli went to help the children.

Suma followed Edina as she wandered around the house. The kitchen was separate from the house, though not far from the dining room, which was accessed by the French door on the veranda and which was well furnished with huge Queen Victorian furniture and high ceilings.

"Suma, how many can we sit at the table?"

"Twelve, Memsahib."

"Twelve?"

"The mine manager before you often entertained."

"That is a lot of work, do we have enough dishes and silverware?"

"We never have to worry, Memsahib, because we have been taught the English Way. Our dinners are often seven courses and servants from the invited guest will help us, bringing what we need to borrow and acting as table servants for the evening. So don't be alarmed if you go to someone's place for an evening meal and you are served by us."

The dining room was very dark, partly because of the veranda and partly because of the dark furniture, walls, and the old Victorian prints on the walls. It was also warm.

"Suma, do the windows open? Does the fireplace work?"

Suma nodded.

"Memsahib, is this your first visit to India?"

"It is, Suma."

"Would it be impolite of me to explain the working of the house?"

"I would welcome it."

"You have already experienced the heat. As you walk around you will notice that all rooms have an entrance to the veranda—that is so we servants can attend to the house and your needs without being seen within the house. Notice the door opens directly opposite that door on the other side; in this case the door goes directly into the girls' bedroom, which has a door to the veranda. Now, if we were to open all the doors, we would have great cross ventilation."

"Yes, yes, I see how ingenious." Edina walked into the girls' room.

"Ma, look at our beds." There were two canopied single beds side by side but with space between, and each was enclosed with a mosquito net. The foot of each bed was close to a fireplace. There were two chairs and a small table to one side, and space for the children to play. A door opened to the back veranda, and another door opened to a bathroom.

"Ma, go into the bathroom, it connects with John's room."

Everlasting Lies | 265

Edina stopped, aghast, at the sight of a zinc bath and a wooden commode.

"That, Memsahib, is the thunder box, which is emptied by a man called the sweeper, and he looks after all the bungalows in this compound."

"How do we have hot water for the bath?"

"Oh, we fill it for you, Memsahib. When you are finished, you pull the plug and it empties onto the floor and runs through that little hole in the bottom of the wall into the soak pit."

Edina peeked into John's room. It was small but adequate and he seemed to be happy to have his own space.

She wandered back into the dining room and then into the living room. Again, it had doors that led to the veranda along with a fireplace, sofa, chair groupings, and a curio cupboard, and it was nicely decorated with flowers.

"Where do you all sleep?"

"We sleep in the godowns—a number of small rooms at the end of the compound."

"Suma, what are the frilly things up in the ceilings?"

"They are punkahs. We have our young children or older boys act as coolies. They sit outside when you are eating and pull the rope and the punkah keeps you cool."

Edina was in the master bedroom with Suma and Belli, who were unpacking. As Charles walked in, the servants seemed to fade away.

"Sugata just left and expects us at his lodge at seven for drinks. The children are not invited. Our staff is here to feed and look after them and put them to bed, and we are only next door. He has some people he wants to introduce us to. I hope you are not too tired, my love."

"I am fine, Charles, and I know you must start working, so it will be great to meet some other ladies who live here. Have you walked around the house yet? You really should go and see the children, they are pretty excited."

✻

Once over on the Ivy Lodge veranda, Charles and Edina met three other couples: two from within the complex and one who did not work at the coal company.

Sugata sat down in the veranda chair next to Edina's. "Charles is a very lucky man to have a wife as beautiful as you are, Edina. It is hard to believe you are the mother of four children and have just given birth a couple of weeks ago—also to have endured a journey such as what you have just done. You look so appealing, I wonder how Charles can keep his hands off you. If you were my wife, I would be pleading with you to pleasure me, knowing that it is still early for you. Tonight in our new marriage bed, I would lay naked before you, willing you to kiss me all over. You see, here in India it is fine for us to take another man's wife, especially one as attractive as you. I can hardly wait until a month has passed and I return here to fulfill my dreams and to pleasure you."

With that Sugata left and announced that dinner would be ready and that he was famished; with this he looked over at Edina and winked.

Fortunately, Edina sat a long way from Sugata, but he had a woman on each side. Charles sat on one side of his wife and James sat on the other. James was the husband of Sue, who was sitting next to Sugata. Charles and James talked across Edina.

"I say, Charles, what do you think of this fellow Gandhi?"

"I am not sure, James, as I have been out of country for several months now, but I have read about his non-cooperation campaign."

Edina said, "Well, I admire him."

Both men looked at her. James was the first to speak. "Why would you admire a man such as he?"

"Because he chooses to be non-violent. After what we have all been through, I think this is admirable. He is taking up the cause for women and untouchables—what ever could be wrong with that?"

"Interesting, Charles, that your beautiful young wife has an opinion on such grave matters—and, I might add, the ability to express herself. What is this world coming to?"

"Hopefully one of equal rights," Edina said firmly.

As the men talked mine business, Edina continued to eat and watched as Sugata and Sue passed knowing glances to each other. Sugata picked up Sue's hand and proceeded, in front of everyone or anyone who was watching, to take each finger one by one into his mouth and suck it. Sue squealed in delight.

"Charles, is Sugata married?"

James was quick to answer. "Not likely, he always calls us married men 'poor buggers' and says he prefers to sample many. Though I hear tell that he has been married. So how many children do you two have?"

"We have four, our youngest not yet a month old," Charles said. "My dear, you look tired. If you will excuse us, we need to go home and sleep, we have had an exhausting month. I need to be bright for my first day on the job tomorrow."

With that Charles took Edina's arm.

"Charles, we do need to thank Sugata."

"I am sure he won't miss our goodbyes, he seems to be well entertained by the women."

"I am very anxious to get home and see how the ayah has handled Manty."

"Edina, you do look beautiful and can hold a wonderful conversation, and I am proud to call you my wife."

Edina smiled. *I should get our contract down in writing as I know he is about to meet up with his lover.*

Chapter 41

Charles worked with Sugata from Monday to Thursday; Sugata was to leave early Friday to catch the train to Calcutta.

Meanwhile, Edina had settled well into being the mistress of the house and had even managed to meet with a young lawyer, who drew up the contract for her. Edina decided that Charles would sign the agreement before going to work on Friday morning.

Breakfast was served on the veranda early. Edina, still in her nightwear, shared this quiet time with Charles.

"My darling, you look very beautiful this morning."

"Thank you. I want to talk to you about something we discussed earlier—our written agreement about this marriage."

"Great idea, we should get a contract written."

"Whilst you have been busy with Sugata, I have had this done."

She passed him the papers along with a copy. Smiling, she said, "I hope you don't mind that I did this."

"Certainly not as we are getting closer to the time when we will become lovers, and as we have both been unfaithful, it is a wise thing we are doing."

Charles read the document.

We, Charles Alfred Vernon and Edina Vernon, have agreed to the following:

That if either of us stray from our marriage vows and have sexual relations with another, this allows the other person to do the same but would not necessarily cause the marriage to end.

However, if Edina decides a divorce is necessary because of Charles's misconduct, he must grant her a divorce and is required to provide support and payment to Edina and children. She would have the right to deny access to the children until they are of age.

However, if Charles decides a divorce is necessary because of Edina's misconduct, she must grant him that divorce, and he can have custody of the children that he fathered. He owes Edina no support to her or bastard children.

I _____ do agree to this contract.

I _____ do agree to this contract.

Dated_____

Witness

Name_____

Signed_____

Date_____

"That is perfect, Edina, who will witness this?"

"Well, Gopan is around, shall we do it now whilst it is quiet?"

Charles nodded. The two copies were duly signed and witnessed.

The car arrived to take Charles to work.

"I shan't be late, it is time for us to have a weekend all together and make plans about the children's schooling. Later, luv."

Charles kissed Edina just as sleepy-headed children came out on the veranda and Aaina brought Manty to be fed.

※

Charles arrived at the office and settled down at his desk. There was a small knock on the door and without looking up, he said, "Enter."

Vallabha waddled in, big with child.

"Vallabha, come sit down, how are you?"

Charles helped her to a chair. He was shocked at her size and at her face, which seemed much, much darker—almost as if she were wearing a mask.

"I am a little tired, Master, but I wanted to see you, especially as I have been watching you from afar, you and all your family."

"From where?"

"In the godowns. My mother—your daughter Manty's ayah—we live together, and hopefully you are going to allow my mother to look after our child so I can come back to work quickly and be with you as before."

"Won't you need to be around the baby to feed it?"

"No, I am presuming that Memsahib and the children will be going to Darjeeling, to the cool of the mountains, soon. That will mean my mother will be going with them and she will take our child as well. She will get a wet nurse for our child. Also there will be things that Memsahib will need to arrange. Meanwhile I will be here with you to look after your every need."

Charles felt stirrings in his body; it had been nearly three months since he last laid with Vallabha.

"In fact, Master, you look like a man who is very, very hungry."

"That I am," he admitted. He spent time telling her the situation with Edina. "So of course I haven't had any sexually relations with my wife."

"I suspect it still will be a couple of weeks before Memsahib will be ready to look after you." She licked her lips, dragged herself out of the chair, and locked the door. "However, I am still available and need to intimately introduce you to your child."

"You can't mean that, you must be very close to having this child."

"We Indian women like to please the fathers of our child and we need the fathers to feel connected to their child. Tell me, is there a better way to introduce you?"

"I can't, I can't do this."

But Vallabha took no notice. She came to Charles and kissed his forehead, slowly moving her soft, luscious lips to his mouth and placing his hands on her breasts. Immediately, her nipples sprang to life. As he

Everlasting Lies | 271

groaned, she slipped her sari off and pushed her breasts towards his open mouth.

He loved it and wanted her now, breathing fast. "Please, Vallabha, stop." He groaned. "Please stop, I can't do this right now."

"That's not what I am feeling against my belly, you want me with every part of your body."

Somehow, Charles managed to struggle to his feet. Pushing Vallabha roughly, he said, "Put your clothes on at once." As he moved towards the door, he recovered his composure. He turned and said, "I will arrange for you to be off work until after the baby is born. I do not want to see you here working. Go home to your mother. I need time to think as to how I shall handle this situation. We will wait until after the birth. Then we will talk, but not a moment before."

Vallabha was dressing. "Your words may tell me to go, Master, but your body was very encouraging."

"I will arrange for my driver to take you home. We will no doubt hear when the child is born."

With that he opened the door and barked instructions to the men in the office, adding, "Vallabha is not to return to this office for anything until I give her permission, is that understood?" The men nodded.

⁂

Charles was greeted by Gopan when he arrived home that night. "Master, I will bring hot water for your bath. Memsahib is out in the garden learning the names of the flowers with the children. I will have cold drinks for you and the children on the veranda. Your usual whiskey and soda?" Charles nodded. "Dinner will be served early at six thirty, Master."

After dinner, the children went off to get ready for bed and Charles and Edina sat quietly on the veranda.

"How was your first day working without Sugata?"

"Pleasant, it is lovely to be working and in control."

"I had no idea how hot this place was going to be. It is like living in an oven."

"I guess when I was in the army I got used to it. However, we do have the option of using the place in Darjeeling for you and the children. It would give you a chance to go and look at the boarding schools for John and Lily. You could take the female staff with you and leave the men to look after me."

"I would miss you terribly and so would the children. At this point I am willing to suffer the heat. Will you be taking any time off?"

"Maybe it would work if you went for July, I came for two weeks at the end of July, and we all returned here together. Then you could go a week before the children start school, get them settled, and return here."

"That sounds a better plan as I do not want us to be separated for long at this point in our lives. Also I have found out that the school year is not the same as in England. I worry about the children's lack of routine and learning."

"Is that true about the school year being different?"

"Yes, it is. Maybe we should have them tutored here."

"That would be a great solution, all three of them could be tutored in the house until school starts."

With that the children came running onto the veranda in their night-clothes, demanding that Charles read them a story. Though both Lily and John could read, Edna got to choose the book.

"So, Lily and John, what are you reading?" Edina enquired as she already knew that Edna would be bring *The Jungle Book*.

"I am reading *Treasure Island*."

"Mine is *Black Beauty*."

Charles enticed Edna over to him. "Oh, you want more of this story, Edna?" She nodded. "Aren't you tired of Mowgli?"

"I like all the animals."

So Charles read as the children gathered round to listen—even Manty, who was suckling from her mother's breast.

"...but I speak the truth." Edna was dozing in Charles's lap and Belli came to put the child to bed.

Charles peered at the two eldest. "On Monday you two will be starting school."

"No...where are we going?" John asked with his eyes wide.

Everlasting Lies | 273

"Right here in your own home. You will be tutored so that when you go to boarding school later, it won't be such a shock for you."

"Boarding school? Why? I don't want to do that. Where?"

"Boarding school will give you a good education. John, you will go to St Joseph's in Darjeeling. You, young lady, will go to Loreto Convent, also in Darjeeling. Your ma and I are planning some time to go there in July as we have a house there and Darjeeling is much cooler than here. It is way up higher, where they grow tea. It will be fun for us, like a holiday."

"We will go first without Pa and visit the schools. Then Pa will come, as he wants to see your schools as well. He will return and you and John will then go straight to the schools as the school year is from the beginning of March until early December. I will stay for a few weeks to make sure all is okay."

"What if we don't like it?"

"Well, Lily, you will have to make the best of it," Charles said.

"All right, children, off to bed. Belli, the children can talk in John's room for fifteen minutes so as not to wake Edna, and then they may read for five to ten minutes."

"Oh, thanks, Ma."

"Ah, there you are, Aaina, I think Manty is ready to settle down too. Could you tell Gopan to bring the master another drink and me a small glass of sherry? Thank you. We will be down the other end on the swinging settee."

Edina took Charles's hand and led him to the swing.

"Um, looking after my needs?"

Somehow, Gopan already had their drinks there waiting. "Well, not quite all your needs, yet. I hear you had a trying morning."

"What do you mean?"

"It wasn't hard for me to put two and two together when the company car brought home a sobbing, very pregnant woman. I was told this was Aaina's daughter who worked at the mine and that she was told not to return to the mine until after the baby was born. I knew you must have done this."

"I did. I am not sure when the baby is due, but I didn't want to have her around."

"Remove temptation?"

"Yes, something like that. I want to give us a chance. We were so in love when we were young. I know I was the one making mistakes by going with other women. Then came the war, and it was very different for us all, you included. We lived in the moment. But I didn't need to today. I am being honest by telling you that I wanted to live in the moment, but I didn't because I want us to have a chance. We have family, we made promises this morning—I wasn't about to break my promise the same morning."

"I want that too—a normal life. Though I can hardly call this normal. Servants, being waited on, this is abnormal for me."

"Welcome to my world."

"Here again, my dear, I know nothing about your world before me."

"Then let me tell you about my family. About my brother Abe. Do you know I met him in the war in the trenches?"

There in the darkness, Charles told his story with his arms wrapped around his wife.

Chapter 42

The Vernon family had been living in Rose Lodge for over a month and were planning their trip to Darjeeling. With their contract signed, Charles and Edina had re-established their relationship and seemed blissfully happy. Manty was growing under the care of Aaina, who now had Vallabha's daughter, Charita, to care for as well. Vallabha was still banned from the mine.

Tonight, the household was holding their very first dinner party as they had now made a number of friends from the British Empire Club and Sugata was back to the mine for the first time since they had arrived.

"Gopan, I am going into the gardens to pick some flowers for tonight. If anyone needs me, send them to the gardens."

"Yes, I certainly will, Memsahib."

Edina loved the gardens; the smells and the colours all delighted her.

"Good afternoon, Mrs. Vernon. I have to say you look even more beautiful than I remembered."

Edina looked up into the lecherous eyes of Sugata.

"Drinks are not until seven."

"I know, that's why I came now, just to see you and have you"—he paused to lick his lips—"to myself."

"I am a little busy right now."

"Let me help you." He came close, taking the flowers from her arms and making sure he touched her breasts as he did. He buried his head into her hair. "You smell wonderful. You look wonderful. I bet you taste wonderful. I might say that I find you erotic." He kissed her neck.

"Don't you do that."

"Oh no, Edina, I want to do a lot more than that. I want to take you for my own. I think you are a person with a great sexual appetite that I might be able to fulfill. After all, I wouldn't be your first lover out of marriage, and with your allure I am sure I won't be the last. Tell me that your heart isn't pounding, tell me you don't feel aroused?"

"I find you disgusting."

"Then a better challenge for me, because I will have you."

Gopan arrived. "Do you need help, Memsahib?"

"Lovely, Gopan, take our guest to the veranda and give him a drink. I will pick up the flowers I dropped. Thank you."

"You will drink with me, Edina, right?"

Edina hurried into the kitchen, quite flustered. Sugata had managed to arouse her; she could feel her heart pounding. She suppressed these thoughts and said, "Where are the children?"

"Finishing their classes, Memsahib."

"Go get them right away and tell them I need them to help me entertain on the porch."

"Yes, Memsahib."

"Gopan, don't make Sugata's drinks strong, I don't want him making a scene."

"Thanks, Ma, for getting us out of class early," John said.

"I need a favour—go and entertain Sugata for me whilst I arrange these flowers. Tell him I will come when I am finished."

The three went off, giggling. Edina wondered what it would be like to make love to a man of colour. Would it be different? Gopan, who returned smiling, interrupted her thoughts. Edina looked at him quizzically.

"Memsahib, he was quite horrified when the children arrived and I gave him your message."

"He is a very indecent, strange man. Gopan, if he happens to come in the kitchen, do not leave—or at least makes sure someone is with me at all times. If necessary, have Aaina come tell me Manty needs me, you understand?" He nodded. Edina smiled to herself as she thought, *Maybe I am strange, as I don't think I would want to push his advances away.*

It wasn't long before Sugata arrived in the kitchen. "My dear, I thought you were coming to entertain me. After all, that is what mine managers' wives are expected to do, not work in the kitchen." As if on cue, Aaina walked in with Manty.

"Memsahib, your baby is looking for her mother's attention."

Edina took Manty in her arms and kissed her as the other children came in.

She saw Sugata physically shudder.

"I shall remember this, Edina."

"Oh, so you are leaving, Sugata? Well, we will see you tonight. Children, say goodbye to Mr. Kumar. Belli, you will be sure that the children are out of the way and finished eating by the time our guests arrive."

※

After cordial drinks on the veranda, Sugata came over to Edina at the table. "My dear, you look ravishing—edible, in fact. Of course I am to be seated next to the lady of the house so I can then explore you."

"Not tonight, Sugata, maybe the next time. But I see my special guest has arrived, I knew she would be a little late. Sugata, this is Don and Mary's niece, Sarah. She just arrived from England three days ago and I invited her to make our table even."

Sarah was a striking redhead, wearing her hair in the latest style with a royal blue band and a silver feather. Her royal blue dress appeared, in this light, to be the only covering for her perky breasts, and with its cut just above her knees, it displayed very shapely legs and high silver sandals.

"Delightful, I must say, and delighted to meet such another perfect woman. Sarah, I shall be happy to escort you anywhere."

"My, Sugata, are you flirting with me?"

"Sugata, you will be at the foot of the table, and Sarah, you are to sit to his left."

"Delighted." Sarah whispered to Sugata as she took his arm, "So this way just maybe we, Sugata, can rub knees and get to know each other."

The dinner was a great success. As everyone was getting ready to leave, Edina overheard Sugata saying to Mary and Don, "Is it all right if Sarah comes to my lodge for a nightcap? I will bring her home in an hour."

"Of course, she is certainly old enough to make her own decisions."

"Thank you, Uncle Don, for pointing out that I am old enough to look after myself."

Sarah smiled at Sugata, then threw her head back, licking and parting her lips. "Now, Sugata," she purred, "what kind of drink will you offer me?"

"I am sure, my dear Sarah, I can find a way to satisfy your needs." With this they walked next door.

Edina was sure Sugata could satisfy Sarah, and she couldn't help wondering again what kind of lover he would be.

※

As Charles and Edina were getting ready for bed, Charles said, "Congratulations, Edina, everything went so well. The flowers were amazing, and you are a perfect hostess. Here, let me help you with your necklace."

Charles moved behind Edina, kissing her neck, undid the necklace, and it dropped to the floor. "Oh, how clumsy of me," he said as he went down on his knees to pick it up. Quickly he was under her dress, one hand holding her bum, the beads dangling from this hand. He reached up with his other hand and took hold of her knickers.

Edina gasped and moved backwards and Charles came from under her dress. Smiling she laid on the bed. " Come on rip them off, darling." Her mind once again settled on Sugata, and how much he had aroused her. "Look at me, darling, can you see how much I want you, how you excite me?" Charles kneeling between her legs, moved his hands upwards under her dress to her bare breasts, and she remembered Sugata's hands touching her. "Don't stop."

"Your nipples are on fire, I want to kiss your breasts."

Rolling off his wife. Quickly she sat up pulled her dress off, and she lay there with her breasts exposed, her garter belt holding her stockings, and her husband now holding her knickers. Groaning, he yanked the knickers off her body, leaving her exposed yet framed by the garter belt and stockings.

"Is that what you wanted?"

Everlasting Lies | 279

"Yes." Her mind was racing; yes, this is what she wanted. Edina now fiddled with the buttons of his shirt, then pushed him to a sitting position and ripped the shirt off, wondering what it would be like if Sugata removed his shirt. Yes, he had certainly aroused her this afternoon. She stood up before Charles could stop her, almost naked and so inviting as she removed his clothes, she continued to be amazed at the size of him for a man so small. What size is Sugata? She wondered.

"Charles, you look like you are ready."

She lay on his stomach kissing his chest, moving up closer to his face so she could kiss him, letting her legs fall off him and onto the bed. "What are you doing? What are—"

Charles groaned as she put her hands just where he wanted them. "

"More, more," he cried. He caressed the bare leg above her stocking. "I must kiss your thigh."

"Oh, Charles, Charles. She panted"

Suddenly Charles could wait no longer. "I have to have you now." His words made her think of the afternoon encounter and she heard I will have you. "Please, please take me now." Her mind could only think what it would be like to do this with Sugata. "Take me, and take me now."

Charles whispering, "You are mine."

In her mind she was lifting her body up to persuasive Sugata, feeling him. Wildly, she said, "Yes. Yes, finally I am yours."

Clothes were scattered around the bed as they climbed under the sheets and both fell into a contented sleep.

Chapter 43

The day arrived for Edina and her four children—accompanied by Chinpan, Suma, Aaina, and Vallabha and her baby, Charita—to depart for the cool of Darjeeling. Once again it was going to be a long journey, as they had to go back to Calcutta and then catch a mail express train. It would travel overnight and arrive in Siliguri with enough time to catch the 9:00 a.m. "Toy Train" to Darjeeling, which would arrive in the evening, travelling forty-six miles and rising high into the mountains.

"We aren't really going on that train, are we?" John exclaimed.

"Memsahib, I have brought food for you and the children. Sit on this bench and eat."

The staff sat on their haunches around the family and ate as well.

"It is so old here."

"True, little memsahib. This station was opened in 1880, forty years ago, and we have your people, who had the vision, and our people, who had the muscle."

"Why did they build it, Chinpan?"

"I suppose it started because of the hill stations and the growing of fine teas."

"Right, Darjeeling tea. Ma, isn't that the best kind of tea in England?"

"Yes, it is."

"I wish I had a map to show you and John and Edna to help you to understand." Chinpan picked up a stick and drew a rough outline of India. He pointed to each side of India. "What's here, Edna?"

"Sea."

Everyone giggled.

"What's up here to the north?"

Everlasting Lies | 281

"Mountains."

"True, John, but there is a country to the north. Guesses?"

"China," Lily said.

"Partly right, it is China's Tibet. Where we are now going used to be a kingdom of Sikkim. The British East India Company adopted this area as a rest and recovery station for soldiers way back in 1835. Now, children, I have another question for you. Tibet is to the north, but what country is to the east?"

"There is a country?"

"Yes, John, there is, and it has a very big mountain in it." Silence "The country is Nepal, and to the west is Bhutan. Originally there was just a track that got larger and now it is a road. But in 1878 the Eastern Bengal Railway submitted a proposal to build a railway from Siliguri. It was approved and they started construction immediately. Looks like we can get on the train now, I must away and see to our luggage."

"Gosh, he knows a lot."

Once settle in their carriage, Chinpan returned. "We are right now at about four hundred feet and here the train goes very, very slowly as we are climbing a mountain!"

"I don't know, Ma, we have been on the train for an hour and quite honestly I feel I could walk faster!"

"Bet you can't, Lily!"

Chinpan left and when he returned, he had drinks for everyone.

"We are just pulling into Sukna village and we have travelled about ten miles and only climbed another one hundred and ten feet."

"I think my husband said there was a wildlife sanctuary here, Chinpan, is that true?"

"Yes, Memsahib, it is called Mahanadi and it is known for its elephant migration, and it is possible to see tigers and Himalayan black bears." Chinpan felt tugging on his legs. "Yes, Missy Edna?"

"We got to ride an elephant."

It was obvious that Chinpan loved the children as he listened to their story.

"Look, look I can see the back of the train."

"Ah, this is the first sharp curve and then we have a loop, you should all be looking out the window."

There were lots of squeals from the children, who knew they were climbing. As they pulled into Rangtong, Chinpan said, "Well, children, we have travelled for four miles and we have gained eight hundred and ninety feet."

"Golly! This is so small compared to our railway stations."

"It gets better now," Chinpan said as the train pulled out of the small station. "We will climb fourteen hundred feet in about seven miles. We are now turning south though we want to travel north. You will know when we have turned north again as you will see breathtaking views of the mountains and valleys."

It didn't seem long before Chinpan was saying, "You see those mountains over there?" The children nodded. "That is the Bhutan range. Wait, wait, look down there, it is the Teesta River. Now, this river begins in Tibet. Before we get to the next station we will experience your first zigzag."

"Zigzag, what is that?" John asked.

"Well, the track makes a zigzag, but to negotiate this it has to reverse and then move forward again."

"Why doesn't it slip?"

"There is a small and dependable native man who sits perched over the forward buffers of the train and scatters sand on the rails when the wheels of the engine lose their grip."

"Oh, I wouldn't want that job."

"I think this is a very scary ride." Lily grimaced.

"Well, I think, little missy, you will have to get used to this as you will be going to school in Darjeeling, as will John also. So you will have to travel this to get home for holidays!"

"Why did you pick schools here in Darjeeling, Ma?"

"Lily, I didn't really. Barrackpore Coal Company decided what would be best. You will be going to Loreto Convent and John will be going to St Joseph's. We will be looking at them while we are here."

The train was shunting back and forth on the track and seemed to be groaning.

"Children, you need watch as we are fast approaching Agony Point, one of the most breathtaking loops. Look down there, you can see where we came from and how much higher we are now. Look out towards the mountains."

"Look at all the black smoke from the engine!" Lily said. "Oh, Ma, look at the mountains, they are so big and beautiful."

"Ah, we are going to fall over the cliff!" John exclaimed.

As they pulled into Gayabari Station, Chinpan said, "Well, we have now climbed over three thousand feet and we have only one zigzag left, but we have about four hours left!" Edna was already curled up on the seat. "My suggestion is to have a nap and I will return in about two hours." At that moment, Aaina arrived with Manty for a feeding and shooed Chinpan out.

The children settled down as Aaina fussed over each of them. Then she took Manty from Edina, saying, "Memsahib, you will do well to sleep a little too."

Shortly after two o'clock, Chinpan returned to find them all awake and gazing out the window.

"Chinpan, what is the name of that road?"

"Hill Cart Road, and we will be travelling beside it for some time now."

"Lily, watch the children running beside our train."

"Look, they are waving back."

Some time later they entered a town called Ghoom. "Everyone, we are at the highest point now—seven thousand four hundred and seven feet. That is over one mile higher than we started!"

"I don't understand," Edna said.

"Let me try to explain. John, please give me your belt. So, Edna, if I lay this on the ground and say to you that this belt is a picture of a mile, can you imagine that?" Edna nodded. "John, I want you to hold the buckle and don't let go. So where John is holding the buckle is where we got on the train." Edna nodded again. "So I am going to slowly lift my end to show you where this station is. You know we have been going up—this station is above where we started by a mile so it is here."

"Oh, I understand, we are a mile closer to the heavens and God."

Everyone smiled.

"Darjeeling is not as close to the heavens as here, but pretty close because like here it is over a mile as well."

※

Everyone was grateful when they finally arrived at the house in Darjeeling. Edina was extremely surprised to find Sugata already there.

"Sugata, I didn't expect to find you here!"

"Welcome, Edina and children. This is a company retreat from the heat, and I knew you were to arrive today to view the schools here. I have been here ever since your party and had planned to leave yesterday, but I decided that as this is a big residence, I would stay on and show you around for a couple of days."

"How very kind of you!" She looked at Sugata with new eyes and saw a very handsome Indian, tall and skinny and most attractive.

"Edina, I am so glad you are not upset at my presence."

Sugata spoke to her staff in his native language; it appeared he gave them orders as they disappeared with the children.

"What did you say to them, Sugata?"

"Told them to unpack and look after all the children while I showed you the grounds. I know you have such a love of flowers."

"That I do!"

"It must be because you look as pretty as a flower yourself."

"You, Sugata are such a flatterer to all women! I have watched you."

"I hope you were jealous, Edina." He took her by the arm. She could feel her heart beating fast and almost wished that his fingers would touch her breast accidentally.

She turned her face and looked up into his. "So how did you get with Sarah?"

"Very well, thank you." He smiled.

"What does that mean? I recall that she was whispering to you about getting to know each other!"

"Oh, we did that at the table!"

"What?"

"Got to know each other intimately."

"At the table?"

"Oh, it is so easy, my dear. We sat down and our knees were touching, so it was very easy for me to touch her knee. I moved my hand away but hers followed mine, and I could feel her parting her legs as she took my hand and place it on her thigh. Her hand then went to my thigh. Now, I have to admit, my dear, that I have no self-control. If someone invites me to be intimate, I am willing to oblige. Her hand managed to find my penis, which, of course, was large and ready."

"I think that is enough detail for me!"

"Why be so shy? Surely you and Charles are having relations again. Or, Edina are you waiting for me or someone else?"

"Charles satisfies my every need!"

"Tell me how Charles satisfies you! I shared some of my encounter with Sarah—and maybe at dinner tonight we could sit the same way so I may show you for future reference!"

Lily came running up to them, asking her mother to come and see the house. Sugata kissed Edina on the cheek and said, "Best I leave you with those thoughts and will see you later when we all sit down for a meal."

Chapter 44

Sugata had taken Edina, Lily, and John to their respective schools that day, each child seeing where they were to sleep and meeting some of the boys and girls they would be with. It was also pointed out that if Edina came to stay in Darjeeling for more than a week during the hot months, they could become a day student during that time.

Once back in the house, Sugata asked, "So what do you think of your new schools?"

Both nodded enthusiastically.

"That is wonderful, children, you are one of the reasons I am still here— to make sure everything is also good for you."

"Sir, when do you go home?"

"I leave tomorrow, early evening. I return on the train that brought you up here. It leaves at six thirty and that gets me into Siliguri in time to catch the morning train back to Calcutta."

"Oh," said Edina. "I didn't realize you were going home quite so soon."

"Well, as soon as I get back, Charles can come up and be with you all before the children start school. In fact the children can start school any time and that way maybe you can both be here to see them settle in. "

"Ma, do we have to stay here or can we go and play?"

"Off you go."

Sugata smiled. "Well, that is a surprise—I thought you preferred someone to chaperone us. Would it be unthinkable for you to perhaps come and dine with me at a restaurant tonight?"

"I would be delighted to spend the evening with you."

"Another surprise."

With that the door opened and Suma came in carrying letters. "The master must have sent this one for you, Memsahib." She set down a letter from her parents and Edina's heart skipped a beat.

"Sir, I placed about five letters for you in your room, I hope that was all right?"

"Wonderful, Suma, could you tell the staff that Mrs. Vernon and I will be dining out tonight so there will only be the children to feed."

Edina went to her bedroom to read her letter. Would it be just from her parents or…? She tore open the letter and another envelope dropped to the floor. She knew it was from Bill.

She tore it open frantically.

"Darling, darling Edina,

How wonderful to have another daughter, I am sure she will grow to be as beautiful as Edna and you. I am thrilled and I love her name and really can't wait to see you all.

How are Lily and John adapting to life in the Empire?

Your family here are well but miss you all—but nowhere as much as I do.

This probably will be my one and only letter to you. I will be leaving for India almost immediately. In fact this letter will probably reach you just before I do as I should arrive in Delhi mid-July, then travel by express train to Calcutta, which will be my base. I am due to visit Darjeeling as I want to experience the "Toy Train." Is there any possibility of you meeting me there? If so write to me at Howrah Station, Calcutta, and give me a date and I will make it work.

I am sure, my darling, that even writing this makes me "stand up" with pleasurable thoughts—of us willingly removing our clothes and once again exploring our bodies until mutual satisfaction is reached. For me this relief of my desires has been so pent up since you left…and I already forgive you, as I know that you are probably having relations with Charles. Did you both sign the form you wrote me about?

It is of no matter to me, as once we are back together I know that you will choose to have me, a loving man, back in your life.

I shall look forward to your letter waiting my arrival in Calcutta. Make our meeting as soon as possible so we can begin our lives together without secrecy.

Your loving soon-to-be-your husband, Bill

Edina was lying on her bed and was so aroused by just thoughts. Imagining Bill, she hardly heard the knock on her door.

"Memsahib, I was asked to remind you that you are going out for dinner, but Master Sugata wants to give you a tour of Darjeeling before you eat. Can you be ready in half an hour?"

"I can and will be down waiting for him."

※

"Ah, Madame Vernon, you looking stunning. I thought, my dear, that we would visit my friends at Tea Enterprise and partake tea and maybe a little crumpet." Edina looked at him to see if a double entendre was intended. As they were driving along, Sugata remarked, "You look quite flushed, my dear, and deep in thought. What are you thinking?"

"Actually, I was thinking about crumpets."

"How so?" Sugata eagerly encouraged her with those thoughts.

"I was thinking back to England and how we smothered the crumpet with butter. It would run all over my hands, and I used to run my tongue over my arm and suck my fingers to clean up the mess before slowly and purposely allowing the crumpet to reach my lips and sucking the delicious crumpet into my mouth and enjoying it deeply."

Sugata's handed drifted toward her thigh. "Maybe we can share this experience together later."

Edina gently took his hand and placed it on the steering wheel. "Maybe. However, it maybe acceptable behaviour in private, but surely we could not do this in a restaurant?"

Sugata roared with laughter. "Would you like me to see if I can arrange something more private?"

"I am fearful that my husband would hear about my common ways."

"It could be our little secret, Edina, as I would love you to show me your common ways."

"You really are a very nice man, Sugata, and appealing too, but I have four children to bring up and a husband to care for and to help him as a hostess. As long as he remains faithful to me, I will remain faithful to him. I have very much enjoyed a little flirting, but that is all it is."

Edina wondered what Charles had been doing while on his own. How could she be playing with fire like this, especially after the wonderful letter she had just received? The two men that she had experienced were so different, and she couldn't help but wonder how it might be different with this man. Why shouldn't she enjoy this experience to make a better decision? And at the moment that was all she could think about—the experience.

Sugata was a perfect gentleman all evening, showing her Darjeeling's restaurants and sights. "Well, Edina, a perfect evening, and I am even more sure that Charles is perfect as a mine manager—we took him without knowing what his wife and family were like. We knew of his digression, and I see you have made mistakes as well. But war is a difficult time for all and you both have overcome the difficulties. You make a great hostess and can banter and hold your own when advances are made, and I can assure you there will be many."

"Thank you for the compliments, and I shall look forward to seeing and entertaining you when next you visit the mine."

"Really, will you entertain me, Edina? I long to take you in my arms, to feel your breasts heaving on my naked chest. I will leave you with these thoughts, hoping that you will contemplate the possibility of us having an affair. I would be very discrete."

"The thought excites me. Women want to be wanted. But Charles has to stray first, for then I have his permission to do the same."

"What do you mean?"

"That is part of our agreement, as we have both strayed. I wanted a divorce, but he wouldn't give it to me. If he strays I have a choice—to stay and do the same and have my needs met by others or to get a divorce and start a new life with someone else. You are very appealing to me,

Sugata. But at this time I don't think Charles is with anyone other than me. He couldn't keep up the pace."

※

Charles arrived a few days later. The children were so excited to see him even though they knew it meant that they would soon be going to school. A wonderful family dinner was enjoyed.

As they were about to go to bed, Edina said, "Charles, we have all really missed you, especially me. Would you like it if I tell Aaina to look after the children and get the staff to serve us breakfast on the veranda at, say, nine thirty so we can catch up with each other?"

"That would be wonderful, Edina, especially if I am reading your mind correctly."

"You are indeed. We need some time alone together."

"Sounds delicious to me, my darling. Especially as I am feeling very needy right now."

"Then, Charles, I will go and speak to the staff now whilst you prepare yourself for a night of continuous love."

※

Charles and Edina were awoken by the sounds of the table being laid outside their doors on the veranda.

"Charles, don't get dressed, let's sit outside in our dressing gowns and eat breakfast."

"What if the children come and see us?"

"They won't, Aaina promised to do something with them all morning and was getting Vallabha to help her, much to her disgust."

As they sat down on the veranda, Charles said, "Speaking of Vallabha, it has been decided by Sugata and myself that we are moving her to a different mine so she will no longer be working with me. I really don't think she understands that it is over. However, this could affect you."

"You mean, I might be busier with you?"

"That could be," he said with a smile. "No, Aaina will probably go with her daughter to look after her own granddaughter, which affects you because you will have to get a new ayah. I can't imagine that Vallabha will leave without Charita."

"I have watched Charita a lot, Charles, she doesn't seem to have much of you in her."

"Funny, Edina, Sugata made that same comment to me during a meeting after he came back from here. He'd already guessed that she and I were involved before I returned to England. So he had made some enquiries about her way back then, but he wanted to wait until after the baby was born before he spoke to me."

"Why?"

"During the war, Indian women liked being with British soldiers because it was an opportunity to better their way of life by perhaps getting married or getting support from the soldier. As Sugata said, there was little chance that the women involved could hope for a better life because most of these women came from a lower caste."

"Why did he want to wait until the baby was born?"

"My dear, he wanted to see if the child had any white features, and Charita, so far, shows none. So whilst he was here, he confronted Vallabha. He told Vallabha that he had been to her village and spoke to people there. She fell to her knees and begged him to keep silent as I had promised her to support her and the child as I believed she was mine."

"So is Charita yours or not?"

"Edina, my darling, because I think we have grown and come to an understanding I want to be very truthful with you. Vallabha and I had relationships too many times for me to deny the possibility. Most other women were a one- or two-night stand only, but Vallabha was there for me daily, always showing me different techniques, different positions. I truly thought she loved me. However, I know I love you. Sugata found out that she had been having a serious relationship with a man in my office, and when they found out she was with child, he persuaded her to come to me. Apparently, once I left for England they lived together. Sugata had a statement from this man saying he encouraged Vallabha to have relations with me as many times as she could make me—even more than once a day—so I would never suspect that the child could be anyone's but mine."

"So is the child yours or not?"

"I am thinking not, though I have not confronted her yet." He paused, looking at his wife of ten years, who was still a beautiful and very desirable woman. He could see tears welling up in her eyes. "What ever is the matter, pet?"

Sobbing, she said, "I feel so terribly guilty that every day you have to look at Manty and see a reminder of my adultery."

"Just because I do not have a child does not mean I am not blameless. I have nothing to show for all the good times I had—as you know, sexual contact outside of marriage is more easily seen on a woman. Let me show you that it means nothing to me that you had another man." With that he pulled her once again towards their bed. "You are mine now." A little roughly, he pushed her onto the bed. "We men always get our way even if you women resist. Let me show you."

"No, Charles, please don't."

"*Don't*, that is not a word I understand," he said as he rolled on top of her, pinning her down.

Edina was enjoying the game and was completely aroused; thinking that if she denied Bill this is not what he would do. "You cannot have me," she whispered, thinking, *I belong to another—my husband, Charles, my lover, Bill, and hopefully my conquest, Sugata*. What a sexy game this was.

As she fought against Charles, she kept touching him to keep him aroused. He said, "I will have you."

Edina's mind jumped to Sugata, who had once said that to her. He was the tallest of the men who had wanted her. Charles was her own size, and Bill was taller—but not the size of Sugata, the unknown.

Edina tried to jump up. Quick as a weasel, Charles pulled her down on him. She allowed the copulation, easily letting the full weight of her body to enjoy the three desired men: The old and unfaithful and well-schooled in the ways of lovemaking. The new, gentle, kind, and loving—would he be enough? She dwelt on the to-be, desirable, handsome, thinking that he would show her ways she never had thought of. Just think: all three men here, wanting her. Her heart pounded and she grabbed Charles, then lay, arms open, and said, "I need more."

Everlasting Lies

Charles smiled. "You're an animal," he said and obliged.

Yes, Edina thought, *this is more like Bill, soft and gentle.*

Charles rolled over and looked at his wife. "Let us have breakfast."

"No, let us have more. I want you to be the teacher, teach me how to make love like a native. Teach me different ways."

Charles smiled and became a teacher. While he schooled her, Edina could only think of Sugata, the native, the experienced teacher, and vowed to place herself next to him at the very next dinner party and give him the opportunity to get to know her much, much better.

Once they were both dressed and sitting on the deck, Charles said, "Well, Mrs. Vernon, you look well satisfied with yourself."

She laughed. "Indeed I am, but I would like to finish the conversation we started this morning."

"All right, fine by me because I know where this will lead."

"Well, I was thinking it would be best to have a new ayah."

"Agreed."

"I think we should put the children into school this coming Monday so I can come home with you when you leave."

"Agreed."

"I think you should go and spend alone time with the children now so I can write a letter to my parents."

"Agreed." Charles got up and kissed his wife on the top of her head.

Edina was left with her thoughts. Charles: the man who fathered her first two children but who was fond of extramarital affairs. Bill: the father of her last two children, her lover, and, as far as she knew, she was his only love—who was soon to arrive in India. Then her thoughts turned to the most attractive man from India. Sugata: tall, dark, handsome, and unknown, with a beautiful brown body that she wanted to explore. Sighing, she got out paper and an inkwell and pen and sat at the desk in the bedroom.

Thank you, Bill, so much for your letter the other day. How exciting, your arrival here in India, so soon, so close, Now, I have to tell you...

Author Notes

Write a novel! Really?

At first a scary thought, but then one day November 2013 I announced to my husband that I was going to write a novel! That day, the most amazing, creative journey began. My novel is based on some known facts of my maternal heritage. My grandfather Vernon, never talked about his past! He would only say that he came from a wealthy family and he disowned them! Though, during the time that I knew him, he occasionally talked about a brother, Abraham, and a sister, Lillian. My grandmother would talk about her family, so that information is correct.

My mother, Mantua Elenor Vernon, was born on the ship going to India, and the christening bowl is already in the safety of the third generation. Names have not been changed. Who knows, maybe somebody will know the whole truth.

My mother's family was shrouded in secrets and lies and this was where the idea came for the novel. William Charlton did live next door to my grandmother as a child, as I have the census records to prove this. Whether or not he fathered two of my grandmother's children is fictional on my part, though I do know that he travelled to India in late 1920, and lived and worked close to my grandmother. He was India until 1932.

The Vernon Family resided in India until May of 1928, docking in Tilbury, United Kingdom.

The lies continued...

When leaving England with the family, Charles had stated he was thirty-four but eight years later said he was fifty-two. Edina, when leaving England, stated she was twenty-eight when indeed she was only twenty-five. Yet when she returned, she stated she was fifty. I have her birth certificate. No birth certificates were ever found for Charles.

The Vernon's returned to County Durham and tried their hand at raising pigs until swine fever wiped them out. They decided to move south to Mountnessing in Essex, though their son, John Vernon did not move with them, staying in the north.

Charles Vernon worked in Marconi Factory in Chelmsford. The three daughters all married, Essex men. Charles died when they said he was seventy-nine. Edina died at age ninety in 1985. There are four true descendants from Charles and Edina—three doubtful, two definitely not.

William Charlton did not leave India until April 1934, aged forty-one. He was still employed by the railways and travelled first class, stating he planned to reside in the British Empire. He married his wife, Clara, fifty-five and a widow with a married daughter, Amelia. They honeymooned on the ss Flandria to Cape Town, again travelling first class. They travelled back to Britain on the ss Kenilworth Castle, arriving in Southampton in 1935.

In Britain, they moved to "Tandoor Cottage," Landseer Road, Brighton Sussex. William died there in 1944, age fifty-one. Clara died there in 1951, age seventy-two.

"I am forever grateful to Tanis Nessler, Revision Editing, for being such a wonderful editor and supporter."